Simon Scarrow lives in Norfolk and is a lecturer at a College in Norwich. He has in the past run a Roman History programme taking parties of students to a number of ruins and museums across Britain. Having enjoyed the novels of Forester, Cornwell and O'Brian, and fired by the knowledge gleaned from his exploration of Roman sites, he decided to write what he wanted to read – military page-turners set during the Roman invasion of Britain in AD 43. His five other action-packed novels featuring Macro and Cato, *The Eagle's Conquest*, *When the Eagle Hunts*, *The Eagle and the Wolves*, *The Eagle's Prey* and *The Eagle's Prophecy* are also available from Headline.

For more information on Simon Scarrow and his novels, visit his website at: www.scarrow.fsnet.co.uk

UNDER THE EAGLE

SIMON SCARROW

headline

Copyright © 2000 Simon Scarrow

The right of Simon Scarrow to be identified as the Author of
the Work has been asserted by him in accordance with
the Copyright, Designs and Patents Act 1988.

First published in 2000
by HEADLINE BOOK PUBLISHING

First published in paperback in 2001
by HEADLINE BOOK PUBLISHING

This paperback edition published in 2005
by HEADLINE BOOK PUBLISHING

1

ISBN 0 7472 6629 8

Typeset in Bembo by Avon DataSet Ltd,
Bidford-on-Avon, Warwickshire

Printed and bound in Great Britain by
Mackays of Chatham plc, Chatham, Kent

Headline's policy is to use papers that are natural, renewable and
recyclable products and made from wood grown in sustainable
forests. The logging and manufacturing processes are expected to
conform to the environmental regulations of the country of origin.

HEADLINE BOOK PUBLISHING
A division of Hodder Headline
338 Euston Road
London NW1 3BH

www.headline.co.uk
www.hodderheadline.com

For Audrey and Tony,
best of parents and best of friends

THE ROMAN ARMY
CHAIN OF COMMAND
IN 43 AD

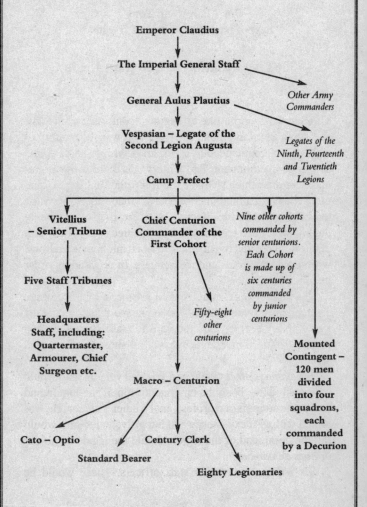

Emperor Claudius

The Imperial General Staff

General Aulus Plautius → *Other Army Commanders*

Vespasian – Legate of the Second Legion Augusta → *Legates of the Ninth, Fourteenth and Twentieth Legions*

Camp Prefect

Vitellius – Senior Tribune

Chief Centurion Commander of the First Cohort

Nine other cohorts commanded by senior centurions. Each Cohort is made up of six centuries commanded by junior centurions

Five Staff Tribunes

Headquarters Staff, including: Quartermaster, Armourer, Chief Surgeon etc.

Fifty-eight other centurions

Mounted Contingent – 120 men divided into four squadrons, each commanded by a Decurion

Macro – Centurion

Cato – Optio

Century Clerk

Standard Bearer

Eighty Legionaries

The Organisation of a Roman Legion

The Second Legion, like all legions, comprised some five and a half thousand men. The basic unit was the century of eighty men commanded by a centurion with an optio acting as second in command. The century was divided into eight-man sections which shared a room together in barracks and a tent when on campaign. Six centuries made up a cohort, and ten cohorts made up a legion, with the first cohort being double-size. Each legion was accompanied by a cavalry unit of one hundred and twenty men, divided into four squadrons, who served as scouts and messengers. In descending order the main ranks were:

The *legate* was a man from an aristocratic background. Typically in his mid thirties, the legate would command the legion for up to five years and hope to make something of a name for himself in order to enhance his subsequent political career.

The *camp prefect* would be a grizzled veteran who would previously have been the chief centurion of the legion and was at the summit of a professional soldier's career. He was armed with vast experience and integrity, and to him would fall the command of the legion should the legate be absent or *hors de combat*.

Six *tribunes* served as staff officers. These would be

men in their early twenties serving in the army for the first time to gain administrative experience before taking up junior posts in civil administration. The senior tribune was different. He was destined for high political office and eventual command of a legion.

Sixty *centurions* provided the disciplinary and training backbone of the legion. They were hand-picked for their command qualities and a willingness to fight to the death. Accordingly their casualty rate far exceeded other ranks. The most senior centurion commanded the first century of the first cohort and was a highly decorated and respected individual.

The four *decurians* of the legion commanded the cavalry squadrons and hoped for promotion to the command of auxiliary cavalry units.

Each centurion was assisted by an *optio* who would act as an orderly, with minor command duties. Optios would be waiting for a vacancy in the centurionate.

Below the optios were the *legionaries,* men who had signed on for twenty-five years. In theory, a man had to be a Roman citizen to quality for enlistment, but recruits were increasingly drawn from local populations and given Roman citizenship on joining the legions.

Lower in status than the legionaries were the men of the *auxiliary cohorts*. These were recruited from the provinces and provided the Roman empire with its cavalry, light infantry and other specialist skills. Roman citizenship was awarded on completion of twenty-five years' service.

ISLE OF THANET

WANTSUM CHANNEL

ROMAN LANDINGS

FOREST

THE MARSH

SOUTH-EAST BRITAIN 43 AD

Prologue

'It's no good, sir, the bastard's well and truly stuck.'

The centurion leaned back against the wagon and paused for breath. Around him a score of bone-weary legionaries stood up to their waists in the foul-smelling ooze of the marsh. From the edge of the track, the general followed their efforts in growing frustration. He had been embarking on to one of the evacuation ships when news arrived that the wagon had run off the narrow path. He had immediately taken one of the few remaining horses and galloped it back through the marsh to investigate the situation at first hand. Weighed down by the heavy chest resting on its bed, the wagon resisted every effort to wrestle it free. There was no further help available now since the rearguard had finished loading and put to sea. Only the general, these men and a thin screen of the last remaining cavalry scouts stood between the wagon and the army of Caswollan snapping at the heels of the erstwhile Roman invaders.

The general let slip an oath and his horse raised its head in alarm from the nearby copse where it had been tethered. The wagon was lost then, that much was evident, and the chest itself was too heavy to carry back

1

to the last ship waiting at anchor. For security's sake the key to the chest had remained with the quartermaster, now well out to sea, and the chest was so constructed as to make it impossible to open without the right tools.

'What now, sir?' the centurion asked.

The general looked long and hard at the chest, in silence. There was nothing he could do – nothing at all. Wagon, chest and contents were not going to move. For a moment he dared not contemplate that, since the loss of the chest would set his political plans back by a year at least. In that agonising moment of indecision a war horn blew close at hand. With terrified expressions, the legionaries started to wade back towards their weapons lying on the track.

'Stay where you bloody are!' the general roared. 'I haven't ordered you to move!'

The legionaries paused, even with the enemy close at hand, such was the depth of their awe and respect for their commander. With a last look at the chest, the general nodded as he made his decision.

'Centurion, get rid of the wagon.'

'Sir?'

'It'll have to stay here until we return next summer. Drag it a little further in so it sinks, mark the spot and then get back to the beach as fast as you can. I'll have them hold a tender ready for you.'

'Yes, sir.'

The general slapped his thigh angrily, then turned to mount his horse and set off back through the marsh towards the beach. Behind him came another burst from the war horn and the sound of swords clashing as the cavalry scouts fought it out with the vanguard of Caswollan's army. From the moment the Romans had landed, to their present flight back to Gaul, Caswollan's men had dogged them every step of the way, harrying stragglers and foragers day and night, and showing no mercy to the invaders.

'Right, lads!' the centurion bellowed. 'One last heave . . . Get your shoulders to the wagon. Ready now . . . Heave!'

Slowly the wagon sank further into the mire; dark brown marsh water flowing up through the seams in the bed of the wagon and rising up the sides of the chest.

'Come on! Heave!'

With a last combined thrust the men eased the wagon further into the marsh and, with a soft gurgling plop, the wagon disappeared beneath the dark water leaving a faint swirl rippling across the oily surface, broken only by the long wagon shaft.

'That's it, lads. Back to the ship. Smartly does it.'

The legionaries waded ashore and snatched up their shields and spears while the centurion hurriedly sketched a map of the location on the wax tablet hanging from his shoulder. When he was done, he snapped the tablet shut and joined his men. But before the column could move off a sudden pounding of hoofbeats on the track caused his men to turn, wide-eyed and afraid. Moments later a handful of cavalry scouts burst out of the mist and galloped by the infantry. One scout leaned forward across his horse's neck which ran with blood from a gaping wound in the man's side. Then they were gone.

Almost at once came the sound of more horses, this

time accompanied by the harsh cries of the natives the legionaries had grown to dread. There was a new triumphant edge to their war cries and a cold finger of dread traced its way down the spines of the Romans.

'Ready javelins!' The centurion called out and his men hefted their throwing spears back, waiting for the order. In the mist, the sounds of their pursuers swept towards them, unseen and terrifying. Then indistinct grey shapes appeared a short way off. 'Release!'

The javelins arced up and out of sight and crashed down on the reckless Britons with a chorus of screams from both man and beast.

'Form up!' the centurion cried out. 'At the command . . . quick march!'

The small column stepped out down the track towards the distant safety of the last evacuation ship, the centurion marching at their side, keeping an anxious watch on the mist that swallowed up the track behind them. The volley of javelins did not delay the Britons for long and soon the sound of hooves closed in on them again, slower and more cautious this time.

The centurion heard a thud and one of his men gasped in pain. He turned to see an arrow shaft protruding from the back of the rearmost legionary. Fighting for breath as his lungs filled with blood, the man fell to his knees and toppled forward.

'At the trot!'

The belts and harnesses of the legionaries jingled as they quickened the pace and tried to increase the distance between themselves and their invisible pursuers. More arrows whirred out of the mist, fired blindly at the

Romans. Still, some found their mark and one by one the column shrank in size as men fell on the track and lay, swords drawn, grimly waiting for the end. By the time the centurion reached the final rise, where the marsh gave way to sand and pebble, only four men remained with him. The faint sound of the seashore was the music of hope to their ears and a slight September breeze worked to thin the mist ahead of them.

All at once the path ahead was clear. Two hundred paces away across the shingle, a small boat waited in the surf. A little way out to sea a trireme lay at anchor in a gentle swell and, far out towards the horizon, the dark specks of the invasion fleet were fading into the gloom of dusk.

'Run for it!' shouted the centurion, throwing down his shield and sword. 'Run!'

The shingle scattered beneath their feet as they sprinted down towards the boat. Immediately the war horn sounded behind them as the Britons also caught sight of the sea, spurring their horses on to run down the surviving men before they could reach safety. Teeth gritted, the centurion hurled himself down the gentle slope, grimly aware of the sounds of their pursuers closing rapidly, but he dared not look back for fear that it might cause him to slow his pace. He could see a tall figure standing in the rear of the boat desperately urging him on, as the general's red cloak rippled out behind him in the gentle breeze. Fifty feet to go, and a sharp cry came from just behind him as one of the Britons thrust his spear through the rearmost legionary.

With every fibre of his body screaming out for life,

the centurion pounded across the wet sand at the sea's edge, splashed through the surf and hurled himself over the bows of the boat. Eager hands grabbed him under the shoulders and bodily pulled him down. An instant later, a legionary crashed down on top of him, snatching his breaths from the sea air. A pair of the general's burly bodyguards jabbed their spears at the pursuers who had reined in at the water's edge now the odds had been evened. But they were already too late and the boat quickly moved into deeper water as the oarsmen bent themselves to their work, rowing the boat back to the safety of the trireme.

'Did you manage to sink the wagon?' the general asked anxiously.

'Y-yes, sir . . .' panted the centurion, and he patted the wax tablet hanging at his side. 'There's a map, sir. Good as I could make in the time we had.'

'Well done, centurion. Well done. I'll have that now.'

As the centurion handed over the tablet he glanced round and saw that only one man had escaped with him. Only one. On the shrinking shoreline he could see a score of horsemen clustered round another of his men, foolish enough to be taken alive, and the centurion shuddered at the thought of what terrors lay in wait for the helpless legionary.

Every man in the boat watched in silence, until finally the general spoke.

'We'll come back, men. We'll come back, and when we do I promise you that we'll make those bastards regret the day they ever took up arms against Rome. I, Caius Julius Caesar, swear this on my father's grave . . .'

The Rhine Frontier

Ninety-six years later, in the second
year of the reign of Emperor Claudius
Late 42 AD

The King's England

Chapter One

An icy blast of wind swept into the latrine with the sentry.

'Wagon's approaching, sir!'

'Shut the bloody door! Anything else?'

'Small column of men.'

'Soldiers?'

'Hardly.' The sentry grimaced. 'Unless there's been some change in marching drill.'

The duty centurion glanced up sharply. 'I don't recall asking for an opinion on policy, soldier.'

'No, sir!' The sentry snapped to attention under the glare of his superior. Only a few months earlier Lucius Cornelius Macro had been an optio and was still finding promotion to the centurionate hard to handle. His former comrades in the ranks were still inclined to treat him as an equal. It was hard to register a respectful attitude to one who so recently had been seen emptying his guts of a skinful of cheap wine. But, for some months before the promotion, Macro had been aware that senior officers were considering him for the first available vacancy in the centurionate and had done his best to keep indiscretions to a minimum. For, when all his qualities were placed in the balance, Macro was a good soldier –

when good soldiering was required – conscientious in his duties, reliably obedient to orders and he could be counted on to hold firm in a fight and inspire others to do the same.

Macro suddenly realised that he had been gazing at the sentry for a while and that the legionary was shifting uncomfortably under his scrutiny, as one tends to in front of a silently staring superior. And officers could be such unpredictable bastards, the sentry thought nervously, first whiff of power and they either don't know what to do with it, or they insist on giving bloody-minded and stupid orders.

'What are your orders, sir?'

'Orders?' Macro frowned for a moment. 'All right then. I'll come. You get back to the gate.'

'Yes, sir.' The sentry turned and hurriedly made his way out of the junior officers' latrine block, pulling the door to as the half-dozen centurions glared after him. It was an unwritten rule that no-one, but no-one, permitted their men to interrupt proceedings in the latrine. Macro applied the sponge stick, pulled up his breeches and apologised to the other centurions before hurrying outside.

It was a filthy night and a cold northerly wind was blowing the rain down from the German forests. It swept across the Rhine, over the fortress walls and was funnelled into icy blasts between the barrack blocks. Macro suspected that he was keenly disapproved of by his new-found peers and was determined to prove them wrong. Not that this resolution was working out terribly successfully. The administrative duties relating to the command of eighty men were proving to be a nightmare – ration-collection details, latrine rotas, sentry rotas, weapons inspections, barrack inspections, punishment ledgers, equipment procurement chits, arranging fodder for the section mules, taking charge of pay, savings and the funeral club.

The only help available for carrying out these duties came in the form of the century's clerk, a wizened old cove named Piso, who Macro suspected of being dishonest or simply incompetent. Macro had no way of finding out for himself, because he was all but illiterate. Brought up with only the most rudimentary knowledge of letters and numbers he could recognise most individually, but more than that was impossible. And now he was a centurion, a rank for whom literacy was a prerequisite. Doubtless the legate had naturally assumed Macro could read and write when he approved the appointment. If it came to light that he was no more literate than a Campanian farm boy, Macro knew he would be demoted at once. So far he had managed to get round the problem by delegating the paperwork to Piso and claiming that his other duties were keeping him too busy, but he was sure that the clerk had begun to suspect the truth. He shook his head as he trudged over to the fortress gate, pulling his red cloak tightly about him.

It was a dark night, made darker by the low clouds that completely obscured the sky; a sure sign that snow was on the way. From the gloom about him, Macro could hear a variety of sounds typical of the fortress existence that had been part of his life for over fourteen years now.

11

Mules brayed from stables at the far end of each barrack block and the voices of soldiers, talking and shouting, drifted out through the wavering light of candlelit windows. A bellow of laughter peeled out of a barrack block he was passing, followed by a lighter female laugh. Macro halted mid-stride and listened. Someone had managed to sneak a woman into the base. The woman laughed again and then began speaking in thickly accented Latin and was quickly hushed by her companion. This was a flagrant breach of regulations and Macro abruptly turned towards the block and laid his hand on the latch. Then paused, thinking. By rights he should burst in, loudly bellowing in parade-ground fashion, send the soldier to the guard-house, and have the woman thrown out of the base. But that meant completing an entry in the punishment book – more bloody writing.

Gritting his teeth, Macro released his grip and quietly stepped back into the street, just as the woman let out a shriek of laughter to prick his conscience. A quick glance about to make sure that no-one else was there to witness his failure to act and Macro hurried on towards the south gate. Bloody soldier deserved a good kicking, and if he had been in Macro's century that's how he'd have been dealt with; no paperwork needed, just a swift kick in the balls to ensure the punishment fitted the crime. Still, from her voice she could only have been one of those nasty German tarts from the native settlement that sprawled just outside the base. Macro consoled himself with the thought of the legionary concerned coming down with a bad dose of the clap.

Although the streets were dark, Macro moved instinctively in the right direction since no legionary base deviated from the standard design used in all camps and fortresses. In a matter of minutes, he had emerged on to the wider thoroughfare of the Via Praetoria and marched towards the gate where the street passed through the walls to the south of the base. The sentry who had interrupted Macro at the latrine was waiting at the foot of the stairs. He led the way into the gatehouse and up the narrow wooden staircase to the battlement level, where a lit brazier cast a warm red glow around the sentry room. Four legionaries were squatting close to the fire playing dice. As soon as they saw the centurion's head appear above the stairs they stood to attention.

'Easy lads,' Macro said. 'Carry on.'

The wooden door to the battlements sprang inwards with the wind as Macro lifted the latch and the brazier blazed momentarily as he stepped outside and slammed the door to. Up on the sentry walk the wind was biting and whipped Macro's cloak behind him, tugging at the clasp on his left shoulder. He shuddered and snatched it back, holding it tightly about his body.

'Where?'

The sentry peered out through the crenellations into the darkness and pointed his javelin at a tiny flickering light swinging from the back of a wagon approaching from the south. Straining his eyes as he stared into the wind, Macro could make out the outline of the wagon and, behind it, a body of men plodding along the track. At the rear of the column came the more orderly progress of the escort whose job was to stop the stragglers slowing the pace. Maybe two hundred men in all.

'Shall I call out the guard, sir?'

Macro turned towards the sentry. 'What did you say?'

'Shall I call out the guard, sir?'

Macro eyed the man wearily. Syrus was one of the youngest men in the century and, although Macro had learned the names of most of his command, he knew little of their characters or histories as yet. 'Been in the army long?'

'No, sir. Only a year in December.'

Not long out of training then, Macro thought. A stickler for regulations, which he no doubt applied in every circumstance. He'd learn in time; how to compromise between following strict procedure and doing what was needed to get by.

'So then, why do we need to call out the guard?'

'Regulations, sir. If an unidentified body of men is approaching the camp in force the guard century should be called out to man the gate and adjacent walls.'

Macro raised his eyebrows in surprise. The quotation was word perfect. Syrus clearly took his training seriously. 'And what then?'

'Sir?'

'What happens next?'

'The duty centurion, after assessing the situation determines whether or not to call a general alarm,' Syrus continued tonelessly, then hurriedly added, 'Sir.'

'Good man.' Macro smiled and the sentry smiled back in relief, before Macro turned back towards the approaching column. 'Now then, exactly how threatening do you think that lot is? Do they scare you, soldier? Do you think all two hundred of them are going to charge over here, climb the walls and slaughter every mother's son of the Second Legion . . . Well, do you?'

The sentry looked at Macro, looked carefully at the flickering lights for a new moments and then turned back sheepishly. 'I don't think so.'

'I don't think so, *sir*,' said Macro gruffly as he punched the lad on the shoulder.

'Sorry, sir.'

'Tell me, Syrus. Did you attend the sentry briefing before the watch?'

'Of course, sir.'

'Did you pay attention to every detail?'

'I think so, sir.'

'Then you would recall me saying that a replacement convoy was due to arrive at the base, wouldn't you? And then you wouldn't have had to haul me out of the latrine and spoil a particularly good shit.'

The sentry was crestfallen and he could not bear the long-suffering expression on his centurion's face. 'I'm sorry, sir. Won't happen again.'

'You see that it doesn't. Or I'll have you on double duties for the rest of the year. Now get the rest of the lads ready at the gate. I'll deal with the recognition call.'

Shamefaced, the sentry saluted and went back into the gatehouse. Soon Macro could hear the sounds of the guard rousing themselves and descending the wooden stairs to the main gate. Macro smiled. The lad was keen and felt guilty about his mistake. Guilty enough to make sure that it never happened again. That was good. That's how dependable soldiers were made – there was no such thing as a born soldier, Macro reflected.

A sudden blast of wind buffeted Macro and he retreated into the shelter of the gatehouse. Inside he positioned himself close to the glowing brazier and let out a sigh of relief as the warmth soaked into his body. After a few moments, Macro opened the small viewing shutter and looked out into the night. The convoy was nearer now and he could make out the wagon in detail as well as the individual men in the following column. A miserable bunch of recruits, he thought, not an ounce of spirit in them. You could tell that by the apathetic way they trudged along, even though they were in sight of shelter.

Then it began to rain, quite suddenly, large drops flung diagonally by the wind that stung the skin. Even that failed to increase the pace of the convoy and, with a despairing shake of the head, Macro began the formalities. He opened the main shutter, leaned his head out of the window and filled his lungs.

'Halt there!' he shouted. 'Identify yourselves!'

The wagon reined in a hundred feet from the wall and a figure beside the driver rose to reply. 'Reinforcement convoy from Aventicum and escort, Lucius Batiacus Bestia commanding.'

'Password?' Macro demanded even though he knew Bestia well enough, the senior centurion of the Second Legion and therefore very much his superior.

'Hedgehog. Permission to approach?'

'Approach, friend.'

With a crack of the whip the wagoneer urged the bullocks up the rise that led to the gateway and Macro crossed over to the shutter that opened on to the inside of the fort. Down below, the sentries were clustered by the sidegate trying to keep out of the rain.

'Open the gate,' Macro called down. One of the soldiers quickly drew out the locking pin and the others slid the beam back into the recess. With a heavy wooden groan, the gates were pulled open just as the wagon reached the top of the rise, its momentum carrying it through the gate into the base. Looking down from the guardhouse, Macro watched the wagon draw up to one side. Bestia jumped down from the driver's bench and waved his vine cane at the sodden procession of new recruits passing by.

'Come on, you bastards! Move! Quickly now! The sooner you're in, the sooner you can get warm and dry.'

The recruits, who had followed the wagon for over two hundred miles, automatically began to mill round it once inside the gate. Most wore travelling cloaks and carried their few belongings in blankets tied across the shoulder. The poorest recruits had nothing, some didn't even have cloaks, and they shivered miserably as the wind drove the freezing rain at them. At the rear stood a small chain-gang of criminals who had opted for the army rather than remain in prison.

Bestia immediately waded into the growing crowd with his cane, beating a clear space for himself.

'Don't just stand there like a herd of sheep! Make way for some real soldiers. Get over to the far side of the street and line up facing this way. NOW!'

The last of the recruits stumbled in through the gate and followed the rest to take up an uneven line opposite the wagon. Finally the escort marched in, twenty men in step, who halted simultaneously at one word of command from Bestia. He paused for effect to let the implicit comparison sink in as Macro ordered the sentries to shut the gate and return to their duties. Bestia turned back to the recruits, legs astride and hands on hips.

'Those men,' Bestia nodded over his shoulder, 'belong to the Second Legion – the Augusta – the toughest in the entire Roman army, and you'd better not forget it. There is no barbarian tribe, however remote, who hasn't heard of us and who doesn't live in mortal fear of us. The Second has killed more of these scum, and conquered more of their land, than any other unit. We have been able to do this because we train men to be the meanest, dirtiest, hardest fighters in the civilised world . . . You, on the other hand, are soft, worthless piles of shit. You are not even men. You are the lowest fucking form of life that ever claimed to be Roman. I despise each and every last fucking one of you, and I will weed out every worthless piece of scum so that only the best join my beloved Second Legion and serve under our eagle. I've watched you all the way from Aventicum – and, ladies, I'm not impressed. You signed up and now you are all mine. I will train you, I will hurt you, I will make men of you. Then – *if* and when I decide you are ready – then I will let you become a legionary. If any one of you doesn't give me every last shred of energy and commitment then I will break him – with this.' He held the gnarled vine cane aloft for all to see. 'Do you shits understand?'

There was a murmured assent from the recruits, some

of whom were so tired they just nodded.

'What was that supposed to be?' Bestia shouted angrily. 'I can hardly fucking hear you!'

He moved into the crowd and grabbed a recruit roughly by the collar of his travelling cloak. Macro noticed for the first time that this recruit was dressed differently from the others. The cut of his cloak was unmistakably expensive – no matter how much mud was caked on to it. The recruit was taller than the rest, but thin and delicate-looking – just the kind of victim to make an example of.

'What the hell is this? What the fuck is a recruit doing with a better cloak than I can afford? You steal it, boy?'

'No,' the recruit replied calmly. 'A friend gave it to me.'

Bestia slammed his vine cane into the boy's stomach and the recruit doubled over and slumped to the ground, hands splashing into a puddle. Bestia stood over him, cane raised for another blow.

'Whenever you open your mouth you call me *sir*! Understand?'

Macro watched the young man gasp for air as he tried to reply, then Bestia swung the cane down on his back and the boy yelped.

'I said, do you understand?'

'Yes, s-sir!' the recruit cried out.

'Louder!'

'YES, SIR!'

'That's better. Now, let's see what else you've got.'

The centurion grabbed the blanket carrier and wrenched it free. The contents spilled out on to the muddy ground; some spare clothes, a small flask, some bread, two scrolls and a leather-bound writing set.

'What the . . . ?' The centurion stared down at the last of the contents. Then he slowly looked up at the new recruit. 'What's this?'

'My writing materials, sir!'

'Writing materials? What does a legionary want with writing materials?'

'I promised my friends in Rome I'd write, sir.'

'Your friends?' Bestia grinned. 'No mother to write to? No father, eh?'

'Dead, sir.'

'Know his name?'

'Of course, sir. He was . . .'

'Quiet!' Bestia interrupted. 'I don't give a toss who he was. Here, you're all bastards as far as I'm concerned. So then, what's your name, bastard?'

'Quintus Licinius Cato . . . sir.'

'Well then, Cato, I know only two types of legionary who can write – spies and those who think they're so bloody wonderful they're going to be officers. Which are you?'

The recruit eyed him warily. 'Neither, sir.'

'Then you won't need this stuff, will you?' Bestia kicked the writing kit and the scrolls towards the drainage gully in the middle of the street.

'Careful, sir!'

'What did you say?' The centurion spun round, cane at the ready. 'What did you say to me?'

'I said careful, sir. One of those scrolls is a personal message for the legate.'

'A personal message for the legate! Well, I . . .'

With a grin, Macro saw that the grizzled centurion was momentarily floored; he'd heard it all before, every excuse, every explanation – but not this one. What on earth could a recruit be doing with a letter for the legate? A first-class mystery, and one that had knocked Bestia off his perch. Not for long though – the centurion stabbed his cane towards the scrolls.

'Bloody well pick that stuff up and bring it here. Just arrived here and you're already messing the base up! Fucking recruits,' he grumbled. 'You make me puke. Well, you heard me. Pick it up!'

As the tall recruit leant down to retrieve his belongings Bestia barked out a series of orders, assigning batches of recruits to members of the escort to be guided to their units.

'Now, get moving! NOT YOU!' Bestia shouted at the lone recruit, who had managed to stuff his belongings back into his pack and had turned towards the safety of the others standing in the pouring rain. 'Over here! What are the rest of you staring at?'

The escort legionaries started to tell off their charges. While the recruits were cajoled and herded into groups, Bestia snatched the scroll Cato held out to him. Taking care to keep it out of the rain as much as possible, he read the address waxed on to it. He checked the seal as well, rechecked the address and paused a moment to consider his next step. He happened to glance up at the gate and saw Macro grinning. That settled it.

'Macro! Get your arse down here.'

Moments later, Macro was standing to attention in

front of Bestia, blinking as the rain dripped down from the brim of his helmet into his eyes.

'This seems genuine.' Bestia wagged the scroll under the junior officer's nose. 'I want you to take this and escort our friend here to headquarters.'

'I'm on sentry duty.'

'Well then, I'll relieve you till you get back. Get going.'

Bastard! Macro swore silently. Bestia had no idea of the letter's significance, or whether it was even genuine. But he dare not take the risk. Communications to legates took strange routes these days, even from the highest sources. Better to let someone else take the blame if the letter proved to be worthless.

'Yes, sir,' Macro replied bitterly as he accepted the scroll.

'Don't be too long, Macro. I've got a warm bed waiting for me.'

Bestia strode off to the gatehouse and climbed the stairs to the shelter of the sentry room. Macro glared after him. Then turned to have a good look at the new recruit who was causing him to make a long trek to the headquarters building through the driving rain. He had to look up to examine the lad who was nearly a foot taller than himself. Under the brim of the travelling cloak, a mop of black hair had been flattened into straggling trails by the rain. Below a flat brow, a pair of piercing brown eyes in deep sockets glinted either side of a long thin nose. The boy's mouth was clamped shut, but the bottom lip trembled slightly. Although the clothes were soaked and splattered with mud from the long journey from the depot at Aventicum, they were of a surprisingly good quality. As for the writing set, the books and this letter for the legate . . . Well, this recruit was something else. Clearly no stranger to money but, if so, then why the hell join the army?

'Cato, wasn't it?'

'Yes.'

'I'm also called sir.' Macro smiled.

Cato stiffened into an approximation of the attention position and Macro laughed. 'At ease, boy. At ease. You're not on parade until tomorrow morning. Now let's get this letter delivered.'

Macro gave the boy a gentle push away from the gate in the direction of the centre of the base, where the headquarters block loomed in the distance. As they walked, he looked at the letter in detail for the first time and let out a low whistle.

'Know what this seal is?'

'Yes – sir. The imperial seal.'

'And why would the imperial service use a recruit as a courier?'

'I've no idea, sir,' Cato replied.

'Who is it from?'

'The Emperor.'

Macro choked back an exclamation. The boy really had his attention now. What the hell was the Emperor doing sending an imperial despatch via a bloody legionary recruit? Unless there was more to this boy than met the eye. Macro decided an uncommonly tactful approach was required if he was to discover more.

'Forgive my asking, but what are you doing here?'

'Doing here, sir? Joining the army, sir.'

'But why?' Macro persisted.

'It's to do with my father, sir. He was in the imperial service before his death.'

'What did he do?'

When the boy didn't answer, Macro turned and saw that his head was bowed low and his expression troubled. 'Well?'

'He was a slave, sir.' The embarrassment of the admission was clear, even to a bluff fellow like Macro. 'Before Tiberius manumitted him. I was born shortly before.'

'That's tough.' Macro sympathised; freed status did not apply to existing heirs. 'I take it you were manumitted soon after. Did your father buy you?'

'He wasn't allowed to, sir. For some reason Tiberius wouldn't let him. My father died a few months ago. In his will, he begged that I be set free on condition that I continue to serve the Empire. Emperor Claudius agreed, provided that I join the army, and here I am.'

'Hmmmm. Not much of a deal.'

'I don't agree, sir. I'm free now. Better than being a slave.'

'You really think so?' Macro smiled. It seemed like a poor exchange in status: the comforts of the palace with the hardship of life in the army – and the occasional opportunity to risk life and limb in battle. Macro had heard that some of the wealthiest and most powerful men in Rome were to be found amongst the slaves and freedmen employed in the imperial service.

'Anyway, sir,' Cato concluded, with a touch of bitterness. 'I didn't have any choice in the matter.'

Chapter Two

The guards on the gate at the headquarters building crossed spears as the two figures squelched out of the darkness, one with the crested helmet of a centurion and the other a bedraggled youth. They stepped into the flickering light of the torches clamped into the portico.

'Password?' a guard asked as he stepped forward.

'Hedgehog.'

'Your business, sir?'

'This boy has a despatch for the legate.'

'Just a moment, sir.' The guard disappeared into the inner courtyard leaving them under the watchful eyes of the other three guards, all large men – hand-picked for the legate's company of bodyguards. Macro undid his chin strap and removed his helmet before tucking it under his arm in preparation for meeting any senior officers. Cato pushed back his hood and brushed his straggling hair to the side. While they waited, Macro was aware of the youth glancing keenly about himself even as he shivered. A spark of sympathy pricked Macro as he recalled his own feelings on admission to the army; the excitement tinged with fear as he entered a completely unknown world with its strict rules, its dangers and its harsh life away from the comforts of his childhood home.

Cato busied himself with wringing water out of his cloak and a puddle soon formed about the boy's feet.

'Stop that!' Macro snapped. 'You're making a mess. You can dry out later.'

Cato looked up, hands wrapped around a tightly squeezed section of the hem. He was about to protest when he was aware that all the soldiers were looking at him with grave disapproval.

'I'm terribly sorry,' he muttered, and let go of the hem.

'Look here, lad,' Macro said as kindly as possible. 'No-one minds a soldier being in a mess when he can't help it. But what they do mind is a soldier who fidgets. It drives the army mad. Isn't that right, boys?' He turned to the guards and they nodded vigorously. 'So from now on, no fidgeting. Get used to standing still and waiting. You'll find that's what we spend most of our time doing.'

The guards sighed in sympathy.

Footsteps approached from the inner courtyard as the guard returned to the portico.

'Sir, please follow me. The boy too.'

'The legate's going to see us?'

'Don't know, sir. I've been ordered to escort you to the senior tribune first. This way please.'

He led them through a broad arch into a courtyard surrounded by a covered walkway. The rain gushed down off the roof tiles into guttering that channelled it out of the building into the street. The guard led them round each side of the courtyard until they reached a further doorway opposite the portico. Through the door, the building opened out into a large hall with offices along each side, except for the far wall where a purple curtain hid the Legion's shrine from view. Two standard bearers with drawn swords stood to attention in front of the curtain. The guard turned left, paused outside a door and tapped twice.

'Come,' a voice called and the guard quickly opened the door. Macro led the way inside, beckoning Cato to follow him. The room was narrow, but it stretched back a fair distance to accommodate a desk along one wall and a rack of scrolls at the end. A brazier glowed just inside the door, filling the room with a warm fug. Seated at the desk was a tribune. Macro knew him by sight, Aulus Vitellius, a former playboy in Rome but now on the path of a political career which began on the staff of a legion. Vitellius was an overweight man with a dark olive complexion that betrayed a southern Italian background. As his visitors entered, he pushed his chair back and faced them.

'Where's this letter?' The voice was deep and tinged with impatience.

Macro handed it over and then took a step back. Cato stood mutely at his side, next to the brazier. A faint smile of contentment played on his lips as the warmth entered his body and the shivering stopped.

Vitellius cast a quick glance at the letter and then ran his fingers over the imperial seal, consumed by curiosity. 'Do you know what this is?'

'Boy says it's . . .'

'I'm not asking you, Centurion . . . Well?'

27

'I believe it to be a personal letter from the Emperor Claudius, sir,' Cato responded.

Cato's stressing of 'personal' was not lost on the tribune and the latter fixed the boy with an icy stare. 'And what do you think could be so personal that the Emperor would trust its delivery to you?'

'I don't know, sir.'

'Exactly. So I think you can safely leave this with me. I'll see that the legate receives it in due course. Dismissed.'

Macro instantly moved towards the door, but the young recruit hesitated. 'Excuse me, sir. The scroll?'

Vitellius stared back, dumbfounded, as Macro quickly grabbed the youth's arm.

'Let's be off, lad. The tribune's a busy man.'

'I was told to deliver the scroll in person, sir.'

'How dare you,' Vitellius said quietly, eyebrows closing together as reflections from the brazier flickered across his dark eyes.

For a moment Macro watched the exchange of expressions; the tribune struggling to contain his anger and the boy, afraid but defiant. Then the tribune's eyes flashed towards the centurion and he forced a smile on to his lips.

'Right then, in person it is.' Vitellius stood up, scroll in hand. 'Come with me.'

Vitellius led them down a short passage into an ante-chamber where the legate's private secretary worked at a desk to one side of a large studded door. He looked up as they approached and, seeing Vitellius, wearily rose to his feet.

'Can I see the legate?' Vitellius asked briskly.

'Is it urgent, sir?'

'Imperial despatch.' Vitellius held out the letter so that the seal could be seen. The secretary instantly knocked on the door of the legate's office and entered without waiting for a reply, closing the door behind him. There was silence for a moment and then the door opened again. The secretary ushered Vitellius inside and held up a hand to the other two. From inside, Macro could clearly hear a raised voice, punctuated by an occasional monosyllable from Vitellius. The dressing down was mercifully brief but the tribune managed to fire a cold, hostile glare at the centurion as he passed out of the office back towards the admin hall.

'He'll see you now.' The secretary waved a finger at them.

Macro silently seethed with anger at Bestia. That bloody letter would do for him. Having been ordered to act as the boy's guide to the headquarters, Macro was about to face the wrath of the legate for imposing on his precious time. If Vitellius, a tribune, could be shouted down only the gods knew what the legate would say to a humble centurion. And it was all the bloody boy's fault. Macro instinctively passed on the look he had received from Vitellius, then gulped nervously as he marched smartly through the door, past the smug expression of the secretary. At that moment he would rather have faced ten howling mad Gaulish warriors single-handed.

The legate's office was unsurprisingly spacious. The far side was dominated by a black marble-topped table behind which sat Titus Flavius Sabinus Vespasian –

scowling as he looked up from the open letter in front of him.

'Right then, Centurion. What are you doing here?'

'Sir?'

'You're supposed to be on duty.'

'Orders, sir. I was told to show this new recruit to headquarters and see you got that letter.'

'Who ordered you?'

'Lucius Batiacus Bestia. He's covering the watch until I return, sir.'

'Oh, is he?' A frown creased the broad brow of Vespasian. Then his gaze switched to the young recruit standing one step behind and to one side of Macro, desperately hoping that immobility was the surest route to invisibility. The legate's eyes quickly looked over the boy, assessing his potential. 'You are Quintus Licinius Cato?'

'Yes, sir.'

'From the palace?'

'Yes, sir.'

'Bit unusual to say the least,' Vespasian mused. 'The palace doesn't generate too many recruits for the legions, my wife excepted – even she's finding it hard to adapt to the squalor of a legate's private accommodation. I doubt you will find our ways much to your taste but you're a soldier now and that's that.'

'Yes, sir.'

'This,' Vespasian waved the letter, 'is a letter of introduction. Normally my secretary deals with such trivial matters because I have better things to do – like, for example, commanding a legion. So you can imagine how annoyed I might have been to have the tribune waste his time and, more importantly, mine, with such a matter.'

Vespasian paused and the two visitors withered under his glare. Then, he continued, in a more moderate tone. 'However, since this letter is from Claudius, as you no doubt know, I must defer to his power to bother one of his legates with petty details. He tells me that, in gratitude for your late father's service to Rome, he has made you a freedman and wishes me to appoint you centurion in my legion.'

'Oh,' Cato replied. 'Is that good, sir?'

Macro spluttered with rage momentarily, before regaining control and bunching his fists hard against his thighs.

'Problem, Centurion?' Vespasian asked.

'No, sir,' Macro managed to respond through clenched teeth.

'Now then, Cato,' the legate continued mildly. 'There is absolutely no possibility of me appointing you centurion, whatever the Emperor wishes. How old are you?'

'Sixteen, sir. Seventeen next month.'

'Sixteen . . . Hardly old enough to be a man. Certainly too young to lead men.'

'Begging your pardon, sir, but Alexander was only sixteen when he commanded his first army in battle.'

Vespasian's eyebrows shot up in amazement. 'You consider yourself to be an Alexander? What do you know about military affairs?'

'I have studied them, sir. I am familiar with the works

31

of Xenophon, Herodotus, Livy and, of course, Caesar.'

'And that makes you an expert on the *modern* Roman army does it?' Vespasian was enjoying the youngster's hubris. 'Well, I must say, I only wish all our recruits were so versed in the arts of war. It would be novel to have an army march on its brains rather than its stomach. Would be quite something, wouldn't it, Centurion?'

'Yes, sir,' Macro replied. 'We'd all be headaching instead of bellyaching, sir.'

Vespasian looked at Macro in surprise. 'Was that meant to be a joke, centurion? I don't hold with junior officers being funny. This is the army, not some Plautus comedy.'

'Yes, sir. Who, sir?'

'A playwright,' Cato patiently explained to Macro. 'Plautus adapted material from Greek theatre—'

'That's enough, son,' Vespasian cut in. 'Save it for the literary salons, should you ever return to Rome. Now then, I've decided. You will not be a centurion.'

'But, sir . . .'

Vespasian held up a hand to silence him and then pointed at Macro. 'You see this man? Now, he's a centurion. The man who escorted you here from Aventicum is also a Centurion. How do you think they came to be centurions?'

Cato shrugged. 'I've absolutely no idea, sir.'

'No idea? Well, just you listen. This man, Macro, has been a legionary for many years – how many, centurion?'

'Fourteen years, sir.'

'Fourteen years. And in that time he has marched halfway across the known world and back. This man has fought in Jupiter knows how many battles and minor engagements. He has been trained to use every weapon in the army. He can march up to twenty miles a day in full armour carrying his kit. He has been trained to swim, build roads, bridges and forts. He has many other qualities besides. This man led his patrol to safety when the Germans cut them off on the far side of the Rhine. Then, and only then, was he even considered for promotion to the centurionate. Now which of these things can you do? Right now?'

Cato thought back a moment. 'I can swim, sir – a bit.'

'Have you considered a career in the navy?' Vespasian asked hopefully.

'No. I get seasick.'

'Oh dear. Well, I'm afraid that swimming doesn't quite qualify you for command, but since we're going to need every man we can train for next year I will allow you to join the Second Legion. Dismissed . . . that's the army way of saying, please be a good fellow and wait outside.'

'Yes, sir.'

Once the door had closed behind the young man, Vespasian shook his head. 'What's the world coming to? Think we can make a soldier out of him, Centurion?'

'No, sir,' Macro replied immediately. 'The army's too dangerous a place for theatre critics.'

'So is Rome,' Vespasian sighed, recalling those who had rashly ventured an opinion on the literary output of the late Caligula. Not that matters were much better under his successor, Claudius. The new Emperor's chief secretary, the freedman Narcissus, had spies everywhere, busy compiling reports on the loyalties of every Roman who might pose the least possible threat to the new regime. The atmosphere in the capital was poisonous following the failure of Scribonianus' coup attempt and Vespasian had recently been informed that several of his wife's friends were among those already arrested. Flavia herself had only recently joined him at the base, anxious and fearful, and not for the first time Vespasian wished that Flavia would be more circumspect in her choice of social companions. But that's what came your way, Vespasian considered, when you married a woman who had been brought up in the highly political atmosphere of the imperial household. Like the young man waiting outside. Vespasian looked up from his desk.

'Well, Centurion, we'll see what we can do for young Cato. Is your century up to strength? Didn't you lose your second-in-command recently?'

'Yes sir. The optio died this morning.'

'Good, that simplifies things. Sign the boy up in your century and make him an optio.'

'But, sir!'

'But nothing. That's my order. We can't make him a centurion and I can't bend an imperial dictate too far. So we're stuck with him. Dismissed.'

'Yes, sir.' Macro saluted, turned smartly and marched out of the office, cursing under his breath. The position of optio was traditionally within the patronage of a centurion and was worth a good deal of money. He would just have to make sure the lad didn't last too long, one way or another. After all, a soft city type who didn't seem to want to be here could easily be induced to seek a discharge given the right kind of prodding.

Cato was waiting for him outside. The lad half smiled and Macro nearly kicked him.

'So what's to happen to me, sir?'

'Just shut up and come with me.'

'Yes, sir.'

'Lads, I'd like you to meet the new optio.'

In the darkened mess room the faces turned towards the centurion, lit in pale orange by the few lamps they could afford to burn. Once their gaze flickered from their centurion to the tall young boy at his side few could conceal their amazement.

'Did you say . . . new optio, sir?' someone asked.

'That's right, Pyrax.'

'Isn't he a little, well, young?'

'Apparently not,' Macro replied bitterly. 'The Emperor's decreed a new selection procedure for junior officers. You have to be tall and skinny and familiar with selected Greek and Latin histories. And those who have bothered to read the odd work of literature are given preferential treatment.'

The men looked at him blankly but Macro was too cross to offer any form of explanation. 'Anyway, here he is. Pyrax, I want you to take him to my clerk. Get him written in and issue him with a seal. He's going to join your section.'

'Sir, I thought recruits could only be written in by officers.'

'Look, I'm too busy right now,' Macro blustered. 'Anyway, that's an order. I'm making him your responsibility. So get on with it.'

Macro rushed from the mess and hurried back down the passage to his quarters. Piso was waiting outside his small office with some papers.

'Sir, if you could just sign . . .'

'Later.' Macro waved a hand at him and snatched up a dry cloak as he made for the outside door. 'Have to get back on duty.'

As the door slammed after him, Piso shrugged and returned to his desk.

Some time later, Cato was sitting bolt upright on the top bunk of a section room. Such was his height that on the top of his head he could feel the straw which lay under the roof tiles. He flinched, suddenly wondering if there were any rats in the rafters, and nervously twisted the small lead ingot that hung from a thong tied around his neck. It bore his name, his legion and the imperial seal. It would be with him until he left the army, or died in battle. Then it would be used to identify his body. Letting his chin rest on his knees, Cato wondered how he was going to get out of this appalling situation. The section room, with cramped bunks for eight men, was no better than one of the stables reserved for work horses at the palace.

And these men!

Well, they were animals. Pyrax had introduced him round the mess and Cato had been hard pressed not to reveal his disgust at the foul-smelling, boozy, farting, belching legionaries. They, for their part, had seemed unsure how to regard him. There was some resentment to be sure. Apparently an optio was a rank many were struggling to achieve. Nominally he was their superior, but he was in no way given to understand that he would be treated as such.

Conversation was limited to a discussion of who had screwed the most women, killed the most barbarians, spat the furthest, farted the loudest – that kind of thing. Stimulating to the senses maybe, but it left the mind a little cold. After what seemed a decent length of time, Cato had asked if Pyrax might be so kind as to show him to his room. Every face in the room had turned towards him, some wide-eyed and open-mouthed. Cato sensed he had somehow put his foot in it and decided that an early night would clear the air.

Chapter Three

Late the following afternoon, as dusk gathered around the fortress and the sharp winter air began to bite, an exhausted Cato hauled his feet into the barracks. The section room was quiet but, as he shut the door, Cato saw that he was not alone. He felt a twinge of irritation at this intrusion into the moment of privacy he had been looking forward to. Pyrax was sitting on his bunk darning a spare tunic by the fading light of the open shutter. He looked up as Cato crossed to his bunk and climbed up on to it fully clothed.

'Hard day, new boy?'

'Yes,' Cato grunted, not wanting to provoke any discussion.

'It only gets worse.'

'Oh.'

'Think you can hack it?'

'Yes,' Cato said firmly. 'I will.'

'Nah!' Pyrax shook his head. 'You're too soft. I give you a month.'

'A month?' Cato replied angrily.

'Yeah. A month if you're sensible . . . More if you're a fool.'

'What are you talking about?'

'There's no point in you being here. You ain't cut out for it – just a wet kid.'

'I'm nearly seventeen. I can be a soldier.'

'Still young for a soldier. And you ain't in shape. Bestia's going to break you in no time.'

'He won't! I promise you that.' Cato unwisely allowed himself a display of adolescent bravado. 'I'd rather die.'

'It may come to that.' Pyrax shrugged. 'Can't say many'd be sorry.'

'What do you mean?'

'Nothing . . .' He shrugged again and continued sewing as Cato glared at him, quite oblivious to the burning shame he had provoked in the youngster. Instead Pyrax concentrated on making sure that he kept the line of stitches quite straight as he worked along the seam. Cato watched without interest; he had seen the palace slaves at work repairing clothes all his life. All the same, spinning, weaving and sewing had always been the work of women and it was something of a novelty to see a man wielding a needle so adroitly.

Cato was sharply aware that his appointment as optio was causing him a lot of enmity. Already he seemed to have fallen foul of Bestia, the centurion in charge of training. Worse still, some of the recruits were openly hostile to him, particularly a group of men sent to the legion from a prison in Perusia, bound in chains for the entire journey. Their self-appointed leader was a thick-set, ugly man who excelled in the latter description, so much so that it was inevitable that he be named Pulcher – the beautiful. One day on the march Cato had found himself immediately behind Pulcher when the man had demanded a drink from Cato's flask of wine. It was a small thing, but the tone with which the demand had been made was so loaded with menace that Cato had handed the flask over at once. Pulcher drank deeply, then, when Cato asked for the flask to be returned, had passed the wine to his friends.

'You want it, boy?' Pulcher had curled his lips into a sneer. 'Then you take it.'

'Give it back to me.'

'Make me.'

Cato winced at the memory and his conscience once again demanded of him whether this was really the behaviour of a proper soldier. A proper soldier would have struck the man at once and taken the flask back. But, the rational side of his mind argued, a man would have to be built like a brick shithouse to take on Pulcher, with his solid limbs and hands like shovels. As if reading his expression, Pulcher had snarled and Cato instinctively stepped back, causing everyone to laugh. He had burned with shame, and still did, even though he told himself that retreat from superior forces was perfectly reasonable, intellectually virtuous in fact. A kindly soldier from the escort had retrieved the flask and tossed it back to Cato with a laugh. Pulcher spat in his direction before the soldier prodded him back into line with the butt of his spear.

'I'll see you in camp, boy,' Pulcher snarled, raising his chains. 'As soon as I get rid of these.'

Since their arrival at the fortress the army had kept the recruits busy and Cato hoped that Pulcher had forgotten about him. He had striven to keep as far from

the man as possible, not even meeting his gaze, in a bid
to become invisible. Now, he had returned to the barracks
rather than remain with the other recruits after they had
been dismissed at the end of the day. It was essential, he
reflected, to make some friends quickly. But how? And
who? The others had bonded into little groups during
the journey from Aventicum – while he had been reading
bloody Virgil, he angrily reminded himself. What he
would give to begin that journey afresh, knowing what
he did now.

Alone, and a long way from his friends back in Rome.
For a moment misery welled up inside him and Cato's
eyes stung with tears. He turned towards the wall and
buried his face in the coarse material of the straw-stuffed
bolster. He felt his chest shudder and suddenly felt angry,
angry at himself, angry that he wasn't man enough to
cope without tears and angry that nothing in his life had
prepared him for this. All his smug Greek tutors and
their stupid admiration for only the finest rhetoric and
poetry – what bloody good were they now? How could
poetry protect him from that animal, Centurion Bestia?
At this moment he would have exchanged all his learning
for a single friend.

Pyrax paused and looked up, needle poised above the
tunic. He had heard the new boy turn over and
recognised the stifled sob for what it was. Pyrax shook
his head sadly. Most recruits were old enough and hardy
enough to cope. Then there were boys, like this one, who
really shouldn't be in the army. It might be the making
of them, as some soldiers argued, but equally it might
destroy them.

The boy sobbed again, muffled as much as possible by the bolster.

'Hey!' Pyrax said harshly. 'Do you mind? I'm trying to concentrate here.'

Cato stirred. 'Sorry. I think I've got a cold.'

'Yeah,' Pyrax nodded. 'Sure. Bound to happen in this weather.'

Cato rubbed his face on the corner of the rough military blanket, drying his tears and trying to make it look as if he was blowing his nose. 'There.'

'Better?'

'Yes, thank you,' Cato replied, grateful that someone was taking interest in him. Then he was immediately worried that his chance to talk to Pyrax alone might be stalled if anyone interrupted. 'Where are all the others?'

'Dice game in the mess room. I'm going to join 'em once I've fixed this. Want to come with me and meet the lads?'

'No thanks. I need some sleep.'

'Suit yourself.'

'Tell me,' Cato suddenly turned and propped himself up, 'is that Centurion Bestia as much of a bastard as he seems?'

'How do you think he got the name Bestia? But don't take it to heart, he treats all recruits the same way.'

'Maybe,' Cato said doubtfully, 'but he seems to have it in for me in particular.'

'What do you expect?' Pyrax said through gritted teeth as he pulled the end of a knot tight and then cut off the spare thread. 'You're in the camp for one night and you're promoted to a rank most of us have to wait years for.'

Cato watched the man closely before speaking. 'You resent it?'

'Of course. You've not proved yourself in any way. You're just a boy.' He shrugged. 'It ain't right.'

Cato flushed with guilt and embarrassment, glad that the dim light partially hid his expression. 'I didn't ask for it.'

'It don't make sense. Direct appointments are made for men with some kind of army experience but you? I'd dearly love to know the reason why.'

'It was a reward for my father.'

'Hah! That's a good one!'

The light had finally died outside and Pyrax put his tunic and sewing kit to one side. 'By the way,' Pyrax paused at the door, 'don't fall asleep in your kit. It'll need to be cleaned for the morning. Bestia hates untidy soldiers. If he has taken a dislike to you, don't give him any opportunity to make the most if it, eh?'

'Thanks.'

'Sleep well, new boy.'

'My name's . . .' Cato started to say, but the door had already closed behind Pyrax and the darkened room swallowed up the protest. He was still for a moment, and nearly fell asleep, but Pyrax's warning jolted him back to consciousness. He sat up, groping with his tired fingers for the buckles at the side of the leather jerkin. The drill instructors had kept the new recruits on their feet since that day's dawn had broken what seemed like an age before. He had been kicked out of bed while it was still dark and pushed outside into the street where the other recruits were being rounded up. Still half asleep, shivering in the chill of the pale dawn light and shrinking from the fine drizzle in the air, their breaths had risen in grey wisps as they were led to the quartermaster's stores where the external trappings of civilian life were peeled away and replaced with the uniform of a legionary.

'Excuse me!' Cato had called out. 'Excuse me.'

The quartermaster's assistant looked back over his shoulder. 'What is it?'

'Well, this tunic, it seems a bit big for me.'

The assistant laughed. 'No, mate. It's the right size. You're the one that's the wrong size. You're in the army now. One size fits all.'

'But look! This is ludicrous.' Cato held the tunic up in front of his body, it was far too wide for his thin frame, and his height drew the hem well above his knees. 'My legs will freeze. Is there nothing else?'

'No. You'll grow into it.'

'What?' Cato replied incredulously. 'I'm the shape I am. I'm not suddenly going to shrink and grow outwards. Now find me something the right size.'

'I told you. That's all there is, and you're stuck with it.'

The raised voices were audible right through the storeroom and all the other recruits and assistants paused to look in their direction. In the small office behind the counter, a chair screeched back on the flagstone floor and a burly man emerged angrily from the door.

'What's all the bloody shouting about?'

'Are you in charge here?' asked Cato, glad to see someone in authority he could make a complaint to. It was as bad as some of the shops in Rome. Everyone was using cheap help these days, staff who neither cared nor knew about their goods. He had been forced to complain about such matters to managers many times before when purchasing for the palace and knew the best approach to adopt. 'I was trying to explain to this man . . .'

'Who the bloody hell are you?' The quartermaster bellowed.

'Quintus Licinius Cato, Optio of the Sixth Century, Fourth Cohort.'

The quartermaster frowned for a moment and then laughed. 'Oh, I've heard all about you! Optio! Hah! Well then, optio,' he smiled. 'What seems to be the problem?'

'Look here. I just want this man to provide me with a garment my size.'

'May I?' The quartermaster reached out for the tunic, and Cato gladly returned it to him. The quartermaster made an elaborate show of examining the tunic, running his hand over the crude stitching and finally holding it up to the light coming in from the open shutters.

'Yes,' he concluded. 'This is a standard-issue tunic all right. Nothing wrong with it.'

'But—'

'Shut it!' The quartermaster flung the tunic back across the counter. 'Now take the bloody thing and don't waste any more of my time.'

'But—'

'And call me "sir" – you snotty little upstart!'

Cato opened his mouth to utter a horrified protest, but managed to bite his tongue at the last moment. 'Yes, sir.'

'Good. Now get the rest of your kit.' The quartermaster turned back to his office, then noticed that everyone had stopped to enjoy the performance. 'What the hell are you lot gawping at?'

The stores building instantly turned back into heaving activity as the new recruits collected their kit allocations. With a shrug, Cato folded the tunic and stood at the counter as the assistant piled his clothing and equipment on to the battered wooden surface. In addition to the tunic was a pair of woollen breeches, a yellow leather jerkin, a thick red cloak waterproofed with animal fat, boots shod with iron nails and a mess tin. The assistant shoved a slate towards him. 'Sign here, or make your mark.'

'What's this?'

'Receipt for your civvy clothes.'

'What?'

'You're not allowed to keep your clothes. You give 'em to me after you change into uniform. We sell them for you in the local market and give you the proceeds.'

'Absolutely not!' Cato said firmly.

The assistant turned back towards the office and opened his mouth to call out.

'Wait!' Cato stopped him. 'I'll sign. But do you have to sell them? I want to keep my boots and travel cloak.'

'Recruits have to be in uniform. Can't just wear any old thing. Anyway there's no room to store clothes. But I promise we'll get you a good price.'

For some reason Cato doubted he would see much of a return on his clothes. 'How can I be sure you'll give me the full sum?'

'Are you accusing me of dishonesty?' the assistant replied in mock horror.

Cato slowly stripped naked and pulled on the standard-issue tunic. It was as ill-fitting as he had feared, reminding him of the short tunics worn by the prostitutes back in Rome. The breeches were uncomfortable and had to be tied tightly above his skinny hips to stop them falling down. And they itched terribly. Almost as uncomfortable were the heavy military boots made of thick-cut leather and laced with tough thongs. The nail studs on the bottom made a clattering sound on the stone floor and some of the younger recruits were amusing themselves by kicking sparks off the paving, until the quartermaster tucked his head round the door and shouted at them to stop. When the boots were laced and tied Cato pulled the heavy leather jerkin over his head and fastened the buckles on each side. It was difficult, as the leather of the new jerkin was stiff. It was hard to bend forward and he could only just reach his laces with a great deal of straining. He noticed that, for some reason, his jerkin had a piece of white linen stitched over the right shoulder – a quick look round the room revealed that his was the only jerkin with a patch.

The main door to the stores building momentarily darkened and Cato looked up to see Centurion Bestia enter and stand just inside the room shaking his head pitifully as he surveyed the new recruits, tapping his silvered greaves with the tip of his cane.

'Stand still!' he shouted and the room instantly fell silent. As he slowly strolled down the length of the storeroom the recruits nervously fell back against the wall.

Bestia snorted derisively. 'Hah! I've never seen such a bunch of women! Right then, girls – outside now!'

The drizzle had cleared away with the dawn and the sun glowed through a slight haze. The air was just cold enough to be fresh to the skin and, all around, the fortress bustled with activity. Training raw recruits was something Bestia greatly enjoyed. Like every drill instructor, he had amassed a collection of useful invective for all occasions and comfortably slipped into the required role of rock-hard intolerance with subtle hints of a warm-hearted concern for his charges. In time they would come to regard him as a father figure – though perhaps not all of them.

As Bestia's eyes swept down the ranks they fixed on Cato, looming nearly half a head above the rest – his height emphasised by the fact he stood immediately to the left of Pulcher.

'You! Yes, you, Mister-I've-got-a-bloody-letter-from-my-friend-the-Emperor!' Bestia bellowed as he strode towards Cato and sharply poked his vine cane into the white shoulder patch. 'What the bloody hell is this?'

Cato winced. 'I don't know, sir.'

'Don't know! How long have you been in the army? Almost half a bloody day and you still can't recognise badges of rank!' Standing right in front of Cato, he glared up into the youngster's face barely a span apart. 'Just what kind of fucking soldier are you?'

'I don't know sir, I . . .'

'Don't look down at me!' Bestia screamed, splattering saliva. 'Keep your fucking eyes straight ahead! At all times. Do you understand me?'

Cato flicked his eyes up and stiffened. 'Yes, sir.'

'So what the hell are you doing with optio's insignia?'

'I am an optio, sir.'

'Bollocks!' Bestia shouted. 'We do not promote ladies overnight.'

'I was, in matter of fact, made an optio last night, sir,' Cato explained.

'So then, optio today, centurion tomorrow, tribune the day after . . . At this rate you'll make fucking Emperor by the end of the week! You take me for a fool, boy?'

'Er, excuse me, sir,' one of the drill instructors said quietly from behind Bestia. 'He *is* an optio, sir.'

'What?' Bestia jerked a thumb at Cato. 'Him?'

'Afraid so, sir. Direct commission from the legate. It's been entered on the new recruit roster, sir.' The drill instructor held out a wax board and pointed out Cato's name.

'Quintus Licinius Cato, optio.' Bestia read out loud. Then he turned back to Cato with clear menace in his eyes. 'So that's what the letter was about! Friends in powerful places, eh? Well, it won't help you. Optio you may be, but while you're on basic training you get the same treatment as the rest. Understand?'

'Yes, sir.'

'In fact,' Bestia leaned close to him, whispering, 'I'll treat you worse. You got the promotion – now you're fucking going to have to earn it.'

Then he spun round and strode away. He took up a position ten paces ahead of the front rank of recruits. 'First lesson, ladies. The attention pose. Your drill instructors have placed you in four ranks, exactly one pace apart from the man beside you, and two paces between ranks. Memorise your position. In future, when I tell you to form ranks you will go to the position you are now in, at once. The correct posture for unarmed attention position is this.'

Bestia dropped his cane and stiffened, his chest thrust out, shoulders back, head up, arms straight down with palms flattened against the sides of his thighs. He paused a moment. 'You all see that? Right then, let's see you do it.'

The recruits self-consciously did their best to adopt the pose while the drill instructors went down the ranks, making adjustments where necessary. Once they were content Bestia continued. 'Next thing. When standing at attention you must at all times fix your eyes straight ahead – whatever happens. And I *mean* whatever happens, ladies. If bloody Venus herself rides past accompanied by a thousand naked virgins and I see any one of you so much as flicker his eyes to one side, I will beat the living shit out of him. Understand? I SAID, DO YOU UNDERSTAND?'

The recruits flinched before nervously replying in an overlapping wave of yesses.

'Louder! I want to fucking hear you this time!'

'YES, SIR!' The recruits roared.

'Better . . .' Bestia smiled. 'Think of yourselves as a part of one body. You will move, talk and think as one from now on . . . Right then, over to the armourer for your weapons. Now, when I say, "Prepare to march . . . march!" you will lead off on your left foot and follow me keeping in position. I will call out the step and I'll keep it slow. Right then, ladies. Prepare to march! March! Left. Right. Left. Right . . . Left . . . Left . . . Left.'

Led by the centurion and flanked by the drill instructors, the recruits ambled off in a long straggling column. Cato tried to keep in time but found that the recruit in front of him, Pulcher, had a short stride, and Cato had to concentrate hard on shortening his pace so as not to collide. It took a considerable act of faith to believe that any army could get two such differently proportioned men to march at the same pace. Almost as if the gods had decided to prove the point Cato scraped his boot down Pulcher's ankle.

'Shit! Watch it, you bastard!' Pulcher turned angrily.

'You! No speaking in ranks!' A drill instructor shouted. 'You're on a charge! Get moving!'

The stocky recruit scowled once at Cato and quickly fell back into step. A moment later Pulcher hissed over his shoulder, 'You'll pay for that, mate.'

'I'm sorry,' Cato whispered back.

'Sorry ain't good enough.'

'It was a mistake.'

'Tough shit.'

'But . . .'

'Shut your fucking mouth, before you get me into any more trouble.'

Cato marched silently behind Pulcher, making sure that his feet kept a safe distance behind the man's heels.

The recruits looked confused, Macro reflected with a smile as he watched them from the chief armourer's desk. They had all received, and signed for, their issue of helmet, mail shirt and dagger, and swaggered around the armoury the way he had seen thousands of new recruits do before. The thrill of wearing a soldier's uniform for the first time was ageless and the recruits looked at each other admiringly. Then, the armourers had started issuing the weighted wooden swords, large rectangular wicker shields and training spears. The recruits were staring at their weapons dumbfounded, holding them at arms' length in disgust.

'Always the same, isn't it?' Macro grinned.

'One-day wonders.' Scaevola complained. 'They never learn. What is wrong with young men today?'

'Same problem as ever. Even you were like them once.'

'Bollocks.' Scaevola spat from his toothless mouth. 'Now tell me, young Macro, what are you doing here? Don't see you from one year to the next. Last time we had a quiet drink, you were a bloody legionary. Now look at you. Centurion Macro. Bloody legion's gone to the dogs.' He looked up and caught sight of the twinkle in the centurion's eyes. 'If you've just come by to wind me up . . . ?'

'Not this time.' Macro smiled and raised his cup. 'Just to share some wine with a veteran, and exchange the odd scrap of news.'

'The odd scrap of news!' Scaevola said contemptuously. 'I know why you're here.'

'Oh yes?'

'It wouldn't be anything to do with the bloody inventory the legate's ordered, would it?'

'Of course not.' Macro reached over with the flask and topped Scaevola up. 'Why would I be interested in that?'

'You'd be the only one in the legion who wasn't.' Scaevola took a swig. 'Anyway, I'm not saying nothing. Orders.'

'Yes,' Macro repeated thoughtfully. 'Orders. I wonder where we're being sent? Hope it's somewhere warm for a change. I'm bloody sick of Germany. Freezing in winter, baking in summer and it's impossible to get any decent wine – cheaply that is.'

The last remark was pointed. The wine they were drinking was from Macro's last jar of Falernian, not the acidic Gaulish brew the local traders peddled. He hoped Scaevola appreciated the gesture, and also hoped that it might loosen the veteran's tongue. It wasn't just for curiosity – a centurion needed to plan ahead. It was useful to know where the Legion was being sent so that he could prepare for the transfer and buy in whatever he needed for the journey before the news broke officially and supplies were snapped up and the local traders charged premium prices. With a tip of his head Scaevola emptied his cup and Macro instantly refilled it. 'Wherever we go, I hope there's something decent to drink.'

'Fat chance!' Scaevola snorted. 'You'd better enjoy this stuff. Won't be much booze over there.'

'None at all?' Macro feigned horror.

'None.' Scaevola replied, then abruptly stood up and shouted over Macro's shoulder. 'There's nothing bloody wrong with that sword! Hold it properly!'

Macro turned on his stool and searched out the target of Scaevola's anger. Standing out, as usual, was that infernal new boy, examining his wooden short sword as he held it by the tip of the point.

'But, sir. This isn't a proper sword. It's wood.'

'Of course it's bloody wood.'

As Centurion Bestia pushed his way through the crowd of recruits to see what the fuss was all about he bawled out. 'What? You causing trouble again? What's the matter now? Sword the wrong size?'

'No, sir. It's wooden. Not a proper sword, sir.'

'Wooden? Of course, it's bloody wooden. It's not a proper sword because you're not a proper soldier. If you become a real soldier, then you get to play with the real thing.'

Bestia filled his lungs to address all the recruits. 'As some of you may have realised, like sonny boy here, the weapons you have been given are not real. Because you do not yet deserve the real thing. If we just handed out dangerous weapons to you ladies you'd be injuring each other in no time. The army does not wish to save our enemies the effort. Before you can hold a sword you must respect it. You must learn how to use it properly. Same goes for the spear. You may find your weapons heavy. That's because they're twice the weight of the standard issue. You are soft, idle scum and we need to build you up and make men of you. We can only do that by training and exercise, and there'll be plenty of it, ladies. So get used to the weight. Now then, the sword belt is fastened with the sword hanging to the right, NOT to the left – like I've got it. That's for officers only . . . Hold your spear in your right hand, shield in the left and get into four ranks outside . . . Now!'

The recruits placed their shields and spears down and struggled with the stiff buckles of their swordbelts before grabbing their equipment and fleeing towards the door.

'Excellent stuff this wine,' Scaevola hinted. 'Shall we have another?'

There was hardly any left in the flask and Macro made sure that Scaevola had the lion's share, saving the dregs for himself.

'What were we talking about?' Scaevola asked.

'Drink. You were saying there's no good drink where the Legion's going.'

'Did I?' Scaevola raised his eyebrows.

'I suppose that means the far east,' Macro carried on casually. 'Nothing decent to drink, just that crap they make out of fermented goat's milk, so I've heard. Or worse, it might even be Judea.'

He watched Scaevola's face for any flicker of response, but the chief armourer merely took another draught of wine and nodded. 'It might be Judea . . . It might not.'

Macro sighed with frustration – getting information out of the canny old veteran was harder than getting the clap off a vestal virgin. He decided to attempt a new line of enquiry.

'Well, have you indented for any lightweight tunics?'

'Now why would I do that?' Scaevola frowned. 'Why on earth would I indent for those?'

Macro took a deep breath, fighting back his growing irritation at Scaevola's smug avoidance of the one answer he sought. 'Look here, Scaevola. Just tell me what you know. Just one word. Just the name of the place we're going. Just the name of the province will do. And I promise I won't tell another soul. You have my word.'

'Sure.' Scaevola smiled. 'Until someone comes up to

you with a flask of wine and tries to loosen your tongue. I have my orders. The legate wants to keep it quiet for as long as possible.'

'But why?'

'Let's just say that the men won't be best pleased when they find out where we're being sent.' Scaevola drained his cup. 'Now I must get back to work. Vespasian wants the inventory completed as soon as possible.'

'Well, thanks,' Macro said bitterly as he rose from the table. 'Thanks for nothing.'

'Not at all!' Scaevola beamed. 'Drop by any time.'

Macro didn't reply as he turned and made for the door.

'Oh, Macro!' Scaevola called after him.

'Yes?'

'If you do drop by, feel free to bring some more of that wine along.'

Macro ground his teeth and stamped out of the armoury.

Chapter Four

Vespasian was wearing the full dress uniform of a legion commander as he mounted the podium at the side of the parade ground. The silvered greaves, breastplate and helmet caught the light of the midday sun and shone brilliantly. The red crest and cloak lifted to a faint breeze. Behind him stood the standard bearers carrying aloft the golden eagle of the Second Legion and the image of the Emperor Claudius – a rather over-flattering likeness, thought Cato, who had last seen the Emperor spluttering food while attempting to conduct a conversation at an imperial dinner. Below the eagle hung a bottom-weighted square of red leather upon which the words 'Augusta' had been embroidered in gold letters.

The recruits faced the podium in four ranks with Bestia and his drill instructors five paces to front. All were standing silently, spears and shields grounded to the sides, as demonstrated to them shortly before. Chests were thrust out, chins raised and shoulders squared, even though Cato couldn't help feeling slightly ridiculous with what seemed to be an over-large wicker basket to one side and a child's wooden toy to the other. But still the sense of occasion filled his breast as he gazed solemnly at the podium where Vespasian was making the ritual offering of two cockerels to the gods. He washed his hands in the ceremonial bowl, dried them on a silk cloth and turned to face the assembled recruits.

'I, Titus Flavius Sabinus Vespasian, Legate of the Second Legion, Augusta, by gracious decree of the Emperor Claudius, pronounce favourable omens on those here assembled for the purpose of enrolment in the Second Legion, and do hereby request and require those here assembled to undertake the oath of allegiance to the Legion, to the legate, to the Senate and People of Rome as vested in the body and person of the Emperor Claudius. Legionaries, raise your spear and recite the oaths with me . . .'

Two hundred right arms swept straight up and sunlight glinted on the shimmering spear tips.

'I swear by the gods of the Capitol, Jupiter, Juno and Minerva . . .'

'That I will faithfully execute the orders of those placed over me . . .'

'By the will of the senate and people of Rome . . .'

'As embodied in the person of the Emperor Claudius . . .'

'Furthermore, I swear by the same gods . . .'

'That I will defend the standards of my legion and my century . . .'

'Unto the last drop of my blood. This I swear!'

As the last echoes died away, all was still for a magical moment and Cato felt a lump rise in his throat. The oaths had made him a different man. He was now set aside from the rest of society, in a new order of existence. He could be ordered to his death on the legate's whim and he would be compelled to obey. He had pledged his life to protect an inanimate lump of gold atop a plain wooden staff. Cato doubted the sanity of the oath he had taken. It was wanton irresponsibility to pledge unquestioning obedience to any man that fate, nepotism or merit placed over him. Nevertheless . . . there was something else, an overwhelming gush of excitement and a feeling of belonging to a group imbued with the mystique of an exclusively male society.

At a gesture from Vespasian, Bestia ordered the recruits to ground spears.

'New recruits to the Second Legion,' said the legate. 'You are joining a unit with a proud tradition and I demand that you honour that tradition every waking moment for the next twenty-six years. The months ahead of you will be hard, as I'm sure Centurion Bestia has already told you.' He smiled. 'But they are crucial in making you into soldiers I can be proud to command. A legionary is the highest trained, hardest fighting man in the known world – and that means we must mould you into a very special kind of person. Years of experience will see to the rest. As I look down at you, I see countrymen and men from the cities. Most of you are volunteers, some conscripted. Your past is your own affair, not the army's. Whatever you were in civilian life you are soldiers now and that is how you will be judged. You are fortunate men. You have joined the Legion at a time when it is about to make history.'

That made Cato's ears prick up.

'In years to come you will be celebrated as conquerors, as men who dared to challenge one of the last great mysteries at the edge of the known world. Think on that, and let it be your inspiration while you train. You are in good hands. You could find no better person to train you than Centurion Bestia. I wish you luck and have every confidence that you will succeed.'

Back to the clichés, Cato groaned inwardly.

'Carry on, Centurion.' Vespasian nodded to Bestia and then left the platform followed by the standard bearers.

'Yes, sir!' Bestia turned to face the recruits. 'Well, ladies, that completes the enrolment. You are all mine now. And training begins immediately after the midday meal. I want you back here then. Any later and I'll stripe your back with my cane. Dismissed!'

The entire afternoon had been spent on basic drill without a moment to sit down and Cato's legs and arms ached abominably from the strain of holding his heavy training equipment. He desperately wanted to sleep, to rest his body and drift away from the hard world he had been forced into. But sleep would not come. Strange surroundings, reflections on the day and anxieties about the future all combined in a whirling bout of mental activity that drove sleep away. He turned on to both sides to try and find the most comfortable arrangement afforded by the uncomfortable bunk, but either way the hard wooden slats could easily be felt through the worn woollen cover of the mattress. His sleeplessness was compounded by the frequent roars and cries from the dice game that was going on in the next section room. Not even the thick bolster pulled over the head could do much to keep the noise out.

But finally sleep came, despite all, and Cato had slowly rolled on to his back, mouth opening in a snore – when a pair of hands roughly shook him back into consciousness. His eyes flickered open to see a thick mop of oily black hair, dark eyes and broken teeth in a mouth stretched into a cruel grin.

'Pulcher . . .'

'On your feet, you bastard!'

'Do you know what time . . . ?' Cato began lamely.

'Fuck the time. We've got business to settle.' Pulcher grabbed Cato's tunic near the throat and hauled him down from the bunk on to the floor. 'I would've got here sooner, but Bestia put me on latrine fatigues, thanks to you. You really did drop me in the shit, didn't you?'

'I-I'm sorry. It was an accident.'

'Well then, let's call what I'm about to do to you an accident. Then we're quits.'

'What do you mean?' Cato asked nervously as he scrambled up off the floor.

'Just this.' Pulcher pulled a short-bladed knife from inside his cloak. 'A little cut to remind you not to fuck with me again.'

'No need!' said Cato. 'I promise I'll keep out of your way!'

'Promises get forgotten. But not scars . . .' Pulcher tossed the knife up and caught it by the handle – the point aimed at Cato's face. 'On the cheek, that way you'll remind others not to mess with me as well.'

Cato glanced around the room, but he was trapped in the corner with nowhere to run to that Pulcher couldn't reach first. A sudden roar of laughter from the next room attracted his eyes to the wall.

'You shout and I'll gut you here and now!' Pulcher hissed. Then he shifted his weight forward.

Cato could see the attack was imminent and, in desperation, lunged forward, grabbing at the wrist behind the blade with both of his hands. Pulcher had not been expecting the terrified boy to move first and tried to withdraw his hand – too late. The boy's grip was surprisingly strong and no amount of shaking and jerking could free his knife arm.

'Let go!' Pulcher snapped. 'Let go, you little piece of shit!'

Cato made no reply and, instead, suddenly sank his teeth into Pulcher's forearm. Pulcher cried out and instinctively smashed his free hand into the side of Cato's head, knocking him back against the bunk. There was an explosion of white inside Cato's skull before the room swirled back into vision. Pulcher was looking down at a dark oval patch on his arm where Cato's teeth had broken the skin.

'You're dead!' Pulcher stooped into a crouch, knife at the ready. 'You're fucking dead!'

Suddenly a broad shaft of light from the corridor flowed into the room as the door was swung open.

'What the hell is this?' Macro growled. 'Is this a fight?'

Pulcher drew himself up. 'No, sir. Just showing the boy how to handle himself in a fight. We're friends, sir.'

'Friends?' Macro repeated doubtfully. 'Then what happened to your arm?'

'Lad got carried away, sir. Didn't mean no harm. Ain't that right?'

Cato rose from the floor. His first instinct was to tell the truth. Then he realised that this wasn't the soldier's way. If he was to earn any respect from his new comrades he couldn't afford to be seen as running to authority for protection. Besides, if he covered for Pulcher now then maybe the thug would have cause to be grateful to him. Any advantage was worth securing at this stage.

'Yes, sir. That's right. We're friends.'

'Hmm.' Macro scratched his chin. 'Well, if you really are friends then I'd hate to be one of your enemies. Right, optio – I want a word with you in my quarters right now, so I'm afraid your friend here will have to leave.'

'Sir!' Pulcher replied smartly. 'I'll see you tomorrow, Cato.'

'Yes . . ?'

'We can continue our practice then.'

Cato smiled weakly then Pulcher turned and left the room, leaving an amused Macro in his wake.

'So that's your friend, is it?'

'Yes, sir.'

'I'd be a little more careful in my selection of friends if I were you.'

'Yes, sir.'

'Now then, we need to talk. Come with me.'

Macro led the way down the corridor to the administration section of the barracks block where his quarters were situated. Cato was ushered, with a friendly

63

wave, into the centurion's office where two desks were set against opposite walls. The larger desk was completely clear while the smaller was covered in neatly arranged piles of papyrus and waxed slates.

'Over there.' Macro pointed to a trestle chair by the larger desk and Cato sat down quietly while the centurion found another chair and placed it behind the desk.

'Drink?' Macro asked. 'It's good stuff.'

'Thank you, sir.'

Macro poured them each a small cup from a large jar and then eased himself back into his chair. A good deal of wine had already passed his lips that day and he felt uncommonly good-natured. Experience should have told him that today's good nature is tomorrow's skull-crunching hangover – but the gods of wine and memory never were on speaking terms.

'I need to talk about your duties, as far as being an optio is concerned. For the moment I just want you to help Piso with the paperwork. There's no way I can let you give orders to the other men in the century – they'd die laughing. I know you outrank them, officially, but you just have to accept that you can't act as an optio for the moment. Understand?'

'Yes, sir.'

'Given time, once you've trained . . . then we'll see. But for now I need a clerk more than I need a second-in-command. Piso will show you what you need to know in the morning.'

'Yes, sir.'

'Now I expect you could use some sleep, you'll need it. You can go.'

'Thank you, sir.'

'I will arrange for Piso to show you the ropes after training ends tomorrow.'

'Yes, sir. I'll look forward to it.'

Chapter Five

The time passed quickly, to Cato's consternation. There simply did not seem to be enough time in the day to do all that the army required of him. Apart from the relentless drilling at the hands of Bestia, Cato had administrative duties to carry out each evening, and then he had to ensure that his equipment was thoroughly cleaned for the next morning. Bestia had the eyes of a hawk and any speck of dirt, broken strap or missing buckle was instantly spotted and resulted in fatigues, or a thrashing with his cane. Wielding a vine cane was something of an art, Cato had discovered. The trick was to inflict as much pain with as little lasting damage as possible – soldiers were supposed to be disciplined, not hospitalised. Accordingly, Bestia restricted his blows to the fleshy parts of the legs, shoulders and buttocks. Cato had occasion to sample Bestia's expertise one day when he had failed to fasten the chin strap of his helmet. Bestia had pounced on him, ripping the helmet off – almost taking one ear with it.

'That's what will bloody happen to you in battle, you stupid bastard!' he shouted into Cato's face. 'Some bloody German will rip your fucking helmet off and smash his sword through the top of your skull. Is that what you want?'

'No, sir.'

'Personally, I don't give a toss about what happens to you. But I will not let the tax-payer's investment in you go to waste just because you're an idle bastard. You we can replace, but a dead soldier means lost equipment and I will not let you give the quartermaster any excuse to get on my back!'

Bestia swung his cane and, before Cato could respond, there was a sharp blow to his left shoulder and his arm went numb. The nerveless fingers loosened their grip on the wicker shield and it fell to the ground.

'Next time you forget to fasten your helmet, it'll be your fucking head.'

'Yes, sir,' Cato gasped.

At the start of every day the recruits had to assemble fully dressed and fully equipped as the dawn trumpet calls blared out across the fortress. Kit inspection was followed by a breakfast of porridge, bread and wine, dolloped into their mess tins by a resentful cook's assistant appointed to rise with the recruits. Then came parade-ground drill. Marching in step, halting, turning, changing face at a word of command. Every mis-step, wrong turn or mistimed movement brought forth a stream of invective from Bestia and his drill instructors and the slash of a vine cane. Eventually the recruits could respond instantly to his commands and training proceeded to the next stage – formation changes. From close order to open order, line to column and back to line. Learning how to march in wedge formation and tortoise formation – and all this while carrying the heavy training equipment.

After the midday meal it was even worse as the drill instructors moved their squads on to fitness training. For the first month, each afternoon was spent marching round the outside of the base, again and again and again until the burnished winter sun dipped into the wispy grey of dusk and, at last, Bestia led them back through the main gate at the same unrelenting pace. In the first weeks, numerous recruits fell out of line only to be promptly pounced on by a drill instructor and thrashed back on to the end of the column.

After the incident in the barracks, Cato made strenuous efforts to keep away from Pulcher and he was quite content to let the other man believe it was through fear. And fear it was, fear tempered by a logic which told him that there could only be one outcome from an open confrontation with Pulcher – being beaten to a pulp. To Cato's mind it made little sense to satisfy one's pride at the expense of one's body. If Pulcher thought him less of a man because Cato denied him the opportunity of beating him up then that was the measure of Pulcher's stupidity, and of any man who felt the same. And yet others did feel the same. Cato slowly became aware of the pitying glances directed at him by other recruits, and the way in which they drew back from him in the few spare moments between training sessions.

'You're going to have to fight him,' said Pyrax one evening as they sat on a bench in the century's mess room.

Cato took a swig of the rancid wine he had bought to

share with Pyrax. The foul liquid rasped down his throat and he coughed.

'You all right?'

Cato nodded. 'Just the wine.'

Pyrax looked down into his cup and took a thoughtful sip. 'Nothing wrong with it.'

'Perhaps if I fight him when I'm drunk I won't notice the pain,' Cato wondered. 'He gets to win easily, I get a few knocks and then it's all over.'

'Maybe. But I wouldn't count on him letting it go at that. I know the type, once they know they've got you beaten they can't resist coming back and doing it again and again. But you keep avoiding Pulcher and people are going to start wondering. I say face him, take a beating – but don't give in too early. Try and stick it to him. Land a few painful blows and he'll leave you alone. Maybe.'

'Maybe? Is that the best I can hope for? Accept a swift kicking on the off chance that Pulcher may decide to leave it at that? What if he doesn't?'

Pyrax shrugged.

'Oh thanks! That's really helpful.'

'Just telling you how it is, son.'

Cato shook his head. 'There must be some other way. Some way of confronting him without a fight.'

'Maybe,' Pyrax shrugged. 'But whatever you do just get it over with soon, before too many people think you're a coward.'

Cato stared at him a moment. 'Is that what they're saying?'

'What d'you expect? That's what it looks like.'

'I'm not a coward.'

'If you say so. But you'd better prove it.'

The door opened with an icy blast and several legionaries entered the mess. In the wildly flickering glow of the mess brazier, Cato recognised them as men from another century. They looked round and then, very deliberately, sat on a bench on the far side of the room. Pyrax quickly downed the last of his wine and rose to his feet.

'Must be off.'

'Why so early?' asked Cato. 'There's plenty left in the flask.'

'True. But I've my reputation to think of,' Pyrax added coldly. 'Remember what I said – do whatever you're going to do, but do it soon.'

Once Pyrax had left the mess Cato brooded over his wine for a while, and then, when he looked up, he momentarily caught the eyes of one of the new arrivals. The man instantly glanced away and carried on talking in low tones to his friends. It was hard not to think that they were talking about him, that they had come to this mess out of curiosity to see the coward who had been appointed an optio.

Cato stood up and, pulling his cloak on, hurried from the mess. The air was freezing and the night sky was threaded with fine clouds rimmed in pale silver from a half moon. Quite beautiful, he thought and paused for a moment to savour the stillness of the moment. But all too soon his mind turned back to the need to confront Pulcher and with a curse he stamped off towards his quarters.

* * *

Nor was Pulcher the only thing troubling his mind. Aside from the relentless drilling during the day Cato had to devote most evenings to learning his duties as an optio. The centurion's secretary, Piso, had been ordered to train the new recruit in the art of military administration. And an art it was, as Cato quickly came to realise. Piso was responsible for the century's records; a file on each legionary itemising every aspect of the soldier's life as far as it affected the Legion. Medical records, leave granted, military awards granted, disciplinary breaches and the appropriate punishments, deductions from pay for food and repayments on equipment issued.

One evening, shortly after the conversation with Pyrax, found Piso and his protégé working in the warm fug of the century's office. The brazier glowed and the wooden fuel crackled pleasantly as the two men examined Cato's latest attempt at writing in the arid style beloved of the army. Piso grunted appreciative noises as he read over the brisk but irrefutably logical requisitions and nodded approvingly at some of the well-turned phrases calculated to provoke a sense of urgency, or implying that an authority well above that of a lowly century clerk was indirectly responsible for the request.

The doorlatch clattered and Macro came into the room rubbing his hands and making straight for the brazier. He stretched his arms out and smiled as the heat soaked into his palms. A vague smell of wine betrayed the fact he had just returned to barracks from the centurion's mess.

'Cold night, sir.' Piso smiled.

'Bloody cold!' Macro nodded. 'How's our new boy working out?'

'Fine, sir. Just fine.' Piso exchanged a look with Cato. 'In fact, he's going to make an excellent clerk one day.'

'So you think young Cato is ready to step into your shoes?'

'I didn't say that, sir. There's still quite a bit to learn. But he's got a talent for it and no mistake. We were just looking over some of his requisition statements. Would you care to have a look, sir?'

Macro shook his head. 'Another time. When I'm not so busy. Anyway, I'm sure he's doing as well as you say. And so you should, what with all that education you've picked up.'

'Yes, sir,' Cato replied, wondering slightly about the change of tone in Macro's voice. 'It's proved to be very useful, sir.'

'Yes.' Macro stared at him silently for a moment, his expression unreadable. 'Anyway, that's not why I'm here. It's about time you got some field experience. There's a detachment being sent to a local settlement tomorrow morning. The local chief sent a Roman tax-collector packing after cutting out his tongue. Seems the chief's related to some troublemaker trying to make a name for himself on the other side of the Rhine. Anyway, Vespasian's sending the Third cohort to arrest the chief and confiscate all precious metals and stones to compensate the tax-collector. One of the centurions of the Third got kicked unconscious by a mule this afternoon and the optio's already in the hospital. I've been ordered to take temporary command of his century – you're coming with me.'

'Oh! Will there be a fight, sir?'

'Doubt it. Why?'

'It's just that we haven't trained with real weapons yet.'

'Don't worry about it. Borrow some kit from one of our lads. Shouldn't need it though – as soon as those Germans see us coming they'll do everything they can to get rid of us. We just go in, make the arrest, requisition whatever we can find and leave. Should be home by nightfall.'

'Oh . . .' Cato could not keep the disappointment from his voice. He had hoped that the excursion might keep him out of Pulcher's reach for a few days at least.

'Don't worry, son,' Macro said kindly, having misread Cato's expression. 'You'll get to see some fighting one day, I promise. But it's good that you're keen to get stuck in. No good being a soldier unless you enjoy your work.'

Cato smiled weakly. 'Yes, sir.'

'Right then!' Macro clapped him on the shoulder, shoving him backwards good-naturedly. 'See you at dawn by the north gate. Full armour, cloak and provisions for the day.'

'Yes, sir. If it's all right with Piso, I'd like to get an early night, sir.'

Macro turned to his clerk, eyebrows raised.

'Certainly!' Piso smiled. 'If the centurion pushes those men like he pushes us you'll need all your energy for tomorrow.'

After the door had closed behind Cato and his

footsteps could be heard fading down the corridor, Macro turned back to his clerk.

'What do you think of him?'

'He's got a knack for paperwork; neat hand and a good memory.' Piso paused for a moment.

'But . . . ?' Macro filled in.

'I'm not sure if he's cut out for army life, sir. Seems a bit too soft.'

'You ever met anyone from the palace who wasn't? Too much good living – that's their trouble. Most of 'em wouldn't last five days in the army, but so far that lad's kept up. What he lacks in fitness he makes up with determination. You know, I think we might be able to make something out of young Cato after all.'

'If you say so, sir.'

'I say so, but you don't think so, eh Piso?'

'To be honest, no, sir. Determination's one thing but fighting requires quite different qualities. I don't think he's got what it takes.' Piso paused. 'There's a rumour going round that he's a coward.'

'Yes, I've heard. But you know how it is with rumours – there's nothing in most of 'em. We have to give the lad a chance.'

Piso was struck by a sudden insight. 'Then you *are* expecting trouble, sir?'

'It's possible, you know what the Germans are like, any excuse for a fight. But I doubt it will amount to more than knocking a couple of heads together. Still, it'll give me a chance to see how Cato reacts.'

'If what I've heard's true, he'll run.'

'Care to make a wager on that?' Macro smiled. 'Five

sestertii? I know you can afford it.'

'Yes, sir. But can you?'

'Five sestertii.' Macro ignored the gibe and spat on his hand. 'Five says that if there's trouble Cato doesn't run. Or are you too scared to take the bet?'

Piso delayed no more than a moment before slapping his centurion's palm. 'Five it is!'

Chapter Six

The night had been cold and, as the soft light of dawn struggled through the morning mist, the fortress of the Second Legion was revealed in a sparkling white frost. The men of the Third cohort were forming into their centuries in a businesslike manner as the air was wreathed in the steam of their breath. Five hundred men, in full armour and heavy cloaks, were gathered in faint filtered shafts of light, rubbing hands and stamping feet in an effort to generate a small bit of warmth against the biting winter air. Jeers and good-humoured insults were exchanged with passing legionaries from other cohorts fortunate enough to be remaining in the fortress for the day. The officers stood apart from the loose columns of men and Cato had no trouble locating Macro's stocky form.

'This your protégé, Macro?' said the man next to him. Macro nodded.

'A little young for an optio, wouldn't you say?'

'We'll see,' Macro grunted, casting his eyes over the optio in his ill-fitting tunic and cloak. The centurion circled slowly, making a close examination of the young man's equipment, testing the buckles with a sharp tug, and tilting Cato's head back to ensure the helmet strap was fastened. 'You'll do. Right, while we're out of the base you stick by me and do whatever I say. No wandering off, no nothing without my say-so. Understand?'

'Yes, sir.'

'Now, join the front of the last century in line – that's the Sixth. Wait for me there.'

'Sir?'

'What is it?'

'How long are we going to stand here?' asked Cato, already shivering.

'You just can't wait, can you?' Macro shook his head. 'Not long now, boy, we're just waiting for the tribune.'

One of the other centurions spat on the frozen ground. 'Bet the bastard's still in bed.'

'Doubt it,' Macro replied. 'The legate's on his case. Seems he wants to test Vitellius. But this little trip's nothing more than an exercise in command. Even Vitellius would struggle to screw it up.'

'Macro, old son, never underestimate the incompetence of staff officers. They're born and bred for disaster . . .'

The exchange fell out of earshot as Cato made his way towards the standard rising over the Sixth Century. A few of the men eyed him curiously as he approached.

'You're Macro's optio?' the standard bearer asked.

'Yes.'

'He mentioned he had a new boy, but I didn't dream he was being so literal.'

Cato opened his mouth to reply before he got control of his feelings. Then he blushed and fumed silently.

'Just stick close to the centurion and me, lad, and you'll be all right.'

As Cato stood at the head of the century the other optios had been given the nod and were now moving down the ranks quietly ordering the men into column of fours, and dressing the lines so that in a short time the cohort was formed up, at ease, and ready to move off. Cato could not help but be aware of the growing sense of impatience as the men stood and waited. The sun had cleared the dawn mist lingering along the battlements and was washing the cohort in a weak orange glow.

And still they waited. For long enough that the cold began to take numbing advantage of their stillness.

At last the clatter of a walking horse sounded from the centre of the fortress and Cato turned to see a red-cloaked officer approaching, feathered plume bouncing from the crest of his helmet. At his approach, the group of centurions broke up and returned to their centuries. Vitellius trotted down the column and took up station at its head. A single word of command later and the lead century marched off, heading through the gate and on to the track beyond the walls. The succeeding centuries followed suit and, as the rear of the Fifth century moved forward, Macro counted off ten paces and then bellowed out the order to advance.

Cato's response, thanks to Bestia's harsh training regime, was automatic, and he instantly broke into the slow measured pace of the standard march two paces behind Macro and abreast the standard bearer. They passed through the gate, iron-shod boots echoing back off the stonework, and out into the half-tamed wilderness of the frontier province. The rising sun cast long shadows across the hoar frost to their left and numerous puffs of steamy breath swirled into the cold air. Underfoot, the ground was frozen hard where, weeks before, muddy channels marked the wagon ruts leading away from the fortress to the many frontier villages in the area. Despite the cold, Cato felt glad to be getting away from the Legion – a whole day without Bestia and Pulcher to occupy his mind.

The head of a column breasted a small rise in the land and, as the Sixth century followed down the reverse slope, Cato took a last look over his shoulder at the fortress stretching out across the landscape – a long stone wall with the red tiles of the headquarters building beyond. A settlement of bars, brothels and squalid hovels sprawled unevenly beneath the walls on the far side of the fortress. Looking ahead, a line of trees marked the end of the land cleared by the Second Legion and the beginning of one of the ancient forests that sprawled across Germany. Beyond the fringe of saplings struggling to recover some of the ground ravaged by the Legion's engineers, enormous pines and oaks reared up, dark and forbidding. Cato shivered, partly from the cold, and partly as he recalled the fate of the three legions General Varus had foolishly led into the depths of just such a forest nearly thirty years earlier. Over fifteen thousand men had been massacred in the gloomy twilight under the tangled boughs, their bodies left by the Germans to rot into the dirt.

As the column advanced down the track and the trees began to close in from the sides and overhead the men fell silent, some glancing anxiously into the depths beyond. Macro could well understand their feelings; there was something innately strange about this far-flung frontier of the Empire. The forests were unlike anything else in the known world, dark and impenetrable. Even the local tribes were afraid of them and told tales of how restless spirits of the dead were cursed to wander as pale wraiths through the shadows and green-filtered light. The track the cohort followed had been hacked through the forest by the Legion's engineers; the locals had preferred to trek round the forest before the Romans arrived. Even now some still refused to enter the woods. The engineers, it seemed, had also been afraid of the place, as the track made no attempt at a straight line and instead curled its way round the thick tree trunks, such had been their determination to get the job done quickly. A short while after the column had entered the forest no more than a score of men could be seen before or behind and Cato felt a trickle of sweat trace its way down his spine beneath his tunic.

'Sir?'

Macro turned his head as he crunched along the frozen track. 'What is it, boy?'

'How far exactly is this village, sir?'

'You mean, how much further through this forest?' Macro smiled.

'Yes, sir.'

'A few miles before the track clears the trees, then we should reach the village by noon. Don't worry about this place, it's harmless enough.'

'But if we should be attacked . . .'

'Attacked?' Macro scoffed. 'Who by? Not the poor sods we're visiting. Bunch of simple-minded farmers. And your nearest German war-band is well to the other side of the Rhine. So relax, boy, you're making the women nervous.' Macro jerked a thumb back at the legionaries of the Sixth century and those in earshot jeered loudly. Cato blushed and merely tried to pull his neck in as far as possible while keeping a close eye on the silvan shadows.

Once the initial oppressive spell of the forest had worn off, the soldiers stopped talking in hushed tones and the column wound its way through the trees accompanied by the usual loud banter of marching soldiers as they swapped jokes and exchanged insults. The deep boughs swallowed up much of the noise and what was left sounded flat and strange to their ears.

At last the column pulled free of the forest and marched out into a bright winter morning as an unobscured sun bathed the land in a warm glow. This side of the forest had been cleared and the cohort passed through primitive farmland dotted with the grim little peat huts of local German settlers, each one marked by a thin trail of smoke reaching up to clear sky. Most of the farmers had taken in their grazing animals and steam clung about the low outbuildings from which the lowing of cattle and the squealing of pigs could be heard as the soldiers passed. There were few signs of human life, the odd face at a door silently watching the column chinkling along the track, but nothing more.

'Friendly lot, aren't they?' the standard bearer commented.

'They don't seem much bothered by us,' Cato replied. 'I'd have thought they'd be a bit more interested. It's not what I imagined the Germans would be like.'

'What did you think they'd be like?'

'Big and aggressive – that's what we heard in Rome.'

'That's exactly what they are like when you're fighting them,' the standard bearer said with feeling. 'But these are just farmers. They're like all civilians when an army passes by. Just keeping their noses clean and hoping we don't have any cause to pay them any attention. Behind that door' – the standard bearer nodded towards a hut they were passing – 'and behind every door sits a family praying we don't stop. Soldiers are bad news for their kind.'

From the head of the column came the shouted order for the cohort to halt and each centurion instantly relayed it to his command. The men stood, silently waiting for the next instruction.

'All officers to the front!'

Macro, having the furthest to go, immediately broke into a trot and made his way along the side of the column towards Vitellius, rising above the First century on horseback. From the rear of the cohort Cato could see that the track passed over a low crest. The officers gathered around Vitellius, at the respectful distance infantry give to horses, as he issued his orders with occasional gestures for clarification. Once dismissed, the officers hurried back into position at the head of their centuries. Macro smiled as he saw the questioning expressions on the faces of the standard bearer and his optio.

'The village is just beyond that rise. The tribune wants to play it low key. He's only taking in the First century. The rest of us are to form up along the crest in sight of the village in case we're needed.'

'Why aren't we all going, sir?' Cato asked. 'Why split the command?'

'Because that's his order, lad,' Macro snapped, but then instantly relented since the optio had made a reasonable point. 'He doesn't want us to make the locals too nervous. We just make the arrest, seize the valuables and leave peacefully. If we all just march in there he thinks we might spook them into doing something foolish.'

'Something foolish?'

'Fuck knows what.' Macro shrugged his wide shoulders dismissively. 'I don't see a bunch of farmers deciding to take us on. Still, it's orders. Ah! Here we go. Back to your position, optio.'

At the head of the First century Vitellius led his men over the crest and out of sight. The following centuries moved to the right and left of the road along the crest. The centurions of the Second and Third centuries paced out the line and marked the positions for each century as they marched at right angles to the road. The gap left for the Sixth century straddled the road and Cato, sticking close to the standard bearer and Macro as ordered, found himself in front of the line of men, formed up four deep, that stretched out over a hundred paces on each side. Ahead, the ground sloped gently down to a village nestling inside a wide loop of river that emerged from the forest surrounding the cleared land.

Cato was surprised at the size of the settlement. He had been expecting a loose collection of mud huts inside a flimsy palisade. Instead there were hundreds of huts and larger buildings crammed within a high turf wall and water-filled ditch. The main gate was closed, flanked by two squat stone towers from which the narrow drawbridge was controlled. A little beyond the gate, the track opened out into a square in front of the largest building in the village.

It was a good half mile from the crest to the drawbridge and the First century had already covered most of the distance on the track while the rest of the cohort had formed up. There seemed to be little response in the village as the soldiers approached and the men waited peacefully as a few faces appeared at the wall to inspect their visitors. While the five centuries stood at ease word was passed that rations could be eaten and the men started feeding on the contents of their haversacks. Cato took out a strip of dried beef and gnawed at the tough but highly flavoured meat. The morning's march had made him more hungry than he realised and he worked his jaws furiously while gazing out across the panorama below.

Cato's eye was suddenly caught by a movement at the far side of the village. Three figures, carrying shields and spears, were running away towards the distant treeline. A greasy smudge of smoke eddied up from where Cato had first seen them as a small camp fire smouldered.

'Sir!' he called out to Macro. 'Over there!'

'What is it?'

'There, sir.' Cato pointed with his javelin. 'Those men running. D'you see 'em?'

'Yes, boy. I see them.'

'What should we do, sir?' Cato asked.

'Do?' Macro frowned. 'Nothing. They're too far away to do anything. Anyway, there's only three of them.'

'Should we tell the tribune?' Cato persisted.

'No point.'

They watched silently as the three armed men disappeared across the farmland towards the trees while Vitellius led his men across the open ground towards the gate and halted the century by the ditch in front of the towers. The tribune waved his arm determinedly and, after a short pause, the gate swung inwards to admit the soldiers. The century passed inside the village and, for a few anxious moments, disappeared from view amongst the huts before emerging into the village square. Vitellius halted the column and sent two men forward to the main door of the largest building facing on to the square. Before they could reach it, the door opened and a tall woman with long flaxen hair emerged. Although those remaining on the hill crest could hear nothing and see precious little from half a mile away, it was clear that some argument was taking place between Vitellius and the woman.

'I thought we were sent to arrest the chief, sir?' Cato commented.

'So we were, boy,' Macro said irritably. 'He shouldn't waste time. There isn't much daylight to waste in winter.' He stared up at the sky where the sun looked longingly towards the horizon. 'Don't much fancy marching home in the darkness.'

Cato involuntarily looked back towards the forest in the distance. The place had been unnerving enough in daylight, Jupiter knows what it would be like in pitch darkness. 'If it gets dark wouldn't it be better to go round the forest, sir?'

Macro shook his head. 'Too far. Besides we can make torches if we need to. You aren't scared, are you, boy?'

'No, sir.'

'Good. Stay that way,' Macro said with relief, hoping that his five sestertii were still safe.

Down in the village the argument was being forced to a conclusion as Vitellius waved his hand at the woman and two soldiers abruptly pinned her arms back. A squad forced their way into the large building, only to emerge a moment later with a large chest. Having deposited it by Vitellius they proceeded to the next building and forced an entry.

'Seems like our man has got away,' Macro remarked, and yawned elaborately. 'The tribune shouldn't have wasted time on the woman.'

'Unless she's the kind of woman the tribune takes a shine to,' the standard bearer muttered. 'You know what Vitellius is like with women, can't resist the impulse to chat 'em up.'

'He should do it on his own time then. Not the army's. And certainly not mine. And not on a bloody cold day like this.'

'Sir!' Cato interrupted. 'Look there! The gate!'

For some reason the gate was slowly being closed and, as Macro watched, the small drawbridge began to rise. A cold feeling of dread, far colder than the trickle of sweat on a winter day, etched its way down his spine. He shifted his gaze to the centre of the village, but Vitellius and his men seemed unconcerned and continued with the house raids. Beyond the far wall of the village a faint movement attracted his gaze. A shadow was emerging from the forest, as if the sun was setting sooner than it should. Then he realised it couldn't be, the sun was behind the cohort.

'Cato! Your eyes are younger than mine. What's happening over there – at the edge of the forest there!' He pointed urgently.

For a moment Cato wasn't sure, a sight haze had risen over the low ground and partially obscured the view. But a moment later the blurry shadow distilled into distinct shapes. 'I think . . . I'm sure, it's a body of men. Coming out of the forest, this way.'

He looked at Macro wide-eyed. 'Germans?'

'What else?' Macro replied dryly.

'But what about the others in the village?' Cato said in alarm. 'They can't see.'

'I know, boy. I know.'

More of the men saw the approaching danger and pointed it out to their comrades. An anxious murmuring swept up and down the line.

'Quiet, there!' Macro bellowed. 'Shut your mouths and stand still!'

The legionaries obeyed instantly the moment discipline was invoked. Puffing down the line came

Centurion Quadratus of the Second – the senior officer present.

'Macro! You see 'em?'

'Yes.'

'We'd better get down there and join the others.'

'We were ordered to remain here,' Macro replied firmly. 'Unless Vitellius signalled us to move.'

'But he can't see them.' Quadratus jabbed a finger towards the approaching Germans, in their thousands now as they poured out of the forest towards the village.

'If we go down there, then we'll all be caught in the trap,' said Macro. 'I suggest we try and attract their attention instead.'

Quadratus stared at Macro a moment and then nodded. He turned to face down the line and cupped his hands to his mouth. 'Standards! Signal recall!'

The remaining five standard bearers raised their standards high and began slowly circling the hanging pendants. Macro looked down at the village where the soldiers of the First century carried on seizing portable items of value, oblivious to the approaching catastrophe.

'Come on, come on!' Quadratus muttered. 'Someone look up . . . this way.'

Finally they saw a soldier gesture towards them with his javelin and Vitellius turned in his saddle. For a moment he sat motionless on his horse, then turned and frantically waved an arm. The soldier who had seen them rushed from the clearing and shortly after reappeared at the top of one of the gate towers. Even as he did so, figures emerged in the spaces between the village buildings surrounding Vitellius and his men. The century quickly formed up in close order and backed out of the clearing towards the gate. Some of the villagers ran forward and threw stones and lumps of wood at the retreating Romans. A sudden shower of javelins from the rearmost ranks rained down on the villagers, leaving half a dozen prostrate as the others fled back into the narrow alleys. The century was soon lost from sight behind the village buildings as it headed back to the gate.

From the hill, the Germans approaching from the forest were now in clear view and it was possible to estimate their numbers and speed of approach.

'Three, maybe four thousand,' Quadratus guessed.

Macro shook his head. 'Barely that I'd say.'

'Vitellius should have time to get out before they reach the village.'

'Easily. They're still nearly a mile from the far side of the village. Once Vitellius clears the gateway he should make the crest before they get anywhere near.'

'Then what?'

'Don't know,' Macro shrugged. 'We'll just have to wait and see what he orders.'

Cato stared at the two officers in disbelief. How on earth could they be so cold-blooded when their comrades faced imminent extinction right under their eyes? And after that, the rest of the cohort would be outnumbered ten to one. He felt a burning desire to turn and run, to shout out to all the others to do the same. But his body refused to move, partly out of shame and partly out of the dread of making the return journey through the forest alone. While he stood motionless, Cato's gaze continued to flicker between the approaching Germans and the village, watching for the progress of the First century. There was a sudden motion in one of the tower gates, the legionary sent there by Vitellius was seized by a group of men, a spear run through him and the body hurled into the ditch.

'Sir!'

'I saw it, boy.'

A series of flashes and glints marked the arrival of the First century at the edge of the village and a brief struggle was fought out for control of the gate. All the while the Germans swarmed nearer to close the trap.

'It's going to be a close thing,' mused Quadratus. 'Better get ready to make a fighting retreat. I'll get the other centuries back on the track. Macro, I want you to stand here and cover our backs until Vitellius arrives.'

'All right.' Macro nodded. 'But you'd better move fast.'

Quadratus made his way down the line shouting out the necessary commands, and one by one the centuries on the crest turned from line into column and marched back towards the track. At the same time, Macro ordered the Sixth ten paces down the slope to clear the head of the track for Quadratus. Down in the village, Cato could see that the First century had managed to overwhelm the villagers at the gate and legionaries were pulling back the thick wooden gate to make their escape. With Vitellius riding at their head, the First doubled up the hill towards the rest of the cohort. A small crowd of villagers followed behind, but quickly gave up once a fresh volley of javelins was hurled back at them.

Once the century was safely away from the village,

Vitellius spurred his horse up the slope to take command of the cohort. He reined in beside Macro, the horse snorting harshly over the frothy bit as a savage gash on its flank bled profusely.

'What the hell's going on here, centurion?' he shouted angrily. 'Where's the rest?'

'Quadratus has moved them back on to the track, sir,' Macro explained.

'What for? Scared of a few bloody villagers? I'm taking the whole cohort back in there and we're going to burn the bastards to the ground!'

'Sir,' Macro interrupted. 'If you care to look over there.'

'Eh? What?'

'Beyond the village, sir.'

For a moment Vitellius froze as the true peril of the situation was at last made clear to him. He studied the dark mass of Germans streaming towards the village and realised what the other officers already knew, that there was no hope of fighting against such odds.

'There's still some distance between us. If we can make the forest in time we can use a rearguard to hold them off.'

'I believe that's what Quadratus had in mind, sir.'

'Good. Right then you stay here. When the First arrives let them through and order them to join on to the end of the column. This century's the rearguard. Only pull back once the cohort is on the move.'

Vitellius took another look back down the slope, gauging the relative positions of both sides. 'They won't reach the village for a little while. With luck, we'll be able to keep far enough ahead of them. Right, centurion, you've got your orders.'

'Yes, sir.' Macro saluted as Vitellius wheeled his horse and rode over the crest towards the head of the column. Once he was sure the tribune was out of earshot, Cato turned to Macro.

'What's going to happen?'

'Just what he said. A quick march back to base. That's all.'

Cato feared that things were not going to work out as simply as that. A nagging feeling at the back of his mind suggested that the worst was yet to come and he silently cursed Macro for ordering him to join the expedition. Instead of the promised bloodless exercise and a reprieve from the attentions of Bestia and Pulcher, he was now faced by a horde of German savages. Barely four weeks into his military career, he reflected bitterly, and already people were queuing up to kill him.

The men of the First century struggled breathlessly up to the line of legionaries below the crest and were quickly ushered on to the track. When the last had passed through the ranks, Macro ordered the line to withdraw ten paces to their original position. The century was about to form up when a faint roar sounded from beyond the head of the column.

Bursting from the distant forest was another swarm of Germans, racing across the farmland to cut off the cohort's retreat. A quick glance was all that Cato needed. Even to his untrained eye it was obvious that the Germans would reach the track well before the nearest century was anywhere near it. Suddenly it was all clear to Cato – the three men running for the forest – the signal fire – the delaying action of the chief's woman. A very neat trap indeed, he conceded, just before the full terror of their plight set the hairs standing on the back of his neck. Looking to Macro for a solution, he was surprised to see the mask of the centurion's composure drop for a moment. He stared at the new threat, then quickly turned back to the first of the German swarms, now hardly three quarters of a mile from the far side of the village.

'Oh great,' muttered Macro. 'Now we're well and truly fucked.'

Chapter Seven

Once the cohort had left the base early in the morning the Second Legion settled into a normal day's routine. Bestia's recruits stamped around the parade ground trying to keep warm in between bouts of drilling, while the commander of the Fifth cohort took his men out of camp for the monthly route march that the army required of all its troops. This day the cohort was joined by the clerical staff from headquarters, grumbling bitterly that their excused-duties status was being ignored by Vespasian.

Watching from an upstairs balcony as the cohort, with the clerks sandwiched between the Third and Fourth centuries, filed down the Via Praetoria, Vespasian could not restrain a grin. The Second Augusta was his first legion command and he aimed to make it a success, even if that meant upsetting the headquarters' clerks. Every man and beast in the Legion would be made fighting fit in readiness for the following year's campaign. Moreover, due to the special nature of the operation outlined to him in the message sent by the imperial general staff, the men of the Second would need training in amphibious warfare. Soldiers, he knew only too well, had an innate suspicion of all things aquatic, let alone nautical. The settled garrison life the Legion had been leading for several years was not going to help matters, he reflected, sipping from a cup of heated wine. A rapid period of adjustment was required and the enforced exercise of the clerks was just the first phase in Vespasian's programme to prepare his troops for the following summer. From now on, route marches and weapons practice would be doubled and no soldier or officer would be permitted excused-duties privileges.

As the tail of the cohort tramped past, Vespasian left the balcony and returned to his private quarters, closing the shutters. Spread across a large wooden table were the inventories he had ordered, as well as a series of missives from Rome providing details of the Legion's relocation – the route they would take across Gaul; the supply depots on which the Second would be permitted to draw while on the march and notification of the amphibious warfare experts to be attached to his command for the duration of the campaign. The document that had set all this in motion was safely secured with his confidential papers in the chest under the table. From constant rereading, Vespasian knew the details by heart. Nevertheless, he removed the key from the chain around his neck and unfastened the lock. The despatch was folded round a scroll and the remains of the broken imperial seal of deep red wax were still fixed to the stiff parchment. Beside the scroll was another, smaller, document marked for his eyes only and written in a personalised code by the Emperor himself. Vespasian considered it for a moment with a pained expression, and then pushed it to the back of the chest before extracting the larger despatch. Flattening it out on the table top, Vespasian took another sip of warm wine and ran his eyes over the finely written script yet again.

The Second and three other legions, together with thirty cohorts of auxiliaries, were to invade Britain the following summer. The imperial clerk who had drafted the despatch had stated the plan as boldly and as simply as that. Then, perhaps a little remorseful about such a staggering degree of understatement, the clerk had struck a rich vein of loquacity and launched into an elegant essay on the significance of the planned campaign. Britain, he noted, had merely been reconnoitred by Julius Caesar; a successful invasion would rekindle the glory of Rome and once again remind the civilised world (and the uncivilised who dwelt without) of the potency of Rome, and its new Emperor.

Vespasian smiled at that. The Claudian accession owed everything to the support of the Praetorian Guard. But for them, the current Emperor would have been swept away in the bloodshed that followed the assassination of Caligula. Claudius might be Emperor, but his suitability for the post was something of an issue among the chattering classes of Rome. Even the plebeians were not entirely convinced that he was up to the job. This campaign plan – the conquest of Britain – was transparently intended to recast Claudius in the heroic mould. A quick victory, a glittering triumph and prolonged public celebration in Rome would firm up Claudius' hold on the affections of Rome's fickle masses.

The clerk continued his outline of the campaign by

stating that the forces allocated to the invasion would more than suffice. Intelligence reports from Britain suggested that armed resistance would be minimal and widely dispersed. The invasion force would quickly brush aside any opposition that might be concentrated and the rest of the campaign would be a simple matter of reducing tribal strongholds by diplomacy or force.

'By diplomacy or force,' Vespasian repeated aloud with a weary shake of his head. Only someone on the imperial staff could make it sound so simple. Any soldier with frontier experience knew just how unlikely it was that diplomacy would succeed. Vespasian doubted if the Britons could even pronounce the word, let alone understand the concept it entailed.

The Britons, according to the imperial clerk's liberal interpretation of Caesar, were an ill-disciplined rabble with a quaint line in chariot tactics. Their hill-forts amounted to little more than mounds of mud supporting flimsy palisades. Few casualties were anticipated and the invaders would have ample opportunity for personal enrichment as a result of the anticipated spoils of war – mainly, slaves. Vespasian was reminded to make that point quite clear to the rank and file of the Legion, who might otherwise be swayed by the superstitious rumours circulating about the mysterious mist-wreathed isle beyond the fringes of the known world. At this point, Vespasian guessed, the clerk became aware that he had rather over-gilded the lily and the despatch switched back into a more objective style. Vespasian was instructed to stamp down harshly on those who spread such rumours and to maintain the highest degree of discipline in the best traditions of the Roman army. The despatch curtly concluded with a schedule of troop movements for the coming months.

Laying the document to one side, Vespasian drained the last of his wine and stared down at the paperwork covering the table. It would be quite an adventure, to say the least. The assembling of a vast force, its daily provisioning and stockpiling of reserves for resupply following the landing, the construction of a fleet, the training of the army for amphibious operations – not to mention the small matter of the campaign itself and the establishing of an entirely new province with all the provision of infrastructure that implied. And for what? The despatch told of vast resources of gold, silver and tin found on the island. From what Vespasian had heard of Britain from the merchants who passed through the fortress, the island was a squalid affair. No cities, no culture, ugly women and preposterous hairstyles. Hardly the kind of place Claudius could proudly introduce to the rest of the empire. But it was a conquest and reputations were built on military success. Vespasian was keenly aware that his political stock needed building up if the ambitions he harboured in his heart were to become any kind of reality. Yes, Britain would do nicely, for all concerned – except the natives, he mused with a smile.

And speaking of natives, there were one or two local arrangements to finalise before the Legion handed over the fortress to the mixed cohort from Macedonia that had been assigned to replace the Second during the campaign. There were some tribal land disputes to settle and that nasty business with the tax-collector which the

Third cohort was presently sorting out. The tongueless tax-collector had filed a petition for compensation with the provincial governor and had stipulated that, unless the sum he claimed was paid in full, he would only be satisfied by the local chief's execution. Mindful that the local tribe had had a poor harvest this year and might need to buy in food over the hard German winter, Vespasian had offered to have the chief's tongue cut out in restitution. But the tax-collector, an uncouth Gaul with an appalling accent and no conversation – a situation unlikely to improve now – had insisted on his blood money, or the chief's death. And so Vitellius had been sent to deal with the situation, a task well in keeping with the tribune's taste for enforcing the Roman peace.

Vespasian found it difficult to warm to his senior tribune but couldn't quite discern why. The fellow was equable enough and popular in the mess. He drank hard, though never to the point of intoxication. He womanised indiscriminately and frequently – as any man should, Vespasian thought approvingly. Moreover, Vitellius loved sports and could drive a chariot as if he had been born with a set of reins in his hands. If he had a vice it was gambling, and even then he was good at it – intuitively knowing when the dice were for or against him. He had a knack for making friends, particularly the kind who were useful politically, and a bright future lay ahead of him. Who knew how far the man would rise? And with that question Vespasian put his finger on the nub of the matter – the man constituted a possible rival in future life.

And then there was that other matter. The coded message unwittingly delivered by that recruit some weeks earlier direct from the personal office of the Emperor, using the personalised cipher Claudius had agreed with Vespasian. It briefly informed Vespasian that someone at the fortress had been implicated in last year's coup attempt by Scribonianus. As soon as the plotter's identity had been obtained from the surviving members of the conspiracy, Vespasian would be told so he could see that the individual concerned disappeared quietly. Fine euphemisms, Vespasian reflected, smiling wryly as he imagined the techniques used by the imperial torturers to extract information and see that people disappeared as discreetly as possible. By way of comfort, the message assured him that at least one – yet again unidentified – imperial agent was present in the camp to assist Vespasian in any way the agent saw fit.

It was all a confounded bloody nuisance, given the exhausting preparations required for the Legion's involvement in a major offensive campaign. A soldier needed to concentrate on military objectives, not high politics, if the army was to operate effectively. And from now on he would have to view every one of his officers with a degree of suspicion, at least until some hapless soul in the Mammertine prison finally cracked and provided a name. Vespasian couldn't help hoping that the name would be that of Vitellius. Now that really would be a neat solution to most of his present anxieties.

Vespasian poured himself some more wine from the jar warming over the glowing embers in the brazier. He sipped carefully at the steaming liquid as he reflected

that it was a shame that he hadn't managed to find a
more dangerous undertaking for Vitellius than turning
over a local village.

Chapter Eight

The tribune's horse came thundering back down the track. Slewing to a halt at the rearmost century, Vitellius thrust an arm out, pointing down the slope to the village.

'Macro! Get your men back there at the double!'

'Sir?' Macro was momentarily startled by the order. His eyes followed the direction the tribune was pointing, and passed rapidly over the village to where Germans were swarming across the flat farmland towards them.

'Just do it, Centurion!' Vitellius shouted. 'At the double.'

'Yes, sir!'

'And when you get to the village, go right through it and secure the far gate.'

'Yes, sir!'

'Stop for nothing! Understand?'

'Sir.'

As Macro turned to the Sixth century to bellow out the command, Vitellius savagely jerked the reins round and kicked his heels into the side of his horse, before racing back down the column which had smartly about-faced and was quick-marching back towards the village. Macro grabbed Cato's arm.

'Stick close. Whatever happens.'

Cato nodded.

'Right, lads, at the trot. Follow me!'

Macro led the century down the track, a small column of panting legionaries gasping out plumes of steamy breath as they looked to the far side of the village and gauged the distance of the German horde sweeping towards them. Even Cato could see that the enemy were sure to reach the far gate ahead of them. What then? A brutal fight in the filthy narrow streets and certain death. And death would be preferable to capture if only a fraction of what Posidonius had written about the Germans was true. Harness straps and scabbards chinked loudly and Cato, who had not yet perfected the technique of running in full battle-dress, struggled to keep hold of shield and javelin while preventing the sword scabbard from being caught between his thighs. Worse, Cato's one-size-fits-all helmet began to tip down over his eyes as he ran, requiring a regular backwards flip of the head.

Glancing back over his shoulder, Macro could see that the other centuries were now coming over the crest and breaking into a run down the slope. He nodded approvingly. The tribune had the good sense not to let them run all the way back to the village and face the Germans while fighting for breath. Macro glanced ahead at the village gate. A small group of Germans, bearing a motley assortment of antique weapons and the more harmful type of agricultural tools, waited uncertainly – quite surprised to see the legionaries hurrying back down the slope towards them. Macro was a few score paces away and saw the frightened expressions on the faces of those who had not yet run away. He filled his lungs with air and drew his sword.

'GRRRAAAARRR!'

Cato leapt to one side in astonishment.

'Keep running, you fool! That was to scare them, not you!'

Sure enough the remaining Germans, rather than face the roaring centurion, turned and ran back into the depths of the village, not even stopping to close the gates. Barely a glance was spared for the Roman body lying untidily by the gate as the legionaries burst in right behind the villagers, screaming with rage and enjoying the effect. Only Cato kept silent, grimly glancing at the roughly constructed huts hemming them in, and quite overwhelmed by the appalling stench of the place.

'Close up!' Macro bellowed over his shoulder. 'And keep shouting!'

The century turned a corner and ran straight into the first steadfast opposition – a dozen hairy men with shields and hunting spears straddling the roadway. Foolishly they had positioned themselves too close to the corner and were run down almost before Cato was aware of their presence. Those that were brushed into a side alley fell out of sight and survived. The others were trampled over and finished off by swift javelin thrusts as the century swept over them. Cato saw only one German go down, his face smashed by the edge of Macro's shield. The man screamed shrilly but the cry was instantly lost in the crushing press that carried Cato forward into the heart of the German village. All sense of fear was lost in the need to concentrate on retaining his footing while remaining as close to Macro as possible. At his side, Cato was aware that the standard bearer was shouting 'On! On!' at the top of his voice, lips drawn back in a grin. By the Gods, Cato thought fleetingly, these men were actually enjoying themselves. Fools! Did they want to get themselves killed?

Suddenly, they were running into the square in front of the chief's hall that Cato had seen from the hillside, villagers scattering before the howling legionaries.

'Leave them!' Macro ordered. 'Keep on! Stay with me!'

He led the century from the village square by the widest route, sure that it led to the village gateway facing the oncoming horde beyond. The way ahead was clear and the only sign of the locals were doors that shut hastily at their approach. Through a gap in the buildings, Cato saw that they were now close to the other gate, rising just above the intervening thatched roofs. Then he was aware of a new sound, the howling of a multitude that rose even above the screams of the legionaries. As they became aware of the noise the legionaries fell silent and the pace slowed momentarily.

'Don't slack, you lazy bastards!' Macro shouted. 'Come on!'

The legionaries sprinted forward in a last effort to secure the gate ahead of the approaching Germans. Cato followed the standard bearer and Macro in a final desperate dash up a slight rise between the stinking German huts and then slammed into the centurion's back as the latter slewed to a halt. Cato's shield slipped from his grasp.

'Shit!' Macro exploded.

'Sorry, sir! I didn't . . .'

'Form line!' Macro shouted, ignoring him. 'Javelins at the ready!'

Retrieving his shield, Cato straightened up and froze. Fifty paces in front stood the gate-house, doors wide open, and swarming through them with a blood-curdling roar, now that they had caught sight of the enemy, were the Germans. They were quite the most hideous creatures that Cato had ever seen; large of body with wild hair, faces disfigured by blood-lust, and their foul animal stench was overwhelming.

'Get to one side, son.' Macro swept Cato to the end of the first line of legionaries where the standard bearer had grounded the standard and drawn his sword. 'First two ranks! Release javelins!'

A dozen javelins were hurled forwards at a high angle and arced towards the Germans, disappearing moments later into the crowd raging down the roadway six abreast. As if a rope had tripped them, the front ranks toppled forward, some impaled on the Roman javelins, others stumbling over the wounded and being pushed to the ground by the pressure from behind.

'Next two ranks, release javelins!' Macro's voice repeated, loud, calm and clear. The second volley turned the front of the German charge into a confused mass of dead and wounded, with the uninjured frantically struggling to get free of the tangle. Macro weighed up the situation in an instant and waved his sword over his head. 'Come on lads! Let's have them! Charge!'

Then he was off, running straight at the Germans,

shield raised to cover his torso and short sword pointed straight at the throat of the nearest enemy. With a shout, the century surged after him and once again Cato found himself being swept helplessly along in this flood of madness. Unlike the front ranks of legionaries, Cato still carried his javelin and, rather than carry the awkward weapon into the heaving melee he decided to hurl it as far forward as possible before drawing his short-sword. But the javelin throwing he had practised on the parade ground bore no resemblance to throwing a javelin in battle conditions. As he drew his right arm back he almost impaled the legionary immediately behind.

'Oi! Watch it, you stupid cunt!' the man shouted angrily, thrusting the butt to one side as he barged past Cato. 'You'll do someone a fucking injury!'

Cato flushed with embarrassment and then quickly hurled the offending weapon forwards at an unfortunately low trajectory, which caused the javelin to glance off Macro's helmet and fly off horizontally over the heaving mass of Germans before dropping out of sight. Cato swallowed nervously as the centurion shot a look of rage back over his shoulder, swore at the top of his voice and then turned to take his anger out on the nearest available German. Cato quickly drew his sword and threw himself forward, trying his hardest not to appear responsible for the errant missile.

The rearmost legionaries were busy shouting encouragement to those further forward, pausing only to finish off any Germans betraying signs of life amongst the tangled bodies stamped into the filthy ground. Cato was shocked to see one or two Roman bodies in among them – men he didn't know. As the legionaries steadily pushed the Germans back towards the gate more Roman bodies appeared, some still staring in surprise at their dreadful wounds. Blood flowed from the wounded, dripping down on to the street where iron-shod boots churned it into the mud. As more Romans fell, the fighting line grew nearer and Cato steeled himself for the moment when he would have to step into the space left by a Roman casualty.

Pressed back against the gate, a handful of Germans desperately tried to broaden the fighting line to take advantage of their numbers, scaling the low walls of the surrounding huts. A shout from Macro brought down a volley of javelins from those legionaries in the rear ranks and the Germans fell back into the mob.

Cato saw the standard waving at the head of the century as the legionaries forced their way step by step towards the gate. Then Macro led a renewed surge that brought the Romans between the huge gate-posts.

'Stand here!' Macro ordered and, with a last thrust of his sword into the enraged German mob, he disengaged and forced his way back through the ranks of the legionaries holding the gateway. Inside he faced the remaining troops. 'You lot. Up on the wall. We need to clear a space in front of the gate. Use your javelins, stones – whatever you can get your hands on.'

As the legionaries scaled the earth ramps to either side of the gate Macro saw Cato and caught his arm. 'Optio! I want you and six men ready with that locking bar. When I give the word, you get it into the gate braces as quick as you can. Understand?'

'Yes, sir.' Cato answered, staring at a crimson gash on the centurion's sword arm.

'Good. Then see to it.'

Then he was gone, thrusting his way back through the lines defending the gateway, shouting encouragement to his men. Cato quickly stirred and saw that the nearest men were watching him, waiting.

'Right!' He tried to sound firm. 'You heard him. Sheath swords and down shields.'

Astonishingly – to Cato at least – they reacted to the order and, unencumbered by the large heavy shields, they reached down and took a firm hold of the rough-hewn locking bar. Cato leaned his shield against the wall of a hut, then he bent and grasped the front of the bar.

'Ready? Lift!'

Cato slowly straightened, gasping with effort as he strained to raise the bar on to his shoulder where it rested uncomfortably. 'Right then,' he said through gritted teeth. 'Over to the gate, easy now!'

They struggled forward, stepping carefully over the prostrate forms of Romans and Germans, and then stood waiting to one side of the gate where the fight seemed to be going the Germans' way. The thin ranks of legionaries were slowly being forced to give ground. With his height Cato could see the Germans beyond, snarling with rage, throwing themselves forward on the Romans.

Macro shouted. 'More fire from the wall there! Use everything you've got!'

The soldiers above desperately rained down the last of their javelins, together with rocks and stones torn from the nearest huts, on to the heads of the helpless Germans.

Instinctively those at the front drew back from the gate, away from the slaughter.

'Back!' Macro turned and shoved the nearest legionaries back through the gate. The remaining Romans hurriedly withdrew, presenting their shields to the enemy. The last men through grabbed the edges of the gate and frantically swung the heavy timbers towards the Germans. Outside there was a howl as the enemy realised what was happening and they rushed forward again, regardless of the stones being hurled down from the walls above. At their head raced a tall warrior, blind rage and hatred etched on to his broad features. As the gates swung out to meet him he lunged for the nearest Roman with his spear.

'No, you fucking don't!' Macro swung his sword down on the head of the spear, knocking it to the ground. Unable to check himself, the German tumbled into the rapidly closing gap and Macro head-butted him, flattening his nose with a sickening crunch. As the German howled, Macro kicked him free of the gate. 'Piss off, you bugger!'

The gates closed with a grinding thud and – before the order could be given – Cato and his men quickly heaved the bar up, over and into the holding brackets where it dropped solidly into place. An instant later the gates suddenly swung in against the bar, which groaned against the strain. Macro watched for a moment to make sure that they were secure and then, posting a guard at the base of the gates, he ordered the remains of the century up on to the wall.

The village wall was a miserable affair, erected mainly

to ward off marauding war-bands from the wilderness beyond the Rhine. The dirt from the ditch surrounding the village had been heaped up to form an interior rampart, faced with turf to hold the soil in place. A narrow walkway, surfaced with a corduroy of logs, ran along the top of the wall beside a chest-high palisade of sharpened stakes, chest-high to a normal man but neck-high to the stocky Macro, who rose on his toes to best view the scene in front of the gate.

A seething mass of Germans stretched out in front of and to the sides of the village, like two arms encircling the Romans trapped within. Immediately below Macro, the Germans were being driven from the gate by a fresh fusillade of stones and a respectful gap, littered with dead and wounded, formed in front of the thick timbers. Further back Macro could see that faggots were already being bundled together from a stock of firewood the villagers had left beyond their walls where it would not be a fire risk. Once those faggots were ready, it would only be a matter of time before the ditch was filled and an approach to the wall was completed. At least the century had bought some time for the rest of the cohort. Macro turned to look for any sign of the other centuries. Dull cries and the faint clash of weapons sounded from elsewhere in the village and, from his slightly elevated position, Macro could see other legionaries stretched out around the wall. The village was secure then. Good. Time to make a report.

Looking down at the carpet of bodies strewn over the street leading up to the gate Macro estimated that almost a fifth of his men were dead, or badly wounded. He glanced up and caught the eye of young Cato, who instantly flashed his gaze over the wall with an expression of rapt attention.

'Cato! Keep your fucking head down, unless you want some German to use it for target practice!'

'Yes, sir.'

'Come here. Job for you.'

Hunched down below the palisade, Macro removed his helmet and wiped his brow with his uninjured arm. As he prepared to give the details of the report to Cato, he ran a finger along a dent across the top of his helmet.

'Wouldn't know anything about that I suppose?'

Cato blushed silently.

'I guessed not. But if anyone tries to spit me like that again I'll have the bastard's hide. Now then I want you to find the tribune. Find him as quick as you can and you tell him we're holding this gate. Tell him I've got about seventy effectives left and then ask him for orders. Understand?'

Cato nodded.

'Get going then!' Macro slapped him on the helmet.

The centurion watched Cato run down the ramp to the street and quickly pick his way over the dead and wounded. As he replaced his helmet, Macro made a mental note to have a word with Bestia if they ever got out of this mess. That boy definitely needed some more javelin practice. He sighed and cautiously peered over the palisade to see how the Germans were progressing with the faggots.

Cato's boots pounded down the street as he ran back

the way the century had come only a little while earlier. Alone, he felt vulnerable and he glanced nervously from side to side as he hurried between the squalid ranks of German huts and buildings. But he saw no-one until he had almost reached the square at the heart of the village. There he ran into a Roman picket guarding the approach. The two legionaries hefted their javelins anxiously at his approach, looking beyond him, but were relieved when Cato drew up, breathing heavily.

'Where's the tribune?'

'What's happening, Optio?'

'Nothing . . . need to find the tribune . . . message for him.'

One of the legionaries gestured over his shoulder. 'Back there, by the chief's hut. What gives at the other gate?'

'It's being held,' Cato called over his shoulder as he ran past.

When he emerged from the narrow street into the square Cato halted in surprise. Hundreds of Germans of all ages were milling around in the centre. Then he saw that they were being herded together by scores of legionaries who pushed with their shields and prodded with javelins to steer their charges into a compact group for easy guarding. Some were still being driven in from the surrounding streets as Cato pushed his way through to the chief's hut where Vitellius was giving orders to a centurion.

'. . . and if they put up any struggle, or try anything on, kill them all.'

'Kill them?' The centurion looked uncertainly at the

villagers, many of whom were wailing loudly. 'Kill them all?'

'That's what I said,' Vitellius snapped, and then sneered. 'Or haven't you got the stomach for it?'

'No, sir!' The centurion seemed surprised. 'Just think it'd be a bit time-consuming to kill them all, sir.'

'Then you'll just have to do it quickly.'

'Sir!' Cato interrupted. 'Message for you, sir! From Macro.'

'What the hell is this, soldier?' Vitellius shouted. 'How dare you come up and yell at me as if I was some market-stall trader! Now, you make your report properly!'

'Excuse me, sir.' The centurion coughed. 'But may I carry on?'

'What? Oh yes. You've got your orders. Get moving.' Vitellius nodded curtly at Cato. 'Now you.'

'Sir. Centurion Macro begs to report that he is holding the other gate and—'

'Casualties?'

'About twenty, sir. He has seventy effectives left, sir. The centurion begs to request if you have any orders for him, sir.'

'Orders?' Vitellius repeated vaguely. 'Right then. You tell him he must hold the gate. We've secured the walls and the interior of the village. Now we've got to hold out until help arrives.' Vitellius looked up at the slowly greying sky. 'We're expected back before dark. The legate will set out as soon as he realises we're in some kind of trouble. If we're lucky, that'll be tomorrow morning. Still, we're better off here than in that forest.'

'Yes, sir,' Cato agreed wholeheartedly.

'You tell Macro what the situation is, and that he is to hold the gate at all costs until relieved. Do you understand me, optio?'

Cato nodded.

'Now go.'

Chapter Nine

Around the German village the day gradually dimmed into the smudged grey of approaching dusk. Once the fighting had died down, the physical heat and frenzied mental preoccupation of battle drained away and the legionaries standing to on the wall shivered in the freezing winter gloom. To make matters worse, snow had begun to fall, large flakes that drifted down lazily in the still air. The initial ambush had failed and now the Germans withdrew out of javelin range and most stood hurling abuse at the village in their harsh tongue. Others busied themselves in constructing faggots and lopping branches off young pine trees to make crude scaling ladders. The Roman defenders watched anxiously from the wall, occasionally sparing hopeless glances in the direction of the Second's fortress, a mere eight miles away. More ominously, the legionaries of the Sixth century could see that a substantial tree had been felled nearby and was well on the way to being converted into a battering ram.

Macro had not been idle either. He had ordered some men to pile small rocks on the wall to supplement the few remaining javelins and another group to pile heavier rocks and earth against the rear of the village gates to absorb the impact of the ram. These were standard counter-measures but if the Germans managed to fully co-ordinate their attack then the thin line of Romans manning the village wall would inevitably be overrun, as Macro patiently explained to his young optio while the latter bound the gash on Macro's forearm.

'What then?' Cato asked.

'What do you think?' Macro smiled thinly as he stamped his feet. 'They'll be all over us, we won't have a chance. We'll be cut to pieces.'

'Keep still please, sir. Will they take prisoners?'

'Best not even think about that,' Macro said gently. 'Believe me, you'd be better off dead.'

'Really?'

'Really.'

'The tribune said Vespasian would send help as soon as he realised something was up. If we can hold out until then . . .'

'Big if,' Macro replied. 'But we might. Just make sure you do your bit.'

'I will.' Cato tore off the excess from the rough dressing and tied the ends firmly. 'There you go, sir. How's it feel?'

'Not bad.' Macro flexed his arm, and winced as a shaft of pain stabbed up to his shoulder. 'It'll do. No worse than I've already had.'

'You've been injured before then, sir?'

'All part of the deal when you join the army. You'll soon get used to it.'

'If we survive.'

'We might yet.' Macro tried to sound reassuring and then, seeing the gloomy expression on the youngster's face, he punched him on the shoulder. 'Chin up lad! We're not dead yet. Not by a long way. But if we do go, well then, there's not a lot we can do about it, so we might as well not worry, eh? Now then, let's see what those bastards are up to.'

A quick inspection of the German lines in the gathering gloom of the snowflake-speckled dusk revealed no significant changes and the dull thuds of axe blows on wood continued unceasingly. Satisfied that the village was safe for the moment, Macro turned back towards Cato.

'Just going to have a word with the rest of the lads. Keep them cheerful. While I'm about it, I want you to take a couple of men and see if you can find something to eat and drink. I'm hungry. Might as well have something while we wait for Herman to stir.'

A quick search through the nearest huts produced a good haul of dried meat, fresh bread and several jars of the local brew.

'Go easy on that stuff,' Macro warned, speaking from bitter experience. 'Make sure no-one gets a skinful or they'll be up on charges when we get back to base.'

Cato looked over the centurion's shoulder. 'Sir! The tribune . . .'

Vitellius and a bodyguard of four burly men emerged from the darkened street and mounted the ramp to the gate. Macro stiffened and was about to call the century to attention but Vitellius shook his head.

'Let the men rest, Centurion. They've earned it.'

'Yes, sir. Thank you.'

'How goes it?'

'Well, as you can see,' Macro swept an arm out to indicate the ring of Germans surrounding the village, 'we're not going to be able to hold that lot off with seventy men, sir. They've been making faggots and assault ladders ever since the last attack. And over there, they've nearly finished a battering ram. Once they bring that up . . .'

'I see.' Vitellius scratched his chin, as if in deep contemplation. 'You'll just have to hold them back, as long as you can.'

'Yes sir . . . How's the rest of the cohort?'

'Our position's not too bad. We control the wall and all able-bodied villagers are being kept under guard. Quadratus's century got the worst of it. That bitch – the chief's wife – opened an outflow grill. Twenty of them got behind Quadratus's men before she was discovered. Just picking us off while the men were keeping the Germans outside the village away from the wall. Lost almost half the century before we flushed them out.'

'You can rely on Quadratus, sir.' Macro smiled.

'Not any more, took a German pike in the guts. Went clean through him.'

'No.'

'Afraid so, centurion. And the Germans managed to take down his optio as well. That's the reason why I'm here. Can you spare someone to take over from Quadratus?'

Five paces away Cato's ears burned and his blood went ice cold in anxious anticipation. He summoned up all his will power not to look at Macro and instead gazed resolutely over the wall at the Germans gathered around the fires, their faces glowing red. Adopting what he hoped was the nonchalant pose of a veteran, Cato continued listening with a pounding heart.

'Hmm.' Macro pondered, looking around, and Cato could almost sense the weight of his gaze as it rested momentarily on his back before passing on.

'What about your optio?' Vitellius asked. 'Is he a good man?'

'Hardly a man, sir. Just a new boy. Can't afford to let him out of my sight. He means well but he's nowhere near ready for what you need.'

'Pity.'

The crushing weight of rejection wrapped itself round Cato's heart. He clamped his teeth tightly and fought back tears of humiliation.

'You have anyone else?'

'Yes, sir. The standard bearer's a good man. Take him.'

'All right then.' Vitellius nodded. 'You know the score, Centurion. Hold the gate at all costs. If we can get through the night Vespasian is bound to send help in the morning. I'm counting on you. Carry on.'

'Thank you, sir.' Macro brought his hand to his chest in salute and then watched as the tribune and his bodyguard picked their way over to where the century's standard drooped above the wall.

'Wanker!' he cursed softly. '*I'm counting on you*' – as if Macro didn't know his duty.

He cast a quick glance round to ensure the indiscretion had not been overheard. The stiff pose of the boy gazing fixedly over the walls was distinctly unnatural.

'Cato!'

'Sir?' The voice sounded aggrieved.

'Any sign of movement?'

'No.'

'Well, keep your eyes peeled.'

'Yes, sir.'

The tribune and his small squad walked back to the gate along the wall, the standard bearer in tow. Vitellius nodded curtly at Macro as he and his men passed.

'Take care, sir,' said the standard bearer.

'You too.' Macro smiled. 'We'll look after the standard while you're gone, Porcius.'

For a moment the standard bearer paused and looked longingly at the Sixth's standard, then with as little show of reluctance as he could muster he thrust the wooden shaft at Macro. 'Here.'

Then they were gone, disappearing into the cold darkness between the dingy German huts, leaving Macro holding the standard with its weighted banner hanging down from the horizontal cross-piece. For a moment Macro felt a strange twinge of excitement as the familiar awkwardness of the standard brought back the memories of his own year served as a standard bearer. He turned the shaft fondly and smiled at the reawakened sensibilities of a far younger man, tantalisingly visceral, then he was aware of Cato again.

'Boy!' he called out softly. 'Come here.'

Cato dutifully came to attention in front of his superior, face hardened with suppressed emotions.

'Relax, son. You've got a new duty. I want you to look after this.'

'Sir?'

'You heard what the tribune said?'

'Yes, sir.'

'And I trust that's all you heard. Now we've lost Porcius I need a good man to take charge of the standard for a while. Are you up to it?'

It was more of an order than a question, however gently said, and Cato felt elated as the bitter shame of a moment before was washed away. Without waiting to reply, he downed his shield and took a firm grasp on the standard with his left hand.

'It's a big responsibility,' Macro said. 'You know that.'

'Yes, sir. Thank you, sir. I'll guard it with my life.'

'You'd better. If Porcius finds so much as a scratch on it when he takes it back, he'll have your balls hanging from the tip the next time we go into action. Got that?'

Cato nodded solemnly.

'Stick close to me and, whatever happens, you hold on to that standard and you keep it high. Up where the men can see it at all times. Understand? . . . Now then, what's up?'

A sudden flow of movement through the men on the wall had caught his eye. All the legionaries were on their feet, shields and swords at the ready. Cato lifted the standard and followed Macro up to the palisade. Beyond the walls, the Germans had risen from their fires and were now moving in a black mass towards the gate. Irregular shapes in the crowd showed where men struggled with the faggots. Some carried torches that lit the faces of the nearest men in a flickering yellow-orange glare.

'Now, remember, lads,' Macro called out as he drew his sword, 'if they get in here then the whole cohort is finished. So give it your all.'

A loud shout rippled along the approaching German horde and quickly grew into a roaring cheer of anger and arrogance. Some of the legionaries shouted back their defiance.

'Steady!' Macro called out above the din. 'They're just wasting their breath! And we've got nothing to prove!'

Beside him, Cato stood rooted to the ground, transfixed by the approaching menace. For some reason, this mass advancing with fierce determination seemed far more threatening in the darkness. His imagination was busy amplifying every noise and every shape. Unlike that afternoon's mad charge through the village, the imminence of desperate conflict gave men space to consider their own courage, their own willingness to fight, and to vividly imagine the worst consequences of what might befall them. Cato shuddered and instantly cursed himself, quickly glancing round at the others on the wall.

'You afraid, lad?' Macro asked quietly.

'Yes, a bit.'

Macro smiled. 'Of course you are. So are the rest of us. But we're here now and there's nothing we can do about it.'

'I know that, sir. But it doesn't make it any easier.'

'Just keep a tight hold on the standard.'

The Germans held a steady pace until they were close

123

to the wall. Then a war horn cried out from somewhere in the night and from all round the village came more horns, and wild warrior roars crashed like a wave against the thin Roman line manning the flimsy palisade. In front of the gate, the dark forms swarmed up to the ditch and hurled the faggots into the deep shadows while others rained down a shower of arrows, spears and rocks on the defenders. With a shield raised over his head, Macro looked up to see that the pile of faggots was filling the ditch in two positions, one on either side of the gate. In a little while the ditch would be filled to a width that would allow the Germans to throw a stream of ladder-bearing men directly up against the wall. Worse still, heaving its way through the horde came the battering ram – the biggest threat to their position.

As long as the legionaries kept their heads, scaling ladders could be dislodged and pushed back, but a ram would inevitably break through the rough-hewn village gate. Then Macro and his men would have no defences to shelter behind and the Germans would overwhelm them by sheer weight of numbers. With reckless bravery, the Germans had quickly filled the ditch and, rather than making a direct assault, Macro was surprised to see them ramping the faggots up against the wall. Those Germans that fell were simply tossed on to the growing pile.

All at once the enemy horde parted in front of the gate and the battering ram, a stout pine trunk with branch stumps for handles, was carried up to the gate by a score of burly men. As the ram crashed against the gate timbers, the impact was felt by all those on the wall above. Macro peered down behind the gate as the second blow thudded home and he saw the crossbar nearly leap from its brace, only just held in place by the frantic efforts of the men he had left on guard. Several pegs were already starting from their sockets.

'This isn't good,' Macro muttered and turned back to look over the wall. Even as the defenders hurled stones down each casualty was instantly replaced and the rhythm maintained. 'This isn't good at all.'

'Isn't there something we can do, sir?' asked Cato.

'Oh yes! If we had Greek fire, we'd fry 'em up nicely.'

Cato dimly recalled what little he had read of the experimental weapon and found it hard to believe that the element burned with a national accent. But from the gleam of longing in Macro's eyes it would appear that the Greek variety was something quite special.

'Would German fire do, sir?'

'What?'

'German fire, sir.'

'What the hell are you talking about?'

'Well, sir, it's just that there were some large ovens still alight in one of the huts over there. Must be a bakery of some kind. No bread though. I suppose they must have been preparing the ovens.'

Macro stared at him for a moment. 'And you didn't think to inform me?'

'No, sir. You just ordered me to find provisions.'

'Right then, we need fire now, so see to it.' Macro replied, trying hard to hide his exasperation. 'Find the men who went looking for food with you and order them to bring coals up to the walls on their shields. Then get back here.'

Once Cato had gone Macro examined the inside of the gate from ground level. The pounding was already opening gaps in the heavy wooden beams through which he could glimpse the Germans beyond. Each new blow dislodged a shower of dust and debris from the wall above and Macro had to blink several times to clear his eyes. Hurrying back up to the wall, he detailed several men to use pitchforks to take straw from nearby huts and pile it on the walkway above the gate. It was not until the first detail returned, shields piled high with red glowing embers, that Cato realised what the centurion's intentions were.

'Get those on the straw!'

The sweating legionaries tipped the embers into the straw and, despite the slight dampness, smoke and small flames flickered into life. As the fire caught and sizzled, Macro pitched more straw on top and smoke began to billow causing the nearest legionaries to break into fits of coughing.

'Right then! Over the wall with it!' Macro shouted. 'Use whatever you've got, but get it over the wall!'

The Romans dived in with pitchforks, the few remaining javelins and even short swords and the burning bundles of straw, sparks crackling high into night, blazed down on to the hapless Germans with the battering ram. Shouts and screams of terror sounded from below and the pounding at the gate ceased. At the foot of the wall Macro could see the ram lying abandoned, almost covered in burning straw. The heat hit his face a stinging blow and Macro stepped back. No-one would be using that battering ram for quite a while, even if it failed to burn completely.

'Hah! Look at them run!' Cato beamed. 'They'll not be trying that again tonight.'

'Maybe.' Macro nodded. 'Maybe. But two can play that game. Look there!'

Cato turned to follow the direction the centurion was indicating. The ramps built by the attackers were finished and, as he watched, torches arced up from the German lines and fell in an explosion of sparks in among the faggots. Within moments the ramps were ablaze and bright orange flames licked up the village walls driving the legionaries back. One hapless soldier, fully illuminated by the flickering glare, was hit by several arrows and pitched forward into the blaze with a scream of terror that abruptly ceased. Cato shuddered, but before he could spare the poor man any more thought a small flame suddenly licked through a gap in the walkway.

'Oh no,' he muttered, then turned towards Macro. 'Sir! Look there!'

Macro looked down just in time to see another, larger, tongue of flame hungrily flicker through the walkway. The gate was on fire. Some of the straw must have landed too near the wall. 'That's just fucking great! So much for German fire.' He glared at Cato.

'We could try to put it out.'

'Shut up! It's too late for that.' The centurion's mind raced. All three fires on the wall had a firm hold and were burning ever more fiercely even as he watched. There was nothing they could do to put them out now. And if they stayed on the wall they would be burned as well as providing nicely lit targets for the German archers.

There was nothing for it. They must give ground until the fire died and they could move back up to defend the wall. But, with the gate already well ablaze and two more openings burning through the wall, in a matter of an hour's time the Sixth century's defence of this side of the village would collapse like a cheap tenement block. And that would be long before dawn and any hope of relief from Vespasian.

'Stand back!' he roared out so that all his men would hear him above the raging crack and roar of the flames. 'Off the wall!'

He waited until the last man had descended the gate ramps and then he took a final look towards the palisade, where sharpened stakes of wood hissed and steamed in the withering heat. Beyond the wall, the front ranks of the Germans were illuminated brilliantly and their triumphant faces wavered and shimmered through the heat-distorted air. Then he ran down to his men and formed the main body up in the street inside the gate, with two smaller sections fronting the stretches of wall ignited by the Germans.

'What do we do now, sir?' Cato asked.

'We have to wait – and pray that the fire lasts.'

Chapter Ten

The fire not only lasted, it raged, sending swirling streams of sparks high up into the night sky where they mingled and melted the falling snowflakes. Most of the sparks slowly glowered into nothingness, but some fell back to earth – landing on the angled thatch roofs of the village. Even as Macro was cursing himself for deciding to burn the ram, and thereby the gate he was intending to save from the ram, Cato drew his attention to the nearest huts. Smoke curled up from the roofs, and here and there an orange twinkle gleamed, then rippled into flames. Macro glanced round anxiously and saw that the huts as far back as fifty paces from the wall were catching fire. Unless they moved they would soon be trapped right in the centre of the blazing inferno to come. A sudden crashing sound drew his gaze to the front, where the entire gateway was collapsing into the roaring flames.

Beyond they could hear the Germans shouting triumphantly. They would be edging towards the blaze, itching for the moment when the fires had subsided enough to allow them to stream into the village and slaughter the cohort. But for now the flames showed no signs of subsiding, indeed the fire was growing ever more intense as it spread amongst the huts. The heat in the street was already intolerable and Cato found himself squinting to protect his eyes, buffeted by the wavering, stinging air. The centurion knew the time had come to retreat, a bitter truth to swallow – but a necessary one.

'All troops to me! All troops to me! Back down the street!'

The legionaries turned and quick-marched until they reached the limit of the fire where Macro ordered them to halt and close up once again. The men looked back in relief, glad to be out of immediate danger. The position they had occupied moments earlier erupted in a shower of sparks as a building collapsed across the street where they had been standing.

'Close one, sir,' muttered one of the men.

'We're not out of it yet,' Macro replied sourly. 'Fire's spreading fast. We'll fall back with it. If we're lucky, we can keep the fire between us and Herman.'

'Until we run out of village,' Cato said softly.

Macro turned quickly, on the point of shouting out some abuse, but the boy was right. 'Until we run out of village,' he agreed. 'Or Vespasian reaches us.'

The fire, let loose like an uncaged beast at some amphitheatre, raged across the village, hungrily devouring all in the path of its blazing jaws. Above it, the sky glowed orange and the snow falling from the sky melted into rain. Little by little the legionaries gave ground and, as they did so, Macro became aware that the blaze at the gateway was dying down far more quickly than it should. He frowned, uncomprehending. Then he saw Germans beyond the falling flames, throwing buckets of water on the ruins of the gate where smoke and steam mingled. As he watched, the men around him became aware of what was happening and a low murmur of despair trickled through the Sixth century. The Germans were clearly not content to leave the Romans to the eventual wrath of the fire, they wanted blood, and the street leading up to the gate was nearly clear of flames due to its relative breadth.

'Silence!' Macro shouted. 'We're not done for yet. Not as long as we can keep the fire between us and them. First two squads with me. Castor!' Macro yelled to the century's veteran. 'See to it that the rest tear down buildings along the street – anything that helps the fire line spread. Got that?'

'Yes, sir.'

'But you keep the line open for us. When you're done you call us back. We'll fall back through you.' Macro turned to the front two squads. 'All right, lads, listen. If Herman gets down the street we have to hold him back long enough for the others to do their work. Then we run like hell. Come on then.'

With Macro and Cato at their head, the two squads marched down the street and stopped as close to the ruins of the gate as the heat permitted. There Macro formed them into an unbroken shield wall and they waited. But not for long. The fire at the gate was quickly extinguished leaving a smouldering heap of ruined timber. The Germans stumbled across it, heedless of the residual heat, and resumed their chain of water jars where the burning building had fallen into the street. As the enemy laboured the Romans waited silently and Cato, in the second rank, held the shaft of the standard tightly to stop himself shaking too obviously. He glanced sidelong at the men around him, silent and still, eyes grimly watching the Germans working towards them.

Suddenly the Germans downed their jars and scrambled over the last blackened ruins between them and the Romans, voices raised in hysterical war-cries.

'Steady, boys!' Macro growled. 'Hold your line. We fight in formation.'

Cato could see over Macro's shoulder the first of the Germans, long hair streaming, running straight at them. Without slowing for a moment, he crashed into the wall of shields and was despatched by a quick thrust. With a gasp he fell dead on the street. But more followed, thudding against the shields, desperately trying to force an opening into which they could thrust their short spears. As the weight piled up, the legionaries gave ground. The first of their number fell, wounded in the side by a spear thrust. Streaming blood, he went down – his place instantly taken by the man behind – and his comrades were powerless to help as they gave ground and left him exposed to the Germans. With a savage cry, the man's throat was ripped open by a spear and the gushing crimson splashed up the shield wall.

Cato ducked as a spear-thrust was aimed at his own head and the standard dipped forward. The Germans eagerly lunged for it and one secured a grip on the banner.

'Hands off, Herman!' Macro shouted, thrusting his sword into the chest the German had foolishly exposed. Abruptly his grip was released and Cato snatched the standard back to the vertical, horrified by the shame of what had nearly happened.

For a second, Macro was able to glance back down the street and saw that the rest of the century had pulled down several buildings, piling the rubble and burning thatch across the street. It was almost time.

'Rear section! Fall back now.'

The men needed no urging and turned to sprint down the street towards the small opening left for them where Castor had some men poised with ropes to pull a wall down across the street. As soon as the Germans saw the rearmost men run back to safety they shouted their contempt and flew at the thin shield wall with renewed fury. Even Cato could see that the last section would be in perilous danger the moment it tried to disengage. But Macro was ready for the moment and, without warning, bellowed an order, 'Break and charge!'

With a shout, the legionaries pushed their shields out and hacked into the Germans before them. The unexpectedness of the move momentarily caught the Germans off guard and they checked and recoiled.

'Run!' Macro shouted.

In an instant the charge turned tail and the soldiers bolted down the street, Cato amongst them, cursing the awkwardness of the standard. As the street narrowed towards the point where the rest of the century was waiting, Macro faced the Germans once again, determined to make sure his men got away. The enemy were still reeling from the sudden turnabout in Roman tactics and, with a grim smile of satisfaction, he ran after the others.

But one German, more alert than the rest, hefted his spear above his head and hurled it after the retreating Romans with all his might.

Cato, awash with relief, was bolting towards the gap being held open by his comrades when he heard Macro shout.

'Ahhh! Fuck!'

Cato turned quickly. Ten paces up the street Macro had tumbled headlong, a spear right through his thigh. His shield had fallen ahead of him and his sword lay to one side. Beyond Macro, the Germans had recovered from their surprise and were running towards the stricken centurion. Macro looked up and saw Cato.

'Run, you fool!'

'Sir . . .'

'Save the fucking standard! RUN!'

In a moment of shocking stillness Cato saw the angry look on Macro's face; the Germans running down towards him; the fire raging in the buildings around them and the sky glowing blood red against the night. Then, before he was aware of any kind of conscious decision, he was running back towards his centurion screaming meaninglessly at the Germans.

Chapter Eleven

'Did you see Titus today?'

'Sorry?' Vespasian looked up from his travel desk. 'What did you say?'

'Your son, Titus. Have you seen him today?' Flavia tapped her finger on his shoulder. 'Or have you been too busy to notice that you have a son?'

'My dear, I really haven't had time.'

'That's what you always say. Always. All this wretched paperwork is taking up your whole life.' She looked into the document chest. 'Don't you think you should make time for the boy?'

Vespasian laid down his stylus and regarded her for a moment, heart heavy with guilt. After three miscarriages and one still-born, Titus had seemed like something of a miracle. The long labour had nearly killed Flavia and the child. Since his birth in Rome two years ago the boy had been treated like a precious vase, wrapped in wool and hardly ever out of his mother's sight. Vespasian had devoted much effort to being as supportive as he could, all the while conscious that time spent with family was time spent away from politics and career advancement – which was ultimately for Titus's benefit, he assured himself.

Accepting the appointment to the Legion had not been an easy choice. He had known Flavia was hugely reluctant to leave Rome, even as she dutifully urged him to accept the post. Like all wives with a respect for tradition, she had accompanied him when Vespasian had left to take up his command. While the fresh air was a pleasant change from clinging stench of Rome, it had not proved beneficial to Titus. Since they had arrived at the base the child had been down with one illness after another. The cold, damp climate was ruinous to a fragile constitution, and many months of long nights at the side of his cradle had exhausted Flavia. The thought of the loss of Titus filled them both with dread, but Vespasian had had the comfort of a full working day while Flavia had not. Removed from her social circle and isolated in the closed world of a military base with only a handful of other officers' wives, Flavia's world had turned inward on her son.

Titus, as is the way with infants, contrived to find every possible way to drive his mother, and her domestic slaves, completely frantic with worry. There was no shelf, table edge or door he had not managed to crash his head against, no chair or chest he had not fallen off and no rug or mat he had not tripped over. The boy's natural inquisitiveness meant that no safety audit of their quarters was ever completed thoroughly enough that Titus did not find something dangerous or unsavoury to stick in his mouth or poke in his eye or when the mood took him – which it frequently did – in the eye of some unfortunate slave. Now his nurses were having to contend with a fine range of needle-sharp teeth that closed unexpectedly on any exposed flesh that ventured within range.

Vespasian smiled at the thought that at least his son had spirit.

'What?' Flavia asked.

'Eh?'

'You're smiling. What are you thinking?'

'I'm thinking it's time I spent some time with my boy.' Vespasian pushed the travel desk back and stood up. 'Come.'

As they left the study and walked along the covered walkway that ran along the private courtyard Vespasian looked at the sky. Beyond the dull flickering light of the courtyard torches the freezing night air was brushed with the first flakes of snow. It occurred to him that Vitellius had not yet returned and the thought of the cocksure tribune marching back from the village in a miserable blizzard would have been gratifying were it not for the poor men he was commanding.

As the door to the little nursery opened, Titus's head swivelled round and, with a shout of pure pleasure, he jumped on to his little legs, pushing his nurse to one side, and ran across to his parents.

'Dada!' he squealed as he wrapped his arms around his father's legs and tipped his head back, wide-eyed and smiling. 'Pick up! Pick up! Pick up!'

Vespasian leant down and, firmly grasping the boy under the arms, swung him up above his head, provoking a fresh bout of excited screaming.

'How's my soldier? Eh? How's my little boy today?'

Vespasian smiled and turned to his wife. 'He's growing up fast. Not long now before he gets to wear his first toga.'

'He's still a baby!' Flavia protested. 'Still my little baby. Aren't you?'

Titus regarded his mother with a disgusted expression and pushed himself back from her tight embrace. Vespasian laughed and leant forward to ruffle the boy's unruly hair. 'That's my little soldier!'

'He's not a soldier!' Flavia said firmly. 'And he's not going to be a soldier, at least he's not going to be one for any longer than is absolutely necessary. If I have anything to do with it, he'll stay in Rome where I can look after him.'

'We'll have to let him decide for himself one day,' Vespasian replied gently. 'The army's a good life for a man.'

'No, it's not! The army's dangerous, uncomfortable and populated by uncouth louts.'

'Provincials like me, I suppose.'

'Oh, I didn't mean . . .'

'Only joking. But seriously, if Titus is to make a career for himself in the Senate then he must serve with the legions first.'

'You could see to it that he gets a posting near home.'

'We've been through this. The appointments get made by the imperial staff. I have no influence there, at least not at the moment. If you want him to be successful he must serve in the army first. You know that's the way it is.'

'Yes.' Flavia nodded sadly and kissed Titus on the

forehead. The infant sensed her mood and suddenly hugged her tightly, crushing his little face into her shoulder. 'I just wish I could have him at this age for longer.'

'I know. I really do. Maybe there'll be more children one day. When you're ready.'

Flavia stared up into his face, dark eyes full of painful memory that threatened to well up into tears. She blinked and then forcefully smiled away the tremble in her lip. 'Oh, I hope so. I want so very many of them. And I want them with you. You promise me you will be careful?'

'Careful?'

'This new campaign of yours in Britain. You will be careful.'

'Britain! How the hell . . .' Vespasian's brow creased angrily. 'That's supposed to be a secret. Where did you hear it?'

'From the officers' wives.' Flavia laughed at his expression. 'You men really do have a great deal to learn about keeping secrets, don't you?'

'Typical,' Vespasian muttered. 'Bloody typical. I swear my most senior officers to strict confidentiality and the next thing I know it's common gossip. Is nothing sacred any more?'

Titus laughed and shook his head violently from side to side.

'Now, don't fuss, dear.' Flavia patted him on the arm. 'I'm sure the secret's safe from everyone else. But don't let's change the subject. I was talking about Britain.'

'So, it seems, is everyone else,' grumbled Vespasian.

'You must promise me you'll be careful. I want your word. Right now.'

'I promise.'

'That's settled, then.' She nodded in satisfaction. 'Now give the boy a hug and put him to bed.'

Vespasian carried the child over to the cot in the corner of the room. Leaning down, he pulled back the soft woollen covers one-handed and removed the warming brick. As he was lowered into the cot, Titus moaned and tightly clenched his hands into the folds of his father's tunic. 'Not tired! Not tired!'

'You must go to sleep now,' Vespasian replied softly as he tried to prise his son's fingers loose. The boy's tiny hands were surprisingly strong and his father struggled to unpick them as the child's eyes welled with tears of anger and frustration. As the last fingers were worked free from the cloth round Vespasian's neck Titus suddenly bit his father on the knuckle. Before he could help himself, Vespasian swore out loud.

'Language!' Flavia hissed. 'Do you want him to pick up such words at his age?'

It occurred to Vespasian that any child brought up in a military garrison was going to pick up a rather wider vocabulary than was deemed appropriate in the polite social circles of Rome.

'That boy,' he continued after a moment, 'has quite a bite on him.'

'But that's good.'

'It is?' Vespasian looked down with raised eyebrows at the small teeth-shaped crescent on the back of his hand.

'Show's he's got strength of character.' Flavia pressed the still struggling boy down into the cot and drew the cover up over his body.

'Shows he's got sharp teeth,' her husband muttered.

With a last whine, Titus succumbed to a child's sense of routine and turned over on to his stomach, closed his eyes and, with a few meaningless mumbles spoken softly into his mattress, fell asleep. Both parents gazed down at him for a moment, wondering at the peaceful, perfectly rounded shape of his face, the final twitches of his curled fingers in the flickering glow of the oil lamps.

Someone hammered on the door. Titus stirred, eyes flickering open for a moment.

'Who the hell?'

'Just shut them up quickly,' Flavia hissed. 'Before they wake Titus.'

Vespasian opened the door on to the courtyard and was confronted by the duty centurion and a shivering legionary.

'Sir!' the centurion barked in best parade-ground manner. 'Beg to report . . .'

'Shhh! Keep your voice down. My boy's asleep.'

The centurion stood open-mouthed for a second, before he managed to force himself to continue in a whisper. 'Beg to report a fire.'

'A fire. How big a fire? Where?'

'In the direction of the forest, sir, towards the Rhine.'

Vespasian eyed the man impatiently. 'And you think that's worth disturbing me for?'

'This sentry says it's a big fire, sir.'

'Big? How big?'

'Dunno, sir,' the legionary replied. 'Can't see the fire as such, sir. Just a glow, on the horizon like.'

A nasty thought struck the legate. 'Third cohort back yet?'

'No, sir.' The centurion shook his head. 'No sign of them.'

'Right, I'm coming. You're dismissed.'

Flavia crossed over to him in small, quiet steps. 'Trouble?'

'Possibly. I'm just going to check. I'll be back soon. You get to bed.'

When Vespasian reached the tower above the eastern gate the parapet had already disappeared under a softly curved layer of snow. Beyond the fortress wall, a dull white landscape stretched out towards the distant fringe of the forest, only dimly visible through the swirling snow. Nevertheless, the duty centurion had been right to summon him; an orange glow reflected off the clouds beyond the tree-line. That had to be quite a fire, Vespasian mused. Moreover, a fire directly in line with the local German settlement.

He turned back to the duty centurion. 'Still no sign of Vitellius?'

'Nothing, sir.'

Worrying, most worrying. Yet what trouble could Vitellius have led the Third cohort into? According to the latest intelligence reports there was little indication of any rebellious sentiment brewing amongst the locals. Still, the cohort should have returned to base by now. And the intensity of the distant glow indicated a sizeable fire. Vespasian considered the damage his reputation would suffer if he sounded the alarm too easily, all too clearly visualising the mocking laughter of his men. But the thought was no sooner in his head than he quickly dismissed it. His pride came a poor second to his feeling of responsibility to the men of the Legion. He turned back to the duty centurion.

'Call out the horse squadron. I want them to scout the route taken by the Third cohort to the local village. They are to report back to me in person the moment they find anything. Then call out the Legion. I want all senior officers at headquarters immediately. Centurions are to have their men in full battle order and ready to move off in line of march. Except the First cohort. They stay and guard the base. Got all that?'

'Yes, sir.'

'Then go. And run!'

After the duty centurion had gone, Vespasian turned back towards the distant fire. Unless Vitellius had lost his way back to the fort, the fire had to be connected with the cohort's absence.

'Sir?'

When he looked up Vespasian saw the concerned look in the young sentry's face. 'What is it, soldier?'

'Do you think our lads are in trouble?'

Behind them the first call to arms shrieked out across the base, to be quickly taken up by others, and out into the night, silhouetted against numerous doorframes, poured the soldiers of the Second Legion. Vespasian forced himself to grin.

'They'd better be in trouble, or else I've just pissed

off four thousand men for nothing. And that wouldn't do, would it?'

Chapter Twelve

Cato was screaming at the top of his voice as he hurtled towards the two Germans closing on his centurion. At the last moment, he lowered the tip of the standard and swept it from side to side. The foremost German standing above Macro, poised for the kill, looked up at the shrill shouts and half turned to face the new danger. Macro didn't hesitate a second and smashed his fist up into the man's crotch. He doubled over and fell to his knees retching, and Cato tumbled over the top, rolling to one side. The remaining German looked quite startled and suddenly burst out laughing. Cato angrily rose to his feet and brandished the standard in his enemy's face.

'Don't you fucking laugh at me!'

For a moment the pair stared into each other's eyes, the German's expression quite cold and calculating now. Suddenly he feinted to Cato's right and, as Cato swung the standard round, the German ducked back and aimed a sword thrust at Cato's armpit. The army standard, like all army standards, was designed for show and not grace and the heavy headpiece swung so far round that the bottom of the shaft came arcing right into the face of the lunging German and stopped him dead. With a stunned groan he slumped on to the ground. Cato, who had been facing the other way, came round – gritting his teeth at the prospect of a fatal wound – and stared in shock at the man collapsing to the ground.

'What?'

'Leave him!' Macro called out. 'Come here, boy! Get this spear out of me!'

'Sir?'

'Just do it!'

Cato took a firm grasp with his spare hand and Macro turned his leg for a better angle. 'Now!'

Cato pulled with all his might and the leaf-shaped spear tip came free of the leg with a gush of blood and torn tissue. Macro howled in agony just once and then, clamping his mouth shut, he painfully raised himself as Cato lifted him by the arm. The wound was bleeding badly, but happily the blood flowed rather than spurted – no fatal wound then. But the pain was the worst he had felt, quite mind-numbing, and it took a great force of will for Macro to swing his arm round the youth's shoulder as Cato helped him back towards the gap between the buildings where the rest of the century waited. Behind them, above the roar of the flames, Cato could hear pounding footsteps and he glanced back to see the Germans rushing forwards, screaming for Roman blood. He renewed his efforts, almost dragging the centurion along with him. Then they stumbled and Macro went down on his knees, crying out as it jarred his wounded leg. The faces ahead filled with despair – they could see that the two would never make it before the Germans were on them.

'Go!' Macro grunted. 'That's an order!'

'Can't hear you, sir.'

'Save the standard.'

At that moment Castor sadly shook his head and gave the order for the building to be pulled down. The legionaries hesitated until the veteran screamed the order out again and then the ropes tightened and the wall crashed down into the street bringing the blazing thatch with it.

'Oh shit!' Cato stopped, then quickly looked back. The Germans were almost on them. To his right was a stone wall with a stout wooden door. Quickly he lifted the latch, kicked the door inwards and bundled the centurion and the standard inside. He ducked through the opening and slammed the door shut, hurriedly throwing the locking bar into its cradle. A crunching thump echoed in the confined space as the first Germans arrived outside and pounded the door. It was dark inside, but light from the flames illuminated the edges of the shutters and gaps in the eaves. The one window in the room faced on to the street, but luckily it had been closed and bolted, and now it too shuddered under the impact of blows from outside.

'See if there's another way out of here,' Macro said as he examined his wound by touch. Blood was still flowing freely and he dare not spill any more than was necessary if he was to keep his wits about him. He undid his sword belt and removed the scabbard before fastening it above the wound as tightly as possible. The bleeding had slowed to an ooze when Cato returned a moment later.

'Well?'

147

'Seems to be some kind of barn, some hay at the back and a ventilation opening, but that's it.'

The pounding at the door was more rhythmic now and, as they both looked at the shuttered window, a long splint of wood flew back into the room where a dark point pierced the shutter. It wriggled, disappeared and moments later more splinters flew and jagged orange shafts of light pierced the gloom.

'We can't stay here.'

'No,' Cato responded. 'Look there!'

A yellow glow had appeared in the raftered thatch over their heads, and then another flaring violently into tiny flickering flames that quickly increased in intensity.

And all the time the shutters were being hacked to pieces.

'We'll have to use the ventilation window,' Cato decided. 'There's a ladder, but with your leg it might be difficult.'

'We haven't got any choice.'

'No. But we have to delay them as long as we can. Can you guard the window, sir?'

'Yes, but—'

'Please, sir, there's no time to explain.'

'Very well.' Macro nodded. 'Help me up and give me your sword.'

Taking the weight off his injured leg, Macro leaned against the wall to one side of the window while Cato disappeared to the back of the barn. Abruptly a large chunk of the shutter finally gave way and tumbled to the floor. Immediately a spear thrust inwards and then hands grabbed the edge of the window frame as a

German prepared to pull himself through. Macro slashed down at the nearest hand and the severed fingers jumped up into the air as the man drew back, screaming.

'Come on, you bastards!' Macro shouted. 'Who's game for some more?'

The attack on the door suddenly increased in frenzy and, solid though it was, the wood began to give way. Defending a window was one thing, but the door would be impossible.

'Cato! Whatever you're going to do, better do it right now!'

'Coming, sir!' Cato grunted, and then staggered towards the front of the barn carrying a twisted mass of straw on the end of a pitchfork. He dumped it between the door and the window and hurriedly spread it out. Then, reaching up to the roof, he used the pitchfork to pull down some of the burning thatch, raising his arm to protect his face from the tumbling sparks that came in its wake. Thick tendrils of smoke curled up. Then the flames took hold and, just as the door gave way, the front of the barn crackled with fire, shrouded in thick choking clouds.

'This way!' Cato called out and coughed violently as he inhaled the foul-tasting smoke.

Propping Macro up as best he could with the hand that was unencumbered by the standard, Cato half supported, half dragged the centurion over to the rear of the barn where a ladder led up into the darkness.

'You go up first, sir. Take the standard with you, but give me the sword. Shout once you're through.'

Macro did not argue with the lad's orders and turned

to make his way up the ladder, cursing his wound and the awkward standard in equal measure. The smoke from the fire was thickening downwards from the apex of the barn, catching in his lungs and stinging his eyes as he climbed the short, but agonising, distance to the ventilation window. He punched it open and quickly hung his head out, gasping for breath. From this raised position, Macro saw that this side of the village was being consumed by brilliant raging flames, rapidly spreading as the fire was fanned by a light breeze. The Germans were picking their way through the twisting alleys, trying to avoid the fire, heading for the open village square where the remains of the cohort were preparing to fight for their lives.

Immediately below was a small closed yard, where two pigs were dashing about in a fine panic. A mound of winter feed lay directly beneath and Macro hefted the standard up and through the window before letting it drop. From inside the barn there was a sudden crash as the door finally gave way and then a rush of feet and harsh shouts.

'Cato!'

'Go, sir!' the boy called. 'Go now!'

The Germans, coughing, were coming towards the rear of the barn, determined to hunt their Roman quarry down, and Macro hurriedly wriggled through the window. Working his way round, he lowered himself down the outside wall until he was hanging full stretch, and then released his grip. The landing was made softer than he had expected as one of the pigs had decided that the hay would make a good shelter from the chaos of the outside world. The last thing that a pig could reasonably expect was a heavily armoured infantryman crashing down from above. Nevertheless, the air was rent with a terrified squeal and a deeper human oath as both struggled to free themselves from the tangle. Macro kicked the beast to one side and sat on the hay, breathing heavily, but otherwise unhurt. The pig had not been so fortunate, its back was broken and the two forelegs worked pathetically to drag the beast over the soiled yard away from danger. And all the while it squealed and screamed so that Macro feared it must attract attention.

Inside the barn, he could hear the Germans shouting angrily as they slashed about in their search for Romans to slaughter. Then came a shout and, immediately after, the scraping of the ladder on the inside of the wall. Macro quickly pulled the standard close to him, swept armfuls of hay across his body and lay still. Through the strands across his face Macro stared anxiously up the wall as a dark head appeared against the orange sky. For a horribly long moment the German's head gazed down, then there was a harsh exchange of words and the head withdrew. Macro kept quite still, listening intently as the voices in the barn faded away, under the screams of the injured pig. When he judged he was safe, he sat up and shook off the stinking hay. One side of the yard seemed to give out on to a street and, from over the wall, he could hear Germans pounding by. The other side was comparatively quiet and, nursing his leg, Macro eased himself up and peered over. Immediately beyond the wall was a large area filled with wicker pig-pens – he could hear the animals grunting inside.

Macro eased back down and, waiting until the street fell momentarily quiet, he called out for Cato beneath the window.

No reply came. He called again, but still nothing.

Damn the boy. He should have followed up the ladder the moment the door gave way. But, with a twinge of guilt, Macro realised that the Germans would have been instantly led to the sound. Cato, he realised, must have know this and sacrificed himself to save Macro and the standard.

The pig's squealing had reached a new, nerve-wracking, pitch of terror and Macro kicked it hard in the side of the head.

'Keep the fucking noise down!' He swung the boot in again. 'Want me to get caught?'

But the pig just renewed its cries with increasing panic. Inevitably, some passing Germans paused in the street to investigate the noise. Macro did not hesitate. The standard went flying over the far wall and he frantically pulled himself over the top and slid down the side into a pile of dung scraped together from the nearest pens. Grabbing the standard and keeping as low to the ground as possible, he crawled between the pens towards the centre of the village, trying not to imagine what he might find even if he did make it back to the cohort.

Chapter Thirteen

When the door crashed open Cato's mind was racing. With Macro safely out of harm's way, he moved along the wall and dived into the huge pile of straw gathered in the corner, burrowing his way deep inside as the Germans advanced into the barn.

Then there were voices close by and, suddenly, a terrible screaming from somewhere just outside the barn. Cato immediately feared for his centurion, before common sense told him that no man could make a noise like that. One of the Germans laughed and then dissolved into a fit of coughing. The smoke in the barn was starting to catch in Cato's throat and he desperately strained to keep his chest still.

Something moved quickly through the straw and there was a dull clang as it struck the barn wall. The noise was repeated, closer this time and, with a feeling of cold dread, Cato realised that they were searching the straw with their spears. He forced himself to remain still, knowing full well that surrender was suicide. More spear-thrusts followed as the Germans hunted for their prey, painfully coughing in the thickening smoke of the burning barn. Someone shouted. Abruptly the search ceased as the Germans hurriedly withdrew from the blazing building.

Only when he was sure that he was alone did Cato cautiously pick his way out of the straw. The room was full of smoke, with only a small decrease in density at floor level. Staying low on his stomach, Cato crawled towards the front of the building where the straw he had lit shortly before was now reduced to glowing embers. Beyond the shattered doorframe the street was swarming with Germans. One voice shouted out a string of orders before they moved on towards the centre of the village. Cato waited until the last sound of the footsteps had gone before he rolled out into the street, coughing loudly and gulping down the fire-warmed night air. His lungs and his eyes stung painfully and it was only after he managed to clear the tears from his eyes that Cato could clearly see the street around him. Although the shouts of Germans could be heard above the crackle and roar of flames he was, for the moment, alone – except for the man he had knocked out earlier with the butt of the standard.

Approaching cautiously, Cato saw that the German was still out cold; a nasty black and blue lump had risen on his forehead. With Germans all around and Romans in short supply, Cato reasoned that a change in appearance would be a prudent move. He undid the clasp on the German's cloak and rolled the helpless man over to pull it free. As he draped it over his own cloak the malodorous mix of sweat, human and animal soiling and waterproofing grease was quite overwhelming, and Cato retched. He struggled for a moment to free the buckle holding his helmet on and then let the cumbersome weight of iron and bronze thud to the ground. There was nothing he could do about his army-cropped hair and, with a distasteful wrinkle of his nose he raised the cloak's hood over his head. With his sword sheathed under the cloak Cato snatched up the German's spear and shield. Looking down at himself he saw that the overall effect, while far from convincing, might at least allow him to look less like a Roman.

What now? The only direction that offered any possibility of safety was towards the village square and what was left of the cohort. But what of Macro and the standard? Cato hurriedly examined the now fiercely blazing barn for access to the rear, but the narrow passage down the side of the barn was filled with flames. The heat scalded his face and Cato recoiled from the passage entrance. Pulling the cloak tightly about his head and body, Cato took a deep breath and plunged headlong into the passage. The heat and light were tremendous and almost at once there was the smell of roasted waterproofing grease. Cato hunched further down and ran on, flames scorching his bare legs, then he was past the side of the barn, out of the fire. The entire cloak was smouldering and Cato hastily beat out the few patches that were alight.

The high wall at the rear of the barn was hard to scale, weighed down and tired as he was. Scrabbling breathlessly up the side, Cato just managed to raise his head above the uneven stonework. The yard behind the barn seemed empty apart from a large pile of winter feed.

'Sir!' Cato called out as loudly as he dared.

Something stirred in the winter feed at the sound of his voice and Cato felt his heart leap with relief. Then the air was cut by a scream of agony.

'Sir! Are you hurt?' Cato cried out anxiously, and then a vague shape twisted out of the winter feed and writhed in screaming fits of agony. A pig. Where was the centurion?

Cato released his grip and sank down beside the wall; young, scared and alone. Bitter tears of hatred at the way the fates had treated him pooled in his eyes for a moment. The roof of the barn suddenly crashed down into the hungry flames. Cato stumbled back as the instinct for self-preservation reasserted itself within him. Very well, he was alone, surrounded by the enemy and a raging fire, but he wasn't going to surrender his life to either without a struggle.

Quickly constructing a mental plan of the village with the relative positions of Romans, Germans and the fire, Cato decided on a direction and hurried away from the barn along the narrow passageway, eyes and ears alert for danger.

Pigs, Macro thought, might be induced to taste well in the hands of a good cook, but in their raw state they were barely tolerable at the best of times, and German pigs – never. As he crawled through the filth between their pens, where the urine and the more liquid variety of shit oozed into a badly dug drainage channel, he strove to keep his mind on saving the standard, which he kept as far from the filth as possible. A quite unbearable stench

156

invaded his nose and overpowered his mind, so that he crawled on, swearing every imaginable oath at each pig he passed.

Macro crawled up to a large wicker gate. Through the crudely woven hazel he peered cautiously into the street beyond. A short distance to one side, the street gave out on to the market area, made up of roughly built stalls, now empty and bare in the depth of winter. The fire had not reached this part of the village and the locals who had escaped Vitellius's round up were carrying away the few precious possessions that time allowed, casting anxious glances beyond Macro to where flames licked high into the night. From what he had seen from the ventilation window, Macro estimated that a little distance beyond the market he would find the village square. The handful of villagers nearby were women, children and older Germans – none of whom seemed to pose too much of a threat. If he got by them as stealthily as possible he might be ignored. And then he would have a short march along the street to the rest of the cohort.

Painfully rising to his feet, Macro withdrew the peg that fastened the wicker gate. Sticking close to the side of the street, he kept the butt of the standard off the ground in a bid to remain as quiet and unobtrusive as possible. Progress was slow as he was beginning to lose any feeling in his wounded leg and, worse, loss of blood was making him feel faint-headed. Breathing deeply he forced himself on, into the market and down the side of the deserted stalls, unobserved or ignored by the villagers retrieving the last of their valuables and helping themselves to those of absent neighbours. It was not in their interest to attract attention any more than it was in Macro's and those who saw him simply eyed him warily as he passed.

Leaving the market, the sound of fighting grew louder and Macro paused for breath at a point where the street bent round sharply towards the village square. His vision was clouding badly and his head started to spin. Macro rubbed his eyes and bit back on the nausea and, gradually, clarity of vision and mind returned. A quick glance around the corner would tell him if the way ahead was clear. The centurion leaned his head out.

The German ran into him so quickly that Macro was only aware that he was suddenly flat on his back, gazing up at the orange sky, winded and gasping for air. To one side of him the German had fallen headlong, spear clattering on to the street. As Macro struggled to roll over and draw his dagger, the German reacted more quickly. In a trice he was on his feet, snatching up the spear and whirling round to plant the broad blade in his enemy's throat. Macro held his dagger out, knowing it was no more than a pathetic gesture of defiance.

'Thanks be to Jupiter!' the German said in perfect Latin.

'Eh?'

The German lowered his spear and offered him a hand. Macro just stared at the man as if he were mad.

'Do come on, sir. We haven't got time,' Cato urged, drawing back the hood, then wrinkling his nose. 'What the hell is that smell?'

Macro slumped back against the wall, smiling with relief, and the moment's loss of determination set his head reeling again. But he didn't really care. Cato was here, bless the lad. Now if he could just rest a moment . . .

'Sir!'

He was being roughly shaken and his eyes flickered open. Above him loomed Cato, hands tightly grasping Macro's harness.

'Up we go, sir!' Cato said, gritting his teeth with exertion as he hauled Macro to his feet. He supported him with one arm while using the spear to steady them both. Macro stubbornly held on to the standard, which trailed behind them, as Cato dragged him along the side of the market to the next street corner. A quick glance revealed more Germans milling about as their front ranks tried to force a way through to the village square.

'This is no good,' Cato said. 'They're in every street. We must try something else.'

'I have to rest.'

'No, sir! You can't.' Cato shook him until his eyes flickered open again. 'There! That's better. Now then.'

Cato kicked open a door and dragged Macro into a small hut. The centurion was only dimly aware of being led through an assortment of dingy rooms and yards before Cato deposited him beside an earth-faced wicker wall. The lad drew out his sword, slipped off the German's cloak and attacked the wall with all his strength.

'What the hell are you doing, boy?' Macro asked weakly.

'I think the square is on the other side of this house. If we can just get through the wall.'

'Then I can rest.'

'Then you can rest, sir.'

Cato grasped the sword handle with both hands and stabbed away at the wall, loosening great lumps of clay, until he had exposed a large section of the wattle. He wiped his brow once, and attacked the slender intertwined branches with desperate energy. Macro watched listlessly, no longer really caring about anything, slowly giving in to his desire to float off into a deep sleep.

The wattle proved a much tougher prospect than the lathe and Cato's heart pounded as he hacked at the wall with single-minded fury. At last he had cut away enough to start attacking the tightly packed earth and clay on the far side. In moments he had thrust through and a dim shaft of light filtered into the room. Cato worked with renewed frenzy and the gap quickly widened. When it was large enough to squeeze through he gently picked up the centurion and dragged him across to the hole.

'You first, boy,' Macro protested.

'No, sir, it'll be easier to get you through now than drag you out after.'

'Fair enough.'

With Cato half supporting him, Macro thrust his head, arms and shoulders through the wall, dislodging a shower of earth which tumbled down over him. He spluttered for breath, shaking the earth from his head, and then someone swung a boot into his side.

'Bloody Germans are coming through the wall!' someone shouted.

'Easy lads! I'm Roman!'

'Oh! Sorry, mate!'

A rough hand reached down to Macro. Moments later, Cato was helping to prop him up and brushing the dust off his head and uniform. The legionary who had kicked him in the side gulped nervously as he caught sight of the centurion's medalled harness.

'Sir, I didn't know . . .'

'No harm done, son. Just take us to the tribune.'

'This way, sir.' The legionary supported Macro on his other side and, with the centurion's arms over the legionaries' shoulders, the trio made their way past the rearmost ranks of the soldiers holding the entrances to the village square. They found Vitellius standing outside the village chief's hut with the trumpeter and the cohort standard-bearer. From inside the hut came the sounds of muffled cries and screams.

'Stop here a moment, lads,' Macro ordered, before extracting his arm from Cato's shoulder and saluting Vitellius.

'Ah! So you're still with us, Macro! I was told the Germans had you, and the optio here, bang to rights.'

'Yes, sir.'

'Nasty wound. Better get it cleaned and dressed.' Vitellius jerked a thumb at the door to the hut. 'The orderlies are a bit busy right now, but you might attract their attention. And get them to wipe some of that shit off you while they're about it.'

'Where's my century, sir?'

'They're holding the main gate at the moment—' Vitellius moved aside as a fresh casualty was carried past into the hut. 'I had them run the villagers outside between assaults. Can't afford to have troops wasted on guard duty.'

'How are we doing?'

Vitellius frowned momentarily before answering. 'Not well. We're down to less than three hundred effectives. The Germans are trying to force an entry to the square down five streets. The fire has cut them off from all other accesses and we still hold the wall and gate on the other side of the village.'

'Can we hold out until Vespasian gets here?'

'Maybe.' Vitellius shrugged, looking up into the snowy sky. 'If the fire keeps channelling them into a limited number of streets. We're holding them back now, but they can afford to lose more men than us. Once they've got the edge in numbers they'll just push us back into the square. Then we make a final stand here, by the injured.'

'And what if the fire gets to us before the Germans?'

'We'll be forced back to the main gate, and then outside into the tender arms of the waiting German horde.'

To be burned to death or gutted by barbarians, thought Cato. Which would he choose when the time came?

'Get your wound seen to, Macro,' Vitellius ordered. He gestured to the trumpeter and the standard-bearer. 'Come!'

'What about me, sir?' Cato asked.

Vitellius glanced back at Macro. '"Me sir" can guard your standard, Centurion.'

'Yes, sir.' Macro smiled grimly, then held out the Sixth

century's standard. 'Hold this, until they fix the wound. I'll take it once I get out.'

Once Macro had been helped inside, an orderly hurried over to inspect the wound. With a casual nod of the head, he decided that no triage mercy killing was required in this case. He flapped his hands at Cato, shooing him out of the hut. When Cato turned at the doorway to take a last look at his centurion, the orderly was cleaning the wound with a bloodstained rag.

Outside the hut, Cato tried to plant the standard with quick thrusts but the frozen ground defeated his every effort. He eventually gave up and rested it against his shoulder. Although he felt relief at being back with the cohort the fight was not going their way. The tightly compacted melees had turned into a heaving scrimmage whose outcome would ultimately depend on which side had the greater weight. Even so, the odd sword or javelin was finding its mark and the occasional casualty emerged from the rearmost legs of the press. Those who were too badly wounded to make their way out of the maul were simply trampled underfoot.

Slowly, but with painful inevitability, the Romans were forced back down the streets towards the square. Cato knew that the moment the Germans spilled out into the square they would swarm around the Romans, who would be annihilated in short order. Much of the night had already passed but there were still some hours until daybreak and then half a day before Vespasian could reach the village.

But even as the Germans pushed forward the fire began to overtake them, spreading rapidly through the combustible dwellings. Distant horns sounded and from the Germans there came a sudden howl of rage and frustration. The horns blew the retreat more insistently and the Germans reluctantly disengaged with a final desperate exchange of blows as they fled from the fire. And then the cohort was alone. But relief was short-lived. The violence of the Germans was swiftly replaced by the wrath of Vulcan as fire swept up to the village square, burning all along its fringes and out towards the village walls. The Romans recoiling before the blaze were lit up in a terrible red glow that cast their long shimmering shadows far behind them. The heat of the fire withered all before it and the men shrank back behind the shelter of their shields.

A legionary came running up, pointing towards the street that led from the square.

'Fall back! Everyone back to the main gate. Now!'

The cohort limped out of the square, a ragged column of exhausted men, some helping support wounded comrades, and others using shields as makeshift stretchers to carry out those too badly injured to walk. But all were silent and despairing. Too many officers had died and unit cohesion had completely broken down as they trudged wearily and painfully through the red-rimmed silhouettes of German huts. At the main gate, Vitellius threw up a defensive cordon with the wounded clustered behind the rear ranks. Then the remains of the cohort quietly waited for the end to come.

Cato had rejoined the Sixth century, after he had made his centurion as comfortable as possible, and from the gate tower he had a fine view of approaching doom. The wind urged the flames on and now they set about consuming the other half of the village. Beyond the wall Cato saw the clustered German villagers watching as their homes and livelihoods were incinerated. Without food and shelter not many of them would survive the winter and the red glow of the fire lit up the expressions of stricken despair etched on their faces. Cato felt a twinge of guilt as he saw the human consequences of war, even though he knew he would be dead soon, one way or another.

Beyond the villagers, the dark ranks of the German warriors stretched into the night as they waited for the fire to drive their enemy out into the open.

As the night grew old, Cato was surprised to see the men of the cohort succumb to a gentle fatalism. The surviving officers and men exchanged words quietly, without any sense of difference in rank. Imminent death was a great social leveller. It was a strange comfort to be with them now, here – just before the final wild charge into oblivion. A warm sense of serenity flushed through him and Cato found that he was smiling. For a moment his eyes met those of a hard-bitten veteran whose expressionless face suddenly returned the smile. No words passed between them; none were necessary.

As the first hint of dawn appeared on the skyline the fire was almost on them and Vitellius ordered the remaining men to form into a column behind the gate. The tribune paused for a moment to consider the fate of those too badly injured to walk unaided. Most had requested that swords be left with them, to allow them to go down fighting, or at least to deprive the Germans of the terrible amusements they reserved for prisoners. Vitellius wondered if it would be more merciful if he ordered them all to be put to death before the cohort left. As he stood pondering, a sentry on the gate tower called down to him.

'They're moving!'

It seemed that the Germans had allowed themselves to be overcome by impatience. It would end with a brief scrap on the walls then, and no final charge, Vitellius concluded with disappointment. Wearily climbing the steps inside the tower, he emerged on to the watch platform where Cato stood with the sentry. The optio looked confused and a moment later the tribune could see why.

The Germans were on the move all right, but instead of moving forwards towards the gate they were marching round the sides of the village, away from the track that led up the slope towards the forest.

'What the hell?' Vitellius frowned.

'Sir . . . What are they doing?'

'I've no idea.'

The Germans increased their pace and already the villagers were standing in pathetic isolation before the gate. Cato could not quite bring himself to believe what his eyes showed him. Then his ears caught a new sound, a sound that rose above the crackling flames licking at their backs. Sharp and clear on the dawn air came the strident sound of trumpets and on the crest of the hill above the village a line of horsemen rode into view; at their head, a party of officers in red cloaks and crested helmets.

Vespasian, it appeared, had not waited for dawn to break before marching to their rescue.

Chapter Fourteen

The hospital orderly cursed under his breath as the sound of the handbell rang down the central corridor of the Legion's infirmary. The patient was being quite impossible. Constantly demanding that messages be sent out, food and wine sent in, fussing that his leg be positioned just so – and moments later asking that it be shifted once again. If it weren't for the fact that he was a centurion, and outranked everyone in the hospital except the surgeon, the orderly would have taken the bell away and let the man stew. But, because he was a centurion, he was entitled to a separate ward, a bell and the undivided attention of any orderly unfortunate enough to be on duty.

All the other ranks wounded in the recent fracas with the Germans were crammed into five-bed wards with the lack of privileges accorded to those of low status: enough food to get by and a scheduled visit by the surgeon, or one of his orderlies, to change dressings, pour off drainage and monitor their recovery. Those that had been immobilised by their injuries were provided with bedpans which the orderlies emptied three times a day; the centurion had his emptied as and when he was pleased to relieve himself.

The injury to his leg had been messy and might have been fatal had Macro not tied a tourniquet above the wound. The surgeon had stitched together the ends of the torn muscle and then the skin – leaving a small burr in place to aid drainage of pus from the wound. He had ordered the centurion to remain in bed until the wound was cleaned and well on the way to healing. Then he had calmly smiled at the consequent stream of invective and reassured the centurion that at a pinch the Second Legion could actually manage without him for a few weeks. The surgeon appointed a personal orderly and, with a nod of professional satisfaction at his handiwork, he left the fuming officer and moved on to the scores of other patients Tribune Vitellius had seen fit to provide him with. Most recovered in a few days, some died – much to the surgeon's disgust, taking each death as a personal affront to his skills – and the remainder recovered at a slower pace dictated by the severity of their injuries. He was only grateful that there were no Germans to tend to: those that hadn't committed suicide, or been killed by their own side, had been mercifully despatched on Vespasian's orders. So the hospital was quite free of any foul-smelling barbarians.

The same couldn't be said for the settlement outside the fortress, which was now swollen with the survivors from the village. The lucky ones had managed to beg for shelter from distant relatives and friends who now repaid the smug disdain they had suffered for adapting to Roman ways. The unlucky ones would be forced to spend the winter in an ugly sprawl of crude huts that sprang up on the fringes of the settlement. Many of them would not survive the harsh northern winter but there would be little sympathy for them from either the Romans or those who lived in the settlement and now bore the weight of the legionaries' rekindled suspicion of all things German.

The bell rang again, more loudly this time, and the orderly slowed his pace as he walked down the corridor towards the better-ventilated end rooms reserved for officers.

'Get a bloody move on, man!' Macro bellowed. 'I've been waving this fucking bell about for ages!'

'So sorry to keep you waiting, sir,' the orderly apologised. 'But I'm afraid one of the other patients was dying and I wanted to make sure his effects went to the right friends before he popped off.'

'And will they get them?'

'The lads and I will do our best to see that the leftovers are sent on.'

'After you've had your pickings.'

'Of course, sir.'

'Bloody vultures.'

'Vultures?' The orderly frowned. 'Just a perk of the job, sir. Now what is it you wanted?'

'Get rid of this.' Macro shoved a bedpan at him. 'And make the fire up. It's freezing in here.'

'Yes, sir.' The orderly nodded as he carefully carried the bedpan over to a low table and set it down. 'Nice day out, sir. Clear blue sky and still air.'

'Oh, is it? Thanks for letting me know. But it's still freezing in here.'

'Not freezing, sir. Just well ventilated. It's good for you.'

'How can it be good? If the wound doesn't get me, the cold will.'

The orderly smiled at that comforting thought as he placed more fuel on the glowing embers in the brazier and blew gently on them to encourage some flames.

'Right, that's fine. Now take the bedpan and piss off.'

'Yes, sir.' The orderly collected the chamber pot and, holding it carefully, made for the door to the corridor. Without any warning, Cato strode into the room and the orderly nimbly stepped to one side without spilling a drop. He tutted at the optio as Cato closed the door behind him.

The optio stood over the bed and smiled down. 'It's good to see you, sir.'

'For the first time in three days.'

'It's been busy without you, sir. I've been trying to keep the century in good order while you recover. How's the leg?'

'Stiff, and it hurts like buggery whenever I try to move it. But the quacks seem to think I'm well on the mend.'

'You look better than the last time I saw you.'

'That was nothing, just some minor infection. The surgeon reckons it's almost gone.'

'When will you be back on duty, sir?'

The non sequitur and the anxiety behind it were not lost on the centurion. He regarded Cato silently while the wood in the brazier hissed softly.

'I'd have thought a young optio might be enjoying the opportunity of having his first command.'

'I am, sir.'

'But . . .' Macro coaxed.

'I had no idea how much there was to do. There's the drilling to organise, barracks inspections, equipment checks, and then there's all the paperwork.'

'You should leave that to Piso. I do.'

'Yes, he's been very helpful, sir. He insisted on handling it. But we've just had orders to conduct a full inventory of equipment and non-portable personal items. And, to make matters worse, headquarters has ordered all money above ten sestertii to be banked by the end of the week. Is it always as hectic as this, sir?' Cato asked helplessly.

'No.'

So the Legion was to be moved in the near future then. The order restricting personal holdings of coinage was to limit the marching load of a legionary, and all non-portable goods would be inventoried for storage or sale. If the latter, then the Legion's transfer was likely to be long term. Interesting. But then, Macro considered, it was likely that the wounded would have to travel in carts and the prospect of the uncomfortable bumps and jolts that that implied filled him with dread. Marching might be tiring, but it was all good exercise and far more comfortable than jolting around on the flat bed of a legionary transport wagon.

'Any word on where we're being sent?'

'Nothing official, sir, but I've heard rumours that we're going to join an army being assembled to invade Britain.'

'Britain! What emperor in his right mind would want to add that dump to the Empire? Wild, savage and filled with bogs – if what I hear is true. Britain! That's ridiculous.'

'That's what I heard,' Cato said defensively. 'And in any case, what emperor is in his right mind these days?'

'Fair point!' Macro lightened up. 'Look, all this admin you're complaining about. It's what running a century is all about. You're just going to have to cope with it, or get Piso to.'

'It's not really the paperwork that's getting me down, sir,' Cato said uncomfortably.

'What is it then?'

'Well, it's the command side of things. I just can't seem to carry off the business of giving people orders.'

'What do you mean?'

Cato shuffled his feet, shamefaced, as he attempted to formulate the problem. 'I know I'm an optio and that means the men have to obey me, but that doesn't mean that they take kindly to having a – well, if I'm honest – a kid telling them what to do. It's not that they don't obey me, they do. Nobody's calling me a coward any more, but they haven't got much respect for me.'

'I'm sure they haven't. It doesn't come automatically – it has to be earned. It's the same for every new officer. The men will obey because they are accustomed to. The trick is to get them to obey willingly and to do that you need to earn their trust. Then they'll respect you.'

'But how do I do that, sir?'

'You stop whining for a start. Then you begin to act like an optio.'

'I can't, sir.'

'What do you mean can't? Can! Fucking will!' Macro propped himself up on his elbows, wincing as he shifted his leg to a more comfortable position.

'Yes, sir.'

'Now then, put some more wood on that fire – some dry stuff – before the bloody thing goes out. And shut the window.'

'Are you sure, sir? Fresh air's supposed to speed recovery.'

'Maybe air that's not quite so fresh. The only thing that window's speeding is exposure, so shut it now.'

'Yes, sir.' Cato quickly obeyed the order and then carefully selected the driest wood he could find for the brazier.

'Did you notice?' Macro asked.

'What, sir?'

'How you instantly did what I said?'

Cato nodded.

'That's what I'm talking about. It's the tone of voice. You need to practise giving orders a while before it feels natural. But once you're there it's a doddle – comes as easy as breathing.'

'If you say so, sir.'

'I do. Now then, what's the news?' Macro eased himself back on the bed so that he was propped up against the bolster. With the window closed the red glow of the brazier added to what little light there was filtering through the shutters. 'Pull up the stool and fill me in. What else have you been up to?'

Cato shifted uneasily. 'I was summoned to headquarters this morning by the legate.'

'Oh yes?' Macro smiled. 'And what did Vespasian have to say?'

'Not much . . . He's investing me with a decoration, a

grass crown. I'm not quite sure why.'

'Because I recommended it,' smiled Macro. 'You saved my life, remember? Even if you did nearly lose the standard while you were at it. You deserve it, and once you get the phalera attached to your harness I think you'll find the men will go easier on you. All good soldiers respect well-earned decorations. How's it feel to be a hero?'

Cato blushed, grateful that the uncomfortable glow in his cheeks was lost in the flickering orange of the brazier. 'Frankly, I feel a bit of a fraud.'

'Why on earth?'

'I can't be a hero on the strength of one battle.'

'Hardly a battle. More of a skirmish actually.'

'Precisely, sir. A skirmish, and one in which I only managed to injure an enemy by accident. Hardly the stuff of heroes.'

'Killing men in battle doesn't necessarily make you a hero,' Macro gently reassured him. 'Admittedly it does help and the more bodies you pile up the better. But there are other ways to be heroic. All the same, I wouldn't go around blabbing about not having knocked a few Germans on the head if I were you. Look, you didn't have to come back for me but you chose to – against the odds. In my book that takes guts and I'm glad you're with us.'

Cato stared at him, searching for the least sign of irony in his superior's face. 'Do you really mean that, sir?'

'Of course. Have I yet said anything to you I didn't mean?'

'No.'

'There you are then. So take it at face value and don't get sentimental on me. I take it there'll be an investiture?'

'Yes, sir. The legate's holding a parade two days from now. There are a number of decorations to hand out, including one for Vitellius.'

'Oh really?' Macro interrupted sourly. 'I'm sure that'll look good on his CV when he gets back to Rome.'

'Then there's a private dinner in the evening. He's invited all officers who served with the Third cohort that day in the village, those of us who survived, that is.'

'Should be rather cosy and intimate then. Typical of Vespasian; always the grand gesture on the cheap.'

'He insisted that you be there as well, sir.'

'Me?' Macro shrugged and pointed at his leg. 'And how am I supposed to attend?'

'That's what I asked the legate, sir.'

'You did? What did he say?'

'He'll send a litter for you.'

'A litter? That's great. I get to play the invalid all night long and have to chase up some social conversation. It'll be a bloody nightmare.'

'Then don't go, sir.'

'Don't go?' Macro raised his eyebrows. 'My lad, a polite invitation from a commander of a legion carries somewhat more weight than a writ issued by Jupiter himself.'

Cato smiled and rose to his feet. 'I'd better go now. Is there anything I can get you for next time? Some reading matter perhaps?'

'No thanks. Need to give my eyes a break. You might

bring me a jar of wine and a dice set. I need to improve my technique.'

'Dice.' Cato was vaguely disappointed as he disapproved of those who refused to accept that dice fell randomly – straight dice at least. He nodded and made to leave.

'One more thing!' Macro called after him as he strode out of the ward.

'Sir?'

'Remind Piso he owes me five sestertii.'

Chapter Fifteen

Centurion Bestia glared into each face as he marched steadily along the ranks. In many ways inspection was the most onerous aspect of training to most recruits. Marching, drilling and weapons practice required no more than effort and the minimum of thought. Preparing for inspection, on the other hand, required a kind of genius that almost elevated it to the level of art. Every item of kit had to be cleaned, polished – where possible rather than where necessary – and in a perfect state of repair. There were few short-cuts, and since they were all known by Bestia it was a foolish or desperate recruit who resorted to them. Thus it was that Cato stood nervously at attention and prayed to every god remotely relevant to the situation that Bestia would miss the varnish he had applied to his belt and straps. The visit to the hospital had left him no time to buff the weathered leather up into a shine and he had simply painted the varnish on instead, on the advice of Pyrax. Standing stiffly with spear grounded to his right and left hand resting on the rim of his shield Cato was acutely aware of the faint smell of varnish wafting around him. If Bestia touched the tacky leather then

Cato's deception would be uncovered and he would be up on charges.

Four men down the line Bestia suddenly caught sight of his prey and skimmed past the intervening men with barely a sidelong glance.

'Ah! Optio.' He laboured the word. 'So very good of you to join us this morning.'

As always the sarcastic greeting was unfair, since Cato had no choice in the matter and was excused drill on alternate days on orders from the Legion's headquarters.

'So then, it appears that you are something of a war hero, Master Cato?'

Cato kept his mouth shut and continued staring straight ahead, eyes unwavering.

'I believe I asked you a fucking question,' Bestia said, then turned to the optio who accompanied him on inspections through the ranks. 'Didn't I just ask him a fucking question?'

'Yes, sir,' the drill optio replied. 'You asked him a fucking question, sir!'

'So answer me!'

'Yes, sir!' Cato shouted.

'Yes, sir what?'

'Yes, I am something of a war hero, sir,' Cato replied in a low voice.

'I do beg your fucking pardon, son!' Bestia shouted. 'But I must be deaf. I can't hear you. Again! Louder!'

'Yes, I am something of a war hero, sir!'

'Oh really? Young lad like you must have really scared the shit out of the Germans. I mean, just looking at you right now is making me bloody nervous. Next thing you know they'll be chucking fucking foetuses into the front line.'

A ripple of laughter spread across the other recruits.

'SHUT UP!' Bestia bellowed. 'I did not give the rest of you ladies permission to laugh, did I? Well, did I?'

'NO, SIR!' the recruits chorused.

'Well then, war hero, now you've really got something to live up to.' Bestia leaned in very close to Cato's face, so that the latter could see every wrinkle and scar of the veteran's face, as well as the red rim of his nostrils. Cato almost smiled with relief as the centurion stepped back a pace, drew out a dirty piece of linen and sneezed into it.

'What you smiling at, boy? Haven't seen a man with a cold before?'

'Yes, sir.'

'I'll be keeping an eye on you, Optio. Make any mistakes from now on and I'll show you no mercy,' Bestia snarled, and then abruptly strode away.

'So what's new?' Cato muttered once the centurion was out of earshot. The drill optio chuckled as he went by and Cato blanched. But the man just winked and hurried to catch up with Bestia.

That morning Bestia changed the routine. Instead of the scheduled weapons-training the recruits were introduced to the rudiments of camp construction, and were marched outside the walls of the fortress to a prepared area where lines of coloured flags marked out a large square with numerous subdivisions. A supply wagon waited at the side of the track; a brace of oxen grazed with dull expressions as they watched the recruits

assemble around Bestia. The centurion had taken a pick
and shovel from the back of the wagon and was holding
them aloft.

'Any of you ladies care to tell me what I'm holding in
my hands?'

The recruits remained silent, not willing to risk the
obvious.

'Just as I thought, dumb as ever. Well, these may look
like horticultural tools but they're the army's secret
weapon. In fact, they are the most important weapon
you are ever likely to handle. With these, you can build
the most formidable fortifications in the known world.
Roman armies get defeated from time to time, Roman
fortifications – never! Some of you may have heard on
the grapevine that the Legion is about to be relocated.'

A low key buzz of excitement greeted the
announcement – the first official confirmation of what
had been doing the rounds of the Legion's mess rooms
for the last ten days. Bestia let it run its course before
continuing.

'Now, you ladies will of course be ignorant of our
final destination, unlike senior officers such as myself.
Suffice to say we're in for an interesting time. But before
you can be let loose outside the base, you're going to
need to know how to build everything from a marching
camp right up to bicircumvallations.'

Now he had really lost them, only the handful who
were familiar with Caesar's account of the siege of Alesia
had the remotest idea what he was talking about.

'Ladies, we're going to start small, since you – barring
our war hero there – will have problems grasping the

tactical defensive potential of anything larger than a ditch. So we begin with the marching camp.

'When the Legion manoeuvres through non-hostile territory it excavates a defensive ditch and turf-mounted palisade. Each legionary, and you ladies, will be issued with one pick and one spade. The yellow flags over there need not concern you – they mark out the tent lines for each century. These red flags mark out the boundary defences. You will dig from that line inwards. You will dig a ditch six feet wide and three feet deep – that's two spades wide by one spade deep – the spoil of which is to be heaped on the inner side of the ditch and then compacted down. Each man digs six feet of ditch, starting with the war hero at the first marker flag. You ladies understand? Then get the equipment issue and get to work.'

Once each man had been issued a pick and spade, for which deductions would be made from their pay, as Cato now knew, and had taken up position along the red-flagged line, Bestia gave the order to dig. A short distance beneath the grass the soil was freezing, if not frozen, and the recruits used their picks to hammer into it with all their might, piling the cold lumps of clay soil immediately beside the ditch. As the morning wore on, the men became oblivious to the chill and sweat poured freely, woollen inner tunics sticking to their backs. Hardened by months of exercise, the recruits nevertheless found the entrenching exhausting, but Bestia allowed them no break from their toils, reminding them that while on the march the Legion would need to make such fortifications every day. Sore hands turned into blistered hands and, when the blisters burst, the palms were rubbed raw by the coarse wood of the wooden handles which would not become smooth through heavy use for some months yet. Cato suffered the agony in tight-lipped silence while those who had joined the Legion from a farming family barely noticed the wood in their calloused hands. As bad luck would have it, Cato was placed immediately next to Pulcher and, while they were out of earshot of the drill instructors, Pulcher resumed his campaign of intimidation.

'War hero? You?' he growled. 'Un-fucking-likely. Who'd you have to be buggered by to get the commendation?'

Cato did not answer, did not even look up from his digging.

'Hey, I'm talking to you!'

Cato ignored him.

'What's this? No manners? And I thought you were so well brought up. I suppose you're too good to speak to the likes of us.' He laughed to the recruit on his other side. 'Seems the war hero's got ideas above his station.'

'Quiet there!' an instructor called out. 'Silence when you work.'

Pulcher fell back to work with exaggerated effort until he was sure that he was no longer being paid any attention. Then he flicked a shovel full of soil at Cato's face.

'You fucking ignore me again, boy and I'll . . .'

'You'll what?' Cato turned angrily, with his pick half raised. 'You tell me what you'll do! C'mon, you bastard!'

Pulcher's hands tightened on his shovel, but some sixth sense warned him to turn back to his ditch just as Bestia strode up to them.

'What's this? Taking a break without orders are we, war hero?'

'No, sir.'

'And why are you covered in dirt, boy?'

'Sir, I . . .'

'Answer my fucking question!'

'I slipped, sir. While I was tossing the soil up into the camp.'

'You tired then, boy?' Bestia asked with an expression of feigned concern.

'Yes, sir, but I . . .'

'Well then, it seems you need a bit more fitness training. You're on latrine fatigues for the next five evenings.'

'But, sir. I'm to attend the legate's party after the investiture.'

'You'll have to shovel shit twice as quick then if you're going to be there on time.' Bestia smiled sweetly. 'And do make sure you're smartly turned out, or Vespasian'll have you on a charge.'

Bestia laughed as he allowed himself to imagine the scene. Then with a hearty clap on Cato's shoulder he wandered back down the line.

'And fuck you, sir,' Cato swore softly at the man's back and then started in horror as the centurion whipped round and pointed a finger at him accusingly.

'Did you say something?' Did you?'

'Just "thank you", sir.'

'You being sarky to me, son?'

'No, sir,' Cato replied, deadpan. 'I'm just grateful that you are offering me an opportunity to improve myself so I can be a legionary you can be proud of, sir.'

Bestia glared at him a moment then whirled round abruptly and strode away, leaving Cato to his digging. Next to him, Pulcher's shoulders rocked with silent laughter.

'I'll remember this,' Cato said quietly.

'Oooh, I'm so scared of you! I'm just pissing my pants,' Pulcher whispered.

Cato stared at him a moment, no longer as terrified of the man as he used to be, only worn down by the anxiety of looking out for Pulcher, wondering when and how the bastard would next find a way to get at him. With an angry sigh he swung the pick back into the ground as hard as possible, then grunted with effort to dislodge the clump of earth. Something had to be done about Pulcher, and soon.

At midday Bestia called for a halt and the men stood at attention as he examined their efforts. The abrupt halt to work allowed the sweat to run cold and clammy beneath their tunics and, in the enforced stillness, most of them were shivering as the drill team strode along tutting at their crude technique. The ditch ran unevenly along its inner side as a number of recruits had forgotten the two-spades-width rule. Others had not yet managed to dig the required amount out of the frozen ground and their sections did not match up to their neighbours. Only a few dozen had performed to Bestia's grudging satisfaction, Pulcher and Cato amongst them.

'Frankly, ladies, I don't think the barbarians out there have much to fear from Rome as long as useless shits like you are manning its legions. If you call this a defensive ditch then I'm a cheap Greek tart. The only thing this'll keep out is the cold. So, ladies, let's fill it in, stop for a quick bite, and then we'll have another go this afternoon.'

Chapter Sixteen

The entrance to the legate's house was brightly lit when Cato arrived, after a fast run from the barracks. He stopped for a moment to catch his breath and place the grass crown back on his head. For the moment, the phalera hung from a ribbon around his neck over the front of his tunic. Later it would be fixed to his harness where it would remain for the rest of his life and be buried with him. Composed, he strode up to the gate where a household steward sat at a desk in the porch behind the two guards. The guards crossed spears to indicate Cato was to halt.

'Name, please?' the steward asked.

'Quintus Licinius Cato.'

'Cato,' murmured the steward as he made a mark on a wax slate with his stylus. 'You're late, Cato, very late. Admit him.'

The spears parted and Cato passed through the gateway to the interior courtyard.

'Straight ahead.' The steward pointed to the main hall, wrinkling his nose and frowning as Cato went by. From the windows above the colonnade came the glow of a brightly lit interior, and the sounds of music and laughter spilled out above the hubbub of general conversation. It was bad form to arrive so late to a party but it would have been unthinkable to have ignored the invitation, just as it was impossible to disobey Bestia's orders to sluice and scrub the latrine channels. Tonight's fatigues had taken longer than usual due to a stomach bug that was going through the Legion at a ferocious rate. Cato had been left with little time to change into his best tunic and run through the fortress to arrive even at this late hour. With a bitter sense of dread for the inevitable interrogation about his tardiness, Cato walked over to the hall at a condemned man's pace. He rapped the door. Instantly the latch leapt up and the door swung inwards to reveal the household's majordomo, hardly able to conceal his irritation.

'There you are at last! You'd better have a good explanation for the legate.'

'I'll apologise as soon as there's a quiet moment,' Cato promised. 'Is there any way I can get to my place unobtrusively?'

'Hardly, young man. Follow me.'

The majordomo shut the door and led Cato through a heavy curtain into a large hall. Though minute by imperial palace standards, Cato mused, the room had been made as comfortable as it could possibly be this close to the ends of the Empire. The hall was brightly lit from scores of oil lamps suspended from the joists. Two long benches ran down each side of the hall, covered with cushions for the diners who ate off the low tables in front of them. Cato was surprised to see that all the tribunes and nearly every centurion was present, together with a number of wives. In the open space between the tables a pair of wrestlers were grunting and straining in a tight embrace as they groped for a decisive hand-hold. At one end of the hall a small group of pipe players strove to be heard above the din of the guests. Cato hurriedly looked for a gap on the nearest bench to quietly slip into, but the majordomo beckoned to him and slowly proceeded down the side of the hall to the head table where Vespasian and his most honoured guests reclined. With horror Cato saw a conspicuous gap between Macro and Vespasian. The legate frowned as they approached, but only for a moment before he forced a smile on to his lips and waved a greeting.

'Optio! I wondered where you had got to.'

'I'm sorry, sir,' Cato replied as he slipped forward on to the couch beside Macro. 'I had some duties I was ordered to complete first.'

'What duties?'

'I'd rather not say over dinner, sir.'

'Not much of that left, I'm afraid. Rufulus! See what you can find for the optio, must be some choice titbits left.'

'Yes, sir.' The majordomo bowed, darting a sharp glare at Cato.

'While you're waiting you might try some of the stuffed dormice.' Vespasian proffered a gold serving dish around which lay an arrangement of tiny baked mice. 'They're filled with some of the local herbs and cheese. Not quite what you're used to at the palace, I suspect, but it's a pleasant enough gastronomic reminder of home. Take one.'

Cato did as he was told. While the mice had been slightly overbaked, they made a pleasant change from standard legionary fare. As Cato happily crunched on the tasty morsels, the legate ordered a slave to bring the late arrival a selection of delicacies.

'Have some wine.' Vespasian pointed out a row of Samian decanters. 'There's a decent Caecuban and a tolerable Massic. I'm saving the last of my Falernian for a toast.'

Cato's eyes glittered at the prospect. 'Your cook has done his Apicius proud. Thank you for inviting me.'

'My pleasure, son. You did well in that little business with the locals. Now I'll leave you to your meal before it goes completely cold. I want to introduce you to a few people later on. Some you will already know.' Vespasian smiled. 'My wife says she is particularly keen to catch up on some of the palace gossip. That is, if I can tear her away from Tribune Vitellius.' He nodded towards the end of the head table where Cato could see the tribune over the shoulder of a slim woman. The pair seemed to be deep in conversation. Suddenly the legate's wife shook with laughter and Vespasian frowned momentarily. He switched his attention back to the waiting optio. 'As I said, that can wait for later. But for now I'm afraid I have to talk shop with the camp prefect. Please excuse me and enjoy the meal.'

The legate turned his back and Cato shifted on to his stomach, feasting his eyes on the spread before him, before he allowed his tastebuds a turn.

'What the hell is that smell?' Macro sniffed accusingly.

'I'm afraid it's me, sir,' Cato replied, filling his cup with a dark red Massic.

'What is it? You stink like a cheap tart.'

'That's because it's a scent Pyrax bought for a cheap tart.'

'You're wearing a scent?' Macro recoiled in horror.

'Had to, sir. I've been up to my knees in shit all afternoon. I cleaned myself down as best I could but there's no shifting the smell. Pyrax suggested I try to cover over it with his scent.'

'He did, did he?'

'Yes, sir. Said it was better to smell like a tart than a turd, or something.'

'That's debatable.'

'How's the leg today, sir?' Cato asked, reaching for another dormouse.

'Getting better. But still a few weeks before I'm allowed back on my feet. I'm not looking forward to spending most of it in a transport wagon.'

'Any idea where the Legion's being sent?'

'Shhh! Keep your mouth shut! We're not supposed to know yet. I think that's why we've all been invited.'

'You think?'

'Why else invite so many if it's just a quiet dinner to celebrate the investiture? There's bound to be more to it than that.'

Flavia laughed politely, but discreetly, at the tribune's joke; one had to be careful when discussing Emperor Claudius. At the same time she wished to probe Vitellius a little further so the amused expression remained on her face.

'That's a good story Vitellius. Very good. But I wonder, do you think Claudius is right for the job?'

'What do I think of Claudius?' He scrutinised her closely before replying. 'It's a bit too early to make a judgement, wouldn't you say?'

'I have friends in Rome who tell me that people are already saying that Claudius won't last long, that he's mad or, at the very least, a simpleton. And that he lets his freedmen run the empire in his name. Particularly that fellow Narcissus.'

'Yes, I've heard that too.' Vitellius smiled, amused by the way in which people discussing the Emperor always voiced their own opinions through the mouths of anonymous friends. 'But it's early days, he's bound to delegate some tasks while he learns the ropes.'

'I suppose you're right,' Flavia replied as she picked a scrap of meat from one of the bones lying on her plate. 'But I wonder how one man can ever be expected to rule the Empire – such a burden. I know I'm only a woman and have a limited perspective on affairs of state, but I would have thought that such a task required the energies of more than one man. Surely there are enough wise heads in the Senate who can be relied on to help the Emperor rule?'

'To help the Emperor rule? Or to rule in his place? And then we're back to the bloodshed of the Republic. Nearly every politician a soldier and every soldier a politician, and once you're in that situation there are no longer any elections – just wars.'

'Not that we have elections any more,' Flavia smiled.

'No. No, we don't. But how long has it been since

Romans slaughtered Romans in the name of their general's political ambitions?'

'As far as I recall, not since the divine Augustus wiped out all his rivals and imposed his dynasty upon us. And, let's face it, the Emperors have rather a lot of blood on their hands. There are many in Rome who suffered at the hands of Augustus, Tiberius and Caligula. And who is to say that the present incumbent won't continue the tradition?'

'Maybe. But how many more might have died if Augustus had not seized control of the army from the Senate and made it the tool of one man?'

'So it's simply a question of the relative death-rates, then?'

'Look here,' Vitellius asked quietly. 'Are you really suggesting that we return to the Republic?'

'No, I don't think so,' Flavia replied sweetly. 'But – just for the sake of argument between friends over a comfortable meal – don't you think a return to senatorial rule would be preferable to the present situation?'

'An interesting question, Flavia. Very interesting. Of course there are arguments that can be made in favour of either arrangement. I'm sure there's a considerable pool of talent that could be drawn on if the Senate had all its powers restored, but I fear that there are rather more senators with designs on accruing power to themselves than there are those who genuinely wish to serve Rome. You only have to look at that nasty business in Dalmatia last year. Poor Claudius had only just been confirmed as Emperor when the mutiny occurred. If a few more legions had joined Scribonianus and the other plotters then who knows how it would have ended? We're lucky Narcissus's agents managed to nip that one in the bud.'

'Nipped in the bud?' Flavia mused. 'That's a nice euphemism for the dozens who were killed. I lost some good friends before I left Rome. I'm sure you did as well. And they're still hunting down the surviving members of the plot. Not a comfortable time in which to live.'

'They brought it on themselves, Flavia. Before you gamble in such affairs you should consider the stakes. It's all or nothing. They lost and Claudius won. Do you think they would have been any more merciful to him if it had worked out the other way round?'

'No. I don't suppose they would.' She nodded thoughtfully.

'Not that there was ever much chance of them succeeding,' Vitellius continued. 'The fools had been old-fashioned enough to appeal to the legionaries' patriotism rather than their purses. The moment Narcissus showed up with Claudius's gold it was all over.'

'It would seem,' Flavia looked him deep in the eyes, 'that the moral of the tale is that the army is only as loyal as the imperial treasury is deep.'

'Why, Flavia!' Vitellius laughed. 'I couldn't have put it better myself! But I'm afraid you are right. At the end of the day it's all down to whoever can offer the troops the most money. Ancestors, wisdom and integrity mean nothing any more. Money is the font of all power. If you have it then the world turns for you, if not then you are quite helpless.'

'Well, then.' Flavia sipped at her wine. 'I hope our Emperor can afford to remain in the job. Otherwise, as you say, it's just a question of time before the army looks to a wealthier patron.'

'Yes,' Vitellius said. 'Just a question of time. But enough of politics, for now. You're an interesting woman. I really do wish I'd had the opportunity to share a decent conversation with you before tonight.'

'That would have been nice. I'm afraid Vespasian does tend to try and keep me under lock and key, army bases being what they are.'

'And I'm sure,' Vitellius leaned closer, 'that you're smart enough to run rings round such restrictions, should you want to.'

'Yes . . . should I want to.'

'And is that why you married him?'

Flavia looked up and saw that his eyes were openly appraising her as his lips melted into the smooth smile of a seducer.

'No.' Flavia shook her head. 'I married Vespasian because I love him. And there's more steel in him than you can imagine. You'd do well to remember that.'

The tribune's brow creased and he was quite still as he accepted the rebuff. Then he refilled his glass, without offering to do the same for Flavia, and raised it.

'To your husband,' he said quietly. 'What you say about him may well be true . . . for now.'

Flavia's eyes flickered up and a warm smile flushed across her face as Vespasian rose to his feet. Vitellius quickly glanced over his shoulder and saw the legate approaching with the newly decorated optio at his shoulder. With a sigh of reluctance he eased himself round and stood up.

'I wondered when you would get round to bringing that poor boy over here.' Flavia laughed as she held out both her hands towards Cato. The optio did a quick double take and gulped.

'Lady Flavia?'

'The same. And how's my little Cato? Not so little these days, it seems. Let me have a good look at you!'

'It seems the optio and my wife were friends back in their palace days,' Vespasian explained to Vitellius. 'So it's something of a reunion.'

'Such a small world, sir,' the tribune replied smoothly. 'We seem to live in a time of great coincidences.'

'Yes. I need a quiet word with you. I'm sure my wife would be only too pleased to join the optio and catch up on several years of gossip. My dear?'

'Of course.' Flavia nodded gracefully and led Cato towards the head of the table.

'Lady Flavia, I had no idea you were here.'

'Why should you?' She smiled. 'Officers' wives are seldom seen out of their quarters. And only a lunatic would expose themselves to the ravages of a German winter by choice.'

'Did you know I was here?'

'Of course. There can't be that many Catos joining the Legion from the palace. And as soon as my husband mentioned the – now what was it he said? – the "bookish beanpole", I knew it had to be you. I've been simply dying for a chance to see you again but Vespasian said I had to let you settle in first – the last thing you needed was some interfering woman mollycoddling you in front of the other men.'

'Yes.' Cato winced at the image. 'My lady, I can't tell you how glad I am to see a familiar face in this place.'

'Come, let's sit.' Flavia settled on to her husband's couch and patted the space beside her. Cato looked around but no-one seemed to be paying undue attention. He had been in the army long enough to feel uncomfortable about social intercourse between widely different ranks.

'Now, Cato, you must tell me how it's going. I can't imagine how you, of all people, have ended up here. It must be quite a change in lifestyle?'

Cato, uncomfortably aware of Macro sitting just to his side, phrased his response carefully.

'Yes, my lady, quite a change. But it seems to be a good enough life, and should be the making of me.'

Flavia raised her eyebrows. 'You really have changed, haven't you?'

'May I introduce my centurion to you?' Cato rose slightly to indicate Macro.

'Ma'am.' Macro nodded politely as he wiped the grease from his lips with the back of his hand. 'Lucius Cornelius Macro, commanding the Sixth Century, Fourth Cohort,' he continued automatically.

'Pleased to meet you, centurion. I trust you are looking after my friend?'

'Hmm. No more or less than any other of my men,' Macro replied resentfully. 'In any case, the lad can look after himself.'

'So I've heard. Now then, Cato, you must fill me in

on what's been going on in the palace since I left.'

As Cato talked, Macro hovered on the brink of the conversation until boredom set in. With a shrug he turned back to his food and made the most of the unaccustomed luxury of the feast before him. For her part Flavia listened intently and interrupted Cato with frequent questions about the endless rise and fall of sundry palace officials. At length she had pumped Cato dry of information and leaned back on one arm.

'So, the same seething hotbed of scandal and intrigue that it ever was. That much has not changed.'

'Indeed, it's almost impossible to avoid the gossip.'

'I have to admit I really miss Rome.'

'You could have stayed there, my lady. It's not unknown for legates to leave their wives at home while on active service.'

'True, but I've found Rome a little uncomfortable since that nasty business with Scribonianus in Dalmatia last year. Too many people spending their time denouncing others as conspirators. It's put quite a dampener on the social scene – you have no idea how much of a challenge it is planning a dinner party while the imperial agents are busy whittling down your guest list.'

Cato nodded. 'By the time I left the palace I'd heard that Claudius had already signed over a hundred death warrants. I'm sure there can't be many conspirators left by now.'

'Narcissus has been a busy man, it would appear.'

'And a very important one since Claudius put him in charge of the imperial general staff.'

'Has Narcissus changed much since I left?'

'Not that you'd notice,' Cato replied. 'But most people are careful what they say around him these days – now that he has the Emperor's ear.'

'Does he still look the same?' asked Flavia, absently gazing at her fingers as they stretched the hem of her palla.

Cato reflected a moment before replying. 'A little greyer around the temples but not so different from when you knew him.'

'I see . . . I see. And I trust our little secret is still safe?' she asked softly.

He had been expecting the question for some time and nodded as he looked her firmly in the eye and replied. 'Quite safe, my lady. I gave you my word. It still stands and will until I die.'

'Thank you.'

An embarrassing silence settled between them as they both thought back to the night of a terrible storm raging over Rome, when a little boy, scared out of his wits by the thunder and lightning, had huddled in the corner of a small ante-room where a man and a woman were coupling in the glare of light flashing through the windows. Later, when the man had gone, Flavia discovered Cato trembling in the corner of the room. For a brief moment she had simply stared at him, afraid of the consequences of what he must have seen. Seizing his shoulders, she had sworn him to secrecy. Then, seeing the elemental terror in his expression, some instinct awoke inside her and she'd shielded his small body from the storm as best she could. Afterwards, despite the social gulf between them, she had felt a sense of responsibility for Cato and seen that he was well cared for by the other palace slaves. Then she had left the imperial household and met Vespasian.

Flavia decided to move the conversation on to safer ground. 'Now, Cato, what do you miss most about Rome?'

'The libraries,' he answered without hesitation. 'The nearest I get to a good read here is some weather-beaten army manual. When I left Rome I was reading Livy's histories. It'll be a while before I get a chance to continue them.'

'Histories!' Flavia exclaimed. 'What on earth are you reading histories for? I thought you young men liked poetry – Lucretius, Catullus, Ovid – that sort of thing.'

'Ovid is a little hard to come by, my lady,' Cato reminded her. 'In any case, I'm afraid my tastes are a bit conservative. I've only really bothered with Virgil.'

'Virgil's such a boring old stick,' Flavia complained. 'Not an ounce of feeling, or empathy. It's just turgid elegance.'

'I really must disagree. I find him quite sublime at times – able to put concepts into words in a timeless way. When all today's cheap romantic poets are mere shadows in the memory of men, Virgil will still be a vibrant influence flowing down through the centuries.'

'Most poetically phrased, Cato, but do you speak of time or legionaries?'

'Hardly the latter.' Cato laughed with the legate's wife. 'Literary aesthetics are not foremost in the minds of such men.'

'Pass the mice,' Macro interrupted.

'Yes, sir,' Cato responded guiltily. 'There you are, sir.'

'Do you read much?' Flavia asked Macro. 'I ask only to reassure myself that Cato here is a bit wide of the mark. I can't believe that my husband's officers would ignore the muses.'

'Ma'am?'

'Do you read poetry, Centurion?'

'Not often, ma'am, I'm too busy most of the time.'

'But you do read poetry,' Flavia insisted.

'Of course, ma'am.'

'So who's your favourite?'

'Who's my favourite? Well, let me think. Probably that chap young Cato just mentioned.'

'Really?' Flavia frowned. 'And which of Virgil's works do you rate most highly?'

'Difficult question, ma'am. I think all of his stuff is good.'

'Coward!' laughed Flavia. 'Frankly, I doubt whether you have read anything of his, or any poet, for that matter. In fact, I doubt whether you read at all.'

She laughed again, but Macro looked down at his food in silence and Cato, sensed his centurion's acute discomfort.

'Shhh!' Flavia raised a finger to her lips. 'I think the legate is about to speak.'

Sure enough Vespasian downed the last of his wine and stood up. He tipped a wink to the majordomo who ordered the servants to quickly distribute the decanters of Falernian to all tables. Then he rapped his staff down on to the mosaic floor. The room slowly fell silent as all eyes turned to the head table. Vespasian waited for complete quiet before he began to speak.

'Gentlemen, and ladies, it cannot have escaped your attention that the Legion has been preparing for relocation in recent weeks. I can tonight confirm that imperial staff has issued us with our marching orders. The Legion is to proceed with all due haste to the west coast of Gaul . . .'

If Vespasian was expecting some excited response he was to be disappointed. Many officers in the room looked away in embarrassment, shuffling uncomfortably. One or two polite souls did try and look surprised, as if this was indeed news to them, but they were seen through in an instant, and Vespasian continued with an evident sourness to his tone.

'On arrival we are to join up with elements of four other legions to train for the invasion of Britain. A fleet is being assembled even now and before the year is out a new province will have been added to the empire in the name of and glorification of Tiberius Claudius Drusus Nero Germanicus. The Legion begins moving in two months' time, our fortress to be garrisoned by a mixed auxiliary cohort from Macedonia in our absence. Right, you know the routine. From tomorrow you get straight to it. All that remains tonight is a toast. So, fill your cups and raise them to the Emperor!'

As the orderly and Cato helped lift Macro off the litter into his bed the centurion grabbed hold of Cato's tunic and dragged him close.

'You stay. I want a word in private.' Macro's face was grim.

Left alone with his superior, his mind sharpened by the cold night air, Cato wondered what on earth he could have done to bring on this sudden change in mood. For a moment Centurion Macro stared up at Cato intently before he could nerve himself to say what was on his mind.

'Cato, can I trust you?'

'Sir?'

'Can I trust you with a secret? Something I dare not tell anyone else?'

Cato gulped nervously, and instinctively took a step away from the centurion's bed. 'Well, that depends, sir. I mean, naturally I'm flattered, but you know how it is, some men do and some don't. It just happens that I don't, sir. No offence or anything.'

'What the fuck are you going on about?' Macro frowned as he raised himself up on an elbow. 'If you think, for one moment, that I'm some kind of arse bandit then I'll take your fucking head off. Understand?'

'Yes, sir.' Cato relaxed. 'So how can I help?'

'You can help . . . You can help by teaching me to read.'

'Read?'

'Yes, read, damn it! You know, all those bloody words and stuff. I want to learn how it all works. All right, that's a bit too strong. I don't want to read any more than the next man. Fact is, I have to read and write, if I'm going to stay a centurion. And that bitch of woman nearly had me by the short and curlies tonight. But some day it'll come out and, when it does, I'll get busted back to the ranks. Unless I learn my words.'

'I see. And you want me to teach you?'

'Yes. And you promise not to tell a soul. Will you do it?'

Cato thought it over a moment and inevitably his nature led him to the answer. 'Of course I'll teach you, sir.'

Chapter Seventeen

The winter wore on towards spring and the snow melted; for several weeks frequent heavy showers of rain turned all unmetalled roadways into muddy quagmires. The only traffic in and out of the fortress was the constant stream of imperial staff messengers rushing to the far-flung Second Legion with the latest instructions for the impending relocation. Having delivered the despatches they returned burdened with requests for permission to buy draught animals, fodder and slaves to cover the spring campaign.

Anticipating the assent of the staff corps in Rome, the Legion had hired a cadre of muleteers to buy up the necessary livestock from the towns and villages in a wide sweep south of the Rhine. The men were hand-picked and could be trusted to select only the fittest animals for the long journey ahead. They could also be trusted to haggle for the lowest possible price and, as long as the cost remained reasonable, those in authority generally overlooked the unofficial 'commission' that found its way into the purses of the muleteers. So it was that the mules, and other draught animals, arrived to swell the ranks grazing in the pastures hastily constructed outside the fortress.

Inside, most of the space between the walls and the barracks was filled with the Legion's transport vehicles. Each century was allocated a wagon for engineering tools, administrative baggage – namely, the centurion's tent and all the personal items he desired to make the campaign comfortable – and the pointed entrenchment stakes. Then there was the medical convoy for the carriage of sick and non-walking wounded, the artillery company with their carriage-mounted catapults and bolt-throwers, large grain wagons for the portable food reserve of barley, the vast headquarters baggage train and, finally, the staff officers' convoy of personal effects. Even as things stood the Legion was travelling light. No time could be spared for foraging and so a number of grain dumps had already been established along the route.

Within the fortress the imminence of events was palpable, even to those soldiers who lived a day at a time, and desperate legionaries were trying to offload their non-portable goods to the merchants who gathered like vultures to take advantage of such occasions. Word of the Legion's relocation had spread far and wide and, over the following weeks, the settlement around the fortress swelled to accommodate the Empire's peripatetic merchants, in search of the bargains that every such buyer's market attracted. Disconsolate legionaries trudged from dealer to dealer with all manner of goods, sentimental, ornamental or simply superfluous, and haggled bitterly for the few coins that escaped the tight purses of the merchants, who made small fortunes every time a major military formation was relocated.

One crisp, clear spring afternoon Cato came

wandering through the hastily erected market, on the lookout for some basic reading matter for Macro.

'Nothing fancy, mind,' Macro had warned him. 'None of your poncy literature. Just something simple you can teach me with.'

'But we'll need to go through some literature eventually, sir.'

'Eventually, but for now let's keep it simple, understand?'

'Sir.'

'Now, there's a month's pay there, so make sure you get me value for money.'

'Of course I will, sir.'

'And you keep this quiet. If anyone asks, just tell them I want something to read in the wagon. Catching up on my military histories, whatever. But just you remember – not one mention of reading lessons.'

'Yes, sir.'

And so it was that Cato pushed his way through a buzzing throng of soldiers and merchants on a cold and windy afternoon. Clutching his military cloak tightly about him Cato made his way down the lines of merchant wagons piled high with a bewildering array of goods; fine Samian ware, lyres and other musical instruments, a variety of chairs, chests, tables and portable libraries.

In one wagon sat a slender slave girl in a thin well-worn tunic, shivering miserably, a For Sale sign leaning against her legs. She must have been sixteen or seventeen, with jet black hair tied back. Perched on the driver's board, she rested her pointed chin on her knees, hugging them tightly and trembling from the cold. She glanced up and Cato was stopped dead in his tracks by a pair of startling green eyes. For a moment he simply stared, then, aware that he was making a fool of himself, he tore his eyes away and scurried off down the line of wagons.

He soon found what he was searching for. The tail of one wagon was piled high with scrolls and, as Cato rummaged through them, a shrewd old Phoenician dragged himself away from his small brazier to greet his customer. In view of the soldier's age and inexperience, the trader tried to interest Cato in a nicely illustrated set of pornographic manuals which, while not anatomically accurate, were at least conceptually diverting. Eventually Cato managed to persuade the Phoenician that his interests were strictly limited to historical studies and they parted company with Cato carrying an armful of books, as the trader added yet more coins to his swelling purse.

Books were not uppermost in Cato's mind as he made his way back down the line of wagons. He found himself drawn back to the girl sitting on the driver's board, driven by the simple desire to set his eyes on her once more. That was all. What else could possibly come of it? And yet he felt his heart quicken as he approached the place he had seen her earlier.

The wagon was still there, piled high with goods, but there was no sign of the girl. Cato pretended to browse through the wares of the next trader, making sidelong glances at the nearby tents set behind the wagons. Casually reversing direction, he sifted through some chipped Samian ware with his spare hand.

'Looking for anything in particular, noble sir?'

Cato looked up quickly. A swarthy merchant in an unseasonally bright cloak stood at his side.

'Oh no! Nothing. Just looking.'

'I see.' The merchant continued to watch him closely, a hint of a smile on his dark lips. 'Just looking, then?'

'Yes. You, uh, you had a girl here earlier.'

The merchant nodded slowly.

'Is she yours? I mean is she family?'

'No, sir. A slave. Bought her from a tribune this morning.'

'Oh, really?'

'Yes. And I just sold her a few moments ago.'

'Sold her!' Cato's heart jumped.

'To a lady, there, sir.' The merchant pointed through the throng to where a tall, slender figure was about to enter the fortress gate. At her side, following her new mistress like a dog, was the girl he had seen earlier. Without another word to the merchant Cato set off in pursuit, not sure of any reason for his behaviour other than a powerful desire to see the girl again. And so he hurried through the crowd, eyes locked on the pair of women ahead as he quickly closed the distance. At the gate, the woman turned to look back and Cato instantly recognised her as the legate's wife. Before he could react, Flavia's eyes met his and she instantly waved a greeting.

'Why! It's young Cato!'

Trying hard not to blush, Cato hurried over, managing to avoid looking at the slave girl as he made his greeting.

'Good morning, my lady.'

'Been buying books I see, rather a lot of books.'

'Not for me, my lady. For my centurion.'

'Ah yes,' Flavia smiled. 'It must be quite pleasant having an officer who shares one's tastes in poetry so completely. Did you find anything for yourself?'

'No, my lady.' Cato let his eyes shift to the slave girl and flushed with embarrassment when he saw her smiling back at him. 'Can't afford any books, my lady.'

'Really? That's too bad. But look here, Cato. I have to leave some of my books behind since there's so little room to spare in the wagons. They might not be to your taste, but you're welcome to have the first pick.'

'Thank you, my lady. That's most kind.'

'Call round to the legate's house later on and we'll see. Do you two know each other?'

Cato had found himself responding to the slave girl's smile while the legate's wife had been speaking and now he snapped his eyes back.

'Oh no, my lady! Never!'

'You could have fooled me!' Flavia laughed. 'You look like a pair of lovestruck puppies. Honestly, you youngsters only ever have one thing on your minds. You're worse than rabbits.'

'No, my lady!' Cato's blush deepened to a most unbecoming crimson. 'I assure you I had no intention—'

'Peace, Cato! Peace!' Flavia raised her hands. 'I didn't mean to offend you. I'm sorry. There, I've embarrassed you. I apologise. Do you forgive me?'

'Yes, my lady.'

'Oh dear! I really have upset you. I just hope I can make amends when you call round later on. Can't leave you walking around the base with that look on your face, it'd damage morale.'

'I'm all right, my lady.'

'Of course you are. Well, I'll see you later on then.'

'Yes, my lady.'

'Come, Lavinia!'

Lavinia. Cato savoured the name a moment and, as he watched Flavia lead her new purchase away, the slave girl glanced back and winked at him.

Chapter Eighteen

The legate's house was in turmoil, packing cases lay strewn about his private quarters and the household slaves laboured to bed down every breakable item between layers of straw. The slaves, fearful of Flavia's wrath – she had a fierce temper when provoked and was not above having a slave flogged when the circumstances warranted it – handled the pottery and china with as much care as possible. Besides the breakables, Flavia had to make arrangements for the packing of the linen and personal items of furniture – all of which was being shipped back to Vespasian's house on the Quirinal in Rome. Flavia and Titus were to accompany him as far as the Gaulish coast and return home once the campaign was launched. By that time the witch-hunt for the surviving members of the Scribonianus conspiracy should have died down and some sort of normality would have returned to the social scene. And Rome was the best place for Titus since they must begin thinking about his education in the near future. Vespasian favoured a strictly vocational training in law and rhetoric and wanted Flavia to begin looking for a tutor as soon as possible.

Through the tangle of packing cases and piles of straw

weaved a maid-servant, trying to catch Flavia's eye.

'What is it?'

'Someone to see you, mistress. One of the soldiers,' she said with evident distaste.

'Who?'

'An optio.'

'Cato?'

'Yes, mistress, that's what he said his name was.'

'Very well. I suppose I could do with a little break from all this packing.'

A nearby slave raised his eyes heavenwards.

'Show the optio through to the study. I'll be there in a minute. Make him at home and offer the boy something to drink.'

'Yes, mistress.'

'I was just thinking about you,' Flavia said as she breezed into the study, wearing a light silk stola. The room, like most rooms in the legate's house, was heated by a hypercaust system and Cato was relishing the warmth it provided in the moments before Flavia's entrance.

'You're fortunate that those fools haven't packed up my study yet. Do sit down.'

Cato resumed his seat as Flavia wafted over to a large shelved cupboard with dozens of scrolls neatly stacked in sections. She paused a moment and fondly ran her hands over some of them before she addressed the optio.

'You're welcome to whatever you want, or at least whatever you can carry. You can take the Philippics – bombastic delivery but with flashes of wit – and the Georgics – fertile reading matter – and here's a few volumes of Livy. Would you like some poetry?'

'Yes, my lady.'

Nearly an hour later a pile of scrolls lay on the couch beside Cato and he was engaged in the heart-breaking task of deciding which of Flavia's offerings he would be able to fit into his marching pack. Flavia watched him thoughtfully as he mentally weighed up each book before deciding which pile to place it in.

'You were quite taken with Lavinia, weren't you?'

'My lady?' Cato looked up, scroll poised in hand.

'The slave girl I bought this morning.'

'Oh, her!'

'Oh, her, indeed. You're not fooling me, young Cato, I know the signs. The question is, what do you want to do about it?'

Cato stared back, mind reeling with shame at the transparency of his feelings and a desire to see Lavinia again, to stare into those emerald eyes.

'Well, maybe I was wrong then,' Flavia teased him. 'Maybe you don't want to see her again.'

'My lady! I . . . I . . .'

'Thought so,' laughed Flavia. 'Honestly, I can read you men like a book almost every time. Don't worry, Cato, I'm not going to stop you seeing her – far from it, but give the girl some time to settle into the household and then I'll see what I can arrange.'

'Yes, my lady . . . Thank you.'

'Now you'd better take those scrolls and leave. I'd love to talk but there's too much work still to be done. Another time, soon. And maybe Lavinia can join us?'

'Of course, my lady. I'd like that.'

'I bet you would!'

As she watched Cato's back disappear down the Via Praetoria Flavia smiled to herself. A lovely boy, she thought, and far too trusting. If she cultivated him carefully he might well be useful to her some day.

'So what is all this stuff?' asked Macro suspiciously as Cato handed over the scrolls, each one neatly encased and labelled.

'Essays and histories mostly.'

'No poetry?'

'None, sir, as you ordered,' Cato replied. 'There's some pretty exciting material here—'

'Exciting? Look, I just want to learn enough to read. That's it, as far as I'm concerned – all right?'

'Yes, sir. If that's what you really want . . . Now then, sir, how have you been managing with the letters I showed you?'

Reaching under his bed, Macro brought out a wooden wax tablet and handed it over to his subordinate. Cato flipped it open and scanned the contents. To the left-hand side of each tablet were the letters of the alphabet that he had neatly inscribed on the wax-coated surface. Immediately to the right of this were the centurion's rough attempts at copying – straggling lines and curves that occasionally bore a passing resemblance to the original.

'It wasn't easy writing on my lap, you know,' explained Macro. 'Bloody thing kept sliding all over the place.'

'So I see. Well, it's a good start. Have you managed to remember what each one sounds like?'

'Of course.'

'Then would you mind going through them with me, sir? Just for practice. Then we'll try a few words.'

Macro ground his teeth. 'Don't you think I can do it?'

'I'm sure you can, sir. But practice makes perfect, as you keep telling me. Shall we?'

As Macro stumbled through the alphabet, Cato kept his comments to a minimum and all the while images of Lavinia trickled into his mind's eye, to be expelled with considerable reluctance. In the end, even Macro could see that the young man's attention was not fully engaged with the task at hand. Abruptly he snapped the tablets shut so that Cato nearly fell off his stool.

'What's on your mind, boy?'

'Sir?'

'Even I know I got some of those words wrong – and you're just sitting there nodding like a chicken. What's so bloody important that you can't concentrate on this?'

'Sir, it's nothing. Just a personal matter. It won't happen again. Shall we continue?'

'Not if your problem's going to get in the way.'

The lesson had become boring and Macro was not keen to continue. Moreover, the boy's evident reluctance to explain the cause of his distraction had provoked Macro's curiosity.

'Spit it out, lad!'

'Really, sir,' protested Cato. 'It's not important.'

'I'll be the judge of that. Speak. That's an order. I'm not having my men walk around like daydreamers. You youngsters spend all your time worrying about bullying and women. So which is it? Who's been having a go at you?'

'No-one, sir.'

'Narrows things down a bit then, doesn't it?' Macro winked salaciously. 'So who's the woman then? It better not be the legate's wife. Might as well write out a suicide note right now.'

'No, sir! Not her,' Cato said, with a look of horror.

'Then who?' Macro demanded.

'A slave girl.'

'You want to get her in the sack, I take it?'

Cato stared at him for a moment and then nodded.

'So what's the problem? Offer her a few goodies and you're in. I've never known a slave woman who wasn't prepared to part her legs for the right gifts. What's she like?'

'Quite beautiful,' Cato replied softly.

'No, you idiot! I meant what does she like?'

'Oh, I see.' Cato blushed. 'I don't really know that much about her.'

'Well, find out. Ask her what she wants in exchange and you're away.'

'It isn't like that, sir. I feel something more than just lust.'

'Lust? Who's talking about lust? You want to screw her, right? So that's your objective. All you need now is deployment of the appropriate tactics to manoeuvre her into an advantageous position and then secure your conquest. Then it's just a question of mopping up.'

'Sir!' Cato, who thought he had become inured to the crude humour of the army, was caught off guard and blushed. 'It's not like that.'

'What are you talking about, lad?'

Cato tried to elaborate, but found it excruciating to talk about his feelings for Lavinia. It wasn't that there were no words – his mind reeled with well-remembered lines from any number of poems – but none seemed to quite capture the essence of the horrible aching pain that twisted his stomach and tore at his heart. Poets, he decided, were poor mirrors of mankind's soul. Precious little pen-scratchers pouring out their petty banalities in order to impress their pals. His feelings for Lavinia went some way beyond mere verse. Or did they? Perhaps Macro was right and his motives were somewhat more prosaic than he thought?

'What's so different about this woman? Spit it out.'

'I think you have to see her to understand.'

'Bit of a looker, eh?'

'Yes, sir.' Cato smiled.

'So let her know you're interested and that you'll pay what it takes to have your way – within reason of course, no sense in inflating her price for the lads who come after you – give her one and be on your way.'

'I was hoping for something a little more meaningful and long-lasting.'

'Don't be so bloody ridiculous.'

'Yes, sir!' Cato replied hurriedly. There was no speaking to the man on such issues, he now realised. 'Shall we continue with the letters, sir? We've quite a long way to go.'

'And some of us are hoping to go all the way,' Macro smirked.

'Yes, sir. The letters, sir?' Cato held out the waxed tablets.

'All bloody right then! I can see you don't want to talk about the woman – that's your business, right?'

'Shall we continue with the letters, sir?'

'Fair enough,' Macro said sulkily, 'bloody letters it is.'

Chapter Nineteen

By nightfall on the eve of the Legion's departure every vehicle had been checked for roadworthiness and all wheels freshly greased with tallow. Now they stood in long ranks loaded with the Legion's equipment and assorted baggage. In their pens outside the fortress the animals contentedly chewed on the last of the winter feed. Most of the headquarters staff, their work done for the next few weeks, were on a serious bender amongst the tents and grimy halls where the locals sold a heady brew that the garrison had grown accustomed to in the years they had been stationed on the Rhine frontier. The more sober-headed veterans were busy waterproofing their boots and making sure that the nail-studded soles were in good shape for the three hundred miles that lay between the Second Legion and the coast.

At headquarters a small staff still laboured over final details in large chambers that echoed with an eerie emptiness now that all records had been carefully ordered and packed in filing chests and loaded on wagons. Sundry debts owed to local traders were still being settled and travel permits written out for those officers' families immediately heading south to Italy. A detachment of the

Legion's cavalry had been assigned to escort the convoy as far south as Corbumentum before turning west to rejoin the Legion.

As Vespasian passed a row of desks where a team of five clerks were bent over their work, writing by the flickering light of oil lamps, he glanced down at the papers strewn before them.

'What's this?'

'Sir?' The senior clerk quickly rose to his feet.

'What's this stuff you're working on?'

'Copies of a letter we're writing for Lady Flavia, sir. They're for slave agents in Rome requesting details of any infant tutors they might have in their catalogues.'

'I see.'

'She said it was on your orders, sir.'

The resentment in the tone was unmistakable and Vespasian felt a twinge of guilt that these men were labouring into the night while their comrades were free to indulge themselves to excess.

'Well, I doubt that a night's delay will ruin her plans. You and your men can finish the letters another time. Off you go then.'

'Thank you, sir. You heard the legate, lads.'

The papers were eagerly shuffled into order, ink pots stopped up and pens wiped clean before the clerks rose to leave the room.

'Wait!' Vespasian called out and they turned towards him anxiously. He fumbled in the purse hanging from his belt and tossed a gold piece to the senior clerk. 'For you and your men – have a few drinks on me. You've done a good job these last few days.'

The clerks mumbled their thanks and hurried away, voices loud with excitement, leaving Vespasian gazing wistfully after them. It seemed a lifetime ago that he had enjoyed a night out with the lads as a newly appointed tribune. Dusty memories of wild nights and hideously painful hangovers amidst the fleshpots of Syria filtered into his mind and Vespasian felt a pang for the sweetness of youth that seemed over almost before it had begun. Now he was forever separated from these men by age and, more fundamentally, by rank.

Vespasian slowly made his way towards the gate of the headquarters building, pausing only to nod as he passed by the door to Vitellius's office where the tribune was still toiling over some paperwork by lamplight. Vitellius had been spending a great deal of time in headquarters of late – more than was required by his duties and more than enough to make Vespasian curious. But he could not ask him outright the reason for his new-found diligence; tribunes were supposed to be diligent and any questioning of the man might look like paranoia, or worse. If Vitellius was indeed up to something, any undue attention would alert him to the legate's suspicion. More curious still was the fact that the tribune had taken on a bodyguard. It was a right due to his rank, but one rarely claimed these days. But there he was – shadowing his master about the base – a stocky thick-set man with the manner of professional killer. It would be sensible to keep a closer eye on Tribune Vitellius from now on.

Since Lavinia had been taken into Vespasian's household,

Cato had had no chance even to speak to her and was only able to catch fleeting glances from time to time as he loitered outside the legate's house after he had finished with his duties for the day. He contrived to visit Flavia a few times in the hope that Lavinia might be present while they reminisced about life in the palace. But she remained out of sight and Cato was loath to reveal the true purpose of his visits, to the barely concealed amusement of the legate's wife. Finally, one day, Flavia could not help laughing.

'Really, Cato! You should be more inventive.'

'What do you mean, my lady?'

'I mean these excuses you have for coming to see me,' she smiled, 'or should I say coming to try and see Lavinia.'

Cato flushed and stammered out a garbled protestation that only provoked further laughter. He frowned.

'Please don't get cross! I'm not making fun of you. Really I'm not. If you wanted to see the girl then you should have said and I'd have arranged something for the two of you. Would you like to see her now?'

Cato nodded.

'All right then. But in a moment. We need to talk first.'

'What about, my lady?'

'I take it you know very little about Lavinia?'

'I only met her the same day you bought her,' admitted Cato.

'So she said.'

'The merchant who sold her said that she used to be owned by one of the tribunes.'

223

'Yes,' Flavia nodded. 'Plinius. Nice man, very intelligent – a quality that is totally wasted on the army.'

'Why did he sell her? Why did he leave her nothing more than those rags?'

'The answer to that depends on who you listen to.'

'What do you mean, my lady?'

'Plinius let it be known that he had sold her because Lavinia was useless as a house-servant. He said she was lazy, dishonest and incapable of learning her duties. The last straw, so he tells the tale, is that she stole one of his silk nightshirts.' Flavia leaned forward and continued, quietly. 'But the story being touted around the officers' wives is far more interesting. They say that Lavinia was something more than a house-servant. With her looks, anything else would be a sheer waste. Anyway, word has it that Plinius bought her from a sex-slave trader and was trying to groom her to while away the long winter evenings.'

'A concubine!'

'Not quite. Our Plinius wanted someone more sophisticated than that. Someone he could converse with afterwards. So, for the last few months he's kept Lavinia hidden away in his quarters teaching her how to read and write so he could introduce her to some literature. Bit of an uphill struggle apparently.'

'Hardly any reason to throw her out like that.'

'Quite.'

'So what happened, my lady?'

'What always happens. While looking up from her studies her head was turned by another tribune, somewhat more handsome and personable than Plinius.

And definitely more cunning and versed in the ways of subterfuge and seduction.'

Cato thought for a moment. 'Vitellius?'

'Who else? He had to have Lavinia as soon as he slapped eyes on her. Being rather new to the game Lavinia hadn't quite cracked playing hard to get and caved in with distasteful celerity – she must have been quite taken by Vitellius. In any event, *she* was taken, quite a few times if rumours are to be believed. Until one day Vitellius over-extended his tryst and in walked Plinius, fresh from a hard day's work and just itching to get stuck into some elementary grammar tuition. Well, you can imagine the scene and the consequences you already know about. He almost gave her away to that merchant.'

'Poor Lavinia.'

'Poor Lavinia?' Flavia's eyebrows arched. 'My dear boy, that's what she was raised for. You must have come across her type at the palace in all those years? They were virtually a fixture under the last two Emperors.'

'That's true enough,' admitted Cato. 'But my father did his best to keep me away from them. He told me to save myself for something better.'

'He did? And you think Lavinia's something better?'

'I don't know what she is, all I know is how I feel about her. Am I making any sense, my lady?'

'Oh yes. It's your first experience of infatuation. Sounds like you've got it bad – but don't worry, it'll soon pass. It always does.'

Cato glared at her and said with bitterness, 'Do all older people think like that?'

'Not all. But young people do. That's their charm and

their curse.' Flavia smiled. 'I understand your feelings, really I do. You'll see that what I say is true in a few years' time. You won't thank me for it now, or then. But let's try another perspective. What do you think Lavinia thinks about you?'

'I don't know,' Cato admitted. 'She hasn't got to know me yet.'

Flavia smiled gently and kept quiet for a moment.

'All right, my lady – I haven't got to know her either.'

'Good boy, you're beginning to see reason. It's important that you try to keep a clear head over this situation. My husband thinks you show promise, so don't do something rash which might return to haunt you later. That's all I'm trying to say. Now then, do you want to see her again?'

'Yes.'

Flavia smiled. 'Just as I thought.'

'You're disappointed with me, my lady.'

'On the contrary. A man who has a passion that overrides logic can be trusted in his principles. Only a fool values logic above feeling; sophists can reason themselves to accept any and all principles and therefore cannot be trusted. You have a heart as well as a mind, Cato. Just be careful how you use it. I will say what I believe to be true: that Lavinia can only hurt you, given what you are and she is. I'll say no more, for now. Just leave it with me. It won't be easy to arrange a meeting; there's not exactly much privacy available in the middle of a legion. In any case, my husband has rather traditional attitudes concerning the handling of his property.'

* * *

When the eagle and the other standards were removed from the fortress strong-room at dawn the next day, the legate and his staff breathed a sigh of relief. Soldiers, being the superstitious lot that they were, interpreted any problem in moving the eagle at the start of a campaign as an ill omen of the worst kind. But today the eagle emerged smoothly from headquarters and marched down the Via Praetoria to take its place in the colour guard at the front of the First cohort. The significance of the moment was observed by all those within sight of the eagle: the Legion was about to go off to war for the first time in years – minor border skirmishes excepted. An expectant hush settled over the fortress as every soldier, muleteer and camp follower waited for the order. Only the animals, insensible as ever to the affairs of mankind, moved; hooves scraped on cobblestones, bits jingled on harnesses and tails flicked to and fro in the spring morning.

The legate lowered his arm and the Legion's senior centurion snapped his head back to bellow out the order.

'First century! First cohort! Second Legion! Advance!'

In fine order, the red-cloaked ranks of the First cohort stepped out along the Via Praetoria, past the vast vehicle park and through the west gate where the rising sun caught them in its light so brightly that their cloaks glowed like fire. Close on the heels of the First cohort marched the headquarters company led by Vespasian and the tribunes mounted on smartly groomed horses.

Cohort followed cohort and then the ponderous lines of baggage trundled into their appointed place in the line of march. The last cohort, assigned for rearguard duties, followed the baggage train out of the fortress and the end of the column crawled up the slope away from the west gate. Many of the locals from the settlement watched the Legion depart with genuine sorrow. The Second Legion would be missed, particularly since they were to be replaced by a mere thousand auxiliary troops, two cohorts from Spain whose poor quality made them fit for garrison duties only. The auxiliaries, not being Roman citizens, were paid only a third as much as the legionaries. The local economy was going to be hit hard in the following years, and even as the final ranks of the Legion disappeared from view, a desultory column of civilians was already heading south to find new army bases to live off.

Chapter Twenty

'Halt!' The command was quickly relayed down the column. 'Packs down!'

The legionaries of the Sixth century shuffled to the side of the road and slumped to the freshly churned grass along the verge, far enough from the road to allow quick access for any messengers passing along the column. With a loud sigh, Macro slumped down and rubbed his leg. He had been discharged, at his own request, after the first two days on the road. Hospital wagons were as comfortable as it was possible to make them but, even so, the regular bone-rattling movement punctuated by jarring crashes from potholes was more than he could bear. Enforced lack of exercise made the march difficult but the dogged determination that came with the post of centurion carried him along. And now, some ten days later, Macro was almost back to his previous good health. The scar was still a livid red welt straddling his thigh but it had healed well enough and, apart from an aching stiffness and itch, it troubled him no more than all the other scars he carried.

'Water-carriers coming up, sir.'

'Any stragglers, Cato?'

'Two, sir. Both been placed on a charge.'

'Good. All right, boy, take a break with the rest of us.' He patted the grass at his side. 'The legate's setting a killing pace. It's a wonder we haven't had any more drop out. That's only seven since we set off.'

Cato glanced down as Macro rubbed his thigh again. 'How's the leg today, sir?'

'Fine. Just takes a bit of getting used to.'

A pair of slaves came down the line, pouring watered wine from animal skins into the mess tins held out by eagerly waiting legionaries. The water-carriers were part of a contingent of slaves Vespasian had brought along to carry out menial duties that might slow the Legion down on its quick march to the sea. They moved swiftly from man to man, pausing just long enough to half fill each mess tin. Once they had passed, Cato gratefully sipped the sour-tasting mixture of water and cheap wine. His legs ached terribly and the yoke from which his kit and non-fighting equipment hung was intolerably heavy. He had only managed to keep his place in the line of march through the fear of being seen as weak and unable to keep up with the veterans – the men whom he outranked by virtue of patronage, not merit.

Macro regarded the young man for a moment as he sipped another mouthful from his mess tin and swilled it around his tongue to fully appreciate the refreshing flavour. Cato sat leaning forwards, forearms resting on his knees and hands hanging limply as he stared fixedly into the mid-distance with a strained expression. Macro smiled with almost paternal affection for the boy. Despite all his earlier fears, Cato had turned out well. There was no doubting his guts and his coolness of mind under pressure. And, at last, he was beginning to sound like an officer. Words of command were coming easily now, albeit stiffly and without humour. But that would come in time. He was proving to be an excellent subordinate; conscientiously carrying out every order Macro issued and able to use his initiative when faced with unanticipated situations.

Macro had more cause to be grateful. At the end of each day, Cato freely gave up time to continue the reading lessons, as discreetly as circumstances allowed. Macro was pleased to find there was less to this literacy lark than he had feared. Those dreadful, indecipherable marks were slowly yielding up their secrets and Macro was able to follow the more simple texts in a halting way, dragging his finger from word to word along the scrolls as his lips framed sounds, and gradually extended them into words.

'Packs on!' The cry repeated itself down the line to the Sixth century where Macro stood to repeat the order at parade-ground volume. The century wearily picked itself up from the roadside and shouldered their yokes while the few men with enough energy to indulge in some ad-hoc foraging ran back from the surrounding countryside with knapsacks crammed with fruit and any small livestock they had managed to buy, or steal, from the local farmers. The century stood in line, while up ahead the column rippled into motion as the lead elements moved forward. They were off again, trudging down the paved road that led from Divodurum to the west of Gaul.

Cato, unseasoned as he was, suffered terribly in

comparison to the grim-faced veterans. The afternoon's march was agony, particularly since the blisters he had acquired early on the road had burst and he was only just getting over the agonising rawness of the last few days. He had found that the best way of coping was to try and think of other things, examining the gently rolling landscape they were marching through, or turning his gaze inwards to try and occupy his mind. And there lay the problem. As much as he tried to concentrate on matters military there was always Lavinia lurking on the periphery of his consciousness.

That evening, after the century had been fed and the miscreants assigned their extra duties, just as Cato was yawning with arms at full stretch, a slave entered the flickering gloom of the oil lamps lighting the centurion's tent. He glanced about him, message tightly grasped to his chest.

Macro looked up from his desk, where the benefits of acquiring rudimentary writing skills were counter-balanced by the tedious paperwork he could now cope with. He held out a hand. 'Here!'

'I'm sorry, sir,' replied the slave withholding the scroll protectively. 'This is for the optio.'

'Fair enough,' Macro said. He watched curiously as Cato tore off the seal and unrolled the message. The contents were brief and Cato dipped his pen and quickly scribbled a reply, thrusting it back into the hands of the slave before ushering him out of the tent.

'That looked rather dodgy,' said Macro.

'It was nothing, sir.'

'Nothing?'

Nothing to do with you, thought Cato, but he managed to smile before replying, 'Just a personal matter, sir. That's all.'

'A personal matter? I see.' Macro nodded with a maddeningly amused expression on his face. 'Nothing to do with that slave girl, then?'

Cato blushed, grateful for the orange hue cast by the oil lamps, but kept his tongue still.

'Have you finished your work for the night?' Macro asked pointedly.

'No, sir. There are still some ration requisitions to complete.'

'Piso can finish them.'

Piso abruptly looked up from his desk in annoyance.

'Off you go, young Cato. Right now. But don't over-exert yourself.' He winked. 'Remember there's another long day ahead.'

'Yes, sir.' Cato forced a smile and then dashed out of the tent, burning with embarrassment.

'Boys, eh?' Macro laughed. 'Same the world over, since the dawn of time. Takes you back a bit, doesn't it, Piso?'

'If you say so, sir,' grumbled Piso, and then he sighed at the heap of scrolls spread out in front of him and looked at his centurion reproachfully.

Chapter Twenty-one

Vespasian smiled, even as he rubbed the red marks on his wrist where Titus had sunk his teeth in. That little boy could use some firm discipline, he decided. He simply had to stop biting, throwing things at people and running off with articles he was forbidden to touch. Earlier in the evening the little terror had burst into the nightly briefing of the tribunes. Scampering under the table he had raided the confidential papers safe-box and run off with Claudius's scroll. If it hadn't been for Plinius barring the tent flap, Titus would have got clean away. As it was, the tribune grabbed the boy and swung him up into his arms to return him to an embarrassed Flavia, who had appeared from the legate's personal quarters. The boy swung his hand out and caught Plinius on the chin, just as his mother wrestled the scroll from Titus's grip. Laughter rolled around the tent as the exasperated mother momentarily lost the scroll in the folds of her gown before handing it to the injured tribune and leaving with the writhing, giggling Titus pinned to her chest.

'May I have that scroll please?' asked Vespasian as evenly as possible.

After a cursory – but not openly curious – examination

Plinius returned it to his legate.

'Thank you.' Vespasian restored it quickly to the safe-box and returned to the matter at hand. 'As you gentlemen know, there have been rumours that the army gathering at Gesoriacum is on the verge of mutiny. I had a message from General Plautius late this afternoon, brought to me by a household slave. I'm afraid there's some substance to the rumours.'

He looked up and met the surprised, and anxious, expressions of his officers. There was a silent pause, broken only by the sound of Titus playing somewhere nearby. The officers shifted uneasily. Many careers were riding on the success of the invasion. If the campaign failed, all those associated with it would have blotted reputations. Worse still, for those with an appreciation of the wider political implications, the authority of the Emperor himself would be questioned. Claudius had survived one attempted coup already and until he won the acclaim of the mob in Rome and of the armies spread across the Empire, his hold on power would be tenuous. A successful invasion would tie down a large body of troops and distract the legions from their recent distasteful interest in politics.

'Six days ago a cohort from the Ninth Legion refused to embark on to ships bound for a squadron reconnaissance of the British coast. When the centurions tried to force the men aboard there was a brief struggle which left two centurions dead and four wounded.'

'Has word of this got out to the rest of the army?' Vitellius asked.

'Of course,' Vespasian said with a smile. 'What did

you expect? I've seen at first hand how well soldiers keep secrets.'

Some of the tribunes blushed as Vitellius continued. 'Do we know why that cohort mutinied?'

'It seems that someone has been stirring up the superstitious fears of our troops about what they may encounter when they land in Britain. The usual stuff and nonsense about fire-breathing monsters and other demons. I know it's rubbish but, even if we don't believe it, most legionaries do. As things stand, the troops have refused to go on any ships, even for training purposes.'

'What's being done about it, sir?'

'We're to continue marching towards Gesoriacum but have been ordered to stop ten miles short, in a holding area, until the mutiny is quelled – with or without our intervention. The new chief of the imperial staff was at Lugdunum when the news broke. He's making for the army at top speed and we're to supply an escort from Durocortorum. Apparently he has asked for men from our unit since they have not yet been contaminated by the mutiny.'

'Contaminated?' Plinius raised his eyebrows.

'His words, Tribune, not mine.'

'Sir!' Plinius protested. 'I didn't mean to imply—'

'That's all right. Narcissus is not the most tactful of men at times, but there we are.'

'Narcissus?' Vitellius muttered, just loud enough to be heard by the others.

'Narcissus.' Vespasian nodded. 'You don't seem to approve, Vitellius.'

'I'm not sure I approve of any man who wields power

disproportionate to his social standing, if I may be so bold, sir.' Some of the other tribunes – those unaware of their legate's provincial origins – laughed.

'What I meant to say, sir,' Vitellius continued, 'is that I'm not sure why the Emperor would find it necessary to send his freedman . . . his chief secretary, to deal with the situation in person. It's not as if it's something the army can't handle for itself.'

'It's a big operation,' Vespasian replied. 'I would have thought Narcissus would want to make sure it ran as smoothly as possible, for the Emperor's sake.'

'Nevertheless, it is peculiar, sir,' Plinius added quietly.

Vespasian leaned back from the table. 'There is nothing peculiar in this. You know the man's reputation – he's more gauche than sinister. Narcissus will be escorted to the coast and that's the end of it. If he's playing a deeper game then it's one I'm not aware of. Or perhaps some of you gentlemen are privy to information that is being withheld from me. Well?'

No one dared meet his eye, either through guilt or fear of seeming guilty, and Vespasian sighed wearily. 'I'm getting just a little sick of high politics at the moment, gentlemen. Whatever our futures hold, we happen to be soldiers under strict orders which I intend to obey to the best of my ability. All other considerations should be pushed from your minds. Do I make myself clear? Good! Now, I don't need to remind you of the need for strict secrecy in this matter. If word of the mutiny spreads to our men then the entire army is as good as useless. Jupiter knows how it'll end. Any questions?'

The tribunes remained silent.

'Your orders for tomorrow will be passed to you before morning assembly. Dismissed.'

Later, with an empty tent to himself, Vespasian lay back on the couch and closed his eyes. From all around came the sounds of the Legion settling in for the night; the shouts of sentries and duty officers, the hubbub of men relaxing after the day's exertion, even some laughter. That was good. As long as the men were happy he could be sure that they remained loyal to the authority that bound them all together. Mutiny was the one thing that a commander feared above everything else. After all, what was it that compelled thousands of men to bend their efforts to his will, even to the point of death? The moment the common soldiery decided to disobey their officers the army ceased to be.

The news from the coast was bad, and by now would be spreading east down the roads. It was only a matter of time before the Legion ran into the rumours seeping out from Gesoriacum. Then he would have to proceed with the utmost caution; a fine balance would be needed between upholding the harsh discipline of everyday army life and not provoking the men into open revolt. He wondered about the loyalty of the rank and file. They seemed to respect him well enough and had done little to disappoint him on the march so far. The grizzled senior centurion had assured him that there were far fewer stragglers than normal for such a hard march. And yet he couldn't help wondering how fickle those men outside his tent headquarters might prove to be if given the chance. The mutiny had to be quashed so the invasion could proceed. Narcissus had better be as good an operator as his reputation suggested. Certainly Flavia believed he would be up to the job, when the matter had been quietly discussed over dinner.

Then there was the other issue. The second part of the message brought to him that afternoon had confirmed the presence of a conspirator in his Legion. But he was to be reassured by the fact that the imperial agent would be able to deal with the traitor. The imperial agent's identity would remain a secret to all but the Emperor's inner circle. This, the message assured him, was to ensure that Vespasian could concentrate on the business of running his Legion.

'As if . . .' Vespasian grumbled. He found that he now thought hard about every word spoken in front of his senior officers for fear of alerting the conspirator, or of voicing thoughts that the imperial agent might possibly construe as disloyal. Although he had his doubts about Vitellius, there was as yet no proof, or any overt indication, that the tribune was plotting against the Emperor. For all Vespasian knew it might just as easily be that bookworm Plinius. The distracted academic behaviour might well be a clever front for his real activities. Try as he might, Vespasian could not picture Plinius as a spy. Yet, in the absence of proof, he had to suspect everyone – not just his senior officers.

The presence of the imperial agent was far from reassuring. Vespasian was certain that the man's job was to keep as close an eye on the Legion's commander as it was to track down any unknown traitors. And he wondered who that agent might be; in the current political turmoil it might be any officer under his command. For that matter, it might well be that youngster who had joined the Legion straight from the imperial palace. He made a mental note to have the lad closely watched and then swore out loud.

Of course he wouldn't do that. Otherwise where would it all end? A legion riven by men spying on men spying on men. A mental image of the Legion marching into battle with every soldier casting suspicious sidelong glances at his neighbour sprang up into his head and he laughed.

Well then, let someone else worry about the espionage. He would try and concentrate on making his Legion fight well in the coming campaign. That was bound to enhance his reputation far more than plotting in dark corners. He smiled at his own naivety and went to bed.

Chapter Twenty-two

Although winter was gone, the spring night was cold and Cato's exhaled breathing plumed into the air as he clasped his cloak about him. The note he had received from Lavinia, or at least on her behalf, had arranged for them to meet at the rear of the headquarters' tentage shortly after the trumpeter sounded the change of watch. A roped-off area surrounded the staff baggage vehicles and two sentries marched slowly around the perimeter. Cato waited until they had passed each other, then he padded softly between them over the beaten-down grass and slipped under the rope, before weaving in among the dark forms of the wagons looming up all around. Some of the tents glowed from the light of lamps still burning within and Cato quietly picked his way through the baggage train until he emerged to find a long wall of leather sidings stretching out before him. It was here that Lavinia had arranged to meet him. And yet, there was no sign of her. He stood quite still and waited, annoyed that his heart pounded so quickly as he strove to listen for any movement. But there was none from the immediate area. Perhaps she had lost her nerve? Or been kept busy with some household task?

His shoulder was suddenly grasped from behind. Cato jumped round and a sharp cry of surprise escaped his lips before he could stop himself.

'Shhh!' Lavinia whispered. 'Quick, under here!'

She tugged his arm, pulling him beneath the wheels of a large wagon. He followed automatically and rolled into her side.

'What—' he whispered, but she pressed a hand to his lips and told him to keep quiet and still. He marvelled at the softness of her skin as it brushed his lips and caught a momentary scent of something fragrant.

'Who goes there?' a voice called out from nearby. 'Come on out, sunshine!'

Cato froze and held his breath, scared – and at the same time excited by the physical closeness of Lavinia. A warm glow flowed into his loins.

'What's up?' another voice called out from slightly further off.

'Think we've got a thief. Heard someone over here.'

A pair of legs and a spear butt appeared in front of the wagon and paused. A moment later the other sentry arrived on the scene.

'Found anything?'

'Not yet.'

Cato fumbled for Lavinia's hand and held it tight as he carefully pulled her body into his with his spare arm. She stiffened in protest for an instant and then allowed herself to be embraced.

'Seems quiet enough.'

'I'm telling you I heard something.'

'Could have been from inside the tent.'

'I don't think so.'

Cato's lips moved across her hair and down her cheek until they met hers. With a delirious sense of pleasure – even in this dangerous situation – Cato kissed her gently, relishing the warmth of her breath and the pounding of his chest against her breasts. Lavinia returned the kiss softly for a moment and then darted her tongue into his mouth. Cato felt a ripple of ecstasy sweep through his body.

'Look, there's no-one here now,' the second sentry said impatiently.

'Maybe.'

'Well, there's no point in stumbling around in the pitch dark looking for someone who's scarpered. We'll just do ourselves an injury. Let's forget it.'

The second sentry marched off. After a short pause, the first reluctantly turned away from the wagon and stamped sourly back towards the perimeter rope, muttering dark curses at his companion.

Under the axle, Cato was wallowing in the throes of a passion he had never experienced before. His right hand slowly slid over the silken curve of Lavinia's hips towards the inside of her thighs. She clamped them together and twisted away from him.

'No!' she hissed.

'Why?'

'Not here!'

'What's wrong with here?' asked Cato desperately.

'It's too cold and uncomfortable. Mistress has found a place where we won't be bothered.' She squeezed his hand tightly. 'Somewhere more cosy where we can get to know each other properly. Come on.'

'Flavia?' Cato wondered aloud. 'Flavia arranged this? Why?'

'Shhh!'

Lavinia tugged his hand and led him out from under the wagon. They paused at the edge of the line of vehicles to make sure all was still, before quietly crossing to the back of a tent. She had unlaced a join to provide a small opening in the heavy leather. The gloom inside was almost impenetrable, but Lavinia seemed to know her way well enough, and led him on by the hand. Underfoot, the grass gave way to a sectioned wooden floor which Cato managed to trip over, almost flattening Lavinia in the process.

'Sorry,' he whispered. 'Where are we going?'

'The quietest place we could find.'

'We?'

'The mistress and me. This way – come on.'

They passed down a long corridor with rolled-down flaps, leading to private sleeping chambers, and came to a large space dominated by the dark forms of a campaign table and various seats and couches. No more detail than that was available in the darkness. Cato found himself being pushed down on to a soft couch and, with a small chuckle, Lavinia collapsed on top of him. Immediately his lips sought hers again and he kissed with a burning passion that flowed to every extremity of his body. As Cato held her close he untied a silk ribbon and ran his hand through the long flowing hair. Suddenly Lavinia pushed herself upright so that she was sitting on his stomach.

'What?'

'Shhh! Lie still.' She placed a finger against his lips and, with her other hand, reached behind her and felt for his crotch.

She giggled as she discovered his excitement. 'Do you want to do it?'

Cato choked out a yes.

'All right then. I hadn't planned to let you. First I need to get something.'

'What do you mean?'

'Something to prevent babies.'

'Do we have to stop now?' Cato asked desperately, stroking and squeezing her thighs with his hands. 'Please.'

'Typical man!' She slapped his hands gently to show she was only joking. 'You don't have to live with the consequences, we do. And I don't want to get pregnant.'

'I don't have to, you know, come inside you,' Cato said shyly.

'Oh sure! That's what you all say. *I can control myself – really I can* but when it comes down to it – wallop! Then what's a poor girl to do?'

'Don't be long,' Cato said, somewhat startled by her forwardness.

'Relax. I'll be right back.'

Lavinia climbed off his chest, gave him a final soft kiss and padded away into the darkness, leaving Cato alone in a thrill of expectation. He lay still, eyes closed, heart pounding, letting his mind dwell on that last kiss and the shocking excitement of the touch of her hand on his crotch. He wanted to treasure this moment for ever and opened his eyes to take in as much of the detail of the chamber as possible. Now that they were fully accustomed to the dark, his eyes could discern more of the surroundings and they passed curiously over the trappings of command.

Lavinia had been gone a little while now and a tinge of doubt slowly swelled in his mind. He wondered if he should go and look for her.

Surely she shouldn't take as long as this? Unless she planned to use the most extreme form of birth-control and not turn up at all. That wasn't funny, he decided. Suddenly some sixth sense made him aware that someone else was in the chamber. He was about to whisper Lavinia's name when he realised that the sound of a tent flap being pushed aside was coming from an altogether different direction to the one Lavinia had taken.

He froze, hardly daring to breathe, and strained his ears and eyes towards the far side of the chamber where a dark form eased itself in through a gap in the sidings. Once the shape was inside the room it paused a moment, crouching down, poised for action. Cato was suddenly afraid for Lavinia and for what the intruder might do to her when she returned. But the night was quite still.

Then the figure moved stealthily towards the table, strewn with the evening's paperwork. Round the table he came and now Cato could see that the man wore a hooded cape over his short and stocky frame. He moved with the balanced agility of a cat. In his hand was the unmistakable shape of a legionary's short sword. Cato only had a dagger, sheathed in a scabbard under his left thigh. The intruder, no more than ten feet away, turned his back and groped blindly beneath the table. He grasped something and pulled. Slowly an awkward dead weight was dragged clear – the man pausing every time it grated on the wooden floor panels – Cato saw that it was a chest. He lay rigid with fear, hardly daring to draw breath as his blood pounded in his ears. Leaning over the box, the intruder worked on the iron lock with faint clicks until the mechanism clunked open. The man rummaged inside – he was clearly after something specific.

Cato suddenly realised that the man would turn round in a moment. He could hardly fail to see his body stretched out flat on the couch. Cato slid his left hand under his thigh and pulled at the dagger handle. It was wedged under him firmly enough to require a sharp tug, and he shifted his buttock to make the task easier. Too much. The blade rasped from its scabbard into his hand. The intruder spun round and raised his sword in one motion, momentarily forgetting his basic training – that a few inches of point is worth any length of edge. The sword slashed down and struck the edge of the couch above Cato's head with a loud splintering crack.

Cato thrust his dagger at the shape looming over him and the weapon penetrated cloth and something a little more yielding beneath.

'Fuck!' The man grunted, leaping backwards. He crashed against the table. Cato ran blindly to the left, towards the flap through which Lavinia had deserted him, and smashed his shin against a low stool. He thrust his arms out as he flew headlong over the stool on to the floor. The intruder came after him in a low crouch, taking care not to repeat his previous mistake. Cato felt an agonising shooting pain along the front of his leg and paused an instant too long before trying to rise. His attacker, recovered from his surprise now, rushed at him, sword point aimed at his throat.

'Help!' Cato cried out and instinctively rolled under the table. 'Help!'

'Quiet, you little fucker!' The man hissed and for a moment Cato was taken back enough to still his tongue – but only for a moment. The sword swiped at him and he rolled against the couch and shouted again.

'Help! In here!'

Groggy voices of men disturbed from sleep sounded in the chambers down the adjoining corridor. With relief Cato heard someone call out the guard. The intruder heard as well and paused, twisting about as he looked for an escape route. A glow suddenly appeared at the front of the tent as a sentry shouted, 'Here! This way!'

The intruder ran fast to the side of the tent flap and raised his sword as Cato leapt to his feet by the table. A spear tip swept the tent flap to one side and suddenly the chamber was flooded with the flickering glow of a torch as a sentry stepped inside. Out of the shadows to his left the intruder swung his sword.

'Look out!' Cato shouted.

The sentry turned to the source of the shout and, an instant later, was struck a savage blow to the back of his head. With a grunt he slumped to his knees and pitched forward as Cato looked on in horror. Sparks flew as the torch thudded down on to the wooden flooring and rolled up against a loosely arranged pile of maps. When Cato looked up the light was fading and he saw the back of the intruder as he dashed from the room. Without any hesitation he followed, sprinting out of the legate's tent into an antechamber lined with collapsible tables for the scribes. Ahead, to the right, the intruder slashed at the tent siding and hurled himself through. From the left came the flares of approaching torches and the shouts and thudding footsteps of those carrying them. Cato stopped at once, panting in a blind terror.

He ran back to the legate's tent and saw that the maps were now alight, orange and yellow flames eagerly lapping across their surfaces. From the other side of the canvas he heard the voices of those roused by the commotion. There was no escape there. He fell to the floor at the opposite end and heaved at the heavy leather siding. A peg suddenly gave and he rolled underneath. He found himself in a kitchen area with trampled grass beneath him – no luxury wooden floors for the slaves then. Terrified by the proximity of the cries behind him, Cato rushed across the kitchen to the far wall and rolled out under the side of the tent.

He was outside, on his back looking up at the stars peacefully twinkling from the serene inky depths of the night sky. Then he was on his feet, running for the gap behind the tribunes' tents and the artillery train, weaving in between them until the headquarters tent was no longer visible. Leaning against the side of a ballista carriage, he paused to catch his breath. His heart pounded as his breathing came in sharp, shaking gasps. Over in the direction of headquarters a tinge of orange was visible and then a stab of flame as voices shouted for water and more guards.

It would be bad to be discovered anywhere near

headquarters, Cato realised. He turned away, hurrying through the artillery train until he emerged on the far side of the camp, into the space in front of the turf wall and palisade. Drawing his cloak around his shoulders, he turned left and headed for his century's line of tents, at what he hoped was a steady pace. If anyone stopped him now he knew he could not trust himself to give a plausible reason for his presence.

The sentries on the wall were turning to look back into the camp but the distance between them, and the darkness, protected Cato and he walked steadily on. After a nerve-shredding age, he reached the cohort standard and then hurried to the tents of the Sixth century. Off in the night, a trumpet sounded the call-out of the watch cohort. Without a glance back over his shoulder, he entered the eight-man tent of his section and lay straight down on his blanket roll, without removing his cloak or boots.

'That you, Cato?' Pyrax asked sleepily from the darkness.

Cato lay still and silent.

'Cato?'

It was no good ignoring Pyrax. Better say something. 'Yes?'

'What's going on out there?'

'How should I know?'

'You've just come in.'

'Just been to the latrines, that's all. Seems like there's some kind of fire up at headquarters.'

'Careless twats,' Pyrax yawned. 'Wake me if it spreads to our tent line. Night.'

'Night then,' Cato muttered sleepily. But there was

no sleep possible as he lay quietly staring up at the roof
of the tent in absolute terror.

Chapter Twenty-three

With hands on hips and head thrown back, Vespasian looked up into the starry night, through a large scorched hole in the roof of his tent. Lowering his eyes he stared at the silent ring of men standing around the table. The sentries looked down in shame.

'So how do you suppose our thief managed to gain entry to this tent? If you were as conscientious in your duties as you claim.'

'Sir, we were keeping a good watch, as always,' the centurion explained. 'Four men at the entrance, another four patrolling the outside of the tentage. I've checked round and we've found two places where the tent sidings have been slashed open. I suspect our man used those to get in and out, sir.'

'You suspect that, do you?' Vespasian said bitterly. 'That's brilliant Centurion, quite brilliant. And while our man was busy cutting his way in, where were the rest of you?'

'Please, sir, we were being spoken to by the tribune.'

'Which tribune?'

'Gaius Plinius, sir. Duty tribune for the night. Came up and demanded a full inspection.'

'And why did he do that, do you suppose?'

'Begging your pardon, sir, but we were talking about the invasion.'

'Oh, were you? What were you saying?'

'Well, sir—' the centurion was embarrassed. 'Some of the lads have heard that there's monsters living on the islands.'

'And where might they have heard such nonsense?' Vespasian asked, trying not to reveal his anxiety.

The centurion shrugged. 'Just the grapevine, sir.'

Vespasian drew a breath. 'So then, Plinius was disciplining you for talking like a bunch of old women, and that's when you think the intruder made his way into my tent?'

'Yes, sir.'

'Right, well, you and the watch will be up on charges. And you're demoted to a line century. Now get out of here.'

As he watched them shuffle out Vespasian knew that the latter punishment was the more telling since the headquarters guard was rightly seen as a cushy number under normal circumstances; better food, lighter duties and a relatively safe position in the line of battle. And now one of them was lying in the hospital tent critically injured. The man had been unconscious and bleeding heavily from a slash wound to the back and side of the head. He was alive, just, but the surgeon had not been convinced that he would survive the night. It was too bad, since the man might have seen his attacker and be able to provide an identification. And that was what

Vespasian desperately needed at the moment.

Upon entering the room, half dressed like the others who had been woken by the crashes and thumps coming from the command tent, the first thing he had checked was his document safe-box. One glance was all he needed – the small scroll bearing the confidential seal of Claudius had gone. Everything else remained; that meant the thief knew precisely what he was after, and now he had it. Someone in the camp had possession of a priceless piece of political intelligence that might be used to help topple the Emperor. Not that Vespasian needed the document – he had long since memorised the contents and made his plans. But now someone else had access to the information it contained.

And what would happen to him once word got back to Rome, to Claudius, that he had allowed someone to steal the scroll? No excuse would be accepted, the responsibility was his, and that was why he had punished the sentries harshly; they had to share in the suffering they had caused him.

At least the thief had to be near. Someone in the Legion, more than likely the traitor Plautius's letter referred to. There might yet be time to recover the letter before the Legion reached the coast and merged into the mass of units gathering for the invasion. Some blood had been discovered near the couch, with more splatters around the table, leading from the tent to the churned-up soil where the trail was lost. The man had been wounded, then. Which struck Vespasian as most odd. Since the sentry had been struck from behind in the doorway to the tent it seemed likely he had been surprised. In which case the intruder must have been injured by someone else.

What had happened to Lavinia? Inwardly Cato squirmed with fear and worry. She had never come back, but surely she wouldn't have encountered the intruder while he lay waiting in the tent? He prayed that she was alive and unhurt. He couldn't risk going near headquarters to try and see her for a while. That guard had got a clear look at him and would surely be able to pick him out without any problem. He would have to get word of Lavinia from Flavia; a message must be got through to her as soon as possible. But he did not know how much the legate's wife would know about the situation and how far she could be trusted. If Vespasian discovered that he had been in the tent, then all the evidence would point to him being directly involved in the theft of whatever it was the intruder had taken from the chest. He was in deep trouble and needed an ally. If he could see Flavia – tell her everything he had seen – then maybe she could protect him. She had befriended him and now he needed her. In the morning he would try and see her.

Next morning Cato was rudely woken from a troubled sleep by a rough shaking of his shoulders. He looked up blearily into Pyrax's face. 'W-what?'

'Centurion wants you right away.'

Cato propped himself up on his elbows and, looking out of the tent-flap, saw that the sun had risen for some time. He shook his head and scrambled up.

'How long since morning call?'

'A while.' Pyrax shrugged. 'You missed breakfast and

we're about to strike the tents.'

'Why didn't someone wake me?'

'You're a grown-up now, lad, it's up to you to look after yourself.'

'Where's the centurion?'

'In his tent. I'd get over there smartish if I were you. Macro doesn't look too chuffed with his lot—' Pyrax glanced down at Cato. 'What happened to your hand?'

Following his gaze, Cato saw that the thumb and forefinger of his hand were smeared with dried blood.

'Oh that! I, er, managed to get a cut of meat from a beast some of the muleteers slaughtered last night. Roasted it on their fire.'

'Nice of them,' Pyrax said grudgingly. 'But you might have cleaned yourself up afterwards.'

'Sorry,' Cato mumbled. 'I have to go.'

He punched through the half-open flaps and washed his hand with some water from a skin hanging on the tent frame. The blood from the intruder had caked on and had to be scratched off with his nails and wiped clear. With a shock he realised that his dagger must be bloody as well and drew it to find the blade heavily soiled by dried blood. That took somewhat longer to clean and by the time Cato pushed his way into Macro's tent the centurion was steaming. Piso stood at the back of the tent, eyebrows raised in warning.

'What took you so bloody long? I sent for you ages ago.'

'I'm sorry, sir.'

'Well?'

'Sir?'

'Why were you late? Explain yourself.'

'I was in the latrines, sir, something I ate last night.'

'Well, take more care over what you eat in future,' Macro said impatiently. 'Now then, we've got work to do. The legate's detached our century from the Legion to perform escort duties. I was given the orders at the morning briefing. We're to advance ahead of the Legion to Durocortorum and meet up with some staff bigwig. Then we're to escort him to General Plautius's headquarters at Gesoriacum. That's all, and since we have to get moving ahead of the column we're going to have to rush. I've already given the orders for the wagon to be loaded and hitched up. I want you to requisition some wine and treats for our guest. The quartermaster's been notified. Piso, you go and get the men moving; I want tents struck and loaded and packs ready before the next watch call. Now get out of here, both of you.'

Outside Cato looked at Piso enquiringly.

'Bad morning,' Piso whispered. 'Some dodgy business up at headquarters last night.'

'Dodgy business?'

'Some thief tried to rob the legate. Managed to knife a guard and get away. Now Vespasian's blowing his stack at the officers for not having their men keep a good enough watch.'

'Oh. Did anyone say what was stolen?'

'Nothing of value, apparently. But the poor sod who discovered the thief won't live long.'

'That's too bad.' Cato tried to sound concerned while his heart lifted slightly at the news, and then, as his cursed imagination summoned up an image of the blameless sentry lying bandaged and scarcely alive, he felt ashamed and guilty.

'Don't take it too badly, son.' Piso laid a hand on his shoulder. 'It happens. Just your good fortune it wasn't you.'

The tribune rested his chin on the palms of his hand and stared across to where Pulcher sat on a folding stool nursing his leg. The upper thigh had been punctured to a finger's depth and had bled profusely until he had got far enough away from the tent to apply pressure on the wound. Pulcher had limped back to the tribune's quarters, where he now sat applying a fresh bandage to the area. Luckily, the wound was high enough that the bandage would be concealed under his breeches and no-one need know that he had been injured. But the day's march would be agony, the tribune reflected with a smile. That would encourage the man not to cock it up next time – if there was a next time. Vespasian had issued orders to double the guard from now on and access to the command tent would be almost impossible. The man opposite did not yet know that another attempt would be required.

'I expect you'll be looking forward to returning to Rome,' the tribune asked as he poured the man a cup of wine.

'Too right!' Pulcher grunted. 'I've had enough of this undercover nonsense. I want to get back to soldiering.'

'I hardly think the Praetorian Guard counts as soldiering,' said the tribune mildly.

'It's the kind of soldiering I like.'

'But you did volunteer for this.'

'True. But for the sum of money we arranged anyone would volunteer.'

'But not everyone has your unique talent for ensuring things happen, encouraging loquacity in the tongue-tied, making people disappear – that sort of thing. Speaking of which, are you sure you can't put a face to the man you saw in the tent, the one who managed to pigstick you so efficiently?'

'No.' The reply was laced with anger. 'But when I do find out who it was, they'll suffer before I let them die. That's something I'll take care of for no extra fee.'

'Well, be sure that you do find him. If he knows who you are, he might manage to make you implicate me.'

'There's no chance of that.'

'Don't ever underestimate the power of effectively applied torture to loosen tongues,' the tribune warned him. The other merely sniffed with derision before the tribune continued, 'Now, I'm afraid I've got some bad news for you.'

'Eh?'

'You've not done your job.'

'What do you mean?' Pulcher jabbed a finger at the scroll. 'That's what you wanted, and that's what you've fucking got.'

'Oh no,' replied the tribune. 'You don't really think I took the trouble of bringing you all the way up from Rome to get a piece of stationery.'

He flattened the scroll out for the other man to read. But there was nothing to read, it was completely blank.

'It seems someone is a step ahead of us. Looks like

Vespasian was smart enough to use his safe-box as a decoy. Or, someone else here has beaten us to the scroll and left this in its place.'

Chapter Twenty-four

The departure of the Sixth century well ahead of the main column caused some little excitement to those who witnessed it, not least the men of the century itself. In the normal course of events no common solider would dare march out of the camp before the senior officers and the colour party. Therefore it was clear to all that the Sixth century was being detached on a special duty. What that duty was remained known only to the centurion, his optio and secretary; the common soldiery could only wonder as the century's baggage wagon creaked out of the main gate and followed the line of men stepping out down the road towards Durocortorum. The curiosity of the onlookers soon disappeared as their officers drove them back to work, preparing to strike the tents for the day's march.

The Sixth century's excitement was palpable and the men noisily speculated about the task before them. At the head of the column Macro could hardly fail to overhear the conversation conducted behind him at a level calculated to attract his attention. He allowed himself a small smile at their all-too-obvious angling for information. Let them have their fun, they would know

261

soon enough. In the meantime there was little to be gained from ordering them to quit babbling like small children and march in silence. While they were happy he was prepared to indulge them. The centurion was glad to be detached from the Legion; no more looking at the same backs he had followed for the best part of two hundred miles. No more frustrating delays for distant bottlenecks, and waiting patiently to be led to and from tent-area allotments by members of the colour party puffed up by their sense of self-importance.

Ahead was an empty road, stretching out in a more or less straight line towards the horizon. Above him the sky was clear and deep blue, while the air was filled with birdsong. In short, it was the kind of morning that filled Macro with an inner glow of delight at simply being alive.

Which made it all the more strange that the optio marching to one side and slightly behind him cast his eyes down to the road surface with a grim expression of concentration, quite oblivious to the general sense of well-being in the world.

Macro dropped back a step and clapped him on the shoulder.

'What on earth is the matter with you this morning, Cato?'

The boy was quite startled by this abrupt intrusion into his thoughts. 'Sir?'

'I asked you what the matter was.'

'Matter sir? Nothing's the matter.'

'Exactly!' Macro beamed. 'So, smile and enjoy life. It's not often you'll get an independent duty. Even if,' he lowered his voice, 'even if all we're told to do is nursemaid some staff officer to army headquarters.'

'If you say so, sir.'

'I do say so, lad. And believe me, I know what I'm talking about. Now be a good sort and try to enjoy things a bit more. You take life too seriously, young Cato.'

The optio fixed him with a bitter glare. 'That's because I find life rather too serious at the moment, sir.'

'Still mooning about over that slip of a girl?' Macro laughed, before giving him a sharp nudge in the side. 'So how did last night go then?'

Cato was startled into breaking his stride for a moment, until a low curse from the front rank of the column made him skip forward again to his position at the centurion's side.

'Well?' Macro winked. 'Did you score?'

'No, sir.'

'Why on earth not? Don't tell me you came over all poetic and romantic. You didn't, did you? Please tell me you didn't.'

'No, sir.' Cato looked down, not trusting himself to mislead Macro effectively. 'We were interrupted before we could . . . get down to anything.'

'Oh that's too bad.' Macro nodded sympathetically. 'So what happened?'

'We had arranged to meet in the wagons behind the legate's tents. We were getting on rather well when all this shouting and commotion broke out. We would have ignored it and carried on with things but Lavinia heard her mistress calling for her.'

'Should have gone for a quickie,' Macro suggested.

'Not even enough time for that, sir,' Cato said

regretfully. 'She had to rush off, without even arranging our next meeting. And now I'm sent off on escort duty and she's stuck back there.'

'Never mind, lad, I'm sure she'll keep it warm for you.'

'Yes, sir.'

'So you were there when that thief was discovered? Did you see anything?'

'Nothing, sir. Nothing at all. Just got out of there and went straight back to my bed.'

'Looks like you missed all the fun.'

'Yes, sir,' Cato replied, quietly enough that Macro mistook it for the boy's continued pining for his first love. A degree of sensitivity was called for to distract young Cato from his woes. Macro grasped at the first idea that crept into his head.

'Let's see how my words are coming on. You say a word and I'll spell it. All right?'

'Whatever you want, sir.'

As Macro stumbled through such tests of his new-found skill as 'rampart', 'sentry' and 'javelin', Cato was consumed by anxiety. If that sentry recovered from his head injury it would only be a matter of time before the investigation closed in around him. And then what? Torture, a confession extracted, and certain humiliating death. But if Lavinia was safe then she would be sure to back up his version of events. Unless – a rather nasty thought struck him – unless she feared that she might implicate herself. And what of Flavia? After all, she had arranged the meeting. She might deny Lavinia's statement for precisely the same reasons. While the

century was detached from the Legion he would not
know how the situation developed.

'Cato?' The centurion had quickly grown tired of
spelling tests.

'Sir?'

'This man we're going to meet.'

'Narcissus?'

'Keep it down,' Macro hissed. 'That lot back there
aren't supposed to know.'

'Sorry, sir. What about him?'

'Did you ever run into him at the palace?'

'Yes, sir. He was a close friend of my father, or at
least he was until he struck it rich.'

'What's he like?' Macro asked, then noticed the
curious expression on his optio's face. 'I just need to
know before we meet so we don't start off on the wrong
foot, that's all. If we're to guard him for the next few
days then I don't want to risk pissing him off, given that
he's one of the Emperor's inner circle. Not that I'm afraid
of him or anything, after all the man's only a bloody
freedman. Just want to make sure he's happy while in
our care. Won't harm our futures any if he gets to like
us. So then, tell me about him.'

'Well sir—' Cato paused for thought. This wasn't going
to be easy. What he knew of Narcissus was far from
flattering, and he had been wise enough to keep what
he knew to himself. The cold shoulder Narcissus had
turned to Cato's father in the latter years of their
friendship had left Cato in no doubt that he could expect
few favours from the leading figure of Claudius's inner
council. After Narcissus, only Messalina – the Emperor's

carelessly ambitious wife – wielded more power under the Emperor.

'Well?'

'He's a good man – I mean a brilliant man – sir. Might seem a bit cold and distant at first, but that's probably because he has a lot on his shoulders. They used to say in the palace that he had more brains and worked harder than any other man in the Empire. We all respected him,' concluded Cato tactfully.

'Well, that's all very nice, but what I want to know is what he's like as a man. What should I do to get on with him?'

'Get on with him?' Cato raised his eyebrows.

'Yes. I mean, is he a man's man? That kind of thing. Does he like a good joke? There's plenty I could tell him.'

'No, sir. Please don't try to be funny,' Cato begged, visions swimming before his eyes of a cosmopolitan sophisticate being regaled with the boorish humour of the ranks. 'Just be yourself, sir. Be professional and keep out of his way as much as possible. And be careful what you say.'

Chapter Twenty-five

Just after dawn, Flavia was sitting at her portable writing desk going through some papers. From the next tent she could hear Titus squealing with laughter as his nurse struggled to feed him his morning meal. Flavia intended to catch up on some correspondence she had been meaning to write since the Legion had set out from the Rhine. She had already despatched a letter to a distant relative commanding a cavalry unit that was joining the invasion force, hoping to meet up with him when the Second Legion arrived in Gesoriacum. Then there were people in Rome she needed to inform of her return. And there were instructions to be issued to the majordomo of the house on the Quirinal, as well as to the steward of Vespasian's villa in Campania. Both establishments needed plenty of warning to ensure that they would be ready to receive Flavia and her retinue.

But the writing of those letters must wait until the present task was meticulously completed. She dipped the tip of her stylus in the inkwell and continued writing with deliberation, pausing occasionally to copy some detail or other from the map on a scroll lying open before her. A salute was shouted outside her tent and Flavia quickly pushed her paperwork into a roughly ordered pile as Vespasian entered. Flavia smiled and laid her stylus down as she rose to give him a kiss.

'I'm afraid you'll have to begin packing in a moment,' apologised Vespasian. 'Even the legate's wife is not permitted to delay the Legion.'

'Surely, after last night's rumpus, you'll allow us time to recover?'

'Recover from what? Lost sleep is a fact of life in the army.'

'I'm not in the army,' she protested.

'No, but you're married to it.'

'Brute!' Flavia scowled. 'I knew I should have married some fat old senator with a consuming interest in viniculture. Instead of roughing it out here in the barbaric wilderness with a man who thinks being a soldier matters.'

'I never forced you to,' Vespasian said quietly.

Flavia took his face between her hands and looked deep into his eyes. 'Just joking, you idiot. You know why I married you. For love – as unfashionable as that may be.'

'But you could have married better.'

'No, I couldn't.' Flavia kissed him. 'One day, you'll be powerful beyond your wildest dreams. I guarantee it.'

'That's reckless talk, Flavia. Please don't. It's too dangerous to even think such things these days.'

Flavia looked deeply into his eyes for a moment and then smiled. 'You're right, of course. I'll be careful what I say. But mark me, history won't remember you merely for commanding a legion. I'll see to that if no-one else will. You really should be more ambitious, or do you still cling to that deep-seated Republican modesty of yours?'

'Maybe.' Vespasian shrugged. 'But right now I think I'll be lucky if I retain command of the Second until the end of the month.'

'Why dear? What's the matter?'

'That incident last night—'

'The fire?'

'The person who caused the fire. The thief. He stole something quite precious – something that Narcissus had trusted me to keep secret. Once Narcissus finds out that it's been stolen I don't think he'll be in much of a mood for any excuses.'

'It's not your fault it was stolen,' Flavia protested. 'Whatever "it" was. He can't replace you just for that.'

'He can. He will. He has to.'

'Why? Whatever can be that important?'

Vespasian allowed himself a small smile. 'That I can't tell you. The orders were quite explicit on that point at least.'

'Were they?' asked Flavia, her face momentarily flushed with anxiety. 'When we join the rest of the army, let me have a word with Narcissus. He was a good friend of mine back at the palace.'

'I'd rather you said nothing to him. Let me continue the investigation here in the Legion. We'll find the thief sooner or later.'

'How is the sentry?'

'Not good. The surgeon says he's lost a lot of blood. He's in no shape to travel and today's journey might just finish him off.'

'Well, why can't we leave him at Durocortorum until he's well enough to follow the Legion – if he lives?'

'We could, with a few men to carry a litter once he's up to it. I had thought of that. But he won't be under the care of the surgeon.'

'Good thing too – if half of what I've heard is true. Look here, why don't I leave Parthenas to care for him? He's a trained physician. I've seen him at work on the other slaves and he seems competent enough.'

'All right,' Vespasian nodded. 'The man would have a far better chance of survival lying still in a bed rather than bouncing along the road in a hospital wagon. Now, if it's not too much trouble, I'd be greatly obliged if you would arrange for your personal effects to be packed immediately.'

'Very well.'

'Oh! One other thing.'

'Yes?'

Vespasian reached inside his tunic and drew out a small silk ribbon. 'I wonder if you've ever seen this before?'

'Let me have a look.' Flavia examined the ribbon a moment before replying. 'This is Lavinia's. Where did you find it?'

'In my command tent, on my couch. Yet there's no reason for her to have been in there and I don't recall seeing it when I left the tent last night. Odd, don't you think?'

'What's odd?'

'Lavinia has no cause to be in my tent. Do you know anything about this?'

'Why should I? It's your tent.'

'She's your maid.' Vespasian looked up, a strange expression on his face – one that alarmed his wife.

'Whatever's the matter?'

'Probably nothing. But I think I might have a word with that girl. There's something funny going on.'

Chapter Twenty-six

'And, if I'm not mistaken, lurking under that monstrously oversized helmet is young Cato.' Narcissus smiled and held out his hands. With an instinctive reluctance Cato responded and Narcissus held the young man's hands in a tight grasp while he stared searchingly into Cato's eyes. 'It's good to see you. But what you are doing dressed up as a solider is quite beyond me.'

'It's because I am a soldier – sir,' Cato said formally. 'As you may recall, I was given my freedom on condition I agreed to enlist.'

'I seem to vaguely recall some such detail,' Narcissus replied airily, as if trying to remember a snack he had once eaten. 'So how are you finding the army? I'd wager a boy of your age would be relishing the outdoor life.'

'Can't complain, sir,' Cato said, bitterly swallowing the indignity of being referred to as a boy in front of his centurion. 'Of course, it is more physically demanding than living in the palace.'

Narcissus produced a thin smile. 'You're right about that, I'm afraid – haven't exercised in years. Policy-making is more my metier these days. But no matter.

I'm glad to see you again, my boy. I trust that he is giving satisfaction, Centurion?'

'Yes, sir. The lad's got the makings of a fine optio. You must be quite proud that the palace can turn out lads as good at soldiering as young Cato.'

'Refresh my memory, if you'd be so kind. What exactly is an optio?'

'Why, he's my second-in-command, sir,' Macro replied, shocked by the civilian's ignorance. 'And good at the job too.'

'It's most gratifying that even the army can appreciate the worth of a good education.'

Macro produced the required flush of anger.

'Just my little joke, Centurion. No harm intended.'

Narcissus took him by the arm and led him into the lodge of the imperial staging post. The imperial secretary was well into his middle years and his eyes peered out of crow's-feet lines formed by a lifetime's worth of smiling. There was no stoop in the way he carried himself and the mobility of his expression clearly matched the speed of his thinking. And yet that dry, caustic wit indicated a mind practised in the art of putting others down. Macro pressed his lips together; as long as the man was under his protection he would have to endure the inevitable slights and barbs. Narcissus, he concluded, was typical of his kind. He treated social superiors as intellectual inferiors and – as his treatment of Cato had shown – he was inclined to treat his intellectual equals as social inferiors. One just could not win with that kind of man. Best try and ignore it.

'What are your orders, Centurion?' Narcissus asked

him when they were alone inside the lodge. 'Your precise orders?'

'To escort you as far as the main body of the army and then wait for the rest of the Legion in a holding area yet to be specified. That was it, sir. Other than to render you assistance should you require it.'

'In other words, you're to obey my orders.'

'Yes, sir,' Macro conceded reluctantly. 'That's about the size of it.'

'Good.' Narcissus nodded. 'Glad to see that Vespasian managed to get that right at least.'

Macro stiffened at this unwarranted slur on his commander's aptitude. Coming from a Roman citizen that would be bad enough – but to hear a freedman speak in this manner was a clear breach of the most basic social etiquette.

'Centurion, we must get on the road immediately,' Narcissus ordered, poking Macro's chest to emphasise the point. 'I have to reach Gesoriacum as soon as possible. Much depends on it. In fact, I can tell you that the entire campaign depends on it, and more. Do we understand one another?'

'I'm not sure what you want me to understand, sir,' Macro replied frankly. 'Why the hurry?'

'That information is given on a strictly need-to-know basis.'

'But a whole century to guard one man?'

'Suffice to say that some political miscreants would prefer me not to make it to Gesoriacum – and that's all you need to know.'

'Yes, sir.'

'Right then,' Narcissus resumed brightly. 'Let's be off. I'm travelling light; just my litter bearers and a personal bodyguard. A number of my porters have succumbed to some local ailment and I'll need a few of your men to replace them. There are two chests outside the stables. See to it now, please, and I'll join your line of men in a moment.'

The grinding of Macro's teeth was almost audible as he emerged from the lodge and approached Cato.

'Detail five men for the freedman. He needs some porters.'

'Porters?'

'You deaf? Just get on with it. The men can stow their yokes on the wagon.'

'Yes, sir.'

'Apparently we're in a bit of a hurry to reach the coast, so we're going to have to give our leisurely stroll through Gaul a miss. Might as well have stayed with the Legion,' Macro grumbled.

Narcissus's litter turned out to be a light travelling model with screens, carried by eight huge Nubians who moved with a strength and litheness born of a lifetime's experience at the job. The litter took up position in the middle of the century, immediately followed by the two chests carried by the five bitterly resentful legionaries who had joined the slave porters. The latter were quite enjoying having someone brought down to their level. Beside the litter stood the bodyguard: a huge, muscular figure with a highly polished black cuirass and short sword. His knotted ponytail, savagely scarred face and black eye-patch announced to the world a long

experience in the arena. Suddenly a hand emerged from
the leather screen and clicked its fingers to attract the
bodyguard's attention.

'You! Polythemus! Tie these back. Might as well see
some of this benighted land while we march. Right then,
Centurion!' Narcissus called out. 'When you're ready.'

Macro sourly gave the order to advance and the
century moved off, marching through the main gate of
Durocortorum, along the plumb-line straight road that
passed through the town to the far gate and the road to
Gesoriacum. As they crested a low ridge, Cato glanced
back and saw, far to the rear, the advance units of the
Legion emerging from the forest road, heading towards
the town they had just left. He felt a twinge of anxiety as
he thought of Lavinia, then vivid memories of the
previous night flooded into his mind and he turned away,
filled with dread.

Chapter Twenty-seven

By midday the baggage train and rearguard of the Second Legion had passed through Durocortorum and Vespasian gave the order for a short rest period. Progress had been slow because some of the local children had taken it into their heads to sling stones at the oxen pulling the artillery carriages. One viciously aimed shot had struck a larger than average beast in the testicles, causing it to try to turn in its traces as it bellowed with rage and pain. Seeing the small crowd of urchins responsible the beast had plunged after them, toppling the bolt thrower and its carriage into the street. While the beast was pacified and the wreckage cleared, word had to be passed up to the front of the column and back down to the rearguard, ordering a halt. Eventually the carriage and the bolt thrower were pushed down a side street where a detachment of engineers set about making repairs and the column started moving again.

Vespasian, riding back to investigate the delay, had cursed the shortage of draught animals that had necessitated using temperamental male oxen. The beast, comforted by a muleteer, was led away to join the small herd of lame animals destined to provide the column's fresh meat, while the young boy concerned was given a thrashing he would remember for the rest of his life. Not that that in any way comforted Vespasian as he raged inwardly at the delay. Nor was he in an improved mood when the Legion halted at midday. Seated at a table, he gave the order to see his wife's new maidservant.

As he snacked on some tough cold chicken washed down with a nameless local wine – when would these Gauls ever learn the art? – Lavinia was brought before him. His mouth full, he indicated that she should stand by the table where he gazed at her while his jaws worked hard to break the chicken down. She was quite a beauty, he decided, now that he had the chance to look her over properly. Completely wasted as a serving maid; a tidy sum could be fetched for her in Rome as a courtesan.

After a quick sip of wine to clear his palate he was ready to begin. He extracted the ribbon from his tunic and laid it down on the table. He was gratified to see that it was instantly recognised.

'Yours?'

'Yes, master. I thought I'd lost it.'

'And well you might, it had nearly slid down behind a cushion on my couch.'

Lavinia reached for it but Vespasian still held it in his grip and her hand dropped back.

'What I'd like to know,' Vespasian smiled, 'is why it was there in the first place?'

'Master?'

'What were you doing in my tent last night?'

'Last night?' Lavinia asked, all wide-eyed innocence.

'That's right. The ribbon wasn't there when I left for

bed. So tell me, Lavinia, and tell me straight, what were you doing there?'

'Nothing master! I swear it.' Her eyes pleaded with him to believe her. 'I just went in there to lie down for a moment. I was tired. I wanted somewhere comfortable to rest. The ribbon must have come off then.'

Vespasian stared long and hard at her before he continued. 'You just wanted to rest on my couch? That's all?'

Lavinia nodded.

'And you didn't take anything from the tent?'

'No, master.'

'And you didn't see anything or anybody while you were there?'

'No, master.'

'I see. Here.' He pushed the ribbon towards her and leaned back in his chair, while he considered her claims. She might be telling the truth or she might tell an altogether different tale if a little physical persuasion was applied. But almost as quickly as the thought of torture entered his head, Vespasian dismissed it. He did not doubt its efficacy in loosening tongues, it was just that he had seen too many victims offer up the version of events they knew their tormentors required of them. Hardly an effective way of finding out what had really happened. A new tack was required.

'You've only recently joined the household, according to my wife.'

'Yes, sir.'

'Who did you belong to before then?'

'Tribune Plinius, master.'

279

'Plinius!' Vespasian's eyebrows shot up. That changed things. What was a former slave of Plinius doing in his household? An agent? A spy trying to gain access to his safe-box? Yet, looking at her, it was hard to imagine that she could manage the guile required for the job. Another facade? It was impossible to tell at this stage.

'Why did Plinius sell you?'

'He grew tired of me.'

'You'll forgive me if I find that hard to believe.'

'It's true, master,' Lavinia protested.

'There must be more to it than that. Speak up, girl, and mind it's the truth.'

'There is more, master,' Lavinia admitted and bowed her head, as Flavia had told her to do, before she continued. 'The tribune wanted to use me . . . in certain ways.'

I bet he did, thought Vespasian.

'But he wanted more than that, he wanted me to have feelings for him. I couldn't bring myself to and he grew angry with me. And when he discovered I loved someone else he flew into a rage and hit me.'

Vespasian tutted in sympathy. 'And who might this other person be, the one you loved?'

'Please, master,' Lavinia looked up, tears glistening at the corners of her eyes. 'I don't want to say.'

'You have to tell me, Lavinia.' Vespasian leaned forward to pat her arm comfortingly. 'I must know who this other man is. It's vital that I know. I can command you to tell me.'

'Vitellius!' she blurted out, and broke down in tears, clutching her hands to her face.

Vitellius. So she loved Vitellius. Enough to do his bidding? A further thought struck Vespasian.

'Have you been seeing Vitellius since you joined our household?'

'Master?'

'You heard me. Are you still seeing him?'

She nodded.

'Did you see him last night? In my tent?'

Lavinia looked up at him with a shocked expression and shook her head.

'But you were planning to. Weren't you?'

'He never turned up, master. I waited, but he never came to me, as he had promised. I waited in the dark and he never came. So I went to bed. I never noticed the ribbon was missing until this morning.'

'I see. Did Vitellius ever ask you to tell him anything about me? Did he ask you anything about my household?'

'We talked,' Lavinia replied carefully. 'But I can't remember much of what we said about my lady Flavia and you, master.'

'And he never asked you to steal, or borrow, anything from my tent?'

'No, master. Never.'

Vespasian stared into her eyes for a long time, trying to determine if she spoke the truth. Lavinia just stared frankly back at him, until she could no longer meet his gaze and stared down at her feet instead. Certainly her story had the ring of truth. But if she still loved Vitellius it was conceivable that she might be persuaded to steal for him, or arrange access to the general's tent so that the senior tribune could steal the secret scroll after she had given up on him and gone to bed.

'You may go now, Lavinia.' Vespasian waved his hand. 'But I want you to remember this: if Vitellius ever asks you for any information about me again, or arranges another meeting, I want to know about it. And I warn you, the consequences of not telling me the truth from now on will be very painful. Very painful indeed. Do we understand one another?'

'Yes, master.'

'Good. Now leave me.'

'So how did it go?' Flavia asked Lavinia that evening as they waited for the tents to be erected.

'I think he believed me, mistress. But why did I have to say that I was meeting Vitellius in the tent that night?'

'Would you rather have told him the truth and got Cato involved?'

'No, mistress. Of course not.'

'Well then, if we're to keep Cato out of the frame we need to put someone else into it. Vitellius fits the bill nicely. Very nicely indeed.'

Lavinia glanced at her mistress in surprise. Clearly there was more to this than simply saving Cato's skin. The pleased expression on Flavia's face as she idly watched the legionaries struggling with the guy ropes went beyond relief for saving the young optio and Lavinia could not help wondering if she, and Cato, might well be small pieces in a deeper game. Flavia suddenly switched her gaze to the slave girl.

'You must remember to stick to the story we agreed,

Lavinia. Stick to that and we're all safe, understand? But don't ask me for any further explanations. The less you know, the more honest you will appear. Trust me.'

'Yes, mistress.'

Chapter Twenty-eight

The Sixth century marched through lush Gaul countryside bursting with the fresh buds of spring. The legionaries joked and chatted happily – with occasional raucous bursts of lewd singing to while away the day. And this mode persisted despite the pace that Macro had set, for he was eager to reach his destination as soon as possible and offload the imperial secretary before the latter tempted Macro to some act of violence. Narcissus had lost no opportunity to make barbed comments about the army in general, and its soldiers and Macro in particular. The centurion would dearly have loved to smack the smug bastard in the mouth just once, to emphasise the fact that you simply did not behave in such a fashion: 'When in Rome do as the Romans do, but when you're in the army keep your mouth shut and show some fucking respect.'

He smiled at the thought but knew it could never be voiced aloud, let alone face to face with a close friend and confidante of the Emperor. And so he had to sullenly endure the sarcasm and criticism in apparent good spirit – the fate of all those exposed to insecure arrivistes. Cato fared somewhat better at the hands of their tormentor since their common background provided a basis for conversation, even though Narcissus made it perfectly clear that, whatever the past, a huge social gulf now existed between them. Fortunately, the only opportunity for conversation occurred at rests in the march and at the end of the day when the century camped for the night. In between, Macro and Cato led the column from the front, though a smoother-tongued, more ambitious officer would have marched by the imperial secretary's litter to engage him in conversation and use every opportunity for flattery. After the first day, Macro insisted that he inspect his troop's equipment at each break in the march. The men regarded this zealous display of duty with curiosity, silently shaking their heads as the centurion tugged at equipment straps and checked that their weapons were being properly maintained.

On the evening of the third day of their escort duty Macro calculated that they would reach the coast the following evening, thanks to the extended length of the marching day that had been possible for the small formation. If they started just before dawn and really pushed the pace they should make the main body of the army by nightfall.

'Very good, Centurion.' Narcissus nodded approvingly. 'And an arrival in the darkness will attract less attention. That would be better in the present circumstances.'

Cato and Macro exchanged a look; precisely what the present circumstances were was still a mystery. Narcissus had said nothing to enlighten them over the last three days and Macro was a good enough soldier not to question his orders. He was also human enough not to

44444444

44444444444

want to give the imperial secretary the satisfaction of turning down a direct request for information. A more subtle tactic was required, thought Macro.

'More wine, sir?' He held out the jug, with a forced smile.

This time it was Cato and Narcissus who exchanged a look, surprised at the transparency of the centurion's approach. Narcissus laughed.

'Yes please, Centurion. But I'm afraid it'll take more wine than we have with us to loosen my tongue. You'll just have to wait.'

Macro's blush was visible even by the glow of the fire. The night air was still chilly and the fire and hot meal at the end of each day was greatly appreciated before the men turned in. The food that Piso had managed to wangle for the century had come from the staff officers' stores, as Vespasian was anxious to create a good impression on the distinguished guest. A rich stew of venison and spring vegetables was being mopped from the silver plates that Narcissus's bodyguard produced from one of the chests. Macro had eaten a double portion and smacked his lips before wiping them on the back of his hairy hand. He caught the disapproving gaze of the other two and shrugged as he knocked back the last of his wine before refilling the cup.

'It's good to see a man enjoy his food,' Narcissus remarked with a sly smile. 'Even if it is only such rude morsels as are provided for the common soldiery. I must say, I almost feel like one of you as we share the hardships of the march, iron rations and outdoor living in the wilds of untamed Gaul.'

'Untamed Gaul?' Macro's eyebrows rose. 'What's so untamed about it?'

'Did you notice any theatres as we passed through Durocortorum? Have we passed any great landscaped estates? The only things I've seen are a handful of struggling farms and a few shabby inns. That's what I mean by untamed, Centurion.'

'Nothing untamed about inns,' Macro replied gruffly.

'Not as such, no. But look at that foul beverage they sell as wine. I wouldn't even use it as a salad dressing.'

'You're drinking it now,' Macro pointed out.

'Only under the strictest sufferance. And you did rather force it on me. Maybe I'll reveal all to avoid inflicting any more on my poor stomach.'

'So make it easy on yourself, sir,' Cato said with a grin. 'And tell us why you're going to Gesoriacum. It can't be to oversee the invasion – all the plans for that must have been made months ago. Something's gone wrong, hasn't it?'

Narcissus looked at him, carefully weighing his thoughts. 'Yes. I can't say too much. I won't. But everything is at stake. I have to reach Gesoriacum – alive. I have certain information for General Plautius. If anything happens to me, I doubt that there will be an invasion, and if there's no invasion then there might be no Emperor in short order.' Narcissus saw the incredulity that his words produced, and he leaned closer to the others, half his face thrown into flickering shadow. 'The Empire is in great danger, greater than it has ever been. Even now there are still some fools in the Senate who think they're capable of running the

Empire. They never cease trying to undermine the Emperor – that's why I have to get to Gesoriacum. There are some who say Claudius is a cruel simpleton.' He smiled sadly. 'I'm sorry if it surprises you to hear me say that. And it might even be true. But he's the only Emperor we have and the Julio-Claudian dynasty may well end with him.'

'I've heard some people argue that it might be as well if it did,' Cato said.

'And then what?' Narcissus asked bitterly. 'A return to the Republic? How would that benefit us? Back to the old factions fighting it out in the Senate with words, and then letting it spill out on to the streets with violence, until the whole of the civilised world is torn apart by civil war. To read the pious nonsense republican historians write you'd think that the days of Sulla, Julius Caesar, Mark Antony and their breed marked some kind of golden age. Well, let me tell you, those "heroes" marched into history over the bodies of three generations of Roman citizens. We need the Emperors, we need the stability of one authority dominating the state. We Romans are no longer capable of anything else.'

'We Romans?'

'All right, we freedmen and the Romans,' conceded Narcissus. 'I admit that my fate is bound up with the Emperor's. Without his patronage, some senator or other would rouse the mob and I'd be torn apart in a matter of days. My destruction would just be the start. Even you people out here on the frontier would suffer the consequences.'

'Makes no difference to me who is in power,' said

Macro. 'I'm just a soldier. There will always be an army and that's all that matters.'

'Maybe. But what kind of an army? If Claudius falls you'll still get your war – but it'll be fought against Romans. You may even be called upon to fight men you now regard as friends. Maybe even each other. Think about it. And then give thanks for the Emperor.'

Cato looked across at his centurion, whose eyes glinted in the light of the fire. The optio smiled unsteadily as he turned back to Narcissus.

'You're testing us, aren't you? To see how we respond.'

'Of course I am,' Narcissus readily admitted. 'A man has to know where other people stand on the fundamental issues.'

'Just as well we kept our peace,' Macro laughed.

'Silence can be every bit as incriminating as the spoken word, Centurion. But I doubt whether you, or the optio here, constitute much of a threat to the Emperor. So you're both safe . . . for now.'

Macro glanced nervously at his optio for reassurance that the imperial secretary was joking with them. But the frozen stare of the young lad was enough to still any attempt at obsequious laughter.

'Anyhow, enough of that.' Narcissus drained his silver cup of the last remnants and set it down in front of the flask of wine. 'One last drink for the road and then to sleep. You know, it's quite a liberating thing to be away from all the intrigues of Rome. A man could get used to this life of yours. I propose a toast,' he said as Macro half-filled the cup proffered to him, and then the centurion filled his to the brim.

'To the good life!' Narcissus raised his cup. 'To the army, who—'

An arrow whistled out of the darkness and the imperial secretary screamed as his cup flew off into the night to clatter down against a rock. Narcissus held his drinking hand tightly against his chest as his face contorted with agony.

'What?' Cato began.

'To arms! TO ARMS!' Macro roared, throwing down his cup. He sprang to his feet and ran to gather his shield and sword propped up against the litter. Only a handful of men had risen to their feet around the century's camp fires when a shower of arrows descended on them. Several were aimed at Narcissus but mercifully missed him, their feathered ends sprouting up in the grass about the fire – and one thudding against a glowing red log, sending a plume of bright sparks swirling into the blackness. The imperial secretary had recovered sufficiently to be aware of the immediate need for self-preservation and he rolled away from the light of the fire towards the century's baggage wagon where he lay flat between the protection of the wheels.

As Cato snatched up his shield and drew his sword, an arrow took a legionary in the back as he struggled to pull his chain-mail shirt over his head. The man grunted as the breath was knocked from him by the impact and he toppled forwards, hands desperately scrabbling for the shaft sunk deep beneath the shoulder blade.

Shield held close to his body, Cato ran over and saw that the injured legionary was starting to cough up frothy gouts of blood.

'Leave him!' Macro shouted and pointed to the other men. 'Get them formed up around the wagon!'

In the flickering red light of the fires, Macro raced through the century kicking men to their feet and pushing them towards the wagon. Some were still dazed and had to have a shield and sword thrust into their hands before they recovered their wits and stumbled off in the direction of the wagon. Two more men had been hit by the time Cato had formed a rough perimeter around the century's baggage wagon, under which the imperial secretary lay, wide-eyed at the action around him. The legionaries knelt down behind their shields as they had been trained to do in the face of missile fire. Except now they wore no armour, merely woollen tunics that would stop neither arrow nor spear-thrust. Most had not been able to strap helmets on and kept their heads ducked down as the arrows continued to whirr in from the darkness, striking shields with a splintering crack. From the nearly flat trajectory, Cato knew their attackers had to be close and tensed himself for a sudden rush. Looking around he saw that he had twenty or so men with him, and more were straggling up from the main line of tents, driven on by Macro.

Suddenly the volley of arrows ceased and, an instant later, there came the wild roar of a battle cry from the darkness all about them. Dark shapes flew out of the night and, in the mid-distance, could be heard the deep thrumming of many hoof beats.

'Stand by to receive cavalry!' Cato shouted. 'Close up on me!'

His little body of men compacted around the wagon

just as a score of huge men burst into the lurid glow of the fires, bearded faces contorted by their screams. They wore thick black cloaks, pointed helmets and carried curved cleaver-like swords. They moved into attack with a fierceness few of the Romans had seen before. The first three crashed into the shields and tumbled to the ground in a tangle of cloaks, shields and flailing limbs and were quickly despatched by the other men around them. The rest of the attackers arrived as one body and a desperate fight began in the flickering red and orange light.

The Roman line dissolved at once into a mass of desperate one-on-one fights and Cato, no longer in command of a cohesive body of troops, found himself facing a large, powerfully built enemy, face twisted into a snarl. Sizing up his young opponent in an instant, the attacker screamed as he feinted forward. Cato flinched momentarily, but kept his position, shield raised and short sword poised by his side. Seeing that his attempt to scare Cato into fleeing had failed, the man laughed and swung his sword in an arc at Cato's head. The raised shield took the blow at an angle and the blade clanged off into the ground, gouging up a long divot of turf. The shock of the blow shot pain down Cato's arm from fingertips to shoulder and he cried out. Then, as the momentum of the blow carried the man forward, Cato went down on one knee, twisting to one side to avoid being crushed by his enemy. Savagely, he thrust his sword deep into the warrior's side. He fell forwards on his face with a dull moan, yanking the sword from Cato's hand. Cato thrust his foot against the man's back and tried to jerk the blade free, grimacing with the effort as the dying warrior groaned in agony. But it was no use, the blade was tightly wedged in the man's ribs and would not come free easily. Glancing around, Cato saw that most of the attackers were down, together with a number of Romans.

Close by, one of his men had lost his shield and could only raise his arm against the sword about to be smashed down on his head. With a howl that bordered on an embarrassing scream, Cato threw himself behind his shield into the attacker's back, sending both of them headlong into the grass. By the time he had risen to his feet, the man he had saved had thrust his dagger into the attacker's throat.

As suddenly as the attackers had burst upon them they were gone, and the surviving Romans stood, bewildered by the speed of events.

'What the fuck are you doing?' Macro shouted from close at hand as he ran up to the wagon with the remainder of the men. 'You heard the optio! Close up to face cavalry!'

For a moment, Cato had forgotten about the horses but now they were close and the legionaries hurriedly closed ranks around the wagon, shields interlocking, with swords and javelins held ready.

As suddenly as the first attack had come, the second raced out of the night; a line of horsemen in the same equipment, some still holding horse-bows while others carried long spears, thrusting out from under their arms, all of them crying out their terrifying battle-cry. Macro quickly looked across at Cato to make sure the optio was unhurt.

'Pick up a fucking sword, you idiot!'

Cato realised that he was unarmed and hastily snatched up the nearest weapon – one of the attackers' curved cleavers. It felt strange to a hand used to the weight and balance of the legionary's short sword, but reassuringly heavy.

'Hold steady, lads!' Macro called out. 'Hold steady and we'll live.'

When the horsemen were almost on them they drew up; those who still carried bows drew arrows and waited for a chance to pepper any Roman foolish enough to expose himself while the spear-carriers moved in on the ring of shields. They brought their horses slamming up against the shield wall, throwing the legionaries back against the wagon, while stabbing down with their long bladed spears. The bulk of their horses and fear of the archers kept the Romans crouched down through sheer instinct for self-preservation. A few of them took every chance to thrust their swords into any part of man or horse that came within reach and an occasional cry or shrill neigh told when a blow had struck home. But time was not on the Romans' side; already four men were down on the ground around the wagon and blood was making the grass slippery.

It was all too obvious to Macro what the outcome of the fight would be if they fought defensively; a whittling away of their numbers and one final rush that would overrun the survivors. Just as he realised this, fate intervened in a peculiar way. Two of the horsemen suddenly spied the imperial secretary sheltering beneath the wagon and hurled their horses through the Romans.

Leaning down from the saddle, they thrust under the wagon. Narcissus rolled away from their spear tips with a scream. Up jumped Macro, teeth parted in a savage snarl, as he automatically leaped to the imperial secretary's defence. He caught one man by the arm and hauled him bodily from his saddle. A slash of the sword into the man's eyes left him helpless as the centurion snatched up the fallen spear and plunged it into the small of the other attacker's back.

Then Cato, too, was on his feet, kicking at the men nearest him. 'Up and at 'em! Come on, get up! Charge!'

Now all the Romans were running at their attackers echoing Cato's call to the charge. The attackers were momentarily shocked into stillness – a fatal failure of nerve, as it turned out. Moments later, the Roman infantry were in amongst them, knocking them from their saddles and finishing them off as they lay helpless on the ground. The bloody skirmish was quickly over, only a handful of the enemy managing to break away and flee into the night.

Cato leaned on his shield, blood pounding through his veins as he breathed heavily. All about him bodies were strewn around the century's camp fires. Legionaries quickly moved among the prostrate forms to finish off the wounded enemy.

'Stop that!' Narcissus shouted as he scrabbled out from under the wagon. 'Don't kill them!'

The shrill tone of his voice caused the men to pause in their grisly work, swords poised, waiting for Macro to countermand this ridiculous instruction.

'Don't kill them?' Macro was astonished. 'These

bastards were about to gut you. And us!'

'Centurion, we must have prisoners! We must find out who is responsible for the attack.'

Macro could see the sense of what Narcissus was saying. He wiped his sword clean on the cloak of one of the attackers before sliding it back into his scabbard. 'Lads! If any of these bastards are still breathing drag them over here. Section leaders! Call the roll of your men, all returns to the optio at once!'

Later, while the Roman injured groaned and cried at the rough first-aid that was meted out to them by their inexpert comrades, Macro gazed down angrily at the three warriors sitting sullenly at his feet. Cato emerged from the night.

'What's the butcher's bill?'

'Eight dead and sixteen wounded, sir.'

'Right. Get the seals off the dead and tell off a burial detail.'

'What about my litter bearers? My bodyguard?' asked Narcissus, nursing his injured hand.

'One dead, one missing and the bodyguard's still unconscious – someone said he'd been kicked by a horse.'

'Right then, you bastards,' growled Macro, and as he kicked the nearest one on his broken arm a shrill scream of agony split the air. 'Eight of my men are dead. Don't think for a moment you aren't going the same way. But we can make it quick for you, or slow and painful. Depends on how you answer this gentleman here.'

He jerked a thumb at Narcissus and stepped to one side. The imperial secretary stared hard at them, hands on hips, but stood beyond arm's reach.

'Who ordered you to kill me?'

'Kill you?' Cato asked. 'I thought they were bandits.'

'Bandits!' Macro laughed harshly. 'Ever heard of bandits attacking a full century? No? Well then, don't be stupid. Besides, look at them, look at the clothes and armour. This lot belong to something far more organised.'

'Like an army unit?'

'Maybe.'

Narcissus raised a hand for silence and asked his question again. 'I said, who ordered you to kill me?'

None of the three looked up, even when he repeated the question more forcefully.

'Centurion?'

Macro stepped up and delivered another kick, this time to the head. The man went down on his back with a sharp cry.

'Well, are you going to tell me?'

The man who had escaped the kicking thus far glared up through bushy brows and said something in a language Cato had not heard before. He emphasised his point by spitting on to the hem of Narcissus' tunic. Macro drew back his boot.

'No!' Narcissus raised his hand. 'There's no need for that. I think I know this tongue. They're from Syria. If they're who I think they are, they won't talk for a while.'

'I wouldn't bet on that, sir,' Macro replied coldly. 'There are ways . . .'

'I haven't got time. We mustn't be delayed in reaching the army. These men will come along as prisoners. When I get to Gesoriacum there'll be plenty of time to go to work on them. See that they're securely bound. They can march behind my litter tomorrow.'

When the century set out the next morning, the full scale of the action became clear. Twelve more bodies were found, as well as the Roman dead, and all were buried in a hastily dug trench before the unit broke camp. Macro had ordered his men to march in full battledress and they moved wearily down the road to Gesoriacum in a box shape around Narcissus's litter and the wagon now carrying the Roman wounded. All surplus baggage had been abandoned to make room for the wounded. That had not endeared the prisoners to the centurion, who had them tied to each other by the ankle, and fastened the line to the back of the wagon. There was no stop for a rest, despite the weariness brought on by a sleepless night, as the column picked its way along the road to the coast. A pair of horsemen appeared in the distance from time to time as they shadowed the century, evidently frustrated by the lack of opportunity to continue the action. Shortly before dusk the horses wheeled away and disappeared over the brow of a narrow ridge that ran alongside the line of the road. As night fell the century's pace quickened and the men glanced nervously into the shadows looming around them, fully expecting the ambush to be renewed the instant darkness could provide enough cover for their strange attackers.

At last they marched over the brow of a hill and Cato let out a gasp of astonishment. Below them was a vast military camp stretching, it seemed, for miles, lit by thousands of camp fires and braziers. Four full legions were concentrated in the area, together with an equal number of specialist auxiliary cohorts, engineers, ship-builders and staff planning-officers – over fifty thousand men all told. But as they approached the gates Macro sensed that something was wrong. Small pockets of men roamed outside the camp, unarmed and out of uniform, others played at dice or just sat drinking themselves insensible.

Before the Sixth century came within speaking range of any of the other legionaries they were intercepted by a staff officer on horseback, escorted by several centurions, who commanded them to halt. Once the identity of the imperial secretary had been confirmed, the officer issued immediate orders for the removal of the prisoners to a secure place, while he escorted the imperial secretary to army headquarters. And that was the last Cato and Macro saw of Narcissus. They received no thanks for their success in preserving his mission and no acknowledgement of the lives that had been lost in his cause.

The camp prefect of the Ninth arrived to arrange for the movement of the wounded to the Ninth Legion's hospital. Then he led the remnants of the century out of the camp to a cleared area some miles distant where the lines for the Second Legion had already been laid out.

The Sixth century set up its tents as quickly as possible and, once the pickets had been positioned, the men fell into an exhausted sleep.

Chapter Twenty-nine

Two days later the Second Legion marched into the site and the vast area was overrun by thousands of soldiers struggling to erect tents. In strict accordance with military protocol, the legate's camp was put up first, followed by the senior officers' and only then was the common soldiery allowed to begin work on their own, far more basic, quarters.

Vespasian sat in his command tent at a small table, screened off from the household slaves as headquarters staff scurried to and fro, laying down wooden flooring and unpacking furniture and other items. Above it all, he could hear Flavia issuing orders and driving them on to greater speed. He knew she was glad the tiresome journey was over and that the hardships of life on the march could be pushed to the back of her mind for a few weeks at least, though soon she would have to undertake the even longer journey south to Rome.

Vespasian was much less content – even though the missing scroll had been returned to him by Flavia a few days earlier. She had found it amongst the toys in Titus's travel chest and saw that it was addressed to her husband. The boy told her he had found it on the floor, so she said, and was incapable of being any more specific, given his age. Vespasian had hugged his wife and immediately locked the document away in the darkest recess of the safe-box. It seemed that whoever had stolen the scroll must have dropped it while fleeing from the command tent. Vespasian was appalled by the breach of security that could have occurred. What if someone else had discovered the scroll before Titus? Jupiter! It didn't bear thinking about. But Vespasian's joy at the recovery of the scroll was now tempered by the forbidding situation that existed beyond the confines of his command tent.

A day's march from Gesoriacum they had been met by a messenger from Plautius with new orders. In the army commander's opinion – and here Vespasian detected the hand of Narcissus – it would not be wise to use the Second Legion to put down the mutiny. It would be more efficacious for the mutiny to be settled by negotiation rather than direct action. For the army to go into a major campaign with the memory of bloody repression fresh in their minds would be foolhardy. A delay in crossing the thin strip of sea between Gaul and Britain would have to be tolerated as the price to be paid for quelling the mutiny.

Worse news, as far as Vespasian was concerned, followed: the Second Legion would not be included in the first wave of the invasion. Two other legions had been training for amphibious operations for several months and to them would fall the honour of fighting their way ashore and establishing a beachhead for the rest of the army. Vespasian knew that if the Britons decided to meet the invaders on the beaches then all the glory and political capital would go to the commanders and officers of the spearhead units. He gloomily foresaw a long period of mopping-up operations stretching ahead of him; a nasty process of attrition that would win no garlands and be a mere footnote to the epic tales of victory that would be told on the streets of Rome.

If the mutiny could be put down, he reflected.

As he had made his way through the main camp to report to Plautius, it had been heart-breaking for the legate to see the collapse of discipline in the other legions. Few of the soldiers he rode past bothered to salute and, although no-one had actually said anything to him, the look of defiance in their eyes – daring him to try and exercise his authority – enraged Vespasian. Only the army commander's personal bodyguard and the officers remained in full uniform, carrying out their normal duties as far as they were able to.

Vespasian was shown into the wooden headquarters building dominating the centre of the huge army camp, where Narcissus was seated at a great map table with General Plautius. Vespasian had known Plautius socially before he had joined the army and he was shocked to see the weary, beaten expression on the general's face.

'Good to see you again,' said Plautius with a smile. 'It's been a long time. I just wish it was under happier circumstances. Have you met Narcissus?'

'No, sir, though his reputation precedes him.'

'A good reputation, I trust?' Narcissus asked.

Vespasian nodded, not willing to perjure his true opinion.

'I must thank you for your unit's protection, legate.'

'I'll pass word of your gratitude on to the men concerned, if you haven't already thanked them.'

'You are most kind.'

'Now, your report please, Vespasian.' Plautius waved him to a seat. 'How is your legion?'

'They are still responding to orders, if that's what you mean, sir.'

'For the moment maybe. In a few days they'll be just like the others.'

'Have you found the ringleaders of the mutiny yet?' Vespasian asked.

'Thanks to Narcissus we have the names. Tribune Aurelius, two centurions and twenty or so legionaries. All were transferred to the Ninth from the Dalmatian legions, complete with their previous loyalties, as you'd expect.'

'Have they made any demands?'

'Only that the invasion be abandoned. They've managed to persuade the others that demons and certain death are the only things waiting for them on the other side of the ocean.'

'Not that it's much of an ocean,' Narcissus added. 'But the word has a certain depressing effect on the imagination of military types. Present company excepted, of course.' He smiled. 'I'm afraid we are dealing with some quite well-thought-through treason, gentlemen. More sophisticated than anything that Tribune Aurelius and his little band of mutineers could come up with. You see, Vespasian, the general and I have already decided to eliminate this group. But first we must try and discover the identity of their masters back in Rome. Aurelius and his men were only exposed when my agents intercepted a message en route to his masters in Rome. Unfortunately, the courier expired before he could be induced to divulge the name of the intended recipient. Such is life – or not, in his case. Then there is the little matter of the ambush on the road from Durocortorum. Evidently the opposition got wind of my travel arrangements and the purpose of my journey. It appears that someone on "our side" is not quite what they seem.'

'I had news of the attack. I heard that you had prisoners. Have they said anything yet?'

'Not much, I'm afraid, before they died,' Narcissus replied, with regret at the inconvenience. 'The interrogators were quite thorough, but only managed to confirm that they were Syrians, supposedly a group of deserters raiding the area. That's all we got before I had their throats cut.'

'A raiding party?' Vespasian shook his head. 'Doubtful enough. But to attack an army unit . . .'

'Quite,' Narcissus replied. 'It's not remotely possible. Their loyalty to their masters does – did – them credit. But there's a more worrying factor. I've had news that a few days ago an entire squadron of Syrian horse-archers supposedly deserted from an auxiliary cohort that was marching from Dalmatia to join this army.'

'Dalmatia?' Vespasian pondered. 'From Scribonianus's command?'

'Exactly.'

'I see. Whose unit?'

'Gaius Marcellus Dexter,' Narcissus replied, watching the legate closely.

'The name's familiar, my wife might know him. Do you think the men who attacked you are from that unit?' Vespasian asked.

'We'll know soon enough. The cohort is due here in three days' time. The bodies will keep until then and someone should be able to identify them.'

'If they are from that unit,' Plautius added, 'then this plot spreads far wider than we first feared. The question is, can we stamp it out in time for an invasion this year?'

'We have to, my dear Plautius,' Narcissus said firmly. 'There's no question of the operation not proceeding. The Emperor himself has arranged to join the army in Britain.'

'Has he?' Vespasian turned to Plautius. 'But I thought you were to be the supreme commander, sir?'

'Apparently not.' Plautius shrugged. 'The Emperor's right-hand man here has told me to summon the Emperor to our "rescue" once the army stands outside the Trinovantes's capital.'

'Relax, General,' Narcissus said with a gentle pat of Plautius's hand, which the other man withdrew as if it had been slithered over by a snake. 'It's just good public relations. You'll be in charge right through the campaign. Claudius is there to act as a figurehead, to lead the triumphant army into their capital, hand out the gongs and then rush back to Rome for the triumph.'

'If the Senate awards one,' Vespasian reminded him.

'It's already in the bag,' Narcissus smiled. 'I like to plan ahead as far as possible, keeps things simple for the historians. So Claudius gets his triumph, the Empire gains a new province, we all avoid a nasty civil war, and our careers are safeguarded for the foreseeable future – which, I admit, is never quite as long as one would like. It all comes up roses, provided—'

'We end the mutiny and get the legions on to the ships,' Plautius finished wearily.

'Precisely.'

'And how,' Vespasian broke in, 'do we achieve that?'

'I have a little plan.' Narcissus tapped his nose. 'Can't let anyone else in on it if it is to stand a chance of working. But, trust me, it's a corker.'

'And if it doesn't work?' asked Vespasian.

'Then I'll save you a space on the cross next to me.'

Once the Second Legion had settled down for the night and the sentries had been issued with strict orders not to permit any men to move in or out of the camp, Vespasian summoned Macro to make his full report. He had received a preliminary account earlier but, in the present hush-hush atmosphere dominating army headquarters, Vespasian wanted to glean as much information as possible. Night had long fallen when the centurion was quietly ushered into the tent and stood at attention before the legate's desk. Vespasian was catching up on some paperwork by the guttering light of a pair of oil lamps. Once the leather tent flap had fallen back into place, the legate set down his stylus and closed the ink pot.

'Tough journey, I hear?'

'Yes, sir.'

'Lose many men?'

'Eight killed, six of the wounded are still in the Ninth's hospital recovering.'

'The losses will be made up from the recruit pool.'

'Yes, sir.'

'Now I want the full story, Centurion. Leave nothing out and tell it just as it happened, no embellishments.'

With Macro standing at attention and staring at the back of the tent above the legate's head, the tale of the march, the ambush and the final day's journey to Gesoriacum was delivered in a prosaic monotone while Vespasian listened attentively. When the centurion had finished Vespasian looked sharply at him.

'And you told no-one the nature of your mission?'

'No-one, sir. The orders were very clear on that.'

'So we can assume that your attackers were not acting on inside information?'

'Yes, sir.' Macro nodded before committing his own opinion on the matter. 'They were no ordinary bunch of thieves and crooks. Those men laid on an excellent ambush and fought like regulars. It was clear they were after the imperial secretary.'

'I see.' Vespasian nodded, hiding his disappointment; nothing the centurion had said added significantly to what he already knew. If Macro was to be believed then Narcissus's attackers had acquired information about his route from outside the Legion. That should narrow things down for the imperial chief secretary – if the centurion was telling the truth.

'Centurion, may I ask you for a personal opinion – strictly off the record?'

Macro shifted uneasily. He would like to have replied 'It depends', but a soldier did not set conditions for his response to a superior officer, so he had to agree – while emphasising his reluctance as far as possible. 'Yes, sir, I suppose so.'

'Do you consider the invasion of Britain to be wise?'

'That's state policy, sir,' Macro replied warily. 'Far too high up for me. I guess the Emperor and his staff have thought it all through and made the right decision. I don't even have an opinion.'

'I did say it was off the record.'

'Yes, sir.' Macro inwardly cursed his legate for placing him in this tortuous situation. Nothing a subordinate ever said was 'off the record', if a superior chose to change his mind later on.

'So?'

'I simply don't know enough about it to voice an opinion that would be useful to you, sir.'

So, that line of enquiry was stalled, Vespasian realised. A more indirect approach was needed, one that would absolve the centurion of responsibility for what he said.

'What are the men saying about it?'

'The men, sir? Well, some of them are worried, quite naturally – none of us likes to be any nearer to water than the next drink. Anything could happen at sea. And then there's stories about the dangers waiting for us.'

'You're not afraid of their army?'

'Not afraid as such, sir. Only concerned, as much as any man facing a new kind of enemy should be. It's, well, more to do with the druids, sir. Them and their kind.'

'What about the druids?'

'The men have heard that they have the power to summon up demons.'

'And you believe this?'

'Of course not, sir.' Macro was offended. 'Anyone with half a mind can see it's a load of bollocks. But you know what the men are like with their superstitions.'

'Not so long ago I believe you were one of the men.'

'Yes, sir.'

'But you're not superstitious? Like them?'

'No, sir. I gave most of that up when I became a centurion. A centurion hasn't much time for that sort of stuff.'

'Where did your men hear about these druids?'

'Some of our foragers ran into men from the main camp yesterday, sir. They told them about the druids, then they let on about the mutiny.'

'They called it a mutiny?' asked Vespasian. 'Be quite sure about that.'

'Well, no, sir. They said they were still loyal to the Emperor and that the invasion must be some crackpot scheme of Narcissus's that no sane man would pursue. Call it what you like, it's still mutiny to me, sir.'

'And the other men feel as you do about this?'

'As far as I can tell, sir.'

'Very good, Centurion. Very good.' Vespasian eased himself back in his chair. So far so good. For the moment at least the Legion was loyal. But, unless Narcissus's little scheme worked its magic, then it would only be a matter of time before the Second Legion was riven by the same contagion that had hit the other units. However, as long as the officers like Macro acted their part, the spread of the mutiny might be contained for a few weeks at least.

Chapter Thirty

While the men of the Sixth century watched the rest of the Legion settle in around them, Cato left the tent lines and hurried between the mass of men, animals and transport wagons to the area allocated for the legate's quarters. The headquarters staff and the wagons allotted to Vespasian's household were just entering the area set aside for vehicles behind the tent site. Since summer was fast approaching and the Legion would only be encamped for two months at most prior to the invasion, the army staff officers had marked the camp out for tents rather than wooden barracks.

Cato kept far enough back from the wagons to avoid attracting attention and looked for any sign of Lavinia. The wagons were drawn up alongside each other by heaving, cursing muleteers. Their passengers climbed down to begin the tiring process of unpacking the travel chests, carrying them into the large tents being hauled up on tall tent poles by teams of legionaries straining on guy ropes. Cato's eyes alighted on the household wagons and his frantically searching gaze was finally rewarded by the sight of Lavinia descending from the legate's personal coach with Titus clenched under one arm. Cato resisted the temptation to wave or call out, and tried to look as inconspicuous as possible as he stood still amongst the crowds of legionaries toiling away. He watched Lavinia follow her mistress as Flavia marched into one of the erected tents. Cato stared at the entrance for a long time before he turned and walked slowly away.

He wandered through the Legion until dusk when the meal call was sounded and he realised he was hungry. Cato had had no appetite at midday as he nervously anticipated the arrival of the Legion and news of Lavinia and the injured sentry; an odd mix of heartache and dread that was peculiarly painful. By the time he had rejoined the century the sun had set and the shapes of men and tents were grey and indistinct against the pale glow of the horizon. Cooking fires had been lit and the first faint odours of yet another stew wafted into the rapidly cooling air. Cato had been assigned to the second watch and wanted a full belly before he had to follow the senior watch officer on his rounds, collecting the tokens from each station on the walls and gates. As he sat by the section fire and mopped up the last remnants of his meal with some freshly baked bread, Macro squatted down by his side.

'Where've you been?'

'I just went for a walk, sir.'

'A walk, eh? I don't suppose you happened to pass the general's quarters?'

Cato smiled.

'I suppose it's that woman of yours. Still carrying the candle for that little bint?' Macro shook his head wonderingly. 'What did I tell you about all this before –

back at the base? A soldier who lets his feelings cloud his thinking is a soldier distracted, and the army can't afford distraction. Put her out of your mind, boy. As a matter of fact, I might be able to help out in that direction. Some of the lads and I are heading into the town later on tonight – I've wangled a pass to purchase barley supplies for the cohort. We've been told where to find a nice little inn that offers something a little more tasty than the local brew. You might want to join us once you've finished your watch.'

'Is that an order, sir?'

Macro stared coldly at him. 'Well, fuck you, lover boy. I'm just trying to help out. But if you want to sit and sulk rather than have a drink with some mates and get your end away, then it's your funeral.'

Cato knew he was in the wrong. The sour note of his reply had been impulsive and now he regretted the offence it had caused.

'Sir. I'm not ungrateful for the offer. I just don't feel like it right now. I can't help it.'

'Can't help it?' snorted Macro. 'Suit yourself then.'

He quickly rose to his feet and stormed off, with one final black look at Cato before entering his tent.

While he waited for his watch to begin, Cato sank into a mood of despair. Perhaps the centurion was right? What kind of romance could he carry on with a girl he could never see? She was, moreover, a dangerous girl to know, given that she could testify that he'd been in the legate's tent that night. If for any reason she was indiscreet, then both of them would be up in front of Vespasian. And the truth, about the other man, was hardly likely to be believed. The best move would be to forget her, forget about love and get on with life. Perhaps he would join Macro and the others after all.

Shortly after the change of the second watch, when all but a few diehards were sound asleep, the sentry on the main gate saw two figures walking down the road towards the camp. He called out for the password and, when he received no immediate reply, he lowered his javelin point and challenged them again.'

'Relax soldier!' a voice called out. 'We're friends.'

'Password!'

'We're friends, I tell you! From the other camp.'

'Keep your fucking distance!' the sentry shouted, slightly relieved that the strangers spoke Latin.

'We want to speak with your commander. We have a pass signed by General Plautius himself. Let us in.'

'No! Stay where you are.' The thickset sentry took a pace back and pointed his javelin at the two figures scarcely ten feet away. Now, by the dim light of the stars, he could see that one man was tall and thin, wearing a dark, hooded cloak. The other was a giant of a man who wore a sword in a scabbard at his side. 'Optio! Optio of the watch! Come down here quick!'

The side-passage gate opened and the optio marched over, munching on a hunk of bread soaked in wine.

'What is it? Better not be another false alarm, I'm still bloody eating.'

'This man wants to speak to the legate.'

'Has he given you the password?'

'No, sir.'

'Then tell him to fuck off – you should bloody well know the regulations by now.'

'If I might interrupt?' The taller figure took two paces nearer.

'Stay exactly where you are, pal,' the optio growled.

'I have business with the legate,' the man insisted, then he brought out a small slate from his cloak. 'See here, I've a pass authorised by Aulus Plautius.'

The optio approached cautiously and quickly took the slate held out to him, before retiring towards the open side-gate, which provided just enough light to read the message. The pass was in order and the ring seal pressed into the wax surface bore the eagle of a commanding general. Still, the optio considered, it might just be a fake. Given the strictness with which camp regulations and restrictions of movement to and from the gates were being enforced, the legate and his senior officers were clearly jumpy about something.

The optio paused: a person bearing a pass authorised by Plautius himself must hold some kind of rank. 'Please wait here, sir.'

'Commendable security you have here,' Narcissus said, somewhat later, as he accepted a drink from Vespasian. 'It was quite difficult persuading the senior watch officer to let us see you, even with the general's pass. Your soldiers are sticklers for the rules.'

'No rules – no order – no civilisation – no Rome.' Vespasian trotted out the old adage and raised his glass to Narcissus. 'But I'm glad you came, for whatever reason of your own. I needed to speak to you alone.'

'Then our interests happily coincide.'

'What about him?' Vespasian nodded at the imperial secretary's bodyguard looming in the shadows, still and silent.

'Ignore him,' said Narcissus. 'I take it we're safe in here?'

'Absolutely. All entrances are well guarded.'

'Oh yes?' Narcissus took a small sip of wine as he fixed Vespasian with his eyes. 'That's not what my sources tell me.'

Vespasian coloured. 'Your spy told you about that?'

'I was informed that a sentry had been injured by an intruder. I take it nothing was stolen. Nothing important that is.'

'Nothing.' Vespasian said firmly, forcing himself to keep his eyes fixed on those of Narcissus.

'So what happened?'

'As far as I know, a slave girl was due to meet her lover in my command tent. He didn't show and she waited a while and then left. Shortly afterwards the guards came across someone in the tent. He injured a sentry and fled the scene. A dropped torch set fire to the tent, but we managed to get it out without too much damage being done. And that is all there is to tell.'

Narcissus stared at him and slowly took another sip. 'You tortured the girl?'

'It wasn't necessary.'

'Really? There are some officers who get a kick out of that sort of thing.'

'If you think—' Vespasian half rose from his chair and the figure in the shadows moved quickly forwards. Narcissus waved the bodyguard back.

'I think nothing of the sort. I just wondered if you had managed to get any more information out of her.'

'Just what I said.'

'And the man's name? The one she said she had arranged to meet.'

'Look here, Narcissus, I run my Legion, and if there are any problems to solve then I'll sort them out. You're a freedman, you don't give orders to a legate. This isn't Saturnalia, you know.'

Narcissus gave him a curious smile. 'It's funny you should say that. But no matter . . . I want the man's name.'

Vespasian did not reply immediately. Much as he disliked Vitellius he was reluctant to give information that might lead an innocent man to his destruction. An innocent man now – but possibly a political rival later. Or an ally. Nothing was written in stone.

'It would be best that you tell me now,' Narcissus said quietly. 'Before I get Polythemus to ask you.'

'How dare you?' Vespasian recoiled in shock. 'You threaten me in my own tent? Why, man, I could call out for my guards now and have you, and your brute there, crucified just like that!' He tried to snap his fingers with a crack but his damp hand made no sound.

The failure of the gesture was not lost on Narcissus and he allowed himself a small smile of satisfaction before he continued in a more conciliatory tone.

'I fear you misunderstand our relative worth in the eyes of the Emperor. Aristocrats with pretensions to political greatness are ten a sestertius. Some undoubtedly have considerable talents – you are such a one – but they are freaks within their own class. Generations of inbreeding have produced nothing more than idle, arrogant idiots. We – the Emperor – can replace you easily enough. I, on the other hand, am irreplaceable. How do you imagine a mere freedman has been able to rise to become the Emperor's right-hand man? There is more intelligence, more cunning and more cruelty in my little finger than in your whole body. Remember that, Vespasian. Remember it before you even think to upbraid me.'

Vespasian clamped his mouth shut to stop up the torrent of rage churning inside him. He gripped the edges of his chair tightly and swallowed.

'Excellent.' Narcissus nodded slowly. 'It's good that you're smart enough to accept an unpalatable truth when it is presented to you. You will grow to understand the importance of that when you return to Rome. I'm glad I was right about you.'

'And how were you right about me?' Vespasian asked through clenched teeth.

'Your brain rules your heart, and your pride knows its place. Now, be a good fellow and tell me the name of the man the slave girl was supposed to meet in your tent.'

'Vitellius. She said it was Vitellius.'

'Vitellius? Now that is very interesting, wouldn't you say? A senior tribune engaged in a liaison with a slave girl in the legate's command tent where, no doubt, some very sensitive documents were being stored. I find that very interesting. Not to mention suggestive. Don't you?'

Vespasian just stared coldly back.

'Do you still have the letter?'

'Yes.'

'You're clear about what has to be done?'

'Of course, but finding a wagon dumped in a bog a hundred years ago won't be easy.'

'Then you'd better get some good men for the job. Keep the numbers down – the less who know what's going on, the better – and make sure they are discreet.'

'I have a few men in mind.'

'Fine. That chest has to be located and once you've got it, guard it with your life. When the Emperor arrives with the reinforcements the chest will be passed over to a special unit of the Praetorian Guard for shipment to Rome. And then you will forget that you ever knew about it. You and those men you choose to carry out the mission.'

Narcissus pushed his cup away and rose to his feet. 'Now, I'm afraid I must go. Thanks for your hospitality, Vespasian. And relax. I'm sure the Emperor will be deeply gratified when I report how co-operative you have been.'

'Before you leave, tell me one thing.'

'Yes.'

'Who is the imperial spy in my legion? I must know who I can trust once we arrive in Britain.'

'Then he would lose his value to me.'

'Like being able to report on me, for instance?'

'Of course.'

'Then, at least tell me who the traitor is,' Vespasian asked. 'I need to know which direction to guard myself against.'

Narcissus tried to look sympathetic. 'I don't know. I

suspect, but I can't be sure yet – I need further proof. If I say anything that causes you to treat the people around you differently then the other side's spy will know we are closing in. Nothing must be done to alert suspicion. You speak to no-one about this matter. Not even your wife. Understand?'

Vespasian nodded. 'I understand that you're putting me in danger.'

'You're a soldier. Get used to it.'

With that, the imperial chief secretary turned his back on the legate and left the tent, summoning his bodyguard from the shadows with a waggle of a finger. Alone, Vespasian fumed with silent frustration. He had managed to get himself off the hook for the theft of the letter, for the moment. But he was no nearer finding a way out of the dark threads of intrigue that bound him so tightly.

Outside, Narcissus paused. There was no sign that Vespasian had ordered them to be followed. He turned to his bodyguard.

'Make sure that I'm not tailed. If I call out, come as quickly as you can.'

He walked off quietly, and a few moments later the bodyguard followed, hugging the shadows and keeping a keen eye on his master. Narcissus walked down the line of tribunes' tents, then paused outside an entrance flap. When he was sure he was unobserved, he entered hurriedly. Inside, the imperial spy was waiting for him, as had been arranged earlier in the day by secret messenger. He rose from his campaign seat to greet the imperial secretary.

'Keeping well, sir?'

Narcissus grasped the hand that was extended towards him and smiled. 'Yes, Vitellius, very well. Now, we need a little talk about that scroll I told you about a few months ago. Moreover, I'm curious to know why you omitted to tell me about your arranging to be in the legate's tent the night it was burgled.'

Vitellius frowned. 'But I wasn't in the tent.'

'That's not what Vespasian says. He questioned some slave girl who said she had arranged to meet you in there.'

'It's not true. I swear it's not true.'

Narcissus watched him closely and then nodded in satisfaction at the response. 'All right. I believe you . . . for the moment. But if it's not true, then why would she say so? Or why would she be told to say so?'

'Told? Who by?'

'That, my dear Vitellius, is what you were sent here to find out.'

Chapter Thirty-one

'Cato! How on earth did you get in here?'

'Brought a report from my centurion to headquarters, my lady. Somehow I lost my way trying to get out. And here I am.'

Flavia laughed as she rose from the floor. She had been busy packing a campaign chest for her husband and the wooden flooring was covered in neat piles of tightly folded clothes. 'You look awful. Rough night?'

'Yes, my lady. I went into Gesoriacum.'

'When will you youngsters learn? Still, I don't suppose you've come here to explain yourself to me. So you might want to go and inspect progress on the nursery I'm having built for Titus.'

'My lady?'

'I've put Lavinia in charge of some household slaves to spruce up the nursery. She wanted a word with you. And I dare say you wouldn't mind seeing her again.' Flavia winked. 'Now run along and let me get back to work. Go out that flap, it's the third entrance on the left. Oh, and don't let anyone catch you in here.'

As Cato walked slowly the way Flavia had indicated, his mind raced. Desperate as he was to see Lavinia, there were still questions in his mind about that night in the legate's tent. He needed to know if she had said anything to anyone about him. Clearly Flavia knew he had been there, but who else? He paused at the entrance to the nursery.

Cato steeled himself and stepped inside. The interior was cluttered with children's toys and clothing. Squatting amongst the mess were several of Flavia's household slaves, busily striving to make a comfortable place for a child to play. Sitting to one side, happily painting a farm animal on to a small screen, was Lavinia. She had not seen Cato enter and jumped when he softly called her name from a few feet away.

'Now look what you've made me do.' She laughed, pointing her brush at the screen. 'There's a tail on my cow's head.'

'Cow?' Cato could have sworn it was a horse.

Lavinia turned to face him. For a moment her expression was serious and his heart sank. Then she reached out for his hands and smiled.

'I was worried about you, after I heard about that sentry.'

'Why didn't you come back?'

'I couldn't. When I got back to my quarters, my lady Flavia said she needed me, said Titus was ill. I couldn't see anything wrong with him but she told me to stay with him while she went to find some medicine. By the time she got back everyone was shouting. I'm glad you got out before that nasty business with the guard happened. I can't tell you how worried I've been. I felt really bad about leaving you alone in the tent. I'm sorry I did, truly I am.'

Cato squeezed her hands. 'It's all right. I'm just glad you were safe. When that man came into the tent I was afraid you'd walk right into him when you came back. I think he'd have killed you.'

'Other man?'

'Yes, you didn't think it was me who attacked that sentry?'

'No . . . but who?'

'I don't know. When he discovered I was there he nearly did for me. I shouted for help and, when the sentry appeared, the man attacked him and vanished. I got out as quickly as I could.'

'I see.'

'Anyway, I was so glad to see you safe when the wagons arrived at the camp.'

'Were you glad? Really?'

'Of course.'

'That's so sweet.' She leaned forward and kissed him on the mouth. 'You do care for me, don't you?'

He said nothing and kissed her back, for longer this time, his heart pounding against the warm softness pressed against his chest. When their lips parted he looked into her eyes, feeling cheap for what he was about to ask.

'Has the sentry identified anyone yet?'

'He's dead. He died back in Durocortorum. My mistress only had word of it this morning. He never spoke a word – so you're safe.'

'Does anyone, apart from Flavia, know that I was there that night?'

'No. But the legate knows I was there. He found my hair ribbon.'

'What did you say to him?' Cato felt a finger of ice trace its way down his spine.

'I told him I was going to meet someone else there and that when he didn't show up I went to bed. That's all I told him. I swear.'

'I believe you. Who did you say you were going to meet?'

'Tribune Vitellius.'

'Why him?' Cato felt uneasy about Vitellius being fitted up in this manner. A vision came to mind of the tribune issuing orders in the flames of the German village. It would be a low thing to do to cast suspicion on him.

'Because my mistress told me to say so. Apparently her husband doesn't like him, and thinks there's something suspicious about him. He seemed the natural choice, she said.'

'It doesn't seem quite right.' Cato started to protest but Lavinia pulled him close and kissed him again.

'Hush! It doesn't matter. As long as no-one suspects you. That's all that matters to me. Now then,' she continued, pulling him to a screened-off area of the tent that was to be used as a changing area, 'we haven't much time and there's a lot we have to catch up on.'

'Wait. What do you mean, we haven't much time?'

'My mistress is returning to Rome soon. She's taking me with her.'

Cato felt sick.

'I'll try and wait for you in Rome,' she said gently.

'I might never return. And even if I do, it might be years from now.'

'It might be . . . It might not. Either way there's not much we can do about it right now.' Lavinia gently took his hand. 'We haven't got long, so come with me.'

'What about them?' Cato nodded at the other slaves.

'They won't mind us.'

She pulled Cato through a pair of curtains into Titus's sleeping chamber and drew the curtains behind them. A soft pile of folded materials had been neatly arranged over the floorboards, and Lavinia gently pushed Cato down on to his back. As he lay still, heart pounding, his eyes travelled down her body to where her hands were lifting the hem of her tunic.

'Now then,' said Lavinia, 'where were we?'

Chapter Thirty-two

A few days later, the cohorts of the three mutinous legions were gathered in the turf amphitheatre that had been built outside the camp. They were guests of Plautius and Narcissus, who had paid for a day's gladiatorial entertainment in the name of the Emperor, and sat with Vespasian and other senior officers in the comfort of the box. Throughout the morning and into the afternoon a lavish display of beasts and men shed their blood on the sand in the arena. The men's enjoyment had been lubricated by a generous issue of wine and a cheerfully boisterous mood filled the amphitheatre as the spectacle drew to a close.

Down on the sand, the last gladiatorial fight reached its inevitable conclusion. As usual, the Retarius had had the best of it and now stood over his victim, trident poised at the throat of the heavily armoured Mirmillo helplessly enmeshed in his net. The Retarius looked towards the audience for a decision. Against the odds, the Mirmillo had put on a decent show and all around the arena thumbs were raised to have him spared. After the briefest hesitation, Narcissus turned his thumb down. The men instantly roared out their disapproval and surged towards the box where the senior officers were sitting. Right on cue, Plautius jumped to his feet and raised his arm high for all to see, thumb up. The howls of outrage abruptly turned into cheers of approval and the crowd turned back to the arena where Narcissus was alarmed to see the Retarius already taking a bow. The fool! If the legionaries got the slightest inkling the thing had been set up . . . but far too much wine had flowed and all but the sharpest minds were dulled to the elaborate performance that was being enacted before them.

Narcissus suddenly rose to his feet and, without any warning, jumped over the edge of the box. Making his way to the centre of the arena, he raised his hands for silence.

The legionaries had not been expecting this and quickly fell silent, waiting with curious expectation, still in high spirits. A few were whispering, but were hushed by their comrades as Narcissus waited for absolute quiet.

When all was still Narcissus raised his arm in a dramatic gesture.

'My friends! Romans! Legionaries! Hear me!' he called out in a deep rolling voice. 'You all know me. I am the Emperor's secretary and, while I do not speak in Claudius's place and am only a freedman, I count myself as being as Roman as any of you.'

A small murmur of disapproval rippled through the audience as Narcissus blatantly assumed the mantle of Rome and ignored the sensitive distinction between Roman citizen and mere freedman.

'I say again, my heart is as Roman as any man's here!' At this, he ripped his tunic open and bared his thin white chest to the audience. A few could not help but titter at the sight. 'And because I am Roman in all but name I come here to say to you that I, Narcissus, am sickened by what I see. That men who I count as fellow Romans should rise in mutiny against the heroic generals of Rome, who you are privileged to serve and to whom you should be honoured to lay down your lives for, chills my blood to ice! That a great man, from one of our greatest families – Aulus Plautius!' Narcissus thrust his hand out towards the general. 'That he should suffer the shame and ignominy of your treacherous mutiny makes me weep!'

Narcissus half turned and buried his face in a fold of his tunic while huge sobs wracked his body. Some of the men were laughing openly now at the freedman's histrionics.

Narcissus took a deep breath and swooped round to face his audience, tears streaming down his face. 'COWARDS! Ungrateful cowards who dare call yourselves Romans! If you shall not follow the brave and honoured Plautius then lend your arms to a man who will! I shall invade Britain! Alone, if I must. So lend me your arms!'

The imperial secretary held out his hands imploring the audience to give him their weapons.

'All right, you old bastard, have this!' A legionary stood and tossed his sword at Narcissus, who ducked back in alarm. Then all at once others followed suit and swords and daggers rained down on to the arena, as Narcissus dived backwards for his own safety, accidentally stepping on the hem of his torn tunic and rolling over backwards. The legionaries roared with laughter.

Vespasian smiled and then forced himself not to laugh as the imperial secretary went down again. His face burning with embarrassment and anger, Narcissus jumped to his feet and snatched up one of the swords.

'Laugh at me? You dare to laugh at me? I'm the one who's prepared to fight. I'm not sitting on my fat arse doing nothing. I'm the only one here worthy to carry the sword and glorious eagles against the barbarian hordes!'

Some of the men were crying with laughter at the ludicrous spectacle, and Narcissus rushed to the front of the stage and swung his sword at them, totally misjudging the swing. He spun round and the sword dug into the sand at his feet. Panting, he struggled to regain his wind.

'Weak, am I, from a lifetime serving Rome, and yet I would do what you are afraid to, and you call yourselves Romans! Why should I beg you to go back to your officers? Why should I even ask? No – I order you to end this mutiny. I command it!'

This was too much for the troops, who hooted with laughter and, from somewhere in the crowd, a voice called out, 'Ho Saturnalia! Ho Saturnalia!' The cry of the public holiday when social ranks were reversed was taken up by others, and spread quickly until all of them chorused, 'Ho Saturnalia!' and pelted the arena with whatever refuse was to hand. With a last shake of his fist and some inaudible cry of defiance, Narcissus turned and ran from the arena.

For some time the legionaries still shouted 'Ho Saturnalia' until it was clear that Narcissus had left the stage for good. Then slowly the men dispersed, trickling, then streaming, out of the amphitheatre and back towards the main camp.

'Well, I hope it's worked,' said Plautius.

'A fascinating team-building exercise,' Vespasian reflected. 'It'll be interesting to see if Narcissus has managed to shame them back to their duties. Can you imagine how the rest of the army will react when word gets out that a freedman has spoken to them like that? Now, if you'll excuse me, sir?'

'What? Oh, all right. Whatever you will. I need a drink.'

Vespasian left his superior and hurried down to the holding cells at the side of the amphitheatre.

'Anyone seen the imperial secretary?'

'Here I am.' A voice piped up and Narcissus emerged from the dark recesses. 'Safe to come out?'

'Only just!' laughed Vespasian. 'That was quite a performance.'

'Thank you.'

'I'm just curious. Is there no indignity you wouldn't suffer to further your cause?'

'My cause? That humiliation you just witnessed wasn't for me. I did it for the Emperor and Rome. One day you'll learn, Vespasian,' Narcissus continued bitterly. 'One day you'll realise that the only thing that keeps any state running is the number of bureaucrats who are prepared to eat shit to keep it going. That's the measure of their commitment. And the fact that they are never mentioned by historians is the measure of their success. You'd do well to remember that.'

'Oh, I will. But what made you think of trying that strategy?'

'It's a cynical age,' Narcissus replied. 'A direct appeal for patriotism was bound to fail, so a different approach was needed. I just pray to the Gods that it's enough. Do you think it'll work?'

'We'll have to wait and see.'

'Yes. Can I take shelter in your camp tonight?'

'No-one else will have you,' said Vespasian with a grin. 'Do you want an escort back to the camp?'

'I need to have a word with someone first. There's still a little matter that needs sorting out. See you later.'

The imperial chief secretary threw a military tunic over his torn clothes, then scuttled off back towards the main army camp. Vespasian returned to his headquarters and passed the word for Macro to be brought to him.

Shortly afterwards a hastily spruced-up centurion was standing to attention in front of the legate's desk.

'Centurion Macro, in view of your proven fighting qualities and discretion over that escort business, the imperial chief secretary and I have got a little job for you once we land in Britain . . .'

The festival atmosphere deriving from the afternoon's events in the amphitheatre lasted well into the night until the riotous soldiers had drunk the army base dry and returned to their quarters to sleep it off. Those too drunk to stand found themselves a quiet corner and slumped down. And so, in the dark hours before dawn, few were around to witness what followed.

A small detail of centurions, led by Vitellius and Pulcher, accompanied a wagon as they made their way through the base arresting men named on a list supplied by Narcissus. Most of the victims were veterans who had joined the eagles in the last years of Augustus's reign and despised the moral decline that had followed when first Tiberius, and then Caligula, became Emperor. Most were too drunk or tired to put up a fight as they were dragged out of their tents. Pulcher saw to it that they were securely bound before being thrown into the back of a wagon. When one of the more alert tried to shout for help, Pulcher promptly cut his throat and threatened to do the same to the very next man who muttered a single word. And so, as the sky lightened in the east, the little procession silently passed through the gates of the camp and made for a distant forest where it halted in a clearing well beyond earshot of the slumbering legions.

While Vitellius went to report back to Narcissus, the bound men were rolled off the back of the wagon and dragged into a rough line. They knelt fearfully eyeing Pulcher as he slowly walked up and down, a dreadful smile fixed on his scarred face. Once the line was complete he casually drew his dagger.

'Right then, traitors, you've had your fun. Now it's my turn. I need names. I need to know who gives you your orders from Rome. Now, while I appreciate that most of you will not be in the know over this, frankly I don't care. If I get names – you live, if I don't – you die. That's all there is to it.'

Pulcher approached a grey-haired veteran at the end of the line.

'You're first. Names?'

The man pursed his lips and spat on Pulcher's feet. Without the slightest hesitation Pulcher grabbed a fistful of hair and yanked the man's head back. The dagger flashed across his throat and a sheet of crimson splashed on to the forest floor. Pulcher let go and the man collapsed, writhed a moment, and then was still.

'Okay, who's next?'

Shortly after dawn, Pulcher returned to the camp of the Second Legion to find Tribune Vitellius. He presented a list of names scratched on to a waxed tablet. Grim-faced, Vitellius ran his finger down the list – there were few surprises – until his finger stopped abruptly.

'Are you sure about this last one?' he asked sharply.

'That's what the man said.'

'That explains how the opposition got to know about Narcissus's visit so speedily. Who gave you this name?'

'Aurelius, senior tribune of the Ninth. He's well connected in Rome.'

'I know that, thank you,' Vitellius replied testily. 'I don't suppose there's any chance of having a word with Tribune Aurelius?'

Pulcher shook his head. 'You said they were to disappear. I've been my usual thorough self, I'm afraid.'

'That's a pity. I would have liked to confirm this name myself. But we'll just have to accept that Aurelius's information is accurate.'

'Should we tell Narcissus?'

'No, I don't think so. Not just yet at any rate.'

'Right. I'd better get back to the woods then. Need to arrange a bit of digging.'

As the mid-morning sun shed its warm glow on the sentries at the main gates of the camp, a wagon emerged from the treeline of the immense forest that stretched inland from the coast. It was escorted by a party of grim-faced centurions, with Pulcher whistling contentedly in the driver's seat. As the wagon passed into the base the sentries saw that it carried just a few picks and shovels – and a dark stain smeared across its wooden boards.

Chapter Thirty-three

The late afternoon sun slanted across the deck, sliced by the shadows of the mast and rigging of the army transport. In the bows, a sailor was casting a weighted line out ahead of the vessel and reading off the depth as the line touched bottom. The ship eased its way through the entrance of the channel as the captain ordered two more reefs to be put in the sail. While the sailors climbed aloft and spread out along the yardarm, Cato gingerly made his way forward to the base of the stubby bowsprit.

As soon as the transport had drawn out of the port at Gesoriacum and met the gentle swell of the channel a wave of seasickness had engulfed him. Cato had joined several other men at the side of the ship as they spewed their guts up into the foaming sea sweeping past the gently rolling vessel. Macro took the opportunity to munch his way through several pastries he had bought from the harbour market shortly before boarding. He couldn't resist offering the last one to his optio and burst out laughing at the look of pure evil that answered his gesture.

As soon as the transport entered the sheltered waters of the anchorage, Cato felt the terrible nausea subside and, with one hand on the stay, he gazed out over the channel where the invasion fleet lay at anchor. Hundreds of vessels crowded the shimmering surface of the sea; sleek warships with their high crenellated towers rising above the banks of oars lining each side, wide troop transports with shallow drafts wallowing close by the shore and hundreds of smaller craft ferrying in supplies and equipment from Gaul.

The legionaries crowded the sides of the transport to get a better view and were pushed and cursed by the sailors, who still had to handle the vessel as it slowly made its way towards the mainland under a slight breeze. The mysterious fog-ridden island of Britain, so long a part of Roman folklore, lay revealed as a dull coastline basking in the heat of a clear midsummer's day. Excitement was therefore tinged with a sense of disappointment at the gently rolling landscape of farms, fields and forest that stretched away into the distant haze. Here and there, small columns of legionaries spread out across the country while far off the faint dust cloud of the rearguard marked where the main body of the first two legions had pressed ahead inland.

During the last two days the men had heard only the sketchiest details of the progress of the invasion. The crew of the transport who had returned for the second division of the army could only report that the first two legions had managed to land unopposed. As Cato could see, there were no signs of heavy fighting, no funeral pyres of fallen comrades, no bodies of the enemy – in fact no sign of the natives whatsoever. It was hard to believe. Caesar's account made great play of the hazards of invading Britain and recorded that the first landing had been bitterly opposed by an enemy who met the Romans on the beach and almost fought them to a bloody standstill in the pounding surf. This, on the other hand, looked almost identical to the last amphibious exercise with which Plautius had engaged the army on the coast of Gaul barely two weeks earlier: Plenty of Romans but a non-existent enemy.

With a shout from the captain, the transport altered course. The great sail was hauled round at an angle to the deck and the bows swung in from the centre of the channel. The bows steadied on a gap in the lines of shipping close to the shore that had been marked out with large red pennants which lifted lazily in the dying breeze. A number of transports carrying elements of the Second Legion had already landed and Cato could see a group of horsemen riding up the beach and into the flattened grass beyond. That would be Vespasian and his command party rushing ahead to mark out the area where the Legion would assemble for the night before moving off in the wake of the Twentieth and the Ninth Legions.

Except that he would not be marching with them, Cato reflected with a sudden tremor of excitement and fear. While the rest of the Legion marched to meet the enemy, he would be with a small detachment under Macro's command carrying out a special duty. As yet the centurion had not confided the details of the mission and sat apart from his men, at the stern of the vessel staring down into the heavily silted sea. As Cato looked aft, Macro spat into the water and turned forward, immediately catching the eye of his subordinate. He paused a moment, then made his way towards the bows through the tightly packed mass of legionaries in the waist of the transport.

'Not so terrifying after all, is it?' He waved a hand at the shore.

'No, sir,' Cato replied. 'Quite pleasant, really. Looks like it'll make decent farm land once we've settled on it.'

'And what could a palace boy possibly know about horticulture?'

'Not much,' admitted Cato. 'Only what I've read of it from Virgil. He makes farming sound quite fascinating.'

'Quite fascinating,' mimicked Macro. 'Real farming's a hard life – there's no poetry in it. Only townie tossers paying the odd visit to their estates could make it sound good.'

Macro immediately regretted his harsh response and smiled as he patted his optio on the arm. 'I'm sorry, that was uncalled for. It's just that I've got things on my mind right now.'

'What things, sir?'

'Things that concern ranks higher than yours. I'm sorry, Cato, I can't say anything until we're well away from the Legion. Those are my orders.'

'Orders from whom, I wonder,' Cato said quietly. 'Our commander – or Narcissus, perhaps?'

'No use fishing for information – I can't tell you. Just be patient. I'd have thought at least the army would have taught you that by now.'

Cato frowned and turned to look at the approaching fortifications that rose above the beach and the surrounding land.

When Vespasian had issued his orders he had placed great emphasis on the need for utmost secrecy. Of the eleven men Macro had selected for the mission Cato alone had been told about it, and even the optio knew only that he had been selected for a dangerous detached duty. As Macro gazed at the slowly approaching shoreline he recalled the previous evening in Vespasian's tent. The legate had regarded him by the dim light of an oil lamp, as rain pattered on the canvas overhead.

'You will, of course, need a cart for the return journey.'

'Yes, sir.'

'So make sure you draw one from the transport pool – I'll have a clerk make up the necessary orders.' Vespasian drained his cup and carefully contemplated the centurion. 'I trust you appreciate the importance of this mission?'

'Yes, sir. With that kind of money you need someone you can trust, sir.'

'Quite.' Vespasian nodded. 'But there's more to it than that. The Emperor desperately needs every scrap of gold and silver that he can find. The only thing that's keeping him in power at the moment is the support of the army, and more importantly those greedy bastards in the Praetorian guard. Claudius will last only for as long as the donatives flow to the troops. Understand?'

'Yes, sir.'

'So it's vital we recover the chest, and' – Vespasian continued with added emphasis – 'the men you select for the job must know *nothing*. It is likely that the Emperor's enemies have already got wind of this and we dare not show our own hand too openly. If one word of this leaks out to the wrong set of ears, you won't be the only ones after the chest. You have to locate it first. I think you'll find that you have enough danger to face from the natives without worrying about your own side.'

'May I ask exactly who I have to worry about, sir?'

Vespasian shook his head. 'I suspect a few of our comrades-in-arms, but right now I have no evidence.'

'I see.' Macro could see all right. He could see that this mission had an additional agenda: to expose those members of the Legion who might constitute a threat to the Emperor – even if that meant staking Macro and his men out as bait. 'And what happens when—'

'If.'

'If we come across these people? What happens then, sir?'

'Then you prove to me that I've selected the right man for the job. You succeed, in either task, and I promise you that you will not find me, or the Emperor, ungrateful.'

Macro allowed the corners of his mouth to lift in appreciation. A desperately dangerous mission then, but one that should pay off well if it went according to the simple plan Vespasian had outlined. Too simple, Macro reflected.

He was to lead a small party of men and a cart south to the marshes, way beyond the protection of the main army. All contact with natives and Roman army scouts was to be avoided. Once at the marshes he was to use the map Vespasian had provided him with to locate the remains of a wagon sunk in a bog almost a hundred

years earlier. Having located the wagon, the detachment
was to retrieve a chest and load it aboard the cart for the
return journey to the Legion where it was to be handed
over to the legate in person. Under no circumstances
was the chest to be opened. The sight of the treasure
that lay within might well corrupt the minds of the
common legionary. And if the inevitable curiosity of his
men was not enough to contend with, then there was
the prospect of having to fight his way through enemy
territory against both the natives and men supposedly
on his own side who were playing a deep political game.

'Is there anything else you need to know, Centurion?'

'One thing, sir. What happens if we fail to locate this
wagon?'

'Don't even think about it,' Vespasian said simply.

'I see.' Macro nodded.

The legate was glad that he didn't se?. Should the
mission fail, then the chest would remain in the marsh,
waiting for someone else to find it. There was no
guarantee that the original map Narcissus had supplied
him with was the only one, and now that he had entrusted
the centurion with a copy there was no guarantee that
further copies would not be made. If the mission failed,
then it would be very inconvenient to have a handful of
soldiers around with even the slightest inkling of what
lurked in the marshes. But that contingency was taken
care of.

'If that's all, Centurion?' Vespasian asked, and Macro
nodded. 'Then you had better go and prepare your men.
We shan't speak again until you return to the legion with
the chest.'

'Yes, sir.'

'Good luck. And goodbye.'

Once Macro was out of the tent he carefully folded the map and tucked it inside his harness, more than a little uneasy about the tone of finality with which he had been dismissed by the legate. But the mission was now in motion and there was no turning back.

The transport's captain shouted to the crew to let go the sheets and the remaining sail was gathered in. The vessel had just enough way on her to glide forward and a slight tremor could be felt through the deck as she grounded a short distance from the beach.

From the stern the captain cupped his hands and shouted. 'Landing ramp out!'

The legionaries gave way as the crewmen lifted a long, hinged ramp and ran it forward, well beyond its fulcrum, until the end was only a few feet from the shore. A seaman gave the signal and the ramp was allowed to fall with a messy splash into the sea. The rear of the ramp was then pegged into place with two iron rods driven through the ramp into sockets on the deck.

'There you are!' The captain clapped Macro on the shoulder. 'Safely delivered across the ocean by yours truly. Hope you enjoyed the voyage.'

'It was all right,' Macro replied without enthusiasm. Like most soldiers, he thought that land was the proper place for men, and the sea was for fish and any idiots who cared to traverse it. 'But thanks.'

'My pleasure. Just make sure you give the natives a good kicking.'

'We'll do our best.'

'Now I'd be grateful if you'd get your men off my ship. We're returning to Gaul straight away. Some horses to bring over for a Syrian cohort tonight.'

'Tonight?' Macro was surprised. 'I thought you sailors never went to sea at night if you could help it.'

'Normally, no.' The captain smiled affably. 'But we're being paid by the trip and there's money to be made. So, if you wouldn't mind?'

Macro faced forward towards the expectant eyes of his men. 'Okay, lads, off you get. Make sure you don't leave anything on board or you won't see it again.'

In single file the legionaries picked their way down the boarding ramp and, lifting their equipment clear of the sea, they jumped into the waist-deep water and surged on to the beach. By the time Macro and Cato had reached the line of shingle along the high-water mark, the ramp was already being stowed as a team of seamen strained on a long thick pole to push the transport free.

'What's the hurry?' Cato nodded at the ship.

'Money.'

'What men won't do for it!' Cato laughed. 'You'd think there was nothing more important in this world.'

'There isn't.'

The hard-edged expression on his centurion's face caught Cato by surprise and, as Macro turned to call the century to order, Cato stared at him. The man was understandably tense, as every officer had been, even after the mutiny slowly crumbled. Word of Narcissus's extraordinary performance quickly spread through the legions causing great hilarity whenever impromptu renditions of the bureaucrat's bravado were performed. As the wily freedman had intended, the joke could be shared by one and all and the atmosphere of mistrust and betrayal soon evaporated in the mysterious absence of Tribune Aurelius and his associates. Plautius had further soothed the situation by having the retinue of exiled British chiefs and princes let slip tales of the great wealth to be found in Britain; gold, silver, slaves – and women, just begging to be taken from the arms of a handful of benighted savages who insisted on fighting in the altogether. Their fearful appearance – painted bodies and hair stiffened into wild spikes of white – and the endless shouting all counted for little in the thick of battle. The great warriors of the legions would sweep them aside with ease and seize the fruits of victory. A firm resolve to do what legionaries do best gripped the army in the last few weeks of preparation for the invasion.

It was well after dark when the final tent had been raised and the men of the century settled down to a light supper of barley gruel and coarse loaves of bread prepared in Gaul and already stale. Around the campfires the talk was about the progress of the campaign, based on snatches of information gleaned from messengers and forward-supply orderlies returning from the front. As yet the only contact with the enemy had been a handful of skirmishes between scouts and, from all accounts, the native charioteers had so far bested the Roman cavalry. The old hands of the Legion grumpily told the new recruits that it would be a completely different story once the heavy infantry of the Romans managed to close with the Britons.

Inside the centurion's tent, Macro quietly addressed the men he had picked for Vespasian's mission. In addition to Cato, he had selected the best ten legionaries of his century for the task. They sat on the grass as he outlined the special duty they had been selected to perform.

'As some of you may have observed, our legion has been honoured by the presence of a number of the local royalty, who have been taking advantage of Roman hospitality in recent years due to some misunderstandings with their subjects.'

The men grinned at this description of the Emperor's clients. It was the same throughout the Empire; the local people threw out their despots, who fled to Rome to plead their cause, only to discover that Rome granted asylum at a high price – perpetual obedience.

'As it happens,' continued Macro, 'one of our friends – Cogidubnus by name – had been a little indiscreet in his earlier years when he first approached Rome to discuss a treaty. Apparently he was so impressed by what he saw that he pledged to completely surrender his nation to the Emperor should the Empire extend to Britain. Well, as you can see, it now has. But Cogidubnus seems to have forgotten his earlier good intentions and is holding out for an improved deal from Rome. Unfortunately for him, when he was thrown out by his people, the wagon carrying his personal papers managed to get lost in a marsh near here. Luckily, the general's spies have found out where that wagon is and it's our job to recover his personal document chests and bring them back to the safety of the Legion. Once Plautius has a record of the man's earlier promises to sell his people out to Rome he will be able to hold Cogidubnus to his word – if he gives us any problems we can threaten to let his people see precisely what he thinks of them. A neat double bind, I'm sure you'll agree.'

Macro paused, quite pleased with himself for making this complete fabrication sound so plausible. 'But first we have to retrieve those documents. And that's where we come in. The twelve of us have been detached from the legion to recover the chest.'

'Sir!' One of the legionaries raised a hand.

'Yes?'

'Is someone really expecting us to go wandering off right in the middle of hostile territory. Twelve men alone?' The soldier spat contemptuously on to the ground. 'It's nothing short of suicide.'

'Let's hope it's something short of that.' Macro smiled reassuringly. 'Vespasian said that the scouts have found very little sign of resistance since the first two legions landed. We should be all right if it's a quick job. No more than a couple of days.'

'When do we leave, sir?'

'Tonight. As soon as the moon rises.'

Chapter Thirty-four

A damp clinging mist rose from the ground during the night and, by the time the second watch was sounded, a thin veil of white cloaked the ground. The watery red smudges of campfires silhouetted the forms of Vitellius and his bodyguard, Pulcher. The tribune handed Macro a small tablet.

'There's your authorisation. It's countersigned by the general so you won't have any trouble with our pickets, though I doubt this will hold much sway over any Britons you may encounter.'

Macro did not smile as he tucked the tablet inside his knapsack. Bloody typical of a staff officer to make fun of men he might well be sending to their deaths.

'Well then, Centurion, I trust you will succeed in your mission – whatever it may be.'

Macro nodded.

'Good luck.'

Macro saluted and turned back to the still shapes of his men waiting like shadows in the ghostly mist. The rearmost man was hissing abuse at the pair of mules detailed to pull the cart. Disturbed from a well-deserved rest after a traumatic day at sea, the mules were not on their best behaviour and their long ears twitched nervously as steamy breath plumed from their nostrils. Macro gave the signal to move off and the driver tapped the lead mule on the rump with a javelin butt. With a grunt, both beasts strained against their harnesses. The cart had been stripped bare of any loose attachments and the axles thoroughly greased so that the only sound came from the soft crunching of the ground under the wheels. The mist further deadened the sounds of the night and to the men of the detachment the swishing of their footsteps through long wet grass seemed abnormally loud. Behind them, the fires of the Second Legion faded into nothingness and before long theirs were the only man-made sounds to break the night.

For Cato, born and raised in the world's greatest city, the quiet was dreadfully oppressive: his keen imagination magnified every owl hoot or faint rustle of grass into a deadly Briton silently stalking the Romans until the moment was ripe for the kill. He marched behind his centurion and, not for the first time, envied the way Macro strode about his business with a confident air of invulnerability – which was ironic, given the number of scars that he bore.

Macro's little column marched on, quietly calling out the required password when they were challenged by a sentry on the picket lines who looked curiously at the looming bulk of the cart gently rumbling along behind. Then the strange patrol was abruptly lost in the clammy fog, and very quickly even the sounds of the cart were swallowed up.

* * *

It was only when the picket came to be relieved that word of the strange detachment filtered back to headquarters. Vespasian was confronted by a puzzled senior watch officer who wanted confirmation that Macro was acting under orders.

'Twelve men and a cart, you say?' Vespasian asked irritably – since there was a more pressing matter that needed immediate attention.

'Yes, sir.'

'That's very strange. Doesn't sound like a reconnaissance patrol to me.'

'No, sir. That's what I thought.' The watch officer nodded. 'Want me to send a cavalry patrol after them?'

'No point. Anyway we can't spare the men right now. The scouts have lost contact with one of the British columns – we need every cavalryman we've got to track them down.'

'I see. So what should I do, sir?'

'Enter them in the watch log, of course. Until we know otherwise, I think it's best that we regard them as deserters.'

'Deserters?' The watch officer almost laughed at the ridiculousness of the idea. 'But they'll be cut down by the very first Britons they come across, sir.'

The cold eyes of the legate warned him against uttering another word.

'Deserters is what I said. And if they're caught then I want them brought straight to me. They're not to be seen or spoken to by anyone.'

'Yes, sir.'

Once the watch officer had left, Vespasian frowned.

He felt guilty about branding Macro and his men as deserters. But if they failed to complete their mission they would have to be silenced to prevent any word of the wagon's existence reaching other ears. The legate tried not to give the centurion and his mission any further thought. At present, the movements of the British were a source of considerably more worry. As soon as the invasion force had landed Plautius had sent out his cavalry scouts to locate the natives' army and keep him supplied with precise information on its size and movements. But the dense fog of last night and the lingering mist at dawn had allowed a large British force of chariots and infantry, some nine or ten thousand, to slip away from the Roman scouts and the army's cavalry commander had been desperately struggling to re-establish contact throughout the night. Word had just come to Vespasian that the missing column was believed to be under Togodumnus – brother of Caratacus, the leader of the British forces, and no fool, if the British émigrés accompanying the Roman army were to be believed.

A shaft of orange light fell across the papers in front of him and Vespasian looked up to see that the rising sun had found a chink in the tent. It was going to be a difficult day but, once he found time, someone was going to answer for the shoddy way the tent had been erected.

As the distant skyline lightened with the coming of dawn, Macro softly ordered a halt and the men slumped down along the side of the track. The night march had taken a heavy toll on their nerves and the men were glad to see

351

the darkness beginning to dissolve into the glow of the coming sunrise. After leaving the pickets behind, they had twice had to hurry from the track at the sound of approaching horses, but none could tell whether it had been Roman or British scouts passing as the hooves thundered by in the darkness. For the rest of the night they had marched along the track as quietly as they might, fully expecting to be attacked at any moment. The first shafts of orange light fell upon Cato's worn expression as he chewed on a strip of dried pork. He turned to Macro.

'Much further to go, sir?'

'Should be there by nightfall. See there.' He pointed out across the rolling countryside into the distance where a low, flat expanse still lay underneath a blanket of fog, save for the odd hummock of land that rose like an island from a sea of milk. 'That's where the marsh begins.'

'And how are we supposed to find the wagon amongst that lot, sir?'

'We follow this track, until we find a depression in the track where it enters a small copse. The wagon's hidden in the marsh by a burned-out oak stump. Shouldn't be too difficult to locate.'

Looking down the track to the point where it finally disappeared into the bank of fog, Cato somehow doubted that the search would be as easily resolved as that. The distant marsh waited for them with a cold, sleepy inertia that filled Cato with sudden superstitious fear. This was the vision of the underworld that he heard of as a child on his father's knee. Wraith-like shadows curled about the darker shapes of dimly seen trees as the thinning mist shifted on the lightest of airs.

Macro stared intently down the track and then quickly scanned the surrounding countryside for any signs of movement. To the left, the land rolled gently away and in the distance the sea shimmered, off to the right the sparsely cleared farmland gave way to a distant forest. Nothing moved. The Britons had made sure that all farm animals had been swept from the invader's path and every store of grain had been torched. Well then, Macro decided, it was safe to move. He stood up.

'On your feet, you idle buggers. There's work to do.'

Rising wearily from the grass the men formed up. The centurion strode off down the track and his men followed, tired and tense. The track sloped down towards the marsh and the mules had to be tightly reined in to prevent the cart from gathering speed. At the edge of the marsh, the track narrowed so that the cart's wheels crushed the grass on either side. The ground beneath was soft and Cato could feel it give slightly under his boots as the little column moved into the mist. In a short space of time the vistas of the British countryside had vanished and an indefinite white horizon hemmed them in on all sides. At their backs, the sun struggled to make itself felt through the dense haze and the air was cold and clammy on their skin. No-one spoke and the only sounds were the snorts of the mules as they hauled their burden through the soft peat sucking at the cart's wheels.

The narrow track wound its way through the marsh. Where the ground was too soft for vehicles to negotiate, a thin corduroy road of logs had been laid down and covered with shingle. With annoying regularity, first one wheel of the cart, and then the other, stuck in the black oozing muck on each side of the path. The legionaries had to down spears and shields to lay their shoulders to the thick wooden spokes and strain every sinew to break the cart free and roll it back astride the track. Soon the men were covered in foul-smelling mud and desperately tired. Macro allowed them a short break and they hunched down miserably on a small mossy hummock surrounded by a dank expanse of shallow water. From the angle of the pale yellow disc hovering over the mist Macro realised that it was nearly midday, yet looking at the exhausted men slumped around him he knew that he could not march them much further and still expect them to dig out the wagon once it had been found. It should be near now, if the directions he had been given were accurate.

A sudden lightness in the air caused him to look up and he saw that the sun was at last making an impact on the mist. Patches of brightness began to break up the white swirls, and here and there the air cleared for two or three hundred paces.

'Cato!'

'Sir?'

'Get up on that mound over there. See if you can spot that tree trunk.' He indicated a mossy lump beside the track and Cato rose reluctantly. Tentatively placing a foot on the soft green surface, he tested it to make sure it would bear his weight.

'Don't fuck about lad!' Macro said irritably. 'Get up.'

With arms stretched out to break his fall Cato tensed his knees and slowly straightened up. The surface beneath the moss was surprisingly firm and he stood erect and stared at the haunting landscape about them. Ahead the track wound down a small slope and all but disappeared into a particularly foul black morass. Even at first glance it was clear that the cart had come as far as it could along the track. Macro wasn't going to like that.

'See anything that looks like our trunk?'

'No, sir.'

'What about that, over there?' Macro pointed to where a gap had opened in the mist to reveal several dead trees, starkly black and crooked against the thick white backdrop.

'I'm not sure, sir.'

'Well look bloody harder then!'

Cato squinted his tired eyes, but it was difficult to make out much detail and the mist was closing in around the dead trees once again. Instinctively he leaned forwards to try and see better. With a muffled crunch the moss suddenly gave way beneath him and Cato pitched headlong on to the track, arms outstretched. He came down hard and the breath was momentarily knocked out of him.

'All right?' Macro leaned over to help him back on to his feet.

'Yes, sir.'

'You know, Cato,' Macro smiled, 'I've met some clumsy soldiers in my time, but you . . .'

'It wasn't me, sir! Bloody ground just gave way.'

'I see.' Macro turned to look at the place Cato had fallen from. A large section of moss had collapsed to reveal a crumbling round mass of decayed vegetation.

'There, sir. See?' a piqued Cato protested. 'The whole thing's rotten.'

He fell silent for a second, and then curiously pulled a clump of moss away, and then another, tossing them excitedly to one side.

Macro smiled. 'No need to take it so personally.'

Cato ignored him and continued to clear the moss away until, a few moments later, the rotten remains of a tree stump became visible. He stood up and quickly glanced around; there were several other similar mounds covered in moss on either side of the track. He hurried over to the nearest and kicked the moss away to reveal the remains of another ancient tree stump, then looked up at Macro with a grin.

'What on earth?' The centurion was startled by the young man's actions, which were eccentric even by his normal standards of behaviour.

'Sir! Don't you see?'

'I see you've finally gone mad.'

'They're tree stumps, sir! Tree stumps!'

Cato paused, waiting for his comments to provoke a reaction, a wide grin splitting his mud-spattered face. For all the world, Macro could not help feeling a pang of paternal affection. Cato looked like a little boy – it was impossible to be angry with him.

'Tree stumps?' Macro replied instead. 'Yes, well, I can see that they're tree stumps. Probably been cut down for use on the track.'

'Exactly, sir! Exactly. Cut down. How many of them would you say?'

Macro looked around. 'Ten, twelve or so.'

'Do you think that ten or twelve trees might be enough to constitute a copse?'

Macro stared at him and a familiar cold tingle traced its way down the back of his neck. 'Everyone on their feet!'

The legionaries, tired and filthy, could have looked even less excited had they put their minds to it, but rose to their feet nonetheless.

'The optio thinks we're at the right spot. Start looking for the remains of the cart off the side of the track.'

The legionaries looked at the dull, gloomy morass surrounding them, and then back to their centurion as if waiting for more helpful directions.

'Well, get on with it!' Macro said firmly. 'It's not going to bloody well find itself!'

Without waiting for the others, the centurion started attacking the nearest mound of moss at the side of the track, wrenching away handfuls of the moist growth and hurling them to one side. The others reluctantly followed suit and soon the pleasant little hummock of grass was well on the way to utter ruin. Clods of moss and earth flew through the air and yet more filth adhered to the legionaries as they struggled to unearth any sign of the lost wagon. The sun slowly declined from its midday position with little further effect on the mist that clung to the vast expanse of marsh. The legionaries had found nothing and one by one they sat down and surveyed the dark brown debris of peat and rotten wood that was all they had to show for their exertions. Macro let them stop without a word and squatted down on his heels, fixing Cato with an accusing stare.

'I only said it might be the place we're looking for,' Cato said guiltily. 'I mean, it seemed a reasonable guess, given the way things are going.'

'Guess?' Pyrax muttered angrily. 'You seemed pretty damn sure of yourself earlier on!'

'Maybe it was a mistake.' Cato shrugged. 'But where else can the wagon have gone? From the look of the track up ahead there's no way it can have gone any further than this, and how many other trees have we passed? None. It has to be close by.'

'Where then?' Macro swept his arm round at the excavations. 'We've looked.'

'Well, we just haven't found it yet.'

'Fuck this!' Pyrax stood up angrily. 'Look, Centurion, the wagon isn't here. Any fool can see that. Either we've missed it earlier on the track, or it was never here in the first place. Why don't we just get back to the Legion?'

The other legionaries grumbled in support.

Macro looked down between his feet and thought for a moment before he rose stiffly. 'No, not yet at least. The lad's right. If it is anywhere then it has to be here. We'll have a rest and have another dig. If we find nothing by dusk we'll head back.'

Pyrax swore and spat at Cato's feet. His fist clenched.

'That's my decision, Pyrax,' Macro intervened firmly. 'Now back down and have a rest. That's an order. Understand me?'

Pyrax remained silent, glaring coldly at the optio. Then he turned towards Macro for a moment and nodded.

'I asked if you understood me?'

'Yes, sir!'

'Good. Now sit down.'

With a last glare at the optio, Pyrax turned away and slumped down with the other legionaries who all looked angrily at Cato.

It was more than the young optio could bear for the moment and he wandered down to the edge of the swamp to escape the immediate aura of hostility assaulting him from all sides. The remains of a sapling protruded out of the dark surface at the edge of the hummock and hung at an angle towards the track. With a deep sigh of frustration Cato leaned back against the sapling, firmly intending to empty his mind of immediate concerns and take in the view, such as it was. The moment the mass of his weight fetched up against the sapling it gave way with a loud creak and fell down on to the grass bank of the hummock. For a moment Cato felt himself toppling forwards for a second time, but a frantic windmill gesture kept him on his feet.

'Cato!' Macro shouted out. 'Oh, for fuck's sake! Can't you keep on your bloody feet for a little longer? I swear I have seen completely pissed sailors less clumsy than you.'

'Sorry, sir. I thought this tree could bear my weight.'

'Tree?' Macro asked, then looked down in the grass where Cato indicated. 'That's no bloody tree.'

He bent down and examined the long shaft of wood. Under the lichen, grime and scraps of moss the wood was far too smooth and regular for a sapling. At the end of the shaft he wiped away the dirt and exposed an iron cap. A little more work revealed a foot-long iron collar with two handles protruding on opposite sides of the shaft.

'Well, Cato,' he began, 'you may not be the most agile lad to have joined the legion, but your clumsiness has its moments. Do you know what this is?'

Cato shook his head, still a little bemused that his sapling had managed to sprout ironware.

'It's a wagon shaft end. And where there's a wagon shaft end it's reasonable to suppose that there might be a wagon. Let's see.'

Macro picked the shaft of wood up and raised it above his head, following its line down to where it disappeared in the marsh. He gave it an experimental tug, but even though the shaft rose up and down it was clearly fixed to something at its base. Macro let it drop back into the grass and turned to face the other legionaries who were watching him with weary curiosity.

'Last time then, lads! On your feet and get over here. Seems the optio was right after all. Not that I ever seriously doubted him.'

Were it not for the unreasonable fact that assaulting a superior officer was a capital offence, Cato would have hit him.

Chapter Thirty-five

Dusk was fast approaching and there was still no sign of Togodumnus's force. By now the cavalry scouts of three legions had been joined by two auxiliary cavalry cohorts and the surrounding country was being systematically swept for any trace of the Britons. Until they were found, the Second Legion would be highly vulnerable and Vespasian was loath to quit a fortified position while the location and strength of the enemy were still unknown. His imagination readily visualised the consequences of his men being attacked in force as they were strung out along the line of march. A determined attack, pushed through resolutely, could cripple the Second. That was why he had placed the scouting sweeps under the direct command of Vitellius. Even now, the tribune was somewhere out there in the British countryside with orders not to rest until Togodumnus was located.

Meanwhile, General Plautius was relentlessly pressing the enemy back and had sent messengers racing to the rear to call up the two fresh legions – the Second and the Fourteenth – and have them rush to the front to sustain the offensive's momentum. A swift crushing blow was required, he told his subordinates. If the four legions could catch the Britons before they managed to place a major river between themselves and the Romans, the resulting battle would surely see the destruction of the Britons' field army. After that, it would just be a question of picking off the odd hill fort and mopping up the surviving forces. The legate smiled bitterly as he had read that. What the general had not mentioned – perhaps had not anticipated – was the guerrilla war that would inevitably follow for many years before the new province could be considered pacified.

Vespasian wished that he could share the general's confidence in the smooth progress of the campaign. But orders were orders and Plautius wanted the Second Legion on the move at daybreak on the morrow. Vespasian could only assume that the general was aware of the risk.

As far as Vespasian could tell from the latest scout reports, the tracks leading west to the front were clear of the enemy and the land to the south had been searched as far as the marsh – which, his British émigrés had told him, was impassable for a force of any size as the old tracks had been abandoned for many years and were all but swallowed up by the bogs. That left the heavily wooded region to the north of the line of march; a rolling mass of trees and thickets criss-crossed by numerous tracks well known to the natives. If an attack came, it was sure to come from that quarter.

The sun was sinking into the rolling banks of mist by the time Macro and his men had cleared away enough of the slimy foul-smelling peat to reveal the bed of the wagon. The men were caked in mud that sucked at them as they struggled, waist deep. Finally they had discovered the chest they had been sent to retrieve. Once it was cleared of mud, Macro excitedly examined the heavy wooden box bound with iron. Aside from the inevitable staining and the dampness of the wood, the chest was in remarkably good condition and still fastened by a heavy lock. The other men, now that they had something to show for all their exertions, shared his excitement and eagerly helped drag the chest to more solid ground. It proved to be far heavier than they expected and nearly sank back into the mud several times before it was heaved on to the grass bank leading up to the track.

'Right, lads, there's no time to waste. We have to load it on to the cart and get back to the Legion.'

Cato looked up at the sky. 'It'll be dark soon. We won't make it back before nightfall, sir.'

'No. But we'll get out of this place at least.' Macro grasped one of the iron handles. 'Come on! Let's get on with it.'

The twelve men struggled around the chest and hauled it up the bank. Then, with a final back-breaking effort, accompanied by loud hisses of strain and exertion, the chest was pushed on to the back of the cart, which creaked under the load. The men leaned against its sides gasping for breath. Cato found himself shivering as his body was overtaken by a degree of tiredness he had never experienced before. His leg and arm muscles ached abominably and the strenuous labour of the previous hours had left him feeling sick. Looking at the faces of the other men he realised that they were all quite done in, and it would be as much as they could manage to haul the cart clear of the marsh by the time night fell.

Macro rested his arms across the top of the chest. He was tired, but elated that he had succeeded in his mission. Once the chest was in the legate's safe keeping, Macro could rest assured that he had at least one friend in high places who might smooth his path to further promotion. He had reached the pinnacle of a career based solely on competence and ability. Further advancement depended on a mix of guile, intelligence and personal connections. Macro knew himself well enough to be aware that he was somewhat lacking in the first two of these qualities; the third he had just taken care of. He patted the chest affectionately.

'Well done, Centurion!' a voice called out of the growing gloom of mist and dusk.

Macro snapped round, his hand going straight to the pommel of his sword. The other men were on their feet in an instant, alert, some with swords already drawn.

A vague shape slowly emerged from the mist and took the form of a Roman staff officer – Tribune Vitellius. Behind him several more figures materialised, men in Syrian garb leading horses. At sight of them, Cato felt a cold chill of recognition and slowly drew his own sword. And there, holding the bridle of the tribune's horse, stood Pulcher.

Vitellius walked up the track towards them and stopped ten paces from the cart.

'I take it that is the chest you were sent to retrieve?'

Macro was still recovering from the shock of the tribune's sudden appearance. He frowned with suspicion, but made no reply.

'Well, Centurion? Is that the chest?'

'Yes, sir. But what . . .'

'That's a job well done. I congratulate you and your men.'

'Thank you, sir—'

'And now I'll take charge of things. The chest needs to be returned to the legate as quickly as possible.' Vitellius turned his head back to the waiting horsemen. 'First two men – here!'

Vitellius walked over to the cart and patted the chest with a smile. 'You must be exhausted. I expect you'll be glad to be relieved of this. Get some rest before you follow us back to the Legion.'

Macro nodded while his mind worked quickly to frame his next words as carefully as possible. He could see the credit for his achievement slipping away. 'Sir, our orders were to hand the chest over to the legate in person.'

'I know. But the orders have been changed.'

'The legate was quite specific, sir. To him in person.'

'Are you questioning my authority, Centurion?' Vitellius asked coldly. 'I'm telling you that the orders have been changed. Now you will hand over the cart to my men, understand?'

Macro stared at him, eyes cold with bitter resentment that his superior was about to snatch the prize from his grasp.

'Tell your men to stay away from the cart, sir,' Macro said quietly.

'What?'

'Tell your men to back off. You're not taking the chest.'

'Centurion,' Vitellius tried to sound reasonable, 'there's nothing you or I can do about it. I'm obeying a direct order from Vespasian.'

'My orders come from Aulus Plautius,' Macro bluffed. 'We're not giving up the chest until I get different orders from the general, in person.'

Vitellius stared at him silently, and his men – sensing a confrontation unresolved – stopped short of the cart. Then Vitellius smiled and backed away a few paces as he spoke.

'Very well, Centurion. You keep the chest for the moment, but this isn't the last you'll hear of the matter – I swear it.'

He turned and beckoned his two men to follow as he retreated from the cart back towards the waiting horsemen. As he watched, Cato saw the tribune move to one side of the track, casually moving out of the line of sight between his men and the cart. A sudden movement from the figures in the mist caught Cato's attention and his eyes returned to the tribune. Vitellius had flicked the cape off his sword arm and was looking back towards the cart. Cato's eyes widened in sudden realisation of the danger.

'Down! Get down!'

He hurled himself at his centurion and they rolled on to the muddy track behind the cart. The other legionaries followed suit as a flight of arrows whistled through the air. One man reacted too slowly and, with a sickening thud, a dark feathered arrow buried itself in his throat. The legionary slumped to his knees, gurgling blood, as he desperately struggled to wrench the barb free from his neck. Two arrows from the second volley caught him in the face and chest and, with a cry he went down.

'Behind the cart!' Macro shouted. 'Get behind the cart!'

The legionaries crouched down in the filth behind the cart as further arrows landed around them. Two men were wounded and gasped in pain as they tried to wrestle the arrows free.

'Leave them!' Macro shouted, only too aware of the damage barbed arrows caused on extraction. If they lived, the arrow heads would have to be cut out by a surgeon.

If they lived.

The Syrians were already fanning out on either side of the track, as far as the marsh would allow, in order to minimise the effective shelter of the cart. The legionaries huddled tightly together. Most had left their shields down on the grass bank and only a couple had leaned them against the cart. Now these were hurriedly passed to the side to protect the men's flanks and deflect the arrows with a harsh clatter. Even so, arrows were finding their mark and another man had been wounded in the leg.

'What the hell are they doing?' Pyrax asked. 'They're on our fucking side.'

'Apparently not,' replied Cato. 'Whatever's in that chest must be bloody priceless.'

'How many of them are there?' Macro asked. 'Did anyone see?'

'I counted eight,' Cato replied. 'Vitellius, Pulcher and six Syrians.'

'Then we're even. If we try and rush them.'

'Rush them?' Pyrax repeated shocked, as he pressed

himself into the ground. 'Sir, they'd cut us down before we could get near them.'

'Only while their arrows last.'

'If we live that long.'

A sudden piercing shriek caused Cato to jump. One of the mules had been hit in the flank and now it bellowed with pain and reared and wrenched in its traces. For a moment it looked as if the animal might panic enough to drag the cart clear of the sheltering legionaries but the other animal had frozen and gazed at its comrade with wide-eyed terror, and the cart stayed still.

'Careful, you fools!' Vitellius screamed out a short way off. 'You're hitting the mules. Pick your targets – only the men!'

'Thank you, Tribune,' Macro said bitterly as the arrows struck the cart and shields with splintering thuds. He caught Cato's eye and gestured towards their attackers with his thumb. 'I'm getting a bit sick of those Syrians. About time we did something about them.'

'But not right now, sir,' Cato implored him. 'Please wait until the odds are a little more even.'

The arrows continued to fall, but at a diminishing rate as the Syrians conserved ammunition. Individually they had closed the distance and were now taking pot shots whenever a target made itself available. But the narrow strip of the hummock made it impossible for the archers to enfilade the legionaries. So, after a little while, it became apparent that a stand-off had been reached. The legionaries, stripped of armour and with only two shields between them, dared not rush the archers; and the archers, lightly armed and a poor match for well-trained heavy infantry, dared not take the legionaries on hand-to-hand. The Syrians only hope was to incapacitate enough of Macro's force to make their numbers decisive.

The arrow fire ceased, but the legionaries remained under cover in case it was a ruse.

'Macro!' Vitellius called out. 'Macro! Still with us?'

'Yes, sir!' the centurion shouted out, automatically responding to his superior.

'That's good. Now look here, Macro, I will have that chest in the long run. You're trapped where you are and I've sent for more men. It'll take them a while to arrive. We can spend that time sitting here staring at each other or you can give me the chest and I'll let you and your men go.'

'Fuck off, sir!' Macro shouted back. 'If you want it, you'll have to fight for it!'

'Hear me out, Centurion! If you make me wait then there will be no mercy. We will over-run you and you'll be killed. Give me the chest now and you'll live. You have my word on it.'

'His word?' Cato raised his eyebrows. 'What kind of idiots does he take us for?'

'My thinking exactly, Optio,' replied Macro.

'Macro!' the tribune called out again. 'I'll give you a few moments to talk it over with your men. Then you choose; delay the inevitable and it's death for all of you, or give me the chest and walk out of here.'

Macro turned back to his men. 'Well?'

'There's no way he's going to let us live,' Pyrax said firmly. 'No matter what we decide.'

'You're right.' Macro nodded. 'So what do we do? A charge is out of the question.'

'Unless we can hit them from two sides,' Cato suggested.

'And how do we achieve that?'

Cato rolled over and propped himself up on an elbow so he could point out directions as he talked.

'Some of us go back down the track. The grass is long on either side, so if you keep low enough you should be screened. Then, where it dips into the marsh, you swim round in a wide arc until you come back on to the trail behind them. Then we charge from both sides – hopefully the surprise should be enough to put them off their aim for just long enough.'

Cato finished, but saw that the others were still looking at him expectantly. 'Sorry, that's it.'

'That's a plan?'

Cato nodded.

'Fair enough. It's that or die, I suppose,' Macro said. He looked around the surviving members of his squad. 'Right then, you take Pyrax, Lentulus and Piso. When you get round behind them you charge and make as much noise as you can.'

Cato shifted with embarrassment. 'Sorry sir, but someone else has to lead the other party.'

'Why?'

'I can't swim.'

'You told Vespasian you could. That night you joined the Legion.'

'I'm afraid I was exaggerating, sir. Sorry.'

'Lying, you mean.'

'Yes.'

Macro glared at him. 'Well, that's just terrific, Optio. Now I'll have to bloody do it.'

'Yes, sir. I'll make sure I learn as soon as we get back to the Legion.'

'Fine.' Macro unfastened the clasp on his cloak and nodded to the others to do the same. The small party checked that their swords and daggers were firmly attached to their belts, then Macro led them down the track away from the Syrians, closely hugging the ground and slithering along the muddy surface. Once they had eased themselves into the water and swum off into the gloomy mist, Cato risked a quick glance round the side of the cart. The Syrians stood as before and, to one side, the unmistakable shadow of Vitellius sat atop a small mound close to where Pulcher tended their mounts. There was a sudden blur as an arrow flew close by and Cato ducked back down. The three other men, still unwounded, held their draw swords tight in their hands and crouched expectantly.

For a while it seemed nothing was happening, all was still and quiet as before. As the light failed Cato began to wonder what had become of his centurion. Then Vitellius stood up and called out impatiently.

'Time's up, Centurion. Surrender the chest now or die. What's it to be?'

Cato looked round at the other legionaries.

'Well, Centurion?'

'Say something!' one of the men hissed.

'What? Say what?' Cato asked helplessly.

'Anything, you fool!'

'That's it, then,' Vitellius concluded angrily. 'You'll bloody well die and like it.'

With a roar of fighting rage, Macro and his four men rose up from the shadows immediately behind the line of archers and raced down the track. The noise momentarily surprised Cato as well, but he recovered in an instant and was up on his feet running for the nearest Syrian, shouting at his party to follow. As he saw Cato running towards him, teeth bared in a feral war face, the Syrian dropped his bow and reached for the cleaver at his side. He fumbled as he unsheathed the blade and it fell to the ground. Cato shouted as loud as he could and the man ran for it leaving his weapon lying in the mud. Cato thrust his sword at the Syrian's back but the point barely penetrated the cloak and caught him in the buttock instead. The man yelped and sprinted down the track as fast as his feet could carry him, frantically weaving round Macro and the others who were mercilessly despatching his comrades.

Frustrated by the enemy's escape, Cato turned wildly about to look for another foe and saw Pulcher heaving Vitellius up into the saddle.

'Over here!' Cato cried out. 'Don't let him get away! Quick!'

Without waiting for the others, Cato dashed towards Pulcher, sword raised high above his head. At the last moment, Pulcher turned and drew his weapon, faster than Cato would have believed possible.

Firmly standing his ground, the stocky legionary aimed the tip of the blade squarely at Cato's throat. Cato instinctively tried to dodge the blade and, to his horror, found his feet losing their grip on the slimy peat. He went down on his knees, sliding in under Pulcher's blade and thrusting up into his guts as hard as he could. His momentum slammed him into Pulcher's legs and both went down in a sprawling heap. Cato pulled himself clear with unbloodied sword still in hand. The thrust had not penetrated Pulcher's armour, only winded him badly, and now he rolled away fighting for breath. Before Cato could finish him off, a sudden swish through the air, close to his ear, caused him to duck. Vitellius loomed above him, raising his sword arm. When it came, Cato had just enough time to raise his sword to parry a jarring blow.

'Here! Quickly!' he cried out.

Vitellius was about to move in for the kill when several shouts close at hand alerted him. Swearing bitterly, he charged his horse at Cato. The optio dived to one side, but not fast enough to avoid being sent sprawling by a blow from the animal's flank as it swept past, and he crumpled to the ground.

With hooves sliding and slithering in the mud, the horse weaved through the loose line of legionaries and pounded down the track, past the cart where the wounded mule still bellowed its pain, and on into the gathering gloom.

Macro hurried over to Cato and hauled him on to his feet.

'You all right?'

'Will be . . . once I get my breath back. Did we get them?'

'Near enough. Five down and three did a runner.

Shame we didn't get that bastard Vitellius.'

Cato quickly looked about but there was no sign of Pulcher either.

'Yes, sir.' Cato drew in a deep lungful of air and felt his chest. Aside from bruises all seemed in order. 'What are we going to do?'

'There's no point in going after him, if that's what you mean. We have to get the chest back to Vespasian as soon as possible. Before the tribune comes after us with more men.'

Once the legionaries had harnessed four of the horses up to the cart, the others were tethered to the back, along with the remaining mule. Concerned that the other mule might attract unwelcome attention with its hoarse bellowing, Macro had led the animal down to the side of the marsh, cut its throat and tipped it into the mire. With the wounded loaded aboard the cart, the small party began to retrace its steps along the track towards the edge of the marsh. Night closed in around them as they drove the horses onwards, grateful that they no longer had to labour at hauling the cart out of every muddy rut along the way.

As they neared the edge of the marsh and could see the dark swell of land rising up above the mist, Macro heard the sound of a horse approaching behind them.

'Halt,' he called out softly. 'Grab your shields and spears and follow me.'

He led them back down the track a small distance and detailed four men to hide each side in an extended line to be sure of providing the approaching rider with no means of escape. Cato lay down close to the ground, too tired by the day's action to be anxious any more. Moments later the dark shape of a rider and horse loomed out of the mist and cantered into the middle of the trap.

'Now!' Macro shouted, and eight shadows detached themselves from the grass on either side of the track and converged on the horseman. Startled by the sudden movement, the horse reared, whinnying in terror, and the rider struggled to regain control of his mount before tumbling to the ground. Macro pounced on him, slamming a punch into his face before hauling the man to his feet.

'Well now!' He laughed. 'What a fucking surprise it is to see you again, sir.'

Vitellius wiped his bloody nose on the back of his hand. 'Get your hands off me, Centurion!'

'Get my hands off you?'

'You have to let me go. I've got to get back to the Legion.'

'Listen, you bastard, if you think—'

'There's no time for this!' Vitellius shouted. 'There's a bloody army coming down the track. Nearly rode right into them. I don't think they saw me, but they'll be here soon. I have to tell Vespasian!'

'He's lying, sir,' Pyrax growled. 'Kill him, and let's go.'

'Wait!' Cato interceded. 'We don't even know what he was after yet.'

Pyrax raised his sword. 'Who needs to know?'

'Lower that sword legionary!' Macro ordered. 'Now!'

'Please!' Vitellius begged. 'You have to let me go. I

have to warn Vespasian. We've found Togodumnus! If that column surprises the Legion we'll lose thousands. Thousands of our comrades.'

'Comrades!' Pyrax spat at him. 'Comrades don't fucking kill each other.'

For a moment they stood in silence, a tableau of crisis and indecision, Vitellius on his knees, Macro with his fist twisted into the tribune's cloak, a look of bitter contempt etched on his face.

'If there is a column,' Cato said softly, 'the legate has to be warned.'

'There's no fucking enemy column!' Pyrax thumped the butt of his spear down. 'He's just trying to save his skin.'

'Then why ride back towards us?'

'He got lost. Why are we even wasting time on this?' Pyrax turned to Macro. 'Kill him, sir!'

Macro glared down at the tribune for a moment, face hardening into a look of pure disgust and resentment at the predicament the tribune's reappearance had placed him in. Then he thrust his fist hard against Vitellius's chest and the tribune went down flat on his back in the mud.

'Go and warn the Legion. But, make no mistake, when this is all over I'll see to it that the general himself knows what you did here. I'm sure he'll be most keen to find out why a senior officer should want to kill his own men to get hold of that chest. Now go! Go, you bastard, before I change my mind.'

Vitellius scrambled to his feet, jumped on to his horse's back and snatched the reins back from the legionary who stood at the beast's side. Without any delay he kicked his heels in and raced up the track, past the cart, and disappeared into the night.

'Right then! Let's move. If he's told us the truth, there's no time to waste. Let's go!'

'Of course he's not telling the truth!' Pyrax snorted.

'You questioning my decision?' Macro asked coldly.

'I'm telling you, we should have killed him.'

'You call me sir when you address me, legionary!'

'Quiet!' Cato raised his hand. 'Listen!'

The small party froze, every ear straining in the direction Cato pointed. For a moment there was nothing to disturb the soft sounds of the night. Then came a distant whinny, then another, accompanied by the unmistakable crack of a whip as someone shouted a Celtic curse.

From somewhere on the track not far behind them.

Chapter Thirty-six

It was clear that the Britons would be upon them before they even made the ridge. There was no hope of outrunning the enemy, that much was evident to Macro as he frantically scanned the immediate area, and found a faint possibility of hope.

'Over there!' He thrust his arm out to one of the larger folds in the land away to the left of the track. In the dim light of a new moon the mist forming in the dip had a cold luminosity that was far from welcoming, but it offered the only hope of quick concealment. 'Get the cart off the track, quick as you fucking can!'

As the men turned the horses into the long grass and hurried across the slope towards the hollow, Macro followed and tried to conceal the worst of the grooves the cart had crushed into the wet grass. Praying that the marks would be missed in the dark, and fearing that the Britons might march into view at any moment, Macro dashed after the cart which had reached the rim of the dip and was being man-handled down the reverse slope. The thrumming of shod hooves in the near distance spurred him on and when he reached the dip he threw himself down and lay there for a moment, panting.

The slope was steep and the cart was well below the level of the mist that covered the ground in a thick unbroken layer. Ordering the others to stay with the wagon and make sure the animals and the injured remained silent, Cato scrambled up the slope to join the centurion.

'We were lucky there, sir. Wagon nearly went over when we came down this.' He thumped the slope.

'Really?' Macro said, and yawned before he could help it. Then he flipped himself over and propped his chin up with his hands. 'Keep down, and do nothing . . . absolutely nothing. On my orders only.'

Cato nodded and lay as still as he could, waiting nervously for the enemy to emerge from the swamp. And then, suddenly, a small column of cavalry trotted into the dim moonlight barely a hundred paces away, a blend of man and horse in the dark shadows. Cato was surprised to see British cavalry since Caesar had claimed that they preferred to use their animals for chariots. Either the Great General was wrong or the Britons had finally discovered the value of cavalry. The horsemen fanned out on either side of the track and trotted up towards the ridge. The left-flank scout passed within twenty paces of their hiding place and Macro and his optio pressed themselves into the ground, hardly daring to breathe. Their tired eyes strained to detect any sign that the passage of their cart across the slope had been discovered. But the scout passed by without breaking his pace.

From the swamp came the sound of jingling and a dark mass of chariots and infantry spilled out on to the track and snaked their way up the slope. The chatter of their queer lilting language carried softly to the ears of the terrified Romans and Cato found himself comparing the sound favourably with the harshness of the German he had grown used to. A sharp order was given as a chariot passed down the line, and the column obediently fell silent until the chariot had passed beyond the line of scouts and over the brow of the hill, then laughter rippled down the line and they continued talking as before.

There seemed to be no end to the soldiers streaming from the marsh, and now the head of the dark mass had passed over the hill. On and on they came, until at long last the rearguard emerged from the swamp. Macro and Cato watched as the last ranks of the enemy marched over the crest of the hill and merged into its dark silhouette as they passed out of sight down the reverse slope.

'How many do you think there were, sir?' Cato whispered, as if afraid his words might yet carry to the ears of the Britons.

Macro looked down at the small stones he was clutching in his hand and quickly counted them up. 'Say the equivalent of twenty cohorts, that's . . .'

'Nine thousand!' Cato whistled.

Macro silently did the necessary maths for himself and nodded. 'More than enough for Vespasian to worry about. Not to mention the chariot force. If that lot gets the drop on the legate . . .'

'Then it's up to Vitellius.'

'Yes,' Macro replied simply. 'Vitellius . . . Look, we'd better get moving. With that lot on the scene we'd better abandon the cart. Bury the chest here, lose the cart somewhere else and use the horses to circle round the column and rejoin the Legion.'

'Bury the chest? After all we've been through?'

'You want it to be captured? Or worse, you want to be captured with it?'

'No, sir.'

'Well then, we'll have to leave it here and return for it, if we ever get back to the Second in one piece.'

It was clear that the horse was badly winded and would drop if he drove it any further. Vitellius swerved off the track and dismounted in the shadows of an ancient grove whose leaf-laden branches stretched out on all sides. While his mount snorted and gasped at the cool night air, Vitellius cursed in anger and frustration. That bloody chest had nearly been in his hands. An emperor's ransom – enough to fund the most lavish of political careers; an endless source for buying the favours of senators and soldiers alike. Maybe enough to buy him the loyalty of the Praetorian Guard. Certainly the services of the Praetorian agent Pulcher had been reasonably priced and the man had been sufficiently impressed by gold to rid himself of any inconvenient principles. And buying the services of the Syrians earlier that day had been easy, once Vitellius had passed himself off as a close friend of Scribonianus.

It was quite astonishing just how much the prospect of riches bent a man's will in new directions. Only a few months earlier he had been a loyal servant of the Emperor, so loyal in fact that Narcissus had shared a good many more secrets with him than was strictly necessary, or wise. But as soon as Narcissus had told him about the chest, deeply repressed ambitions began to whisper sinister thoughts to him. The recovery of the chest was supposed to be a test of Vespasian's loyalty to Claudius, and Vitellius had been ordered to watch the legate closely for signs of treachery. However, Vespasian had behaved impeccably and in his strict adherence to duty Vitellius had found his opportunity. Secure in the knowledge that the legate would do all in his power to carry out his instructions, it simply remained for Vitellius to be equivocal in his reports to Narcissus. Once the treasure disappeared the finger of blame would unswervingly be directed at Vespasian whose every protestation of innocence would condemn him all the more. And Vitellius, armed with his fortune, would watch quietly and bide his time.

That had been the plan up until a short while ago.

Rosy dreams of that future were now dashed, and he impulsively swore out loud, then nervously glanced about – but the night remained quite still. Vitellius sighed. He had failed and, worse, he had left witnesses to his failure. Once that squat little centurion and his precocious optio got back to the Legion he would be compromised. If only there was some way of ensuring that they never made it back alive. It was possible that the column of Britons he had run into back in the marsh had already caught up with the cart and massacred its escort; Vitellius sincerely hoped that they had. But he knew it would be foolish to count on it – that fellow Macro had just about enough luck and guile to see him through any peril.

Memories of the desperate fight in the German village flooded back into Vitellius's mind, particularly the vision of the centurion bleeding from a savage spear wound. If only that bloody German had paused long enough to take a proper aim.

While Vitellius reflected on his circumstances, his horse had recovered enough to graze contentedly on a patch of grass at the fringe of an oak tree's boughs. Suddenly it lifted its head and stared intently into the night. It was a moment before the tribune was aware of the horse's change of mood and then he hurried over and placed a reassuring hand on the animal's neck. The horse flinched.

'What is it, girl?'

Nostrils flaring and ears twitching the horse took a step back into the shadows. As Vitellius looked into the night he saw a thinly spread line of horsemen approaching along the treeline, barely a hundred paces away. His heart raced as he silently struggled to get up on his mount but the horse, already nervous, reared back with a loud whinny.

'Stupid bastard!' Vitellius yanked the reins savagely as he steadied the horse and hauled himself on to its back. Already there was shouting from a short distance off and Vitellius kicked his heels into the flanks of his mount, turning it away from the dark figures hurrying in his direction. Panic and the desire to flee gripped him and, shouting at his mount, Vitellius galloped away into the night, dimly aware that the direction he was heading in would take him away from the Second Legion. Very well, he'd try and make for the Fourteenth instead, already well down the road as it marched to join Plautius. Vespasian would have to deal with the enemy column on his own and Vitellius would live to be a hero another day.

At the foot of the oak tree where the tribune had taken shelter the dark shapes of his pursuers watched the figure fleeing as fast as his horse could gallop – the drumming of the hooves clearly audible.

'Who the hell was that?' asked a legionary. 'Thought he looked like one of ours.'

'Probably some idiot messenger,' his decurion replied. 'Got himself lost most like.'

'Should we go after him, sir?'

The decurion thought about it a moment and shook his head. 'Nah! Not worth it. If he's one of ours he'll find his way soon enough.'

'What if it's one of them, sir?'

'Then he's had a lucky escape. I'm not risking breaking any of our necks on some wild chase in the dark. Anyway, we'd best get back to the Legion.'

The decurion turned his squadron round and led them at a walk back towards the Second Legion, somewhat concerned about the negative report he would have to give to Vespasian. There had been no sign of Togodumnus and his forces. Frankly, the decurion doubted whether there had ever been any enemy column attempting to flank the army. It was probably just some paranoid staff officer over-reacting. The decurion shrugged wearily. So far the campaign had been a huge disappointment; no enemy, no spoils and no women. It had hardly been worth turning up for, and he had already resigned himself to the fact that Plautius and the vanguard legions would have defeated the Britons long before the Second could get into the action.

Shame, he thought. A nice little battle would have been most welcome, especially in view of the promotional opportunities provided by combat deaths. But, he sighed to himself bitterly, there wasn't going to be a battle, because there wasn't a single bloody Briton for miles.

For Macro and his men, the ride through the night was proving to be a disaster. The Syrian horses were light frisky things; ideal for darting in and out of the fringes of a battle while their riders loosed off volleys of arrows, but totally impractical for carrying more than one man at a time. In the end, after much swearing and kicking of heels, Macro ordered the men to dismount and use the horses just to carry the wounded. His legionaries were far more content on foot in any case.

So the small group quietly made their way through the night, trying as far as Macro could guess the route, to march round the British column and locate the Second Legion before the Britons. Macro had decided to keep his party to the seaward side of the enemy, to be as near as possible to the fortified beachhead. With luck they might even be picked up by a patrol and escorted back.

Vitellius might already have reached the Legion and raised the alarm, so their comrades would at least be safe from surprise attack. Even so, Macro's gut instinct told him that Vitellius would be planning a nasty surprise for them on their return and he cursed himself for letting the man go. They should have slit his throat and dumped the body in the marsh. That was more than the treacherous bastard deserved. The question plaguing Macro's mind was why the tribune had been there in the first place. Vespasian had assured him that the real reason for the mission was a closely guarded secret. Yet, not only was Vitellius in the know, he had also had time to enlist his band of helpers – presumably the same bunch of Syrians who had jumped Macro's century on the road to Gesoriacum. Someone was playing a deep game and Macro was uncomfortably aware that he was just a small thread in a much greater tangle of conspiracy.

He forced himself to concentrate; this was not the time to let his mind wander. Every fibre of his body must be bent towards ensuring that his men returned safely to the Legion. Looking round he could see that the legionaries were completely done in – he had to keep his mind clear and his eyes and ears open as they passed through this hostile landscape. Even as he thought this, a warm aching weariness was flowing through his limbs. In a moment he knew his head would begin to swim. He rubbed his eyes, momentarily rocking on his feet, and then felt a hand grasp his elbow and hold him steady.

'Careful, sir!' Cato whispered. 'You almost fell over. You need to rest.'

'No – I'm fine.'

'You could sit on one of the horses and let me lead the way for a while, sir.'

'I said no. I can't do that.' Macro wanted to explain that no officer could even think of doing such a thing, but he could not frame the words and merely mumbled his thanks, freeing himself from Cato's grip.

As the night wore on, the small band of legionaries carefully picked their way through the shadows of the rolling countryside. They dared not pause for fear that an irresistible desire to sleep would overwhelm them the moment they stopped. They were all aware of the danger they were in, cut off from the Legion and wandering through the dark in hostile country. On they trudged until, just as the sky was beginning to lighten away to the east, they reached the top of a small hill. In the distance they could see the mass of small fires that identified it as the marching camp of a Roman legion. In the glow of the distant light tiny figures moved about in a frenzy of activity.

'Just in time it seems,' Macro grinned wearily. 'Looks like they're already on the march. Vespasian always was an early bird. No rest for us today.'

Cato smiled at Macro.

But Macro was no longer looking at the camp. He was staring fixedly away to that part of the horizon furthest from the coming of dawn. Disappearing into a dense wood that bestrode the Legion's line of march was a thick black shadow of men, horses and chariots moving with the silent stealth of a serpent stalking its prey.

Chapter Thirty-seven

Vespasian had left orders that he be woken well before dawn; the Second Legion was about to move through enemy territory and, although the staff officers had issued orders to every unit, there was still a host of details that needed his personal attention. That, he smiled to himself, was the biggest burden of command. The public in Rome pictured their generals as masters of the battlefield, heroically charging into overwhelming odds at the head of the legions. The mass of paperwork and petty bureaucratic tasks that were also part of the job remained largely invisible, yet it was this dedication to discipline and order that made the army work. Whatever the public may think, the secret of being a good general was having a good army, and the very best armies were composed of men who could wage war with methodical efficiency.

Rolling out of his camp bed, Vespasian pulled on a robe and sat at his desk. His personal slave had left a cup of heated wine and bread soaked in olive oil on a small silver tray and Vespasian gratefully gulped both down as he cast an eye over the latest papers. The century returns were initialled and thrust to one side before he scanned a few requisitions awaiting his approval. Finally he read through the night log. Still no sign of Togodumnus, and the thinly spread cavalry patrols had been shifted to the west and north. It was most puzzling – unless of course there was no column. That possibility looked increasingly likely, but Vespasian was wise to the tricks of fate and refused to discount the existence of the Britons just yet. And so the orders to march closed up would stand, however much the men grumbled. It was far better to be cautious than reckless – like that idiot Vitellius who had ridden off with the scouts and completely disappeared, together with a squadron of badly needed auxiliary cavalry. No doubt he was floundering about in the dark, scared out of his wits. Serve him right.

Having completed the paperwork, Vespasian summoned his armourer and stood still, pensive, as the man fastened the contoured breastplate and carefully looped the ribbons at the front. While the man fussed over the final accoutrements, the legate's eyes wandered across the cameo images of his wife and son on his desk and a nagging sense of guilt caused him to frown. It had been some days since he had last paused to even think about them; the sheer volume of the demands placed upon the commander of a legion in the field left no room for any private thought or deed. Vespasian was suddenly aware how much he missed them. It was only ten days since he had seen them set off on the wagon convoy to Rome, yet so much time seemed to have passed already. And the prospect of a long campaign meant it might be years before he saw them again. Titus would be a young boy, no longer the little toddler with his awkward sentences and manic humour. Flavia . . . what would

Flavia be like? More strands of grey in her hair? An extra crease around her eyes and mouth when she smiled? Suddenly he wanted to hold them both close to him and never let them go for as long as he lived. For a moment he was unaware of the stinging sensation in his eyes, then he quickly blinked before tears could betray his inner feelings.

'Too tight, sir?'

'What? Oh no, it's fine. You can leave me now.'

'Yes, sir.'

Once he was alone Vespasian pinched his arm painfully. That had been close – a moment more of wallowing in his homesickness and he would actually have shed tears in front of a bloody slave. He burned with shame at the thought that even now the slave might be confiding with his cronies about the legate's moment of sentimentality. All the work that had gone into constructing an image of a hard, disciplined commander with a heart of stone, coldly aloof from his men, all of that was for nothing if he allowed his emotions to show. Well, he was damned if he would let it happen again. Angrily he snapped shut the hinged likenesses of Flavia and Titus and made a mental note to have his slave stow them at the bottom of a travelling chest for the duration of the campaign.

His foul mood persisted long after dawn and the surly way in which he snapped out his orders was not entirely an attempt to undo the damage of his earlier moment of weakness. As the headquarters tent was packed away none dared even meet the eye of the legate, such was the dark expression that knitted his brow together and twisted down the corners of his mouth.

After a quick meal of barley gruel the legionaries hurriedly packed their equipment. As the sun struggled above the horizon, the men formed up into their centuries ready to march.

The instructions for the order of progress filtered down to the centuries and the men groaned inwardly. Vespasian had elected to march in two divisions, either side of the baggage train, with a cohort at each end to act as vanguard and rearguard. The veterans quietly cursed their commander's excessive caution and then patiently explained to the new recruits that, although the baggage train would have a nice easy passage along the track, the poor sods on each flank would have to negotiate all the obstacles that nature threw in their way. By the end of the day, the flank columns would be scratched, tired and wet, and all because the legate was worried about a few poxy Britons.

'Now then, you stop for nothing, understand?'

Cato nodded and tried to steady the horse.

'You get to Vespasian and tell him it's a trap. Tell him their numbers and tell him where you last saw them entering that wood.' Macro had severe misgivings about sending the lad but none of the others were up to it.

'What about you, sir?'

'Don't worry about me, lad. Just warn Vespasian. Well, what are you fucking waiting for? GO!'

Macro slapped the horse's rump as hard as he could and the animal started forwards, nearly throwing Cato from its back. At the last moment the optio grabbed the reins and pressed his thighs and heels into the horse. He stayed on, after a fashion. With a last look over his shoulder at the little knot of men gazing anxiously after him, Cato urged his horse down the slope towards the Roman camp in the distance. Cato had never been terribly good in the saddle and now he just knotted his fingers in the flowing mane and pulled sharply on the reins to alter direction. For its part, the horse reacted much to be expected having been parted from its usual rider. It didn't respond easily to his commands and man and horse continued at a slow gallop each regarding the other with antipathy.

As he reached the bottom of the hill Cato looked up in a panic and saw that the camp had disappeared from sight. However, a quick check on the direction of the sun and the lie of the land convinced him that he was still heading in the right direction and he kicked his heels in. As he rode, he wondered if Vitellius had managed to reach the camp ahead of him and if this wild gallop was a waste of time. But unpleasant as this ride might be, Cato could see that it was vital to alert Vespasian to the peril ahead. Visions of the grateful reception of his news filled his imagination and Cato drove his little horse on as he clung to the reins.

A movement to the left drew his attention. To his horror, he saw several horsemen in the wild attire of the Britons racing at an angle to intercept him. They were scarcely a quarter of a mile away and urging their horses on to cut in front of Cato before he reached the top of the next hill. With a savage kick at the flanks of his horse, Cato shouted at it to run, run fast as the wind, run for its life. The beast sensed the new urgency, pricked its ears back and lowered its neck as it burst into a headlong gallop up the side of the hill. Cato glanced again to the left and saw that the Britons had closed the distance. With a chilling clarity he knew that he would not make it, the camp was just too far away, and in a few moments he would be dead – already he anticipated the sensation of a sudden spear thrust from behind.

The crest of the hill was barely more than a few hundred feet away and Cato begged his horse to make more speed. But even as he did so, he could sense that it was running on its last reserves of strength. Cato looked over his shoulders. His pursuers were right behind him, close enough for him to see their feral expressions of triumph as they too realised that he would not escape them. It would be over in moments. Then his horse carried him on to the crest of the hill – two miles away lay the Roman camp, two miles too far. Cato let one hand fall from the reins to draw his sword. Fear had gone now, in its place was a frustrated rage. There was no escape now and death was certain, but he would not let them take his life without a brief, bitter struggle.

Cato looked over his shoulder again, fully expecting to see the Britons hefting their spears, but to his amazement he saw that they were reining in, the leading man pointing his spear directly beyond Cato. He looked ahead and saw what the Britons had already spotted. At the base of the hill, a small patrol of infantry were marching back towards the camp. Heart thumping with a surge of joy, Cato slapped the sword on the horse's rump and pounded down the hill. Looking back he was surprised to see the Britons had gone, vanishing over the crest of the hill as their prey escaped.

The men of the patrol heard the approaching sound of hooves and turned quickly, shields to the front and javelins held ready. A short distance from the patrol Cato reined in a few feet from the rearmost men. Slipping from the horse's back, Cato ran into them.

'Who the hell are you?' demanded the optio in command.

'Doesn't matter,' Cato panted. 'Have to see the legate! Now!'

'Who are you?'

'Quintus Licinius Cato, Optio, Sixth Century, Fourth Cohort. I have to report to Vespasian.'

'Report?'

'The enemy are preparing an ambush, ahead in the woods.'

'Enemy? Where?'

'They were right behind me. You must have seen them.'

The optio shook his head.

'But they were there!' Cato pointed to the top of the hill. 'Right behind me. Someone must have seen them!'

The men of the patrol watched him in silence and Cato stared back in disbelief.

'How could you not have seen them? Look, I have to see the legate.'

He turned and reached for the horse's reins and was about to throw himself up on to its back when the optio grabbed his arm and pulled him away from the horse.

'Not so fast! You're coming with us.'

'What? Look, you don't understand! I have to warn Vespasian!'

'I'm sorry, but I have my orders. Now, you're coming with us.'

As Cato stood in numbed disbelief the optio ordered one of his patrol to take charge of the horse, and then Cato was pushed into the centre of the patrol and forced to march with two men behind him to guard him.

'What the fuck is going on?' he shouted at the optio.

The patrol's commander stepped closer, so that his words would not be overheard.

'You're not to speak to anyone until we get back to the camp.'

'Why? What's this all about?'

'All patrols have been ordered by headquarters to look out for you and your mates, and told to bring you in quietly. Between you and me, it seems you're in deep shit. Now, don't make it worse. One more word out of you and I'll have you knocked on the head and thrown over that horse for the rest of the way to camp. Clear?'

Cato opened his mouth to protest and the optio raised his eyebrows in warning. Cato just nodded.

As the patrol approached the camp, Cato saw that the bulk of the Legion had already moved off towards the forest. Only the rearguard remained, forming up and ready to depart. Unless Vespasian was told about the Britons lying in wait, the disaster was unavoidable. Cato searched for any sight of the legate, but in the milling mass of soldiers, artillery trains and baggage wagons there was no sign of the Legion's commander. The patrol wound its way through the turmoil to report to the officer commanding the Legion's rearguard. Tribune Plinius looked up from his campaign desk as the patrol approached.

'What have we here then?'

'Captured a deserter, sir,' replied the optio. 'Rode right into us on some horse he stole.'

'I'm not a deserter!'

'Seems the boy wants to deny the charge. Well?'

'We're not deserters, sir,' Cato said quietly. 'We were on a secret mission for the legate.'

'A secret mission for the legate – I see.' Tribune Plinius let his amusement show, and winked at the optio. 'So you were on a secret mission, were you? What kind of a mission?'

'It doesn't matter, sir. I have to warn the legate. Before it's too late!'

'Too late for what?'

'There's an ambush, sir, right up ahead in the forest.' Cato pointed desperately at the back of the column disappearing into the trees. 'Togodumnus and his column are right there waiting. Thousands of them, sir. We have to warn Vespasian now!'

Tribune Plinius stared at him in silence for a moment, weighing up the information. There was no reason why he should believe the wild tale told by the boy. How could Togodumnus possibly have evaded the cavalry screen?

'You've seen these Britons personally?'

'Yes, sir! I beg you to tell the legate—'

'Silence!'

Whatever the boy had seen was clearly enough to scare him into this state, Plinius reasoned. But what if it turned out to be a false alarm? What damage would that do to his career? On the other hand what would be the damage of not acting on the information should it prove to be accurate? The reputation of a tribune could not be allowed to weigh against the safety of a legion.

'Very well, get on your horse and go after the legate as fast as you can. Tell him I'm getting the rearguard formed up for battle and will close up with him as soon as I can.'

'Yes, sir!' Cato's heart lifted, and he immediately turned to retrieve his horse from the patrol.

'One last thing!' Plinius called out.

'Sir?'

'If this proves to be a false alarm then I will personally crucify you on the nearest tree. Understand?'

Chapter Thirty-eight

The Second Legion had advanced well into the forest and the vanguard and colour party moved steadily down the track towards General Plautius and the three other legions. The artillery and baggage followed as the two flanking divisions formed a line of march fifty yards either side of the heaving mass of wagons, carts and draught animals. Even as they moved out, it was clear to Vespasian that the order of march was going to run into immediate difficulties. Ahead on the track, trees closed in on either side so the path was constricted to a width of less than thirty paces. Vespasian had foreseen the problem and instructed the senior centurion of each division to thin the flank divisions down to permit as swift as possible a passage through the wooded area. It might well leave the Legion temporarily vulnerable but it was that or face a long march around the forest and Plautius's instructions had required his legates to bring the legions up to the front by the speediest possible route. As the vanguard moved into the forest, the flank cohorts were ordered to form a column of twos to avoid any entanglement with the baggage train.

The manoeuvre was carried out without problem and

Vespasian took pleasure in seeing his troops perform with the effortless ease of an elite unit as they funnelled into the forest. Although Plautius's engineers had done a good job of clearing the foliage from the track, they had not had time to clear it the regulation distance of an arrow shot. Once the men had emerged from the trees the double files would be halted, formed back columns of regular width and moved forward to wait for the rest of the Legion to catch up. Routine as the task was, and the legionaries had carried out many such drills on training marches, the fact that they were in hostile territory lent a tense edginess to the officers as they hurried their men through the forest, eager to return their units to a more secure formation.

Although it was midsummer, when the forest should be bursting with wildlife, a gloomy silence hung in the trees and the dark shadows beneath their boughs. Vespasian was keenly aware of it as he rode forward along the column to check that the units were maintaining cohesion.

By the time he had travelled the length of the column Vespasian was content that all was going tolerably well. He allowed himself to relax, with the confidence that the rest of the day's march should be a formality. Even the legionaries had brightened up and some greeted him as he rode past. The sky was a deep blue that reminded him of the Mediterranean; brilliant white clouds towered above the horizon and the sun blazed down on a myriad of flowers alongside the track. Beyond the lines of men, the green woods shimmered in the sunlight and a faint breeze stirred the topmost branches into a soothing rustle. It was a good day to be alive and the thrill of it all flowed through his veins, so Vespasian was delighted when a stag suddenly plunged out of the trees ahead and froze as it encountered the thousands of men marching towards it along the forest track.

'Look!' Vespasian pointed, the severe facade of a legate momentarily slipping to reveal a boyish excitement.

His staff, who had suffered his foul temper for most of the morning, were keen to make the most of his sudden change of mood and eagerly followed his direction. The stag raised its antlers high and sniffed the air to its front and rear, undecided which way to run. Vespasian was struck by the grace of the animal and its lofty air of natural superiority.

'Bound to be some good meat on that one!' one of the officers said. 'Sir, may I?'

Vespasian nodded. It would be a shame to break the spell of the moment, but after all one couldn't eat spells, and the prospect of a venison supper was too alluring to pass up.

The officer spurred his horse on and yanked the reins round to head for the stag, the line of legionaries hurriedly parting to let him by. Pausing only to snatch a javelin from one of the men, the officer charged off in pursuit of the stag. The animal stood its ground for a moment before it sprang into the air and bounded into the trees. Shouting out his hunting call, the officer raced after the beast and disappeared into the shadows, and Vespasian smiled as he heard the crackle of small branches as the officer crashed through the undergrowth to get at his quarry.

Then the excited cries of the young man were suddenly cut short and, with one last crack of breaking branches, the forest fell silent. The staff officers exchanged looks of alarm. Vespasian craned his neck and stared into the darkness of the forest.

'Shall I go after him, sir?' someone volunteered. 'Sir?'

But Vespasian was no longer listening. His eyes were fixed on the space beneath the broad boughs of the trees. Shadows were moving there, moving all along the treeline. As the cold certainty of realisation clutched at his heart, he knew that he and his men were in the gravest danger. And, in damning proof of the foolishness of the Legion's dispositions, the enemy emerged from the forest into the bright light of day with a silence that was more shocking still. Before Vespasian could respond, a horn sounded and the Britons unleashed a volley of arrows that arced up into the clear sky and swept down on to the Romans. The legionaries dropped their marching yokes and desperately snatched at the shields slung across their backs. Some were too slow and slumped to their knees as they were struck down by the rain of arrows which rattled down on shields and carts and pierced their unprotected skins.

Then the danger was over for a brief instant as the Britons notched arrows ready for their next volley. Vespasian turned in his saddle to see that, miraculously, his staff remained uninjured. Already, the centurions and other line officers were bellowing at their men to form up and face the enemy. Their endless training paid off as the legionaries hurriedly turned from column to line and presented their broad rectangular shields to the enemy, even as a second, ragged, volley fell on to the Legion. Those who had been hit in the first shower, men and animals, were now mercilessly exposed and many were struck again, some killed outright. The area between the cohorts and the baggage train was littered with the still bodies of the dead, and the writhing, screaming forms of injured men and beasts. But the men who had formed up and now sheltered behind their shields were comparatively safe. Vespasian hurriedly issued orders for the north-facing cohorts to prepare to advance and staff officers spurred their horses to each end of the division. Looking across the baggage train to the other cohorts Vespasian was relieved to see that their officers had already formed them up and were clearing gaps in the baggage to allow their men to pass through to the other side. With the legionaries in position, they would be able to make short work of the lightly armed archers. Now that the initial shock had run its course, Vespasian found himself looking forward to the coming fight and inevitable victory.

That was when the Britons unleashed their real attack.

At the very moment the southern cohorts were forcing a way through the baggage train, a deep note blasted from a horn behind them in the forest, and the sound was taken up by other horns up and down the length of the track. And with an ear-splitting roar, the Britons erupted from the forest and hurtled towards the disorganised cohorts, who had frozen at the sound of the horns and now gaped in terror at sight of their impending doom. Some centurions with presence of mind shouted out a string of orders and bodily turned their men to face the charge, but the coherent battle line so typical of the Roman army had simply disintegrated. Vespasian watched in horror as the screaming wave of Britons engulfed his men in a shattering crash. The impact immediately drove the legionaries back on to the baggage train and scores were cut down as they tried to escape through the gaps between the vehicles. Those who turned to face the enemy fought in isolation and, with the Britons still pouring from the forest, the legate could see that the unequal numbers would lead to a massacre of his men unless a battle line could be established within the next few moments.

'Out of the bloody way!' Cato shrieked as he desperately yanked at the reins and the exhausted horse swerved round a legionary who had stepped into his path. Ahead he could see Vespasian amongst his staff. The group had stopped and were looking into the forest on the right-hand side of the track. Suddenly Cato was aware of movement all along the treeline as the Britons emerged from the shadows.

An icy dread washed over him as he realised his warning had arrived too late.

A war horn blasted out and the air was filled with a whirring sound. Before Cato could react, his horse let out a piercing shriek and threw him to one side as it tumbled. Cato scrambled away from the animal and, looking back, saw that it had been struck in the neck by two arrows and now thrashed about in agony. Other victims littered the ground as more arrows thudded down pitilessly. Some men had already abandoned their yokes and were running back down the column towards the camp.

But Cato had no intention of fleeing. He crouched down and glanced around. He felt vulnerable out of armour and hurried over to a dead legionary, quickly stripping the body of shield, helmet and sword. Thus protected, Cato plunged into the nearest mass of men still struggling to organise a resistance against the enemy. It was a desperately unequal fight since the legionaries were not formed up and were engaged in hand-to-hand combat against superior numbers. Only those men who managed to form shield to shield in little knots stood a chance against the sweeping, hacking strokes of the Britons' long swords. Two utterly different fighting styles were in play and as long as the Britons could maintain a loose melee the shorter swords of the legionaries were badly outranged.

Cato rushed into battle, screaming a savage war cry he was not even conscious of. Exhausted to the point of delirium, bitter at his treatment and driven by a keen awareness that this was a fight for survival, he sought the nearest enemy. A tall man of his own height and stature stood in his path, long sword raised and face painted to resemble a many-fanged mouth. Lowering his point and raising his shield Cato deflected the blow and thrust his sword deep into the man's guts. The Briton went down with a piercing cry as Cato wrenched the blade free and knocked him flat with the shield boss. He quickly glanced round, looking for the next target alert to the danger. Three paces ahead of him a Briton stood over a prone legionary whose sword arm had almost been hacked through. The Briton raised his sword to despatch his enemy but before the sword reached the zenith of its arc Cato caught him high in the back between his shoulder blades. With a puzzled expression the man toppled to one side of his intended victim.

'Here!' Cato grabbed the legionary's good hand and, covering them both with his shield dragged the man a short distance to where a group of Romans had formed a tight line with their backs to a pair of wagons. At the centre of the line stood Bestia, bellowing out encouragement to the others in his best parade-ground voice. Cato flung the man he had rescued down with the other injured and turned to take his place among the legionaries.

'Cato!' Bestia shouted, snatching a sidelong glance. 'Time for you to show me what you're really made of.'

Cato nodded grimly as he faced the enemy, thrusting out at any Britons who came close enough, and deflecting the blows of the wicked long swords that carried enough momentum to cut through a man's head in one blow. Indeed, as he fought shoulder to shoulder with his comrades, Cato saw a Roman lean down to finish off a wounded enemy, oblivious in his moment of triumph to the Briton standing to one side, sword raised high in the air. It flashed down, straight through the legionary's neck, before the tip buried itself in the bloody grass beside the track. The legionary's helmeted head shot forward and, with a rattling thud landed several feet away as arterial crimson exploded into the air from the stump of the man's neck.

It was a detail lost in an instant as Cato stabbed at

405

the Britons surrounding the little group. Now that the initial momentum of the charge had subsided, the two sides were locked in thousands of individual struggles whose minutest details would be etched forever in the minds of those who survived. Centurion Bestia laying about with all the ferocious efficiency of a veteran – an anguished expression on an enemy's face – the exotic pattern of the Britons' body paint – the stiffened spiky hair and strangely patterned tattoos. All these impressions burned into the mind's eye even as they passed in a flash. For Cato, an inner calmness seemed to consume him as his mind divorced itself from his body and he fought by instinct. For the first time he felt he really belonged to the Second Legion. If the rearguard arrived in time he might even live to enjoy the feeling.

The battle was going badly and Vespasian saw that the southern line of cohorts – if it could, in truth, be described as a line – would completely disintegrate at any moment unless it could be strengthened. Two cohorts who faced the archers had been ordered forward to clear the treeline and deny them any further opportunity to pepper the Romans. The two remaining cohorts of the main force, some eight hundred men, were all that was left to him now and he hurriedly formed them into a double line facing the baggage train. Then, as their comrades fell back through the tangle of wagons and draught animals, gaps were made in the lines to permit them passage to the rear, where staff officers were hurriedly reforming the survivors of the southernmost cohorts into a reserve.

As things stood, Vespasian knew that the battle could only have one outcome. Sheer weight of numbers, and the loss of a third of his command, meant that the Britons would eventually overwhelm even the stoutest defence. For a moment he considered ordering his men to break formation and flee into the forest to the north but, scattered and lost, they would be easy pickings for the inevitable pursuit. The destruction of the Legion would take place more quickly if they stood their ground, but they would take more of the enemy with them. Then, at least, his posthumous reputation would be salvaged and the name Vespasian would not be linked to that of Varus, who had led three legions to a similar fate many years ago in the dark depths of the German forests.

The reserve line held steady as their comrades were forced back through the baggage train, slowly yielding ground before the enemy onslaught. Once the retreating Romans were safely within javelin range, Vespasian nodded to the trumpeter who blared out the prearranged signal. The men of the two cohorts readied their javelins.

'Release!' Vespasian roared out and the centurions instantly echoed the command. Eight hundred arms hurled their javelins in a high-angled arc over the heads of their comrades, beyond the baggage train, where they fell on the lightly armoured bodies of the Britons massing on the far side. From the volume of cries and screams, the Romans knew that they had hit the enemy hard and the men exchanged grins of satisfaction as they readied their final javelins. The second volley caused a fresh crescendo of screams and cries to rend the air. The legionaries drew their swords, waiting for the Britons to

resume their attack on the thin Roman lines. The Legion
had shot its bolt and now prepared to renew the vicious
hand-to-hand fighting that would decide the matter.

Dismounting from his horse, Vespasian undid the clasp
at his shoulder and let his legate's cloak slide to the
ground in an untidy heap. An orderly held out a shield
and Vespasian slipped his left hand through the strap,
took a firm hold of the iron handle and drew his ivory-
handled short sword. He drew himself up to his full
height and pushed his way forward until he stood in the
middle of the front rank of men facing the enemy. If this
was the day ordained for his death, then he would go
down as his breeding and respect for Roman tradition
dictated he should: with his face to the enemy and a
sword in his hand.

Chapter Thirty-nine

From the crest of a hill at the southern edge of the forest, Macro stood at the base of a vast oak tree and stared up through its leafy branches. The track from the marsh had brought them to this point and Macro could wait no longer to find out how things stood with the Second Legion.

'Well?'

'I can't quite make it out, sir,' Pyrax called down to him.

'Just tell me what you can see.'

'I can see the baggage train right enough, but there's men all over it – can't tell who's who though.'

Macro balled his hand into a fist and struck the rough bark in frustration. 'This is no good,' he muttered and then, grabbing a low branch, he began scaling the broad trunk. He reached Pyrax, sitting astride a limb growing perpendicularly from the trunk.

'Next time I need information,' Macro gasped, 'I'll bloody well do the job myself, and not get somebody who's half blind.'

Beside Pyrax, Macro had his first view of the distant battle and saw with horror that the thin scarlet lines of the Legion were engulfed by a multicoloured wave of enemy troops. Only the rearguard retained any appearance of order. Vitellius and Cato had failed then and Vespasian had unwittingly led his men into an ambush. From the look of things, the ambush was about to become a massacre.

'What shall we do, sir?'

'Do? What can we do?'

'Should we try and find one of the other legions, sir? Or maybe head back to the fortress on the coast.'

'Well, we're hardly going to reinforce that lot,' Macro said bitterly and jabbed his thumb towards the forest. 'But we'll wait. Something might happen.'

'Like what, sir?'

'Haven't got a fucking clue. So we wait.'

They sat in silence, watching their comrades, men they had known for most of their lives, as they were gradually pushed back from the baggage train. It was a struggle for survival, the bloody intensity of which they could only helplessly imagine. It was almost more than Macro could bear and he tried to stop tears forming in his eyes as he witnessed the death of the Second Legion.

'Sir?'

'What?'

'Over there. Look.' Pyrax pointed to the west of the forest, eyes straining to make out the detail in the extreme distance. Following the direction of his finger Macro saw the dark mass which had escaped his attention earlier, when he had been battling to fight back his tears. But now as he looked, the dead hand of fate closed its fingers on any last hopes he may have entertained for the Second

410

Legion. A second column of Britons was flowing down the forest track to seal the Legion's fate.

The hard-pressed men of the Second Legion had been forced to steadily yield ground to the Britons and now their backs were almost up against the treeline from which the archers had emerged. The last reserves of Cato's strength had almost run their course; the weight of the shield on his arm seemed to have increased ten-fold and now he could barely raise it off the ground. His sword thrusts had been reduced to feeble jabs at the faces of the enemy and he could barely parry the blows that were aimed at him. But still he fought on, determined to resist to the last. And that time, he knew, was fast approaching. Bestia had fallen, cut down when three of the enemy had jumped him together and he now lay on the bloodied grass, face laid open to the bone. The fact that the legate was fighting alongside his men was eloquent proof that he too believed that the Second Legion was about to be wiped out. Separated from vanguard and rearguard by the cleverly worked ambush, the cohorts of the main column fought on alone. The ground before them was covered with the fallen and the moans of the injured mingled with the overall cacophony of war cries, shouts of rage and the incoherent roars of men who had surrendered to the blood-lust of battle. There were no cries from Roman wounded, any who fell to the ground at the mercy of the Britons were quickly despatched with the bitter anger that is reserved for all invaders. All around the grass was splashed with slippery crimson gore that presented yet another peril to the men engaged in the deadly struggle waged all along the forest track.

To Cato's left, the Second's legate fought with a savage abandon that filled those around him with surprise, so used were they to the quiet-mannered disciplinarian. But with death so imminent, Vespasian saw little point in preserving any sense of decorum. What the men needed now was not the cold reserve of aristocratic command, it was an example of fighting spirit to sustain them to the end. So he threw himself at all comers, hacking and slashing at the enemy with wanton disregard for his own safety. Yet he still lived, apparently charmed against the blows of the enemy, while men about him were struck down.

In spite of the fact that the Romans showed no signs of breaking, and only seemed to fight harder the more they were pressed back, the Britons scented victory. After the initial surprise of the ambush, the Legion had exacted a terrible toll on them such that only the complete destruction of every Roman would suffice. Vespasian saw a chariot careering along behind the Britons. It carried a richly dressed man of some stature who was wildly exhorting his men, driving them onwards as he pointed his war spear again and again at the Roman lines. For a moment, the legate considered leading a small group against the Britons' commander, in the hope that the elimination of Togodumnus would knock the fight out of them. But every Roman was already committed to the battle and could not be extricated to form such a force. Vespasian despaired as he watched the chariot pass by unharmed and then, his rage further inflamed, he slammed his shield into the body of a Briton engaged with the legionary next to him and thrust a sword into the man's side. No doubt Togodumnus would be considered a great hero by his own people when the day was out, and the thought spurred Vespasian on to fight with even greater ferocity.

When the Roman line finally gave under the relentless pressure, the Legion broke into small groups fighting independently of each other, no longer a part of any coherent military formation, simply fighting to live a little longer yet – and make the enemy pay for the privilege.

Cato found himself in a knot of fifty or so men holding off several times that number of Britons. As he dragged himself round to face the latest attacker he was suddenly confronted by a huge man, naked but painted in strange Celtic patterns from head to toe. With a roar, the man swung a great two-handed sword at Cato's head. Summoning up all his energy, Cato jerked his shield up just in time. With a terrible jarring crash the sword splintered the shield and instantly numbed Cato's shield arm from his fingertips through to his shoulder. His grip failed him and the shield slipped from his useless fingers leaving Cato at the mercy of the towering British warrior, who laughed into the face of his helpless victim. He brutally shoved Cato backwards and the optio sprawled on the ground, the force of the impact winding him as his sword fell beyond his reach. Raising the great sword up for the final blow, the Briton bellowed his war cry. But before he could strike Cato saw a figure come between them – Vespasian. With a snarl the legate thrust himself forward, coming in under the Briton's sword and warding it off with his shield. Then he thrust out, and up, at the Briton's throat, but the warrior reacted with a lithe sidestep that bespoke a mastery of close combat. Pulling back, each man sized the other up, ready to spring to the attack in an instant.

For a moment a stillness surrounded the pair as Britons and Romans alike watched for the outcome of the fight between the giant Briton and the legate. The decisive moment of the battle had been reached. But even as they paused, they became aware of a new sound – the blare of distant instruments. Both men heard the noise though their eyes remained firmly fixed on each other. Lying on the ground, Cato wondered at first if his tired ears had deceived him, but he saw that his comrades shared his reaction. Could it be possible?

The sound was repeated almost at once and Vespasian felt his heart lift – there was no mistaking the trumpet call for the charge. Help was at hand, but from whom? The thought was over in an instant as the British warrior stepped back a pace, instinctively following the rest of his comrades, who broke contact with their enemy as the first terrible doubts began to sow themselves. Seizing the opportunity of the moment, Vespasian thrust his sword-point deep into the Briton's throat and quickly ripped it free. Dropping his sword, the British warrior grabbed at his wound in an attempt to stem the flow of blood. Vespasian ignored him and craned his neck in the direction of the trumpets, now definitely closer at hand. Then, over the heads of the Britons, far down the track, a line of horsemen appeared, cloaked in red, at their head the unmistakable silhouette of a Roman standard.

And from the other direction came the roar of the Second Legion's rearguard as they renewed their attack from the other end of the forest track.

A palpable shiver of anxiety rippled through the Britons as the cavalry began to roll up their flank. A handful of men began to retreat towards the southern treeline. As others followed their lead, the chariot bearing Togodumnus raced up the line and the Britons' leader shouted harshly at his men to hold, but the infectious sense of fear was already turning to panic and his men swept by him. Seeing that a hard core of Britons were holding their ground, Vespasian raised his sword high above his head. No eloquent speech was needed, and none came.

'Get them! Get them!'

The Roman line surged forward in pursuit of the men who, a moment ago, had been utterly assured of victory. Now they ran like rabbits, bolting for the safety of the forest on the far side of the track, all sense of arrogant self-belief gone in an instant. Cato, still lying on the ground, could only marvel at the suddenness of the change in circumstances.

Vespasian kept his eye on Togodumnus and, collecting a handful of men about him, he launched himself through the bloody pursuit, straight at the chariot. But the Britons' leader was no fool and knew when he had lost control of a battle. He barked an order at the driver and, with a crack of a whip, the chariot turned round and raced back down the forest track, away from the rapidly approaching cavalry. Vespasian could only watch in despair as the chariot accelerated away from him, the driver recklessly mowing down everything in his path to ensure that Togodumnus reached safety.

The legate called his men to a halt at the side of the baggage train and climbed on to the driver's seat of the nearest wagon to try and get an overview of the battle. Everywhere he looked, the Britons were on the run and, from the west, the Roman cavalry he had spied moments earlier, mercilessly swept along the forest track slaughtering all the enemy before them. As they approached, a tall figure on a white horse tore itself away from the pursuit and made his way over to Vespasian.

'Vitellius?' Vespasian muttered to himself doubtfully. But a moment later the likeness was clear enough and Vespasian shook his head in surprise. Vitellius reined in by the wagon and saluted.

'What the hell are you doing here, tribune?'

'It's a long story, sir.'

'I bet it is. And once this little lot's over I want a full report.'

High on the hill overlooking the forest, Macro almost fell out of the tree with excitement. He bobbed up and down on the bough, smacking his fist into his other hand as he saw the lead elements of the Fourteenth – it could only be the Fourteenth, he surmised – plough into the enemy surrounding the Second's vanguard, just as the Second's rearguard rushed at the other flank of the fleeing Britons. As soon as the enemy broke, the cavalry was released for the merciless pursuit that followed, the troopers sweeping all before them as panic flooded through the enemy who turned and streamed from the battlefield.

'Brilliant! Bloody brilliant, I tell you!' He slapped Pyrax on the shoulder.

'Easy, sir!' Pyrax shouted as he desperately grabbed the bough.

Macro just smiled at him and then continued his rejoicing. 'Bastards are all over the place! Look at 'em running from the forest. They must have gone through the trees like shit through a goose!'

'Some of them are running this way, sir,' Pyrax observed quietly.

'Of course they are. They're going to try and reach the marsh while they can. Oh . . .' Macro looked down through the branches to the track below that meandered over to the forest in one direction and the distant marsh in the other. 'I see what you mean.'

'We'd better not be here when they come by. I don't imagine they'd be too chuffed to encounter any more Romans.'

'Point taken.' Macro nodded to the men lying in the grass at the foot of the oak tree. 'You'd better go down and get them up here. And lose the horses, they're no good to us now.'

'Right, sir.' Pyrax quickly clambered down and left Macro to watch the final phase of the fight unfolding panoramically before him.

The pursuing cavalry and rearguard troops were emerging from the forest to run down the rearmost Britons as they attempted to stumble for safety. Some dropped their weapons and threw themselves at the mercy of their pursuers, but few were spared. Those taken alive were swiftly rounded up and herded together under

417

the watchful eyes of a handful of sturdy men appointed for the task. Pyrax had been right, many of the figures fleeing from the Romans were heading up the track leading back to the marsh they had used to outflank the Second Legion and they would be passing under the tree in a few moments. Macro looked down and saw that his squad was scrambling up into the oak tree, the uninjured hauling up their less fortunate comrades until all were hidden in the leafy boughs.

Satisfied that they were safe from the Britons, Macro once more watched the pursuit. His eye caught a movement from the edge of the forest nearest the remains of the Second's marching camp and saw a chariot tear round the edge of the trees and head directly up the hill towards the track. As the charioteer thrashed his horses, Macro saw that the man standing behind him, clutching at the wicker handholds, was a superbly built individual in richly decorated robes, sporting a gleaming bronze helmet. Clearly he was a warrior of some significance. A pair of Roman cavalrymen took advantage of the slope and charged after the chariot. Nimbly knocking aside the cavalryman's spear-thrust, the Briton smashed the heavily weighted butt of his spear into the man's face and he tumbled from his horse. The second cavalryman was equally reckless and he paid for it with his life as the British chieftain ran him clean through then ripped his spear free.

As the chariot lumbered up the slope, Macro could see that its present course would take it under the oak tree.

'We'll have him! That bastard there!' He pointed out

the chariot and ordered those of his patrol who were still armed and uninjured to follow him down to the ground. Breathing heavily, with swords drawn, they crouched low and waited. A handful of British infantry ran by but took to their heels with a fresh burst of energy as soon as they saw the grim-faced huddle of legionaries with glinting short swords. Then the pounding of hooves and rattle of wheels heralded the approach of the chariot and Macro tensed, ready to pounce. The harsh shouts of the charioteer rose above the din and Macro risked a peek round the tree trunk to make sure of his timing.

'Ready, lads? Go for the charioteer and the horses first. Then we'll deal with the big one.'

He waited until the chariot was almost level with the oak tree.

'Now! At 'em, lads!'

Macro rushed out, directly into the path of the horses, and made a grab for the traces. The men on the chariot were taken completely by surprise and had no time to steer round the Romans. Macro pulled down hard and the horses stumbled to a halt. Pyrax took down the charioteer with a quick thrust before the man could even drop the reins. He fell off the chariot and his head was crushed under a wheel as his nervous horses sidestepped. The chieftain recovered his wits and leaped down, spear in hand, and made for the broad trunk of the oak tree. He turned, presented his spear and dared the Romans to fight him with a harsh laugh. Macro looked at him admiringly; the fellow was certainly game for a fight, whatever the odds.

'Spread out!' he ordered his men. 'And watch that bloody spear!'

As the half circle of legionaries cautiously approached, the Briton kept the tip of his war spear on the move, thrusting it at one man after another as they crept too close. With a howl of pain, one of Macro's tired men was stabbed in the guts and tumbled to the ground, bleeding profusely.

'All right then!' Macro called out, keeping his eyes firmly on the Briton. 'We'll rush him. Ready? Now!'

Six men threw themselves at the Briton and, with a wild stab, he caught one man in the leg before the others crashed into him, knocking him flat. But, hopelessly outnumbered as he was, the Briton hurled two men to one side, grabbed a Roman sword and rolled on to his feet, crouching low, with the unaccustomed blade held ready to slash at his enemies.

'Leave him to me!' Macro waved the others back. 'Bastard wants a fight, then he can have one with me.'

Readying his short sword, Macro bent his knees and slowly circled the Briton, sizing him up. And all the time the chieftain stared back, coldly assessing the stocky Roman.

'Fancy yourself, don't you?' Macro said quietly. 'Big bastard you may be, but you haven't got a bloody clue how to use that sword. Designed for thrusting . . . it's not a bloody cleaver.'

He feinted forwards and, as he had anticipated, the Briton swung the sword up above his head, rushing at Macro with a savage howl of rage. Macro simply dropped to his knee, straightened his arm and let the Briton's momentum do the rest. With a grunt the man doubled over the sword and flung his arms forward, his hands searching for Macro's neck. He got a grip and pressed down on the windpipe. Gasping, Macro tumbled on to the ground with the Briton on top of him, huge hands grasping ever more tightly on Macro's throat. Their faces were less than a foot apart and Macro saw the man's eyes brighten in triumph as he gritted his teeth and tightened his grip. The sword was still in Macro's grip and he worked it furiously inside his opponent trying for a vital organ. His head felt as if it would explode under the pressure of the man's grip until, at last, the fire in the Briton's eyes faded and after a last spasm, the man's grip loosened. Macro wrenched the hands from his throat and desperately gulped down air. He heaved the body to one side and struggled on to his feet before fixing his men with an angry glare.

'Why the fuck didn't you help me?'

'You told us not to,' Pyrax protested.

Macro rubbed his neck, wincing at its tenderness. 'Well, next time use your bloody initiative. If some sod's about to croak your centurion you get stuck in and stop him, whatever you've been told to do. Get it?'

'Yes, sir.'

'Right then, might as well put the chariot to good use. Load the wounded on, and sling him over one of the horses. Then, my lads, it's back to the safety of the Second Legion and the drinks are on me, if anyone's still awake tonight.'

Chapter Forty

The Second Legion moved no further that day as the surviving officers re-formed their units and took stock of their losses. They had answered grievously for Plautius' orders to join him as quickly as possible. Nearly a third of the Legion had been killed or injured and half the baggage train destroyed or immobilised by the loss of draught animals. A rough perimeter was in the process of being erected around the survivors although no-one seriously believed that the Britons would be able to regroup enough men to mount another attack. In any case, Togodumnus had been slain and his body was displayed, spread-eagled across his chariot, in front of the pen holding the British prisoners. They gazed at the body of their commander in sullen silence and wept, quite unashamed.

The Roman wounded lay in long rows waiting their turn for treatment as the Legion's hospital orderlies moved amongst them, sorting out the triage cases from those that stood a good chance of surviving their injuries. The air was filled with their moans and cries. To one side of the track, a huge pyre had nearly been completed and a growing pile of Roman bodies was being heaped on top: the pyre would be lit once night fell. In front of the hastily erected headquarters tent the pile of identity seals taken from the dead was mute testament to the price the Legion had paid. The dead Britons were unceremoniously thrown into a series of pits dug along the length of the track. Although a victory had been won, the men of the Second Legion had no desire to join the rejoicing of their comrades in the Fourteenth, whose distant cries of celebration could be heard from their camp at the edge of the forest.

In Vespasian's tent, an altogether different mood pervaded. He sat at his desk staring at the three men before him – Vitellius, seated, with a sickening hint of a smile playing about his lips as he listened to the account being given by the centurion and the optio standing to one side. Every so often he was aware of the hate-filled glances shot at him by the other two, but it only seemed to amuse him all the more as be bided his time.

Macro, filthy and exhausted, tried to make his report as clearly as possible but the intense weariness of the last few days clouded his mind and every so often he would turn to his optio to clarify a point, or to recall a detail. Cato stood stiffly at attention, his arm in a sling, still numb and useless from the blow he had received earlier.

The pair looked quite done in, reflected Vespasian, but he was secretly delighted with them. They had recovered the chest from the wagon in the marsh and even now the Legion's cavalry squadron had been despatched to retrieve it from its new hiding place. Not only that, but Macro had brought the body of

Togodumnus into the camp and the corpse was identified by one of the British exiles accompanying the Fourteenth legion, a vile rat-faced man by the name of Adminius. With Togodumnus dead, only his brother Caratacus remained to co-ordinate the British resistance to the invaders. All in all, the legate decided, a disaster had been neatly averted, and had in fact been turned into something of a victory. In that light, his career was safe.

But there remained the sticky problem of the accusations being made against Vitellius by the centurion and his optio. As they spoke of Vitellius's attack on them in the marsh, their words were spoken with the simplicity of truth and all the doubts that Vespasian had ever entertained about the tribune seemed to be vindicated.

Macro finished his report and, after a moment's silence, Vespasian weighed up the evidence, while he stared intently at each of the three in turn.

'Are you quite sure about this, Centurion? Do you really wish to prefer charges against the tribune here?'

'Yes, sir!'

'What you say will sound quite incredible in a court of law. You know that, don't you?'

'Yes, sir.'

'Very well then. Very well. I will give your statements the fullest consideration and let you know my decision at the earliest convenience. You two are dismissed.'

'Sir?'

'What is it, optio?'

The young optio paused to consider his next words carefully. 'I still don't quite understand why we were listed as deserters, sir.'

'The charges have been dropped,' Vespasian said curtly. 'No harm done.'

'Yes, sir, but why were the charges made in the first place? Who—'

'A mistake, Optio. Leave it at that. Now you're dismissed.'

As Macro and Cato made for the tent flap, Vespasian called after them. 'One last thing. You have my thanks for alerting the rearguard. I doubt we'd have lasted long enough for the Fourteenth to rescue us, if Plinius hadn't been able to hold that end of the column. Now, make sure you get some rest. Wait outside and I'll have my orderly fix you and your men some hot food.'

'Thank you, sir,' Macro replied.

Alone in the tent with Vitellius, the legate considered his next interview carefully. Already the established version of events had Vitellius down as the hero who had single-handedly found Togodumnus's column. Unable to fight his way back to warn the Second Legion, he had caught up with the Fourteenth causing them to turn and intervene, just in time to save the Second Legion from annihilation. Consequently the tribune had won fulsome praise from nearly all quarters for his gallant action. Yet the two men who had left talked of treachery and betrayal.

'I take it you will not be pursuing their wild claims any further, sir?'

'It's quite a story. Wouldn't you agree?'

'Yes, but still a story. And, like all the best stories, there isn't a shred of truth in it.'

'But if the rest of their patrol says the same then you're in a bit of a fix.'

425

'Not at all,' Vitellius protested smoothly. 'It's my word against theirs. The word of the son of a consul against a bunch of squaddies. Who do you think a court will believe, especially after I've risked my life to save the Legion from certain defeat? At best it'll look like sour grapes. At worst, it will look like a political prosecution and that's hardly likely to go down well with the plebes in Rome – they're rather partial to heroes, I understand. I'd let it go if I were you.'

Vespasian smiled. 'Even heroes still have to call their superiors "sir",' he said quietly.

'My apologies – sir.'

'Let's, for the moment, agree that the centurion spoke the truth. How did you find out about the chest?'

Vitellius did not reply immediately as he sized up the legate. 'You know, I could deny all knowledge of the chest. I was, after all, acting on your orders to scout for sign of Togodumnus. I could say I just happened to be in the marsh at the same time as your little team. A thick mist, a case of mistaken identity . . . all perfectly understandable.'

'Understandable, but not true.'

'Of course it's not true, sir. But it doesn't really matter.'

'Why?'

'Because nothing will ever come of it. Not one word of what passes between us now will ever be uttered outside this tent.'

'And why might that be, tribune?' Vespasian smiled.

'I'll come to that, in a little while. Since you seem to be quite keen to know the truth about things then I'll indulge you. Actually, Narcissus told me about the chest.'

'Narcissus?'

'He told me before we'd even left the base on the Rhine. You see, I'm the imperial spy you were told about. He wasn't entirely sure about you and wanted me to keep an eye on the operation. Of course, I was only too happy to oblige.'

Vespasian managed to smile at the irony of the situation. Even the cunning Narcissus had his blind spots. Motive and alibi had been handed to Vitellius on a plate.

'But while he told me about the wagon, he didn't tell me where it was. That's why I needed to see the map on that scroll. Unfortunately someone beat me to it. Not only that but they tried to frame me for its theft. Still, it was simple enough to have Pulcher follow your men down into the marsh and send for some assistance the moment they started digging. I genuinely hoped to avoid any bloodshed, amongst my men that is. If I'd managed to persuade Macro to give up the chest we'd only have had to kill them afterwards. As it was, he demonstrated an unfortunate penchant for the most resourceful soldiering in adverse circumstances. And so the chest has been won for Claudius.'

'But why would you want the chest in the first place?' Vespasian asked. 'You couldn't possibly have hoped to use such a vast sum without attracting attention.'

'Absolutely. I hope you don't take me for that much of a fool, sir. I never intended to spend the money on myself.'

'Then why go to such lengths to obtain it?'

'For the same reason the Emperor wants that chest.

Gold is power; and with that kind of wealth I could buy the loyalty of pretty much any, and every, man I wanted to.'

'I see.' Vespasian nodded. 'Then that would make you the traitor Narcissus warned me about. It never occurred to me that the imperial spy and the traitor were the same person. I think Narcissus will be equally surprised when I tell him.'

'Me the traitor? Is that what you think?' Vitellius laughed. 'Hardly! As it happens, I am still the imperial spy – always have been. At least that's what Narcissus believes.'

'So why try to kill him?'

'Kill him?' Vitellius frowned. 'Oh, that business on the road to Gesoriacum. Not guilty, I'm afraid. And anyway what could I possibly gain from his death? I needed him to get to the army and help crush the mutiny. After all, how could I hope to get to the chest unless the invasion went ahead? No, that ambush was the work of someone else. My guess is that the person behind the ambush wanted to prevent the invasion. You know as well as anyone how important it is for Claudius to win approval for his elevation to Emperor. With Narcissus dead, the mutiny in full flow, the invasion abandoned, and the fortune in the chest denied him, how long do you think Claudius would last? Believe me, until I could get my hands on the chest I was only too keen to further the Emperor's aims.'

'And what then?' Vespasian asked. 'You could hardly produce such a large fortune all at once.'

'Of course not. I don't need it right now. I'm just

planning for my future. Claudius won't last for ever and someone has to be Emperor – why not me one day?'

'You?' It was Vespasian's turn to laugh.

'Why not? Come to that, why not you?'

'You can't be serious?'

'I'm serious. Deadly serious.'

'But Claudius has heirs, a family to ensure someone succeeds him.'

'That's very true,' agreed Vitellius. 'But you must have noticed how easily members of the imperial family succumb to all manner of peculiar deaths. They're quite a tragic lot. And if something is to happen to them, I intend to be there when the vacancy is announced. But I'm in no hurry just now. I can bide my time and make sure that I move only when I have the resources to buy the necessary support. Thanks to those two outside I'll just have to wait a little longer.'

Vespasian was shocked by the tribune's naked ambition. Was there no limit to what the man would do in his desire for power? Yet there was a more immediate question that demanded an answer.

'If you aren't the spy acting for the traitors, then who is?'

'I was wondering when you would ask that.' Vitellius leaned back. 'The truth is, it took me a long time to find out. I should have known much earlier, certainly before my man Pulcher beat it out of the ring-leader of the mutiny.'

Vespasian suddenly recalled the way in which Plinius had looked at the scroll he had retrieved from Titus that evening back in the command tent, and the convenient way Plinius had distracted the guards at just the moment when the thief had been searching through his document chest. 'Plinius?'

'Plinius!' Vitellius laughed. 'Him? Oh, do be serious, sir.'

'If not Plinius, then who?'

'I would be wary about someone much closer to home if I were you.'

'What do you mean?' Vespasian felt a cold, sick feeling rise in his throat.

'If what Narcissus tells me is true then it seems that someone was trying to frame me over that business in the tent.'

'You deny that you tried to steal the scroll?'

'No,' admitted Vitellius. 'But the scroll I had Pulcher steal from you was blank. Someone had made the switch before I could get to it.'

'It couldn't have been blank,' Vespasian countered with a smile. 'Because it couldn't have been switched in the first place. It was already out of the safe-box, Flavia found it, she said Titus had . . .' Vespasian felt his blood turn icy cold.

'Flavia found it. How convenient.' Vitellius smiled at the legate.

'It's not possible,' muttered Vespasian.

'That's what I thought at first. You have to hand it to her, Flavia is a slick operator.'

'But . . . but why?'

'Why? I can't pretend to fully understand her motives. I don't suppose for a moment that she's half the Republican she pretends to be. I'd say it was more likely that she was easing the way for you, to advance your career.'

'Me?' Vespasian was shocked.

'My dear legate, you may think that your moral integrity does you great credit, and that to serve the Emperor unquestioningly is the first duty of your office, but the very fact that you don't suspect your wife makes you all the more useful as a political pawn. What better candidate to step into the gap following Claudius's fall than a man who honestly believed he had served the old boy to the fullest extent of his ability and loyalty. The plebes would love you. I bet you could have given Antony's funeral oration over Caesar a run for its money.'

'How dare you?' Vespasian said quietly, struggling to control his rising temper. 'How dare you suggest that Flavia – could even begin to do the things you accuse her of?'

'You never suspected? I suppose that's to your credit as a husband. And I'm sure you'd make a great statesman, but you'd be a lousy politician. The men who attacked Narcissus came from a cavalry unit commanded by Gaius Marcellus Dexter, one of Scribonianus's officers and, as it happens, a distant cousin of your wife. You don't think that's a coincidence, I hope. Face it, Flavia's cover is almost blown. I'd have a word with your wife very soon. Encourage her to cease her meddling in power games and Narcissus might just miss her part in all this. If you want to keep your wife in good health, I suggest you make sure that I never feel the need to tell anyone about her extra-curricular activities. I haven't yet told Narcissus what I know. You give me your silence about all that we've said in here and I give you Flavia's life. A fair bargain, wouldn't you say?'

Vespasian stared at him, his mind still trying to deny the evidence his memory relentlessly reassembled from the events of the last few months. That moment in the tent when she fumbled the scroll she had retrieved from Titus. It had been deftly swapped, he now realised.

'Sir, I don't expect you to agree to my offer right now. But think it over carefully. I won't deny that I've been rather careless in many respects. And I might just be able to persuade Narcissus that any charges you bring against me are unfounded, or even unscrupulous. But the merest suggestion that I have been anything but the good and faithful servant he believes me to be, will surely undermine my position. So you see, if you force all this out into the open we'll both suffer the consequences. Moreover, I'll be forced to reveal what I know about Flavia. I'm sure you'll accept that it's in all our interests to be discreet about every detail of the last few months.'

Vitellius waited for a reply but Vespasian was looking down, wrapped in a growing despair and oblivious to the tribune's final comments. He raised a hand to rest his head on, still shattered by the revelations.

'Oh, Flavia . . .' he whispered. 'How could you?'

'Now, sir, if I may go? I have my duties to attend to.' Vitellius rose to leave the tent. 'And I trust we'll hear no more about Centurion Macro's charges against me.' For a moment Vespasian struggled for words to continue the interview. Words to express his shame and fear – and rage at the smug superiority of the tribune. Some words to put Vitellius in his place. But no words came and he simply nodded in the direction of the tent flap.

Outside, Cato and Macro were sitting on some forage left out for the staff horses. Macro was fast asleep, head bowed down on his chest and snoring heavily, having finally surrendered to a terrible need for rest. The loud snores drew disapproving glances from passing orderlies bustling in and out of headquarters. The peat-soiled clothes, grimy skin and dark dried blood of Togodumnus smeared over his hands and face had reduced the centurion to a pitiful state. Yet Cato regarded him with affection as he recalled Macro's honest delight at finding him alive and well on his return to the Second Legion. The sense of belonging that Cato had been so clearly aware of during the battle had remained with him and he sensed that this was how it felt to be a legionary, at one with his comrades and the unforgiving way of life he had been thrust into. The army was his home now. He belonged body and soul to the Second Legion.

And it was as well, he reflected, as he looked up and caught the eye of one of the hundreds of Britons sitting quietly in the prisoners' pen, spoils of war destined to be shipped back to Rome and sold into slavery. But for his late father's request, Cato might still have been a slave, like that poor savage in the pen. A lifetime of the worst kind of slavery awaited them all. Back-breaking agricultural labour on some huge estate, or a faster death on a chain-gang in a lead mine was all that uncivilised prisoners taken in battle could expect.

Yet there was something in the prisoner's eyes that spoke of an unbroken spirit, of a will to fight to the bitter end at any cost, of a fire that burned within as long as one man bore arms against the invaders. Cato knew that the campaign to subdue these people was going to be a long and bloody struggle.

Now you can buy any of these other bestselling books by **Simon Scarrow** from your bookshop or *direct from his publisher*.

SOUL TO SOUL

DONNA HILL

Genesis Press, Inc.

Indigo Love Stories

An imprint of Genesis Press, Inc.
Publishing Company

Genesis Press, Inc.
P.O. Box 101
Columbus, MS 39703

ISBN: 1-58571-211-6
Manufactured in the United States of America

First Edition 2000
Second Edition 2006

Visit us at www.genesis-press.com or call at 1-888-Indigo-1

ONE

It was lunchtime and the black folks of Clinton Hill tumbled out onto the Brooklyn streets, meandering in and out of antique shops, Afrocentric boutiques, and almost upscale restaurants in search of something to do for that one blessed hour.

Leone Weathers had her own agenda as she weaved in and out of the foot traffic on Fulton Street. Her spirits felt as light as the September air that gently tussled her recently cut hair. Her bandleader, and after-hours lover, Cole Fleming, had called to tell her to hurry down to the club and listen to the sax player he'd found.

The club had been without a permanent saxophone player for almost two months, after the last one got a gig touring Europe. She had listened to so many "potential" candidates her ears were crossing. It's not that they weren't good, they just weren't great. They didn't have that "somethin' somethin'" that took your breath away. Leone had grown so weary of the search, she'd turned the whole process over to Cole and warned him not to call her until he was positive he'd found "the one." This time he was certain, he'd assured her less than an hour earlier. "Come in and hear him for yourself. You won't be disappointed."

So, she'd thrown on a pair of jeans, a long-sleeve white cotton blouse and her sneakers and hurried over to the club, which was only five blocks away from her house.

Leone stopped in front of the smoked glass door and couldn't help smiling with pride as she looked at the gold leaf lettering on the door: Soul to Soul Nightclub and Restaurant.

Soul to Soul was her baby. She'd worked twenty years as a registered nurse, saved her money and purchased her dream five years earlier—her very own nightclub. She'd put a lot of work into rehabbing the abandoned building and making it into one of the fastest growing hot spots in downtown Brooklyn.

The first year had been a struggle, and between the growing pains of her teenage daughter Raven, the disintegration of her marriage to Steven, and trying to get her business off the ground, there were many days when Leone wanted to throw in the towel and go back to nursing. It was people like Cole, and her best friend and business consultant, Antoinette Lewis, who kept her believing in her dream.

Leone dug into her canvas bag and pulled out her keys. Antoinette had been pressuring her into considering opening for lunch, but Leone had balked at the idea. Dealing with the after-work and dinner crowd was quite enough, she'd said. Maybe in another year, but now was too soon. She'd had enough changes to deal with over the past year or two. With her daughter rapidly approaching eighteen and developing a life of her own, the business pretty much self-sufficient, she'd had a bit more time to look at her own life and where she was. What she was discovering day-by-day had led her to begin rethinking her direction.

She was getting older and in a few more years her forties would be a thing of the past. Cole had been pressuring her to get married, but she'd coyly been able to put him off and wasn't certain why. He was a wonderful man and they had a decent relationship, but at the heart of it, she didn't really think she loved Cole. At least not the kind of love to build a marriage on. She'd been down that road and maybe her disastrous marriage had jaded her to the sanctity of union. But the more she examined her feelings, the more she realized that what she wanted in a relationship was that spark, that total feeling of compatibility that was more than just great sex and someone good to look at in the morning. Yet, the thought of being alone again kept her locked in place.

Unlocking the door, Leone slipped her sunglasses from her nose and stepped into the dim, cool interior.

"Hi Terry," Leone said, waving to her hostess. Leone continued toward the back of the nightclub. "Where's Cole?" she asked over her shoulder.

"I think he's in the office," Terry said over the din of glasses and dishes clattering in the kitchen.

"Thanks."

Leone walked around the circular tables until she'd made her way to the office. The door was partially opened and she could hear male voices coming from inside. One she knew with her eyes closed, the other she didn't recognize, its deep pulsing quality suddenly making her feel warm all over. Leone pushed the door open and stepped inside.

Cole was seated behind the desk. He looked up when Leone walked in. A slow smile and a hint of something a bit more intimate spread across his dark brown face. The one with the voice had his back turned toward her. The shoulders were wide, stretched beneath a blue denim shirt, she quickly observed. His hair was neatly trimmed, cut close to his head and she knew the almost carnal scent she smelled was not Cole. Her stomach did an inexplicable tumble before settling down.

Leone closed the door and stepped fully into the room. "Hey, Cole."

Cole stood and the stranger turned in his seat. The dark probing eyes with the slightly hooded brow and slick black lashes, made an all too appealing picture set against his warm brandy-toned skin. His full mouth, lined by a thin mustache, dipped in the center like a heart to tease the lush bottom lip that he languidly licked with a swipe of his tongue.

"Leone, this is the man I was talking to you about. Ray Taylor. Ray, Leone Weathers."

The stranger stood, extending his hand simultaneously. "You're definitely the lady of the house. Cole, here," he added with a toss of his head, "has been singing your praises all morning."

Leone felt her hand become enveloped by his. "Cole tends to exaggerate," she said derisively, trying to ignore the warm pressure of his hand. "But in your case I hope he proves me wrong. He says you're the player we've been looking for."

"I believe I am," Ray said without pretext. "It's what I do." His gaze of challenge burned into her eyes.

She raised her chin a notch. "And how long have you been doing it?"

The corner of his mouth curved in a wicked grin and his eyes suddenly picked up the light. "Since I was big enough to hold the instrument in my hands and make it do what I wanted—or what was asked." The challenge in his voice, the languid assurance of his body, the unfathomable thing in his eyes, held her on the precipice of temptation, almost daring her to take the leap. Right then. Don't look back.

Leone felt her face heat, and the flush spread through her body. The conversation was benign, she reasoned, over the frightening racing of her heart. It was the tone and the double entendre of the banter that raised the stakes to something infinitely more dangerous.

Cole chuckled and came from behind the desk, effectively short-circuiting the electric current that zinged back and forth between Leone and Ray. "If you like what you hear, I figured Ray could sit in on a set tonight," Cole said, watching Leone closely.

She turned to him, freeing herself of the erotic web of words. "I don't think he needs an audition." Did they hear the breathlessness in her voice? she wondered. "If you say he's good, I'll take your word for it. The audience will be the final judge." She threw down the gauntlet. "Give him a solo tonight. Let's see what he can do."

Leone gave Ray a cursory glance. "Nice meeting you. If it works out you'll be dealing with Cole. What he says goes."

"I'm sure it will," Ray offered.

Leone turned to leave. The room had grown infinitely smaller. "Cole, can I see you outside?"

Cole stepped out of the office and shut the door behind him. His cool brown complexion had hints of red undertones, an early indication that he was upset about something.

"What the hell was that about in there?" he asked from between his teeth, hooking his finger over his shoulder toward the office.

Leone's eyes sharpened. "What are you talking about?"

"You know perfectly well what I'm talking about. You two were no more talking about playing the sax than you were about the theory of evolution."

"What?" She planted her hands on her hips. "Now you've really lost it."

"Lost it. Didn't you see him coming on to you—and you letting him? How's that supposed to make me feel, Leone, huh? What am I, the invisible man or something?"

Leone let out a sigh, knowing full well that Cole had hit the ark. The very idea that she'd been so transparent made her feel every bit like the kind of woman other women whisper about in not so pleasant terms. She'd just about made a fool of herself in there and made a fool of him as well. She and Cole had been an item for more than a year. They were more than business partners, they were lovers. It was a comfortable relationship. She didn't see rockets go off every time they made love, or feel her stomach do flips when she heard his voice on the phone, but Cole was good to her and to Raven. He was solid, the kind of man women spend their lives looking for. Sure, he had his faults, shortcomings and baggage; but didn't everyone? She had no reason to look elsewhere, and she wasn't quite sure why, for that moment in the office, she did.

She stepped up to Cole, reached out and stroked his cheek, the beginning of afternoon stubble tickling her palm. She ran her hand across his short salt and pepper hair, looked into his soft brown eyes. Yes, she was content. Wasn't she?

"Cole, babe, you're letting your imagination play tricks on you. There's no more happening between me and that man than me and that broomstick in the corner. This is business. Simple." Her voice grew softer. "Don't take this someplace it doesn't need to go."

Cole stared at her a moment, trying to see beyond the words. He laughed softly. "Maybe it is me. I'm kinda old to be playing the jealous lover, huh?"

"Tell you the truth, I'm flattered. I can't remember the last time a man got jealous about me."

Cole stepped closer, cutting off all available space between them. "Any man in their right mind should know what a catch you are, Lee. They'd be a fool if they didn't." He let his hand trail down her arm. "It would make a man crazy to think that someone else had their eye on you."

"Well, that's not something you have to worry about," she said, pressing her finger to his chest. She checked her watch. "I need to run home. I want to see Raven before she goes out tonight. It's a double date thing and I want to be sure everything is correct."

"She still crazy about that guy Ron?"

They began to walk toward the exit.

"She is for this week," Leone laughed. "Who knows? I must admit, he has hung around longer than some of the others." She looked thoughtful for a moment, then gazed up at Cole. "I don't know if that's a good thing or not. I mean, she's only seventeen. She's still too young to become serious with anyone. That only spells trouble."

Cole draped his arm around her shoulder. "Raven is a good kid, Leone. You raised her right. She'll keep her head on straight."

"I hope so. I just pray that she doesn't become a statistic like so many young girls."

"Raven gets plenty of love and support. She doesn't have to go out looking for it. Just relax and let her be a teenager."

Leone sighed. "I guess you're right." She raised up and pecked his lips. "You usually are."

Cole opened the door for her. "I know," he teased.

"I'll see you later. About ten." She walked outside, slid on her shades and headed home. But even as she did, thoughts of Ray Taylor dogged her trail.

TWO

Ray Taylor sat with his right ankle resting on his left knee, staring at the posters and flyers tacked to the office wall. There was also a row of framed portraits capturing a variety of media stars and musicians who'd visited the club at one time or another. In each of them there was a picture of Leone Weathers, in outfits from casual to sequin-studded.

The montage of pictures gave Ray some insight into a very intriguing woman. She appeared to be just as comfortable in paint-spattered jeans as she was in formal dinner wear, and everything in-between.

He ran his index finger along the line of his mustache, wondering just exactly what the relationship was between Cole and Leone. He sensed something. Cole took on a proprietary air when Leone entered the room. Interesting, he'd thought, when he watched Cole stake out his territory. But was it really his, or only wishful thinking?

"Sorry I took so long," Cole said, entering the room and derailing Ray's thoughts. He turned in his chair.

"No problem, man. I was just checking out the pictures. A lot of big names have come through here."

Cole chuckled. "That's all Leone's doing. She's a master at getting beyond the secretaries and right to the source. Once she gets it in her head she wants to invite someone to Soul to Soul, believe me, it's a done deal. After the first year or so, folks started calling her, wanting to know when it was a good night to drop by, or they'd stop in when they were in town."

"She seems like a very determined lady."

Cole assessed Ray a moment, trying to hear something beneath the words, see some giveaway in his eyes. Ray's expression remained relaxed and open. "Yes. That she is." He came around the desk. "We start rehearsal at three. Happy hour starts at five, but we just play CDs until the band comes on at nine."

Ray nodded. "No problem." He stood. "I'll be here. I'm just going to grab some lunch."

Cole reached into his desk and pulled out a sheaf of papers. "Do you read music?"

"Enough."

Cole handed the stack to Ray. "Here's what we'll be playing tonight. Take a look, and if you have any questions, we'll go over them at rehearsal."

Ray tucked the folder under his arm. "See you in a few."

Cole watched Ray walk out and wondered if he'd just hired pure brilliance or just plain trouble.

Leone stopped in the cleaners to pick up the dress for Raven and realized she was starving. She still had at least an hour before Raven got in and began to panic about her dress. So she decided to visit her favorite African restaurant and grab one of their famous steamed vegetable pita sandwiches and some fruit juice.

The décor was simple and airy with small round tables strategically placed around the room. African artwork and straw mats hung from the walls. The entire side of the building was glass, giving the diners a great view of the passersby and the art gallery across the street.

Having been served with her meal, Leone pulled a copy of the *Amsterdam News* out of her bag and sat back to enjoy her food. The things she liked most about the small eatery were that it was pristine clean, never too crowded and the food was excellent. And she secretly wanted to find out the recipe for the steamed veggies.

Leone glanced up from her reading just as Ray Taylor strolled by the window. Her insides suddenly knotted, the same way they'd felt whenever she would see Chris Lawrence, the senior basketball star, walk through the halls of her high school, and pray that he would notice her and say hello.

And then Ray was gone, moving casually down the street, blending in with the other pedestrians. Leone released a breath she hadn't realized she'd held. An overwhelming urge to leave and try to catch up with him, ask him where he was going, where he'd been, what his plans were for the future, mysteriously pushed her up out of her seat.

She shook her head, snapping good sense back into place. *What is wrong with you?* she silently chastised herself. *You don't know that man from a banana plant.* She slowly sat back down and tried to concentrate on her food, but had lost her appetite. Distracted, she pushed the plate away, dug in her purse for some money and paid the check.

When she came outside, she secretly hoped that perhaps he might be standing outside peering into a shop window. Casually, she looked up and down the block. Ray Taylor was nowhere to be seen. It was probably for the best anyway.

"You look beautiful, sweetheart," Leone told her daughter.

Raven twirled around in her teal mini-dress and grinned broadly, displaying the deep dimples she'd inherited from her father. She planted her hands on her hips. "But I don't want to be beautiful, I want to be fly," she announced with flair.

"Excuse me. Fly, then," Leone conceded drolly. "What time are they picking you up?"

"Six-thirty. Terry said they were on their way."

"What's the name of this place you're going to again?"

"Gee Ma, you must be getting old. I told you like three times already. Harvest House. Terry's mom rented a room for the night for Terry's brother's twenty-first birthday party. Dinner at eight, party after. Remember?"

"Right." Leone tucked her hair behind her ears and stared unseeing at the magazine on her lap.

"Is something wrong? You've been acting weird since you came home."

Leone looked up and pasted a bland look on her face. "No. I'm fine."

Raven stared at her mother for a minute longer. "Daddy didn't call and upset you again, did he?"

"No, your father didn't call. And what makes you think his calls upset me?"

"Because they do. You know it and I know it."

"Maybe you know too much. Ever think of that?"

"I only wish."

The doorbell rang.

"That must be them," Raven said, grabbing her bag from the glass table and dashing toward the door, her shoulder-length hair swinging behind her.

Leone pulled herself up from the comfort of her couch and walked toward the door.

"Hi, Ms. Weathers," Terry greeted, giving Leone a quick kiss on the cheek.

"Hi, honey. How's your mom?"

"Fine. She's downstairs in the van."

Ron stepped out from behind Terry. "Hi, Ms. Weathers," he said in his getting-manly voice.

Leone gave him a quick once-over. As usual, he was impeccably dressed in his oversized designer clothes that made his long, lanky body even longer and lankier.

"Hello, Ronald. Good to see you."

"Hi, Ron," Raven cooed, and took his hand, which caused him to blush beneath his cool olive tones.

"Hey, you look fly," he mumbled, and Raven turned a triumphant smile on her mother.

"We better get going," Raven said.

"Your mother is going to bring you all back, right?" Leone asked, directing her question to Terry.

"Yes, Ms. Weathers."

"All right, then. Have a good time. And don't forget to act like a lady, Raven."

Raven kissed her mother's cheek. "You sure know how to take the fun out of an evening," she joked. "See you later and don't work too hard tonight."

"Night, Ms. Weathers," Terry and Ron said in unison and the trio bounded off down the stairs.

Leone returned to the living room, picked up the magazine from the black couch and returned it to the wicker magazine rack near the loveseat. She fluffed the mud-cloth pillows and returned them to couch. Walking around the table, she headed into her bedroom to get ready for her evening.

While she showered and then spent some time applying lotion to her damp body, her thoughts continued to drift back to Ray Taylor. She hadn't thought to ask Cole too many questions about him. Since she'd implemented her hands-off policy, she'd left all the details up to Cole. Now she wished she hadn't.

Leone stood and stared at her nude body in the mirror. What was it about Ray Taylor that had captured her imagination? A better and more troubling question was, why didn't she feel the same charge when she looked into Cole's eyes?

"This is ridiculous." She slipped on her underwear. "I have a man," she fussed. "A good man at that. Other women would kill to have someone like Cole." She sat on the bed and put on her stockings. "He loves me and he loves Raven. Ray Taylor is just an interesting stranger." *Who am I trying to convince?*

She took her gray knit dress from the hanger and slid it over her head. The clingy fabric caressed the curves of her long body. Leone smiled at her reflection. "Not bad for a woman pushing fifty."

Twenty minutes later she was walking out the door.

By the time Leone arrived at Soul to Soul, the club was quite full. The bar was lined from one end to the other and there were fewer than a dozen tables available.

She greeted some of the familiar faces as she made her way around the club. Her first stop, as always, was the kitchen, to ensure that everything was running smoothly and that the cooks weren't on the brink of slicing each other to bits arguing over a recipe.

Confident that everything was under control, she made a quick pit stop to chat with her head hostess, Kelly. Kelly had been with the club since the beginning, although her real love was modeling. She'd actually landed some print-ads and more jobs had begun to crop up everyday. Leone knew it was only a matter of time before Kelly made it big and moved on. She dreaded the moment. Kelly wasn't only great to look at, she had a dynamite personality and knew how to run the club with her eyes closed.

"How's everything going?" Leone asked, catching up with Kelly at the check-in table.

Kelly looked up from the list of reservations and smiled brightly, her green eyes sparkling in the light.

"Hi, Lee. Busy as usual, girl. I had to put Percy in check about the menu. It seems he had his own ideas about what jerk shrimp was supposed to be. I got that straight quick."

Leone chuckled, imagining the throw down between her head hostess and her head chef. Egos to go. "I know you did. Anything else I need to know?"

"Yeah, you need to get a bigger place. In another year, we'll be busting at the seams. Every week it seems that ten more people hear about Soul to Soul and bring ten of their friends."

"Word of mouth is the best advertiser."

"Well, folks need to stop talkin' just for a minute, so I can catch my breath."

The two women laughed.

"Ooh, have you met the new sax player?" Kelly asked under her breath.

Leone's chest tightened for a moment. "Yeah, I…uh…met him this afternoon. Is there a problem?"

"Other than the brother being too fine for his own good and the fact that every unescorted, red-blooded woman coming through here has tried to get his attention? No, there's no problem."

"I'm sure the interest will dwindle once he's been here for a while and folks get used to seeing him," Leone offered, hoping more than stating fact.

"Humph. I doubt it."

A young couple approached the table and Leone made her quick goodbye and moved on.

So, Ray Taylor was making an impression already, Leone mused, her heels clicking rhythmically as she headed for the back office. She wondered if he played half as good as he looked. She twisted her wrist and checked the time. Well, another half hour and she'd know for herself.

THREE

"Hey, babe," Cole greeted, looking up from the payroll sheets when Leone entered the office.

"How's everything?" She came into the room and put her purse on the desk, then gave Cole a light peck on the cheek.

"Another busy night," he said. "Did Raven get off okay?"

Leone propped her hip on the edge of the desk. "Terry and Ron came to pick her up. What are you doing?" she asked, peeking over his bent head.

"Adding Ray Taylor's name to the payroll sheet. I'll put all the particulars in the computer tomorrow. I didn't get a chance today."

"I could do it. I'll be in early tomorrow," she offered, hoping she didn't sound too anxious.

He glanced up at her. "Sure, if you want to." He leaned back in the seat. "I think he'll work out great. We had a fantastic rehearsal and he fit right it." He slowly shook his head in amazement. "Taylor has a style that is totally unique. He's a combination of Dexter Gordon and Coltrane. Lethal. Hope we can hold on to him. I can see big things in his future."

"Really," Leone stated, reaching for a blasé tone. "If you believe it, then it must be so."

"Thanks for the vote of confidence, Madame Boss Lady. And on that note, I need to get ready for the first set."

He stood, looking at her with desire brimming in his eyes. "You look fabulous, babe." He leaned down and kissed her exposed neck. "Can't wait for the night to be over," he whispered against her flesh. "Is Raven coming home or spending the night at Terry's?"

"She's coming home."

"Hmmm. So much for that idea. Maybe you can make some time for me later. I promise I won't keep you up too late."

She managed a shaky smile. "Let's see how the night goes." She stroked his cheek. "And take it from there."

Cole angled his head to the side. "Are you all right? You seem distracted."

She quickly stood, averting her gaze. "I'm fine."

He waited a beat. "Okay. But think about what I said." He ran his hand down her arm. "It's been awhile, and I'm missing you. Know what I mean?"

"I know. Me, too. We'll see, okay?"

"All right. Let me get going. Check with you later."

Leone watched him walk out and a kind of sadness settled over her when she quietly admitted to herself that she wasn't looking forward to spending the latter part of her night in Cole's arms.

The house lights dimmed and the spot shone on the six piece band. The packed house settled down, reducing conversation to a low hum as Cole stepped up to the microphone.

"Welcome, sisters and brothers. As always, I can guarantee you're in for a night of soulful entertainment. I want you to put your hands together for our newest band member who, I know, will delight you. Let's hear it for Ray Taylor on sax."

To the sound of applause and foot stomping, Ray moved like a lapping wave, smooth and easy, toward the front of the stage, his long, lean body outfitted in all-black. His smile was enough to dazzle the crowd, but he took them to another level as he led off with a solo of "In a Sentimental Mood," by John Coltrane.

Heads rocked and feet tapped as he took them through the strains of the moody classic before being joined by the rest of the band. They played non-stop for more than an hour, tossing in some Miles Davis, Illinois Jacquet, Lionel Hampton, Wynton Marsalis, Earl "Fatha" Hynes, Dizzy Gillespie, and Lester Young. The crowd roared their approval and Cole promised more of the same during the second set.

Leone enjoyed the music with everyone else, but her attention was riveted on Ray. When he stepped to the microphone and began to play, something akin to magic filled the air. He mesmerized the audience—not only with the sound of his sax, but with his very presence. There was an undeniable charisma about Ray that couldn't be ignored. Ray Taylor had star quality and the women in the room smelled it from miles away.

Leone stayed in the corner of the room, where she'd taken up her post when the band came on, and watched the hungry females go on the prowl. The instant he set foot off-stage and walked onto the floor, three women from various points in the club made their way to him.

They looked to be not much older than their late twenties, with the tight bodies of youth and no childbirth. Leone glanced at her profile in the walled mirror. There was no doubt that she'd passed twenty a couple of times and that her once dancer-trim body had bid her a fond farewell. She sucked in her stomach. It helped a little, but she obviously couldn't hold her breath for the entire night.

"The new guy is on the money," Kelly shouted over the din, easing alongside Leone.

Leone snapped her head in Kelly's direction. "Not bad."

"Not bad? Girl, he has it going on. And look at the women trying to get next to him," she added, angling her head toward the bar.

Ray was leaning casually against the bar, with a glass in one hand, his other tucked in his pocket while he held court. One woman, who easily resembled Tyra Banks, was close enough to see the pores in his skin, Leone observed with a twinge. Two others braced him on the opposite side. What was even more amazing was that Ray seemed totally unfazed by the attention. He appeared to truly enjoy it, as if it were commonplace, even expected somehow. The very notion rubbed Leone the wrong way.

She pursed her lips. With all that talent, all his looks and personality, why was he working in a small club like Soul to Soul? she suddenly wondered. It would seem that someone like Ray Taylor would be with a big band or recording on his own somewhere. Curious, she thought.

"Well, let me tend to the masses," Kelly said. "See you later." She moved away, then stopped and shouted over her shoulder, "Cole was looking for you. I think he's up front."

Leone waved her thanks. She took a breath and peered over heads in search of Cole and spotted him at a booth talking with two of the band members. Leone wound her way around the plaster pillars and tables until she reached where Cole was sitting.

Cole smiled broadly when she approached and slid over on the red leather seat to make room for her.

"So what did you think, babe? He as good as I said he was?"

"You were right. He definitely has talent," she said aloud. In more ways than one, she wanted to add but didn't. "All of you were fantastic tonight. Turned the place out." She smiled at Keith, the piano player, and Mark, the drummer.

"This is the man," Keith said, raising his glass to Cole. "He's the one who puts the sounds together. We're just his humble servants."

The group chuckled.

Leone slid her arm around his shoulder. "Don't work your humble servants too hard. You all were throwing off so much energy, you practically had folks levitating."

"I hope that's a good thing," Ray said, suddenly standing above them.

Leone's stomach did a quick dive then settled. Unconsciously, she eased closer to Cole. "Congratulations," she offered. "The crowd loves you."

Ray's mouth cocked into a half smile. "I feed off their energy," he said, staring intently at Leone. His eyes picked up the light and shimmered. "And then I try to give it back to them."

She took a quick sip of Cole's rum and coke to ease the sudden dryness in her throat. "Whatever works, and apparently it does." She briefly glanced around the table. "Gentleman, you'll have to excuse me, but some of us have work to do and can't lounge around for hours at a stretch."

A moan rounded the table.

She had to squeeze by Ray in order to get past him, and she caught the scent of his cologne mixed with exertion and raw animal energy. Her heart knocked. "Have a great set," she said and walked away.

For the rest of the evening, Leone caught glimpses of Ray as he mingled with the guests as if he were the resident celebrity. And the more she saw of him, the more she decided he was nothing more than a pretty boy with some talent. It was obvious that he was out to make as many conquests as possible without breaking any speed laws. She'd lost count of the number of women who'd slipped him their number. He's a player, as Raven would say, which was fine with her as long as it didn't interfere with his performance, her business, or her, she thought, slapping down a packet of receipts and tallying up the first set of numbers for the night. Business was booming.

"Hey, why don't you leave that until tomorrow, babe," Cole said, stepping into the office and closing the door behind him. "I know you have to be beat. It was crazy in here tonight."

Leone forced a smile. "I'd rather get it out of the way."

Cole came around to her side of the desk. "It's not a request, Lee." He covered her hand with his to still her fingers on the calculator.

"You know how I hate leaving things half done…"

"This one time won't matter. It's nearly two o'clock. Put everything in the safe and let me take you home. It'll keep."

She sucked on her bottom lip with her teeth.

"Come on. Let me take care of you for a change." He began to massage her neck, something he knew she loved, and he was rewarded with the sound of her heavy sigh.

Leone let her eyes slide shut and allowed Cole to work his magic.

"You know you need to let me take the stress out of your whole body, not just this beautiful neck," Cole uttered, sliding his fingers along her collarbone.

Leone's eyes flew open and she halted the steady trail of his hands toward her breasts. "Not tonight, Cole. Really."

His hands stopped their exploration but didn't release her. "I see." Slowly he stepped back and came around to look at her. "What is it, Lee, really? For weeks now you've been getting more and more distant. When I come near you lately, you act like I shouldn't. What have I done?"

Her throat tightened. She didn't want to hurt Cole. Heaven knows she didn't. She wished she did have some pat answer, some quick solution to what was happening between them, to her, but she didn't.

Briefly she lowered her head. "I don't know what it is, Cole," she said barely above a whisper.

"Do you still have feelings for me, Lee?"

She looked into his eyes. "Of course I do. You know that. I...I'm just tired. Nothing's changed between us, really."

Cole nodded. "Then that's all I have to go on." He tilted up her chin with the tip of his finger. "I'm a patient man, Lee. And you know I love you. I'm willing to wait it out. Just not too long." He paused a beat. "Good night. I'll call you in the morning, see how Raven's date was." He turned to leave, closing the door softly behind him.

Guilt stabbed her with his last comment. She sat there for several minutes thinking about what Cole had said, trying to search out what was in her heart, but the image wouldn't come clear.

Over the next few weeks, Leone would have sworn in court that Ray Taylor had a built-in magnet that drew the women to the club. Some nights it was standing room only and Ray continued to charm everyone who crossed his path. She should have been elated that the club was doing such phenomenal business. Cole couldn't seem to stop raving about Ray Taylor, which only added to her angst.

Fortunately, between rehearsals and Leone's often hectic schedule she rarely saw Ray alone, until one afternoon when he came to the club early while Leone was going over the inventory.

"Hello, Ms. Lady," he greeted, coming up behind her as she stood at the bar.

Her pulse quickened as she slowly turned toward the sound of his voice. "It's Leone and you're early, Mr. Taylor." She turned back to what she was doing, and was certain the room had grown warmer.

He eased alongside her and leaned against the bar. "I wanted to get some practice time in before the rest of the guys got here. It's not a problem, is it…Leone?" He half-smiled at her.

Leone kept her eyes focused on her paperwork. "I don't see how it should be."

He dipped his head to get beneath her gaze. Startled, her head jerked upward. A frown planted itself on her face.

"That's better. It's really hard talking to someone who seems to be ignoring you."

Leone blew out a breath and rested a hand on her hip. "I'm really busy, Mr. Taylor."

"Ray."

"Hmm. You said you came to practice. So…"

"Have I done something to you? I mean everyone else is friendly, chatty, except you. Since my first day you've barely said two words to me. What is it?"

"Are you saying I'm rude, that I've somehow treated you unfairly?"

"No. That's not what I'm saying at all. It's just that—"

"Then we don't have a problem. Perhaps I may seem distracted, or inattentive, but I have a business to run, which I take very seriously. I'm sure you're accustomed to people running behind you, but I'm not that kind of woman...person."

He looked at her for a moment. "Actually, I'm glad you're not. Don't work too hard." He turned and headed for the stage.

Leone took slow breaths, in and out. She put pen to paper and noticed that her hand trembled ever so slightly. Reluctantly, she turned in Ray's direction and watched him as he sauntered toward the stage. She'd done everything in her power to stay as far out of Ray Taylor's reach as possible. She couldn't deny the attraction she felt for him, right from the beginning. But she was too old to be "one of many" for any man. Besides, she had a man. A good one. *Why do I have to keep reminding myself of that?* she wondered.

Ray stepped on stage, as comfortable there as in his own skin, and took a seat on the lone stool. The music came then, like a lullaby, soft, sweet. The notes of "The Masquerade Is Over" floated through the room as gentle as a breeze, as clear and sharp as if the notes were actually being sung by Sarah Vaughan.

Ray closed his eyes, becoming one with the music, and one by one everybody stopped what they were doing, transfixed by the serene beauty of his playing.

Leone felt her chest fill with an incredible warmth, as captivated as everyone else by the power of his delivery.

Could anyone who had such a sense of perfection, who could transform symbols on a piece of paper into something magical, be as shallow as he projected himself to be? Even as she considered the question, Ray took them on another musical odyssey with "Smoke Gets in Your Eyes."

It was just the music, she told herself, picking up her papers and heading toward her office. It wasn't Ray Taylor, the man, who was appealing, who awakened her senses. He was just talented that's all, and she wouldn't fool herself into believing anything else. No matter what her emotions were saying.

FOUR

"So how long has it been this way with you and Cole?" Antoinette asked as she and Leone shared lunch several days later. She chewed on a stalk of celery with blue cheese dressing.

Leone shrugged helplessly, toying with her salad. "Long enough for it to be a problem." She took a sip of her iced tea and let her gaze wander off. "It's not that I don't care, I do. It's just that..." She fumbled for an explanation.

"There's no spark," Antoinette filled in and signaled the waitress for another diet Coke.

"Exactly. Cole is wonderful, don't get me wrong, but..." She hesitated and turned searching eyes on her friend. "Is it wrong for me, at my age, to want to be thrilled by the sight of my man, totally turned on by the thought of his touch? Am I wrong to want that?"

"Of course not." Antoinette's honey brown eyes focused on Leone. "We all deserve to be totally happy in our relationships, Lee, to feel fulfilled, especially at our age. We don't have as much time for the hit and miss of youth. You don't want to simply settle because it's easy and comfortable."

Leone and Antoinette had been friends since high school. For some inexplicable reason they'd gravitated toward each other, as opposites often do. Where Leone was reserved and conventional, Antoinette lived life without restrictions. They were just as opposite in their appearance.

Leone was tall, dark brown and moderately built. Antoinette, on the other hand, was a mere five-foot, four with a brick-house body that she had no problem showing off. Yet in every way they complemented each other.

"So what do you think I should do about Cole?" Leone finally asked.

"I think you need to decide if you want to be happy or just satisfied. And when you decide—is Cole the man that can do the trick?"

She watched Leone over the top of her glass. "There's something else going on with you. You know I can always tell from that line." She pointed toward Leone's head. "The one that runs right between your brows. Dead giveaway. Just because I've been away for a month doesn't mean I've forgotten the signs."

Leone tried to shrug it off but knew it was pointless. Antoinette would harass her until she spilled the beans. She had missed talking with Antoinette, especially during the last few weeks. There had been no one with whom she could share her confusion. Yet, sitting in front of her now, it was hard to get the words out. She inhaled deeply and plunged in.

"You know Cole was looking for a new sax player?" she asked, a slight hitch of hesitation in her voice.

"Yes…" Antoinette dragged out, eyeing her suspiciously.

Leone cleared her throat. "Well, I met him and…"

"And what?"

"Something happened to me inside," she blurted out. "Something I haven't felt in ages—never felt for Cole, at least not like this."

Antoinette leaned back in her seat, momentarily speechless. Several moments ticked by.

"Don't just sit there. Say something," Leone snapped.

"I'm trying. I'm trying. Every clear thought in my head just took a hike. You, Ms. Cool and in control, having your heart go pitter patter is enough to shut anyone up. Even me."

Leone folded her arm. "I knew I shouldn't have said anything."

"Hey, I'm sorry. You surprised me, that's all. You've always kept your feelings on a short leash. Even on your wedding day, your bridal party seemed more excited than you."

"That doesn't mean I don't feel anything," she said truculently. "I've just never been that way, especially over a man."

Antoinette ignored the bite in her tone and posed her question in soothing strokes, knowing that it was pure anxiety that had Lee on edge. "So what makes this one any different?"

Leone forced herself to relax and regroup, silently embarrassed by her short burst of irrational temper. "I don't really know, Nettie," she said, using the pet name in lieu of an outright apology—an olive branch. "Something just hit me and I haven't been able to get him out of my mind."

"What's his name?"

"Ray Taylor." She hesitated about telling her the last bit of information. As she'd promised Cole, she'd updated the employee files with Ray's background information and to her great dismay discovered that he was ten years younger than she. She'd been walking around for weeks with that little tidbit, and perhaps it contributed to her anxiety over her feelings, knowing that he was younger. As a result, she'd been standoffish and distant while she battled with the right and wrong of it. But she figured she might as well spill the beans at this point. After all, Antoinette was her best friend. "He's only thirty-eight," she said almost to herself.

Antoinette's eyes formed two perfect circles. "Say what?"

"Don't make me say it again." She shoved a plum tomato into her mouth.

Antoinette threw her head back and howled with laughter. The couple at the next table looked at her with disdain for disturbing them.

"I'm leaving," Leone said in a huff, wiping her mouth with the napkin and tossing it on the table.

"No...no, wait... I'm sorry," Antoinette mumbled over her laughter, struggling to get it under control. She wiped her eyes, which had begun to tear up. "Whew, girl ...when you have a story to tell it's a whopper." She held up her slender, always manicured hands. "Okay, okay, I'm cool now." She took a breath. "So you got a thing for this young brother?"

"You don't have to put it like that."

"Hey, the way I look at it, if you can do it, why not? Men do it all the time. Look at you. You look just as good if not better than some of those women that run in and out of the club. And you're mature. You have something to offer."

"Whoa, slow down. I didn't say I was going to pursue anything with him."

"Why not?"

"For one thing, I'm with someone."

"Someone that doesn't particularly rock your world, if I remember correctly."

"But he's good to me and to Raven. I don't want to hurt Cole. And I don't really know anything about Ray Taylor. Other than I think he's a player," she mumbled, but not low enough to keep it from Antoinette's eagle ears.

"A player? You've got to be kidding. What makes you say that?"

Leone ran down the events of the club from the time she and Ray formally met to the all-out pursuit of him throughout every night and his apparent enjoyment of it.

"Hmmm. Brother must have it going on," she said with a crooked smile. "I need to meet him."

Leone rolled her eyes. "Which is all the more reason for me to keep my distance."

"But you said he came on to you. Didn't he?"

"Yes, sort of but…"

"Hey, let me tell you something. You only live once. And during that one lifetime you're entitled to some happiness. If you like the guy, go for it." She dipped another celery stalk and pointed it at Leone for emphasis. "Don't let age be a factor. You never know. He could be the one."

Leone pondered her friend's not necessarily wise words. "But what about Cole?"

"Maybe it's time you and Cole had a real talk about how you feel and where the relationship is going...or isn't."

Leone knew Antoinette was right and she dreaded the thought.

Ray was lounging on the couch watching Sunday afternoon football with his buddy Parker, but his mind wasn't on the game. He adjusted his body and the soft leather moved with him. The twenty-seven inch television was one big blur of color.

"Touchdown!" Parker shouted, leaping from the chair and doing his own version of a victory dance. "Did you see that? My man rushed for one hundred yards!"

His exclamation was met with silence. Parker craned his neck to stare at Ray.

"Whatsup, man? Did you see that?"

"I wasn't really paying attention," Ray answered absently.

Parker stepped over and placed his hand on Ray's forehead. "No fever," he said sarcastically. "But something's wrong. You've been in a daze since I got here." He sat down. "What? The ladies got you down? Hit a wrong note on the sax? What?"

He shook his head in dismissal. "It's nothing."

Parker stared at him a minute. He and Ray had been running partners since college. Ray pursued his musical career, and Parker went on to business management and financial planning, serving as a consultant for several Fortune 500 corporations, foregoing a solid music career as a pianist. He was instrumental in keeping Ray's finances straight and steering him toward the right stocks and investments. As a result, Ray's future was secure. He would never have to worry about money if he lived two lifetimes. Yet, Ray lived his life as if each day was his last—wanting to get the most, the best, the fastest—from cars and clothes to women. For a man who had so much going for him, he never seemed truly settled inside. He was still the insecure guy from the projects who was never sure what tomorrow was going to bring.

"Hey, if you say it's nothing then I have to go by that. Even though I don't believe it." He leaned toward the coffee table and picked up his beer.

Ray cupped his hands behind his head and stared up at the stucco ceiling. "I'm tired, Parker."

Parker cocked his head. "Tired of what, playing?"

"Everything. Just tired of running from one club to the next, one woman to the next."

"Humph. I thought you loved that life, man. That's what you've been telling me for the past ten years. You love the idea of not being tied down. Hitting and running as you put it."

"Yeah, I did. At least I thought I did."

"So what's different now?"

"I've been doing some thinking for a while. I want to slow down and really see life, ya know. Not have it run past me."

"You're too young for a mid-life crisis. So that's not it. You have some problem with a woman? Somebody snag you and you didn't tell me?"

Ray chuckled half-heartedly. "Naw. The other night at the club—man, it was just like all the others. I got the rush from being on stage. I felt charged, ya know. But then when I was finished the women were everywhere. I played along. At first it was fun, flattering. But it got tiring real quick." He turned and looked at Parker. "The scary part was, I didn't know any other way to be but 'on'. And I just didn't feel like playing the game."

"I think I need another beer." Parker got up and went into the kitchen, returning shortly with two icy cold beers. He handed one to Ray.

"Now that you've reached this pivotal crossroads, what are you going to do? Let's be for real, Ray. You're a musician, a damned good one. You have enough charm to bottle and sell. Women have been on your tail for as long as I've known you, and watching you play is enticing to them. It's all part of the program, the life. It's what brings them back to pack the house."

"Yeah, I know. But I'd like to be able to come home to someone at night, Parker, not bring someone home for the night."

"You're serious, aren't you?"

Ray nodded.

"Wow." He paused, momentarily speechless by this revelation. Finally he collected his thoughts. "So, what are you going to do?"

Ray chuckled. "That's the hard part. I don't know how to play it straight. It's like a foreign language."

"Yeah, the hardest part of anything is getting started. Set your sights on someone—sincerely—and see where it goes. There has to be someone out of the dozens of women you date that you really care about."

Ray did a mental checklist. "Not really. At least not like that." He thought about Leone Weathers, that smile, the challenge in her eyes. That was a woman, and nothing like what he'd been used to.

"Okay, spill it. Who is she? I can tell by the look in your eyes, brother." Parker turned off the television with the remote. The game could wait.

The corner of Ray's mouth quirked briefly upward. "She's the owner of the club."

"So what's the problem? You see something you like, you go after it. That's been the deal with you all along. She married?"

"Not that I know of. Didn't see any rings."

"Then I'm not getting it, Ray."

"I don't know, man…it's like I was saying, I guess I was wondering what it would be like to have just one woman, someone I could depend on from one day to the next and not want to forget her name as soon as possible."

Parker suddenly roared with laughter. "Man, this is serious. What did you do, fall and hit your head or some-

thing?" He took a swallow of beer to wash down his disbelief.

Now Ray felt like a fool. He knew he shouldn't have
said anything to Parker. In Parker's mind, he would be forever young, forever single, forever on the prowl.

"I'll tell you what it would be like to be with the same
woman day in and out—boring. Besides, you don't stay put
long enough to stick to one woman," he added as if his last
statement defined the mysteries of the universe.

Ray sat up, bracing his arms on his knees. As much as
he hated to admit it, Parker was probably right. He'd spent
the better part of his adult life roaming from one club, one
city to the next. On a whole, it was a good life, an exciting
one. There were never any two days that were the same.
Maybe that was the trouble, what was finally getting to
him. Some mornings not only didn't he know who was
lying next to him, but even what city or hotel he was in.
Unfortunately, it was the only life he knew, or understood.
With no family ties to bind him, he was free. Yeah, right,
free.

"Hey, man, you're probably right," Ray finally conceded. "Guess I was having a moment." He chuckled half-
heartedly.

"That's more like it." Parker slapped Ray on the thigh.
"Now can we get back to the game?" He pointed the
remote and the roar from the stadium crowd filled the
room. "Yes!" Parker shouted. "Giants, seven, Redskins, zip.
My kinda game." He lifted his beer bottle in salute.

Ray decided to take Parker's advice on more than one level: his life and the game.

Usually after a Sunday football game, Ray and Parker drove into the Village to check out the jazz clubs, listen for any potential new talent that they should keep their ears on, or sometimes they'd sit in on a set and play with the band.

Parker was a master on keyboards, and many had compared him to Herbie Hancock, adding the fact that he looked like Herbie as well. Ray had lost count of how many times they'd used that ploy to get the best seats in the clubs or pick up women. However, Parker played only because it gave him entrée into another lifestyle. But not one in which he permanently wanted to live.

In Parker's real world he was an investment banker and a damned good one. Parker liked music and the attention that it brought. Ray loved it. Without it, he would be incomplete. Music defined who he was.

But tonight when Parker asked what time he wanted to head into the Village, Ray declined.

"You sure you're all right?" Parker asked.

"Yeah, yeah, I'm sure. I want to go home and practice this new piece for the band."

Parker frowned in suspicion, then shrugged. "Whatever you say."

Ray stood and slipped on his light brown leather jacket and grabbed his car keys from the coffee table, dumping them in his pocket.

Parker walked with him to the door. "I'll check you during the week."

Ray nodded. "Cool. Later." He jogged down the steps to the street.

Parker watched until Ray had pulled off in his black Maxima. Slowly, he shook his head and wondered what had gotten into his partner. It sounded like maturity, and all Parker could hope was that it wasn't catching.

Ray cruised for a bit, taking in the twilight sights of Brooklyn on the still warm fall evening. He wasn't sure why or how he found himself easing into the block of Soul to Soul. He knew the club wasn't open on Sunday, but he parked right out front anyway.

Sitting there, he wondered why he'd taken the job in the first place. The hours were more than he was used to putting in, and the money wasn't that great. But when he'd walked in for the first time, the atmosphere of the club called out to him. He easily sensed the warmth and friendship among everyone on the staff, especially the camaraderie of the band members. And Cole was a true gentleman. Yet, even after he'd accepted the spot, he'd had twinges of doubt. Until he'd seen Leone.

That's what his problem was. He knew it. There was something about Leone that had escalated the questions and doubts that had been rolling around in his head lately, even if she did keep him at a distance. But it was pretty obvious that Leone was Cole's woman. And as much as he might want to do otherwise, he never moved in on another man's woman.

FIVE

Every now and then, Leone would get the overwhelming urge to be alone in the club. Tonight was one of those nights. She needed to walk around in its emptiness, absorb the scents, imagine the sounds and remember that it was hers. It grounded her, reminded her that the sacrifices she'd made had been worth it. Somehow, being there validated her, reinforced the fact that she could stand on her own, could fulfill her dreams, something Steven had insisted would never happen.

She straightened an autographed picture of Spike Lee with Denzel Washington, which had been taken when they were in town for the filming of Lee's last movie. She smiled. The music, the service and the food had made such an impression on Spike that whenever he wasn't at a Knicks game, he could be found with his wife at one of the back tables on a Friday night.

Leone walked toward the stage and stepped up. She looked upward at the spotlight, then closed her eyes, wondering what it would feel like to be the center of adoration, hear the rush of applause and shouts for more. How did it feel?

The sudden pounding on the glass door made her leap a good foot off the floor, her scream caught behind the hand that flew to her mouth. Wide-eyed and with her heart pounding, she peered in the direction of the entrance to see the outline of someone peering back at her.

Inhaling deeply, she jumped down off the stage and marched over to the door. Probably someone wanting to know if they were open, she fumed, trying to regulate her racing pulse.

She pressed her face to the glass and looked dead into the eyes of Ray Taylor, who was frowning at her as if she'd stolen the crown jewels. Her entire body went on full alert. A million thoughts tumbled through her head at once: the primary one being, did he see her making a fool of herself on stage?

Putting on her nonchalant expression, she twisted the locks on the door and cracked it open.

"Hi. What can I do for you, Ray?"

Ray peered over her shoulder trying to get a peek inside. "Everything okay?"

Leone put her hand on her hip, trying to regain some semblance of authority. "Of course. Why?"

His eyes narrowed. "I didn't know the club was open on Sunday."

"It's not. I just...I was here...doing... checking on the inventory." She cleared her throat and felt more ridiculous by the moment. This was her damned club and she could come in it whenever she pleased. So why did she feel like a bumbling idiot explaining this to Ray?

He stared at her a moment, then took another glance over her shoulder. "Well, if you're sure everything is all right," he said, his statement hanging like an unanswered question between them.

"Absolutely. Thanks."

Ray nodded and started to back off, then stopped. "You know, Leone, I'd feel a helluva lot better if you'd let me take a look inside...just to be sure."

Her brow wrinkled. "You're serious, aren't you?"

"Very."

With a huff, she stepped back and opened the door. "Come on in. See for yourself."

Ray eased by her and went inside. Slowly he perused the club, checking the kitchen, behind the bar, the storeroom and the office. Satisfied, he returned to the center of the club where Leone was seated at one of the tables, legs crossed and fingers tapping on the tabletop. She looked up when he approached.

"All clear?"

Ray grinned and her stomach see-sawed. "Yeah." He stuck his hands in his pockets. "I guess you must think I'm a bit nuts?"

Leone couldn't help smiling. "Not nuts...exactly. Just a bit over-zealous."

"If you'd been to as many spots as I have and seen as much, you'd understand my concern. I wouldn't have been able to forgive myself if somebody was in here and you had to play it off and I just walked away. It happens, you know."

Leone pursed her lips. "I guess you're right," she conceded, feeling suddenly foolish for being so short with him. "Thanks."

"Not a problem. Sorry if I took you away from what you were doing." He shrugged. "See you tomorrow." He began walking toward the door.

"What were you doing around this way?" Leone asked, stopping him in his tracks. She knew he lived in the Canarsie section of Brooklyn by the Pier. This was a bit out of the way simply to be passing along.

Ray turned. "I was hanging out with my man, Parker, watching the game." He came toward her. "Tell you the truth, I'm not sure what made me come over here. I looked up and I was on the block, so I stopped. Then I saw movement inside. At first I was going to call the cops." He chuckled. "Glad I didn't."

"You and me both."

"That would've made for an interesting Sunday evening."

"I can see it all now. Both of us being carted away with raincoats over our faces so we wouldn't be recognized when the news van pulls up and the police haul us away."

"That would be a hoot. I can see you now trying to explain to your staff."

Leone shook her head, laughing. "It would definitely ruin my image."

Ray pulled up a seat. "Do you always come here when the place is closed?"

"Sometimes," she confessed.

"Want to remind yourself that it's real, huh?"

Leone angled her head to the side. "Yes. How did you know?"

Ray shrugged. "I do the same thing sometimes, pick up my sax and blow a few notes just to see if I can do it." He made little circles on the table with his finger.

"Why? You seem so confident on the stage… and off. Almost cocky," she added.

Ray inhaled deeply, trying to put his thoughts into words without coming off as if he were full of himself. He didn't want Leone to have that kind of impression about him. What she thought was suddenly important.

He tilted his head up toward the ceiling as he spoke. "When I get up on that stage, every nerve in my body feels like it's on fire, ready to leap out—or worse, strangle me. Sometimes I feel as if I can't breathe, that I'll get out there and forget everything I've ever learned. But when I come up to the mike or that spotlight hits me, something inside sparks with life and this rush, like a tidal wave roaring through me, pushes all the anxiety aside and it's just me and my sax playing like it was my first and last time. Everything just comes together." He lowered his gaze and looked at her, returning from the trip he'd taken.

"Wow," was all Leone could find to say. To watch Ray Taylor, you would never think that he would have an instant of doubt, a moment of vulnerability, she thought. Maybe he wasn't as shallow as he appeared.

Ray went back to making circles on the table with his fingertip.

Leone propped her chin up on her palm. "How did you get started? Were you forced into music lessons?" She laughed lightly.

"Not exactly. But it was a way to stay out of trouble. My math teacher got me involved with the school band to keep me from getting suspended."

"Oh." Her eyes widened in mock alarm. "So you were causing a stir even in your youth," she teased.

"One way or the other," he admitted, thinking back to his harrowing days as a gang member in D.C.

"But you must have liked it because you stuck with it."

"Yeah." He nodded. "I kind of dug it, especially when the girls—" He halted.

"Especially when the girls just drooled all over you, right?" Leone filled in.

Ray flashed an embarrassed smile and shrugged.

"It's apparent you haven't lost your touch."

"I don't know about all that. It's all an illusion. People see what they want to see." He looked directly at her.

Leone looked away, then stood. "Since we're here, would you like a drink—on the house?"

"Sure. Scotch and soda." He rose as well and followed her to the bar. "Let me do the honors." He stepped behind the bar. "What will you be having this evening, Ms. Weathers?"

The last thing she needed was to get lightheaded around Ray Taylor, but since she had made the suggestion...

"A rum and coke. Plenty of coke and plenty of ice."

He glanced up at her as he reached for the glasses beneath the counter. "Coming right up."

Leone slid onto one of the bar stools.

"So, tell me about you. How did you get into the nightclub business? Better yet, why? It can't be easy." He handed her the drink.

"Thanks." She took a sip and nodded her approval. "Why? Hmmm. Good question. I guess it came from watching so many old movies. It seemed like some of the greatest scenes took place in a nightclub," she said wistfully. "They always had this air of mystery about them, like anything could happen, anyone could walk in." She took another sip of her drink. "But of course, growing up to be a nightclub owner wasn't something my folks sent me to college to do. So I went into nursing."

"Nursing?"

"Yep. Twenty years."

Leone told him how much she loved nursing, but how she'd always dreamed of having a business of her own. She mentioned as quickly as possible her marriage to Steven and described in loving terms her daughter, Raven.

Ray leaned against the bar totally fascinated by Leone. He watched her eyes light up when she talked about her daughter, saw the lines of tension cross her face when she spoke of her marriage, heard the joy in her voice when she talked about the club and how proud she was of it.

He wanted to ask her about Cole. He wanted to know how old she was, especially since she had a seventeen year old daughter. He wanted to ask her about her childhood, her favorite book, movie, what she did in her spare time. He wanted to know what she thought about him. He wanted to know how serious it was between her and Cole Fleming. That question burned most of all.

But he asked none of that. Instead, he told her about his youth in D.C., the places he'd been and the clubs he'd played in. He shared with her his long-time friendship with Parker and his own passion for cooking and foreign movies.

As Leone listened, she realized with every passing minute that Ray Taylor was truly a complex man, an intelligent and sensitive man. He even had a wicked sense of humor. One by one all of her preconceived notions began to crumble and the restraining wall she'd built rocked on its foundation.

Ray paused briefly in the midst of his storytelling and smiled at her.

Leone knew in that instant that she was in big trouble.

SIX

Leone needed to get out of there. As much as she wanted to stay, as good as being with Ray made her feel, she knew she had to leave. But she couldn't seem to get her body to do anything other than surrender to the warm glow that Ray had thrown over her like a blanket.

As Ray drew to a close his tale of a college prank he and Parker had pulled on a girls' dorm, he glanced at Leone. She was quite pretty, he thought. Understated but pretty. There was a naturalness about her, a solid feeling that she exuded. There was no question in his mind that she was intelligent and determined. Otherwise she would have never been able to leave one career and start another one—and do it successfully. Leone had goals and a focus, qualities that were blatantly absent in most of the women he met. For the majority of them, their major concern was finding a man by any means necessary, and they'd go through all the hoops and whistles to get one. And then their true colors would show. Sure, he'd had his share of women, but one thing he always did was be up front. There was never a question dangling between him and any woman about what the extent of their relationship was to be.

Leone was unlike all the others. She had her own life. She didn't need him as a means to an end. If anything did jump off between them it would be because it was what they both wanted—more importantly, what Leone wanted.

The sound of her glass against the wood table drew him from his reverie.

"Hey, I didn't mean to keep you all this time running my mouth," Ray said, with a sheepish grin. "I know you must need to get home."

Leone checked her watch. She couldn't believe it. They'd been talking for nearly three hours. She looked toward the front door. It was pitch black outside. Night had definitely fallen. She pushed back from her seat and stood.

"I really do need to get moving. My daughter's going to be wondering—where's dinner?" she joked.

Ray stood. "You mean she's not going to be worried about where mom is?"

Leone twisted her mouth in a way that Ray found amusing. "Not hardly. She probably thinks I'm with Cole." Her heart suddenly thudded in her chest at the mention of Cole's name, and the spell that held her and Ray in place was broken.

"Cole's a lucky man."

She flashed him a brief smile. "I'm the lucky one."

They began to walk toward the door, while Leone checked lights and locks.

"How long have the two of you been together? If you don't mind my asking."

Leone punched in the alarm code. "About a year." She opened the door. "Hurry, hurry," she warned. "Or this thing will go off."

He walked to the other side of the door.

Leone came outside directly behind him and locked the door. Confident that all was secure, she turned to Ray. He stood barely a breath away.

"I had a nice time tonight. It's the first chance we've had to really talk, get to know each other," Ray said.

Leone felt as if all the available air was being sucked from her lungs. She was close enough to him to see the hairline scar that ran across his right eyebrow and the brown rim that circled his eyes.

She swallowed. "I had a good time too, but I—"

"I know, you have to get home." He looked around. "Where's your car?"

"I walked. I only live a few blocks away."

"I'll drive you. It's late."

"No, really—"

"I insist. Come on. I'm parked right here."

Being alone with him in the club was one thing, in close quarters inside his car was another story, she worried.

Ray saw her uncertainty, the doubt that made her twist her lips in thought.

"I promise you, I'll keep both hands on the wheel," he said laughing.

Leone bit back a smile. "Well, in that case—okay."

She slid into the sleek car seat and immediately put on her belt, positioning herself as close to the passenger door as possible. Quickly, she folded her hands on her lap as Ray hopped in.

The air suddenly became close and tight, Leone realized. The masculine scent of Ray assaulted her senses. She could feel his body heat as surely as if he stroked her with it. She crossed her legs to stem the smoldering fire.

"Where to?" He stuck the key in the ignition and the Maxima hummed like a vibrator beneath them.

"Greene and Clinton."

Ray snatched a glance at her before pulling away from the curb. "You really do live close. By the time the car warms up good, you'll be home."

"I tried to tell you," she said in the same, 'I told-you-so' tone she used with Raven when her daughter would finally concede that her mother knew what she was talking about.

Ray grumbled something in his throat before switching the radio station to CD 101.9, the local jazz station. Nancy Wilson's voice filled the space.

Majestic brownstones, refurbished to their original glory, proudly stood side-by-side on the tree-lined streets. No more than twenty years earlier, this entire area of Brooklyn had been a "runaway" zone—everyone who lived there wanted to run away from the crime and decay. Somehow word got out that there was prime property falling by the wayside and money and loans that were previously unavailable slowly began to materialize. Now, homes that at one time couldn't be given away, were some of the most highly priced, desirable properties in the borough.

"How long have you lived in the area?" Ray asked, making a right onto Clinton Avenue.

Leone couldn't help noticing the way his body became one with the car, moving in perfect harmony. She swallowed. "We moved out here from Queens when my ex-husband was assigned to manage part of the construction of Metrotech."

"Really? That's the collection of businesses and corporate offices further downtown, right?"

"Yes."

"Your husband—"

"Ex," she quickly corrected.

"Ex ...is a builder?"

"Yep. Pretty good at it, too." She adjusted her purse on her lap and glanced out her window.

"He, uh, still around?"

Leone cut her eyes in his direction. Ray stared straight ahead.

"Make a right at the next corner." She paused another beat. "He's in North Carolina last I heard."

"Oh."

Leone watched the lines of tension ease from around his eyes and the corners of his mouth. The fierce grip he had on the steering wheel lessened. She smiled to herself and suddenly felt bold.

"Where's your wife, or significant other?"

"Don't have one," he answered without blinking an eye.

"Intentional or circumstantial?"

He glanced briefly in her direction. "A little of both."

"I'm three houses from the corner. On your left." She'd heard his response, but felt it best not to pursue it. It would be so easy to fall into a comfortable banter with him, exchange information, pasts, ideas…kisses. That was the problem. "Thanks a lot. I'm right here."

Ray eased to the curb and cut the engine. When Leone turned to say goodnight, she caught him peering up at the darkened windows of her building.

"You need me to go up with you? Check everything out?"

This time she did laugh. "No. But thanks, anyway." She unbuckled her belt. "I'll be fine. Scout's honor."

His left eyebrow rose in question. "Hmm. If you say so. But you'll have to ignore me while I sit here and make sure you get inside safely."

"You're really quite a gentleman," she said, her tone sounding as if she'd grasped a new realization.

"Why is that so hard to believe—about me?"

The bottomless level that his voice had reached settled in the center of Leone's stomach and radiated like sunbeams through her body. A trickle of perspiration wiggled its way down her spine.

She swallowed. "It's just…nice to know, I suppose. Finding men that go that extra distance is a treat."

Ray unfastened his belt and angled his body toward her. Leone's belly fluttered, her body tensed.

"There's probably a lot of things about me that would surprise you." His gaze danced over her face, stopped briefly at the pulse in her throat, then returned to rest on her eyes.

"Like what?" She sounded almost breathless to her own ears and the realization unnerved her even more.

He raised his arm and for an instant, Leone knew he was going to touch her. She wanted him to. Instead, he stretched his arm along the back of the headrest, which was ultimately worse. The proximity of his hand to the exposed flesh of her neck was more tantalizing than if he'd kissed her.

The corner of his mouth curved in a tempting, almost boyish grin.

"Besides being a gentleman, I—"

The loud rapping on the passenger window made Leone gasp with fear. Startled eyes snapped toward the sound of the intrusion. Staring her in the face was Raven.

Leone quickly shut her eyes and inhaled. "Twice in one day," she mumbled.

"Who's that?"

"My daughter," she said, depressing the diagramed button to lower the window.

"Hi, Ma." Raven greeted, staring at Ray and ignoring her mother.

"Are you just getting home?" Leone questioned, knowing full well that the answer was obvious.

"Uh huh. Hi, I'm Raven." She brazenly introduced herself when it seemed that her mother had no intention of crossing that bridge.

"Ray Taylor. I work at the club."

"Really?" she chirped in the high pitch that only teen girls can reach.

Ray chuckled. "Really."

Raven poked her mother in the shoulder. "You didn't tell me."

Leone struggled to maintain her calm demeanor. "Didn't think I had to." She turned to Ray. "Thanks for the lift, Ray. I'll see you tomorrow." She opened the door and Raven leaped back to avoid getting knocked down.

"What's wrong with you?" Raven hissed from between her teeth. Leone ignored her.

Ray lowered his head to better see the departure of his riding companion. "Yeah, see ya. Nice meeting you, Raven."

"You, too," she replied, a bit too sweetly for Leone's tastes.

"Let's go, Raven. You should have been home a half hour ago. Tomorrow's a school day," Leone continued to fuss, thankful for the distraction.

"M—a," she complained before grudgingly trailing behind her mother.

Leone ignored her and marched up the steps to the glass and wood front door. All the while she was keenly aware that Ray hadn't moved from his sentinel position in front of her door. She stuck the key in the lock and quickly stepped inside, shutting the door and Ray firmly behind her.

Ray watched as the house came to illuminated life. Hmm. He'd seen Leone the businesswoman, Leone the mother and disciplinarian. He was impressed with what he saw and wondered what Leone the woman was like.

SEVEN

"He is fine," Raven announced, emphasizing each word. She dropped her purse on the kitchen counter.

"Instead of worrying about who's fine and who isn't, you need to get yourself together for school tomorrow." Leone pulled open the refrigerator door and removed a can of soda. The telltale sound of fizz shortly followed and she took a short, cool swallow.

"What is wrong with you?" Raven asked in that sing-song cadence that belied the challenge in her voice.

Leone cut her eyes in her daughter's direction.

"Nothing."

"Really?"

"Yes. Really."

Raven stared at her mother, trying to find a way around the barrier. "Where's Cole?" Her tone became accusatory. "How come I haven't seen him lately?"

"Cole is wherever he is. People do get busy, Raven."

"Too busy to see me? He always comes to see me. He hasn't even called. Did you run him away, too?"

Leone flashed her a warning look. Raven was treading on dangerous ground, and Leone knew if she didn't nip this in the bud, the conversation would rapidly segue to her ex-husband, Steven. And he was a topic she refused to discuss.

She pressed her palm to her forehead and spoke through tight lips. "Raven—please—go see about your clothes for tomorrow, pack your books and take your shower."

"Fine. Every time I want to talk about something, it's a problem." She snatched her bag from the counter and stomped up the stairs to her bedroom.

An instant later, the house rocked in its hinges with the inevitable slamming of Raven's bedroom door.

Leone shut her eyes, inhaling deeply. Like all the other storms before, this one would pass as well. She opened an overhead cabinet and extracted a teacup. The caffeine in the soda would only make her more agitated than she already was. She rifled around in the cabinet for her box of chamomile tea, and put a pot of water on to boil.

Even though Raven was old enough to understand that her parents' marriage wasn't working, there were days like this one that she would lash out at being "a statistic," Leone thought, watching the water begin to bubble in the pot.

Cole was the only man she'd allowed into her life since her divorce from Steven. And Raven, although tenuous at first, slowly formed a bond with him that she'd never had with her own father. At times Raven seemed closer to Cole than to her. According to Antoinette, it was Raven's need to have a positive male role model that helped seal the bond.

Cole loved Raven, and thought of her as the daughter he never had, Leone reflected, pouring the hot water over the tea bag. The three of them made a great team, and for the most part she was happy. Yet, for the life of her, she couldn't understand her growing restlessness, her dissatisfaction. Even more disturbing was the steady beat of sensory arousal whenever she thought of or saw Ray Taylor.

Why? Why? Why? she questioned, taking a sip of her tea. But even as she posed the silent question, she knew that the answer rested inside herself.

Cole watched the black Maxima pull away from the curb and something deep inside of him twisted like wet clothes being wrung dry.

One by one the lights in the house filled the windows. He should get out of his car, cross the street and ring Leone's bell as he'd intended to do in the first place, until he saw her pull up with Ray.

He turned the key in the ignition, switched on his headlights and pulled away. He didn't want to see the lies in her eyes, or hear them from her lips.

EIGHT

Cole slowly walked into his Manhattan co-op and switched on the light. He tossed his car keys onto the small circular table in the short foyer and went straight to the mini-bar.

He didn't usually drink alone, but felt as if he needed one now. He poured some Scotch over ice and stretched out on the couch, taking a long swallow. The amber liquid burned all the way down and settled in the pit of his belly. Yet, it couldn't melt the chill that had settled there.

What was happening between him and Leone? Where had their relationship taken a wrong turn?

He leaned his head back against the cushions and closed his eyes.

They'd met when she'd put an ad in Backstage Magazine just before she opened the club, looking for a small band.

At first he thought about ignoring it. He knew the difficulty of working with folks who were just starting out. He'd been through enough "start up" operations and wanted something solid. But on the other hand, he'd grown weary of the short stints at one club or the other, never sure from week to week where the next check was coming from. The saving grace for him was that he had no family to concern himself with. The same couldn't be said for the rest of the band members, and he felt responsible for that, responsible for them. They all worked other jobs to make ends meet, but music was their first love. If a permanent gig could be set up, they'd give up their day jobs in a heartbeat.

So, finally he called and set up a meeting for the following afternoon. He wasn't sure what he expected, but it certainly wasn't Leone Williams.

"We can talk in the office," Leone said as she led him through what would become Soul to Soul once the construction was completed.

Cole took in the surroundings, the solidness of the structure, which had once been an antique shop, and marveled at what was being done with the place.

The vastness of the central room was being totally reconfigured with several pillars and a drop ceiling with recessed track lighting around the perimeter.

The old floor had been completely ripped out and replaced with a black marble-like surface except for the dance area which was a hi-gloss parquet. Mirrors lined one wall, giving the illusion of even more space. The once dreary walls were being painted in a soft teal with a deeper teal molding.

"Please excuse the mess," she said, laughing lightly. "We still have a way to go before everything is the way I want it."

"It looks like it's going to be great," he answered, stepping around a crate of framed artwork. "You've put a lot into this place. I remember it being dark and gloomy and crammed with furniture."

She turned to him and flashed the most exquisite smile he'd ever seen. "You've been here before?" Her eyes sparkled.

"Yeah, a few years ago. I was searching for an old roll-back desk and a friend of mine told me about this place." He glanced around again.

"Changed a bit," she teased.

"I'd say so. And for the better."

Leone opened the door to the office. "Welcome to operation central." She extended her hand to wave him inside.

Cole stepped into the sparse room. There was one age-old desk and two wooden chairs that looked as if they'd been left behind by the last tenants. It quickly reminded him of those sinister back rooms from the old black and white movies. But when Leone stepped in and closed the door behind her, everything became colorized and Cole was instantly taken aback by the sudden rush that overtook him.

Leone came around the desk and sat down. "Please, sit."

Cole took the lone available seat. "Looks like you have your hands full, Ms. Weathers." He crossed his right ankle over his left knee.

"It's hectic, crazed and totally insane, but I'm loving every minute. If everything stays on schedule, I should be ready to open in a month." She cleared her throat and leaned slightly forward. "So, tell me a little about yourself and what you've done."

"What haven't I done?" he said with a short laugh. "I guess it goes all the way back to high school. My folks insisted that I take piano lessons, which, of course, I hated. But in my junior year a friend of my father wanted to put a band together. I tried out and the rest is history. I did local stuff until I got out of school. By then I had the bug and wanted my own band." The corner of his mouth curved upward. "Not too good at taking orders and playing other people's music. Started writing my own and recruiting the band."

"How long has your band been together?"

"About fifteen years, give or take a few personnel changes."

Leone nodded. "When do you think you could come in so I can hear you?"

"Whenever you're ready."

"How about Friday evening, around eight."

"Sounds good."

Leone stood. "So, we'll meet on Friday and take it from there." She extended her hand. "Thank you for coming."

The first thing he thought was how soft, almost fragile her hand was. Yet Leone Weathers was anything but fragile. Reluctantly he released her hand. "My pleasure."

He followed her to the door. "Are you taking on this whole project yourself?"

"Pretty much. Everyone thinks I'm crazy, but it's what I want. I want to see it work out."

There was something in her voice, more than determination. She had something to prove to herself and he wondered what it was. "I'm sure it will," he said finally.

They reached the front door and faced each other. When she looked up at him, he felt that rush again, that heat in the center of his stomach.

"Listen, uh, if there's anything I can help you with, don't hesitate to ask. Whether I get the job or not, the offer is still good."

"I just might take you up on that, Mr. Fleming."

"See you on Friday."

"Eight o'clock."

As promised, Cole arrived with the band on Friday night, and before they'd finished the third number Leone said they had the job if they wanted it.

"I can't pay much to start," she said when she and Cole had retreated to her office. "But the pay is guaranteed and steady."

"I'll talk it over with the guys, but I don't think it'll be a problem."

"Great. I'll have the contract ready for you to sign in the next couple of days. Do you want to come and pick it up or should I mail it to your home?"

Mailing it would save him a drive, but coming to pick it up would give him the chance to see her again.

Since their first meeting, Leone had dominated his thoughts. He'd tried to conceive of all types of reasons to call her, just to hear her voice, but had decided against it. There was no point in making a fool of himself. Besides, a woman as lovely and together as Leone surely had a man of her own. But if she did, where was he?

"I can drop by and pick it up. Give me a call when it's ready."

"I'll do that."

Her face lit up when she smiled. "Welcome aboard."

"I have a feeling it's going to be a great ride. Maybe, if you're not busy, we can celebrate after we get all the paperwork out of the way."

She tilted her head a bit to the side. "I'd like that. What did you have in mind?"

Even though he'd hoped she'd say yes, the actuality caught him off guard. This woman didn't play games.

"Let me surprise you," he said, recovering quickly.

"I like surprises."

"Then I'll have to make it a good one. See you in a couple of days."

"I'm looking forward to it—Cole."

And so it began.

NINE

Cole intended to make that first night memorable. Every time Leone thought about one of the great evenings of her life, he wanted her to think of him.

He'd gotten tickets for a midnight cruise around Manhattan Island, complete with dinner and dancing under the stars. The evening was magical. They ate lobster and drank champagne amidst a warm sea breeze and the gentle undulations of waves beneath them. From there it was a series of romantic interludes: talks long into the night, drives upstate for middle-of-the-week picnics. And when they made love for the very first time, it left him weak with an unnamed joy.

Maybe that was when he realized he was falling in love with Leone. But that couldn't be, he reasoned. He was a rational man. He thought things through logically. But when it came to Leone, nothing made sense.

It was the little things she did: a gentle touch or a look, like slipping loving notes into his shirt pockets, or giving him a massage, right in the office.

The first six months of their relationship was like being a kid again. He was in love. Really in love. And it scared him. The last time he'd turned his heart over to someone, he'd been burned. He still carried the scars of Tara Bentley.

Humph. Tara. She was pretty, smart, sexy, driven by her career as a television producer and totally self-absorbed. Tara gave the illusion of caring about others. She could even say the words "I love you," without flinching. But Cole found out the hard way that the only person Tara loved was herself and what someone else could do for her.

"I'm getting married," Tara had calmly announced as they lay in bed together. Cole's body still vibrated from the lovemaking session they'd just concluded.

He chuckled deep in his throat. "I didn't know we'd set a date, babe." He stroked her bare back.

Tara stretched her long, tan legs toward the ceiling, then lowered them to the damp sheets.

"Not to you, silly." She eased off the bed and paraded her perfect body toward the chair where she'd tossed her clothes.

For an instant his mind went blank. Nothing was there. He saw everything around him, but couldn't process the information. Then that sudden rush of realization, that free-fall feeling in your belly pushed its way upward, trapping his breath in his throat, and wouldn't let go.

Fear of choking forced the words out. "What are you talking about?" It was all he could think coherently to ask.

She wouldn't look at him as she put one foot, then the other, through the openings in her panties and wiggled them in place.

"Paul and I are getting married."

Cole blinked as if smacked. All he could see in that instant was the helpless look on his father's face when his mom took the kids and walked out, and that sick sensation of loss that he, himself, felt and was never able to fill. He shook his head, then suddenly jumped up and crossed the room. He grabbed Tara by the arms and spun her around.

"What the fuck are you saying to me? Don't play." His eyes narrowed to two single slits. He could feel the pull in his chest as his heart banged viciously.

She glared down at his hands. "You're hurting me," she said matter-of-factly. "I'm marrying Paul Howell in two weeks. I thought you should know. She looked into his eyes as innocently as if she'd just relayed the forecast for a sunny, cloudless day.

He wanted to hurt her, knock the smug, self-satisfied look off her face. Most of all he wanted to make her hurt the way he was hurting now. But standing there, staring into her soulless eyes, he understood as never before that making Tara feel anything was beyond anyone's ability.

He pushed her away from him and laughed, a deep belly laugh that filled the bedroom and the one beyond. "Think you can get dressed a little faster? I have some music I want to work on." He shook his head trying to catch his breath and pulled on his shorts.

Tara pulled her top over her braless torso and looked at him in stunned disbelief. "Cole, I'm not kidding. What we had was nice. But it could never go anywhere."

"Of course not." He crossed the room to the dresser. "Don't forget your purse."

"You hop from one job to the next. All you ever talk about is music and that rag-tag band of yours." Her voice rose in confrontation. "What can you offer me? Huh? What?"

Cole ignored her as he flipped through his phone book. He needed something to do with his hands to keep them from wrapping around her neck.

"You barely make enough money to pay your rent," she said, needing to penetrate this unfamiliar wall he'd erected. She fastened her skirt and stepped into her pumps.

His mother had spat those same words to his father as she walked out the door. Heat rushed to his head and took on a life of its own as it throbbed.

"It was good, Cole," she flung at him in a last ditch effort. "But it's not what I want."

He picked up the phone. "Oh, just pull the door behind you," he said over his shoulder. "And don't forget to leave the keys on the kitchen table."

Tara glared at him one last time, snatched up her purse and stormed out.

That was nearly ten years ago. Yet, even now, the thought of that night made him feel worthless and used. It made him wary and uncertain. Anger and frustration would fill him and he'd pick up a drink. He did that just about everyday until he saw the ad in the paper and met Leone.

From that first day, his life began to change. He found his humanity again, his self-esteem. And it was because of

Leone—her kindness, her love, her acceptance of who he was began to heal him. He started to trust again—love again.

Cole blinked and looked around his neat, contemporarily furnished apartment. It had gone through some major overhauling since he'd started working at Soul to Soul. His drink had gone flat. He poured it out and refreshed it.

Now, he was right back where he started ten years ago. He'd opened himself up, turned over his emotions, and it was happening again. Again.

Suddenly he hurled the glass against the wall. It splintered and fell in a pile of sparkling rubble, while tears of Scotch streaked down the white surface.

He wouldn't go down that road. Not this time.

TEN

The following morning, Raven barely spoke to her mother before leaving for school. There was a near audible grunt, which could have meant hello or goodbye, depending on which way Raven was going.

Leone pushed her scrambled eggs around on her plate, then stared into her coffee cup.

Last night, if Raven hadn't walked up when she did—she didn't want to think about it. But what truly unnerved her was that she would have let Ray kiss her. She wanted him to. That same exhilaration that you experience when you play tag and you can feel the kid who's "it" right on your heels. And you run and run, excited and scared at the same time.

That's the way she'd felt in the car, like something unseen, untapped was racing behind her, ready to catch her.

There was something mysterious, inaccessible about Ray Taylor. For all his affability, warm smile and good looks, he was undefined, yet to be discovered. That was the attraction, the challenge.

Ray awakened the core of her, the Leone who'd never been allowed to "go off the block," "attend the public school," "wear lipstick or mini skirts," "date before high school graduation." Ray represented "yes you can."

Leone took a sip of her cool coffee and stared out the kitchen window that looked upon a small, untended backyard. Steven had promised to cement part of it and trim the unruly trees so that they could use it in the summer. Never happened. And she refused to do it. She knew it was childish, but it was one of the few ways to show her displeasure. What had been the pattern during their marriage was for Leone to always pick up where Steven left off—from paying the bills to repairs on the house to disciplining Raven. The list went on. She supposed it was just easier that way; easier not to complain, not to make an issue, not to nag. She'd been conditioned to follow protocol. Why would her marriage be any different?

Leaving her job of twenty years, divorcing Steven and finally opening the club had all been acts of long overdue rebellion. She knew that. It had been terrifying and everyday she knew she'd gone completely crazy. And at the same time she felt rejuvenated as if she'd been asleep and just going through the motions for most of her life.

Meeting and settling into a relationship with Cole had been the equivalent of reaching for a life preserver after you've dived off the side of the ship and realize you can't swim. He was safe, secure, the calm during the storm of change in her life—what she needed—what she'd been conditioned to be accustomed to—the status quo.

Now she felt torn. Torn between the Leone who would never jump ship and the one who'd learned how to swim.

Ray had gotten up at first light, tossed some water on his face, brushed his teeth and donned his jogging clothes—nothing fancy—just a ragged pair of navy blue sweatpants and a cut-off T-shirt.

He stood on his front porch and looked out across the water. The air was crisp, sharp like a paper's edge when he stepped outside, pulling in a lungful of air. The blue-green waves rolled gently, one massaging the other. In the distance, he spotted several small pleasure boats out for an early morning sail.

Parker had been instrumental in securing the house for him. With his transient lifestyle and sporadic, though bountiful, financial situation, the bank was reluctant to approve the mortgage. Parker, "Mr. Negotiator," was somehow able to convince the bank to give Ray the loan. It wasn't until later that Ray discovered Parker had used his own home as collateral.

Ray inhaled deeply of the sea-touched air. This was the first place he'd called home since he left his folks and went to college. Most of his adult life had been moving from one city to the next. One kitchenette or studio to another. And as much as Parker might profess his love for the prowl and new adventures, he was probably the most settled, stable guy Ray knew. Parker might run a good game, but at the heart of it he was a seriously practical man. He owned his house, his car, had a huge stash in the bank and wore a suit and tie five days a week.

Ray trotted out of the cul-de-sac of houses and onto the unpaved road, jogging along the shoreline.

At times, especially lately, he envied Parker, envied him more than he'd ever admit. The funny thing was, as quiet as it was kept, Parker felt the same way about him. The grass is always greener on the other side, he mused, catching sight of a sailboat on the horizon.

But Parker was the kind of guy a woman settled down with, made a life with—even though he'd never get Parker to agree.

He on the other hand could always fill "the temp" position. Do it well for a little while, just not forever. For the most part it was fine. It worked with the kind of life he'd been living. But more and more, he realized that what had always been was no longer enough. He gazed out toward a grassy patch shaded by an overhanging tree and noticed an embracing couple simply sitting together enjoying the view.

That's what he wanted. Right there.

An image of Leone's face, the expectation in her eyes last night, materialized before him and that tightness in his chest took hold again.

That's who he wanted. But she belonged to someone else.

ELEVEN

"What are you doing after work today?" Leone asked, hugging the phone between her shoulder and her left ear, as she polished her toes a pearly peach. She knew Antoinette usually finished her day anywhere between two and three in the afternoon. But sometimes, she'd get a last minute call for a job that could run well into the night. She hoped today wouldn't be one of them.

Antoinette's slim fingers quickly typed in a string of programming commands on the computer. She'd gone into computer programming and repair about eight years earlier and loved it. Between the incredible pay, a flex schedule, access to a company car, frequent flyer miles for all the trips she had to take, she couldn't ask for more. Not to mention all of the eligible men.

"This is where the guys are, Lee," she'd said when she entered the training program. "Short, tall, dark, light, fat, thin. They all have brains and will have bucks."

"Been there, done that."

"Let's do it again and again," Antoinette sang off-key.

Now she was head of the programming division and free-lanced for major companies across the country. She'd set up Leone's computer system at the club and it had been a management lifesaver.

"So, what are you doing later?" Leone asked again.

"Sorry, drifted for a minute. Can't seem to get this damned system to run right." She sucked her teeth in disgust. "I don't have any plans. What's up?"

Leone sighed. "Just thought you could hang out for a while before I went to work."

"Sure. Where?"

"Can you come by the house?"

"This doesn't sound like a girls' night out to me."

"I just want some quiet time, that's all."

"Hmm. Okay. I'm sure you'll give me the scoop later. I'll come if you promise to fix the breaded chicken breasts for dinner."

"Nettie," Leone whined.

"Then I ain't comin'."

"All right, all right. Six o'clock. Don't be late."

"Yes, ma'am."

Leone hung up the phone and smiled. Antoinette had some wild ideas about love and life, but she had a good ear, and what she needed right now was someone to listen to all the scattered thoughts that were running rampant in her head.

"Where's Raven?" Antoinette asked later that evening as she swiped a celery stick from the salad bowl.

"Sequestered in her room." Leone checked the chicken in the oven.

Antoinette flicked an eyebrow at the sarcastic tone. "Why is that?"

"We had words last night and she apparently hasn't gotten over it yet."

The oven door banged shut. Leone tossed the pot holder on the counter and grabbed her glass of iced tea.

"You and Raven have been doing great lately. She's keeping up her grades, has a good group of friends, does her thing around the house. What happened?"

Leone's gaze bounced around the kitchen as if the answers could be found in one of the many wood cabinets. She released a sigh and lowered herself onto a stool opposite Antoinette.

"I was with Ray last night," she began, filling Antoinette in on all the details up to when Raven tapped on the window.

Antoinette stared at Leone's averted profile. "It sounds to me that you felt guilty—for whatever reason—and took it out on Raven," she said pragmatically.

"Guilty about what?"

"You tell me."

Leone huffed and sipped her drink. "There's nothing to tell. Nothing went on."

"So then why take it out on Raven?"

"She was being rude and out of place," Leone snapped.

"Raven was being seventeen." Antoinette stretched her hand across the table and covered Leone's. "Let's cut through all the bull, Lee. We've been friends too long to play games. The bottom line is, you're confused about your feelings for this guy, don't know what to do about them, and Raven was the most accessible target for venting your frustration."

Leone remained silent.

"Am I right?"

"I hate it when you're right," Leone conceded and rolled her eyes.

"Yeah, I know. So, what's going on, girl? You're making yourself crazy."

"A part of me wants to see what it would be like with Ray. Take a chance, you know. I see him with the other women in the club. I know I can't compete with that. And at the same time when I see all those young girls all over him, it really ticks me off, because it's not me. I don't know what it is about Ray Taylor that sets my blood boiling. Maybe it's just the challenge, the desire to be noticed, to not be looked at as a woman moving out of her forties. But at the same time, I don't want to hurt Cole. He doesn't deserve that. He's been good to me and for me. I mean, I've only known Ray for a little more than two months. And we never really talked until last night. I've been working real hard to stay away from him. But when we finally did talk, I began to see that he's nothing like I thought." She lowered her head. "Which only makes things worse."

"Listen, maybe I was jumping the gun the last time we talked about this. It's not up to me to tell you to drop your man for some other guy. You know me, talk faster than I can think sometimes. Cole is a damned good man. Maybe this Ray guy is, too. Only you know who and what is right for you, Lee."

"It wasn't anything you said. It's me. I'm at a crossroads in my life. If I settle down again, like Cole wants, I need to be absolutely sure. I don't want to wake up in six months after saying 'I do' and wonder 'what if.'"

"Hey, I know what you mean. That would be the worse mistake you could make. Maybe the whole notion of getting married again has you running scared. Scared enough that you've started talking yourself out of your relationship with Cole, finding things wrong that aren't. Maybe what you need is a short break, give yourself some time and space to think."

"I've been thinking the same thing. A break may be just what I need."

TWELVE

When Leone arrived at the club later that day, the band was on stage going over a new number. Cole's back was turned to her while he gave out instructions about how he wanted each section played.

He never ceased to amaze her, she mused, a soft smile of pride softening her mouth. He was not only an incredible musician, but a wonderful manager. The guys in the band practically worshipped him. He was always fair and open-minded and was eager to give each of them a shot at a solo. He'd even helped them compose some of their own pieces. Yeah, she was lucky to have a man like Cole Fleming, and she was going to remind him of that— tonight. She didn't need a break, she'd decided after a long talk with her heart. What she needed was to start acting like a grown woman, get her love life back on track and stop thinking like a college coed. Cole was her man. Period. Simple as that. She leaned against a pillar and watched him do his thing. She smiled. Yeah, her man.

"Come in slow and easy, Ray, right above Zach's bass," Cole guided. "Think of yourself as the ship sailing across the water. We're the water, Ray," he coaxed. "Take us sailing."

Cole hit the first chords on the piano and one by one the rest of the band joined in.

Ray nodded, closed his eyes and brought the sax to his lips, the plaintive cry rolling on along the crest of the waves.

The music rippled through Leone, scurried along her spine, and she trembled as if some erotic zone had been entered and caressed. Music always had the power to do that to her, reach her somehow. It was, beyond his charm, one of the things that had attracted her to Cole. The more she heard him play and experienced the deep-seated passion he had for his craft, the more enchanted she became. Then, getting to know Cole the man away from the music was even more enlightening.

She supposed it really hit her just how good a man he was when he met Raven for the first time.

She'd decided that since it was no longer hush-hush around the club about their relationship, it was time she introduced "her man" to her daughter.

Leone had been reluctant at first, partly out of fear that Raven would hate him simply because he wasn't her father, or turn on her because there was now someone in her life besides Raven.

"Listen, babe," Cole had said one late night at his apartment. "I've never been the kind of man who sneaks around, and that's what this feels like to me." He eased closer on the couch, put his arm around her rigid shoulders and pulled her near. "I don't want to be the family secret. I think we're great together, and I want to see how far things can go with us. But I won't commit myself to the program if we can't be up front with your daughter. I know once we meet and she sees how much I care about you, it will be fine."

Leone glanced up at him from the corner of her eye. She knew he was right, but…

"Cole," she blew out. "It's just that I've never, I mean I haven't dated anyone since my divorce." There, she'd said it—finally.

"No one?" he asked incredulously.

She shook her head. "Not a soul." She waited a beat, collected her thoughts. "So, I have no clue as to how Raven will react. Although things were strained in the household, she adored her father."

"Most girls do."

"But you understand what I'm saying, right?"

"Sure. You don't want Raven to think I'm trying to take her father's place."

She nodded slowly.

"I couldn't, Lee. And I wouldn't want to. There isn't anything I could do in this lifetime to be able to step into your ex-husband's shoes. No matter what I did, the shoes would never fit. All I can be is who I am. And be the best I can at it. I don't expect Raven to love me on sight, but I tend to grow on people." He gently tickled her side. She giggled. "Besides, we'll never know if we don't give it a shot."

She released a short breath. "I guess you're right." She turned fully toward him, needing to see assurance in his dark eyes.

"It'll be all right," he said, reading her thoughts as he was prone to do. He stroked her hair, then tucked it behind her ears. "Raven couldn't really believe that you've given up living, given up your womanhood because your husband is no longer in your life."

She pursed her lips.

"It might help Raven to see that her mom is still loveable, still beautiful," he added, his voice dropping to a caress. He tilted her chin upward with the tip of his finger. "And very desirable," he murmured before bringing his mouth to hers.

It was a sweet sensation, Leone thought, letting her lids slide shut and easing into the secure comfort of Cole's embrace. He made her feel good from the inside out. Cole had a natural way of making her believe that everything would be all right, no matter what. He could make love to her body as well as her mind.

Neither of them was as young as they once were, but their loving was strong, filled not only with passion, but the maturity of experience. They understood the act of pleasuring each other, the power of the slow hand and hot spring words.

They fit each other physically and mentally. They accepted the extra pounds, the touches of gray, the skin that was smooth, if not workout firm. It was good. It was easy.

Yet for all the assertions Cole made that everything would be fine, it didn't keep Leone's stomach from running an unwinable marathon that fateful Sunday afternoon.

She'd spent the entire morning cleaning, dusting, organizing and cooking. She'd broken out some of her favorite cookbooks and had prepared a head-spinning array of exotic platters from French finger foods to West Indian delicacies.

Every time a door closed, the phone rang or Raven called her name, she leaped from the inside out. She felt the way she did when she was preparing for her first solo date and knew her father and mother would interrogate her new beau and embarrass her the way they always did around her friends. She was so nervous waiting to be picked up that she'd thrown up and developed a raging headache. She never thought she'd feel like that again—until now.

By the time four o'clock rolled around—the time she'd invited Cole—she was on the verge of tossing down some Pepto Bismol.

She checked every room, one last time. Turning from fluffing the couch pillows, she gasped at finding Raven standing behind her.

"Who is this dude, anyway—the President's half brother?" Raven suspiciously scanned the counter as she sauntered into the kitchen. It was lined from one end to the other with food.

"No, smarty. He's just a friend. I told you that," Leone said entering the kitchen.

"He's the band leader, right?"

"Yes."

Raven picked up a buffalo wing and took a bite.

"Any other questions?"

Raven shrugged. "I don't have to hang around all afternoon do I? Ron asked me to go to the movies later."

Leone arched a brow. "I suppose it'll be all right. He has to come and pick you up and you need to be home by eleven."

"But, Ma, it's summertime," she whined.

"Raven, I—"

The doorbell rang, cutting her off. She quickly wiped her hands on a towel and headed for the door. "Midnight," she tossed over her shoulder.

Whatever anxiety she'd harbored about Raven's reaction to Cole quickly dissolved.

After the initial introductions, Cole and Raven launched into a quick and easy banter about music, music videos, rap groups she'd never heard of, the latest singing sensations, books, movies, cars, clothes.

Cole was "up" on everything it seemed, Leone mused as she mixed the salad and listened to their laughter from the living room. She couldn't remember the last time she and Raven talked for more than twenty minutes without getting into a conflict about something. She tossed the salad a bit faster. Humph.

Raven popped up behind her and snatched a carrot from the bowl. "He's cool, Ma." She grinned. "And he even knows Maxwell! Can you believe it?" Maxwell, this R&B generation's heir apparent to the late Marvin Gaye, was, according to Raven, the cousin of a friend's ex-in-law. Go figure.

"That's great. I'm glad you two are getting along. Would you take the tray of sandwiches inside for me and ask Cole if he wants anything to drink?"

"He says he likes Coke with lemon." She spun away toward the refrigerator. "I'll fix it."

Leone blinked. Who was this child in front of her and what did they do with her real daughter? She shook her head in amazement.

And that's how it always was between Raven and Cole. He'd drop by and they'd talk for hours. He'd slip extra money in her pocket when she'd spent her allowance. He'd drive her and her friends to the mall without complaint. Pick her and Ron up from a date. He even got along with Ron, who she'd always believed couldn't put three whole sentences together. And she was certain Raven shared secrets with Cole that she wouldn't dare tell her.

Yes, Cole Fleming had eased into their lives, like the missing piece of a puzzle, she thought, as the music in the club came to a climactic finish.

Leone blinked and the past receded. A quiet sense of peace moved slowly through her. She had a good thing with Cole, a damned good thing. Ray Taylor was simply wishful thinking.

She crossed the room as the band put away their equipment.

Cole and Ray stood facing one another, deep in conversation, both apparently unaware of her presence. She glanced from one to the other.

Cole represented time-tested certainty. Ray was the deep blue sea, uncharted and unconquerable. She was too old to start testing the waters again. Wasn't she?

Leone walked toward the duo, stepped up to Cole and kissed his cheek.

When he turned to her the light that she expected to be there was missing. In its place was a look of resolve. A look that settles over someone who has wrestled long and hard with a decision.

The muscles of her stomach tightened as a flash of heat spread through her limbs.

She touched his shoulder, suddenly afraid and uncertain. Glancing briefly at Ray, she offered him a tight smile.

"Hello, fellas," she said, forcing a lightness into her voice. "You all were sounding really good."

"Ray and I were discussing some changes I'm making." His voice was flat, devoid of the warmth he usually reserved for her.

"Changes?" She looked anxiously from one to the other. Ray glanced away.

"I'll talk with you about it in the office," Cole said. "Okay, guys, that's it until later."

Rather than the usual exuberance the band displayed after rehearsal, they were extremely subdued, Leone noticed, a warning bell sounding in her head. But nothing could have prepared her for Cole's bombshell.

THIRTEEN

"What's going on?" Leone asked the instant the office door closed behind her. She put her purse on the desk and eyed Cole—waiting.

He kept his back to her. "I've been doing a lot of thinking, Lee, and I've decided it's time for some changes—around here and in my life."

Slowly he turned around and she felt her stomach flutter as if butterflies had been let loose.

"What kind of changes?" She stepped closer, her fingers worrying the bottom button of her blouse. The desk separated them, but it felt like a shaky bridge.

Cole straightened and inhaled deeply. All night he'd debated with himself about his decision, about what all this would mean, if he was doing the right thing. By sunrise he understood he had no other choice.

"I'm leaving the club, Leone."

The air stuck in her throat. The room suddenly grew warm, uncomfortable.

"What do you mean, leaving? I—don't—" She swallowed, tried to still the erratic pounding of her heart. "Why?" She came around to his side of the desk and placed her palm on his chest. "What is it, Cole? Talk to me. Are you ill?"

"No. I'm not sick. It's nothing like that," he said with that same emptiness that was terrifying her.

He turned away, moving toward the far side of the room. It was easier if he didn't have to look into her eyes.

"Cole." Her confusion escalated to panic. How would she manage without him? And with that question, she knew with certainty that it wasn't the club she was thinking about. The thought that he was leaving her terrified her. Terrified her the same way the dissolution of her marriage had terrified her. For all the years of her marriage she'd been brainwashed by Steven into believing that she was nothing without him. That she'd never make it if he was out of her life. She'd begun to believe it, accepted it as true. And when the divorce was final, he had glared at her in the courtroom, and said, "Wait and see. Before long you'll come back. You'll never make it on your own. All you know how to do is empty bedpans."

For months after, she was in a trance, moving through her days by rote. Expecting at any moment that the rug of life would be pulled out from under her. But it wasn't, and little by little she realized that she could stand on her own, could make a life without Steven. Yet, there was always that nagging doubt in the back of her mind, lying dormant, waiting for an opportunity to remind her how weak she really was.

That's how she felt right at that moment, weak and vulnerable. The rug of life was slipping from beneath her feet. And all she could do to keep from falling was retaliate.

"So out of the blue you tell me you're leaving. Just like that, with no thought to anything or anyone but yourself," she lashed out.

"It's time I started thinking about myself." He faced her. "I want to move on, move forward. I can't do that here. I can't do that with you."

The sting of his words held her paralyzed. There was so much she wanted to say. All the words were there, in her head, in her heart. But she couldn't get them out. All she could think of was that, again, in some way, she hadn't measured up. Couldn't cut it. A wave of nausea lifted her stomach.

"Cole…"

"We want two different things, Leone, you and I. I love you and…maybe you love me, too, in your own way. But I want more than just some time, Lee. I want more than just a few exhausted hours every now and then. And right now that's all you're willing to give." He drew in a breath. "And knowing how I feel and what I want, I can't stay on at the club—seeing you—it wouldn't work."

She reached out to him, and a sadness such as she'd never known filled her when he moved away, her fingers brushing air. "Please. Let's talk about this."

"What is there to say, Lee? If you can tell me I'm wrong, look me in the eye and tell me I'm wrong—I'll stay."

She started to say the words, wanted to say the words, just blurt them out, tell him he was wrong. But pride held her back. Once in her life she'd pleaded, begged, given in, just to be loved, have someone, and Steven had left her broken. She was still picking up the pieces.

"I—"

He held up his palm. "Don't, Lee," he said, his voice heavy with regret. There was that small corner, that one part of his soul that had hoped she'd tell him how wrong he was. "You don't have to make me feel better. It's cool." He looked away. "I'll finish out the rest of the month, give you a chance to find a replacement."

Suddenly she snapped out of her bout of self-recrimination, and retaliated with anger—an emotion she could handle. "A replacement? You seem to have this all figured out, some preconceived plan going according to your schedule. Things didn't happen in your time frame so you leave. Is that it?" she demanded, needing to attack him, turn the tide away from her and drown him in her pain.

"You know it's not that simple."

"Then why don't you explain it to me, since I'm too dumb to understand." Her eyes began to fill. Don't just walk out on me like Steven did, she thought. Not that.

"Lee, for you things are the way you've dreamed they'd be. The club is prosperous, your life is in order." He swallowed. "I've done all I can. It's time for me now."

Her head felt cloudy, her thoughts fuzzy, as if she were struggling with the after-effects of sleeping pills. She looked at Cole. Really looked at him and saw the unhappiness etched onto his rugged face. A heaviness that resided beneath his eyes from a lack of sleep, she was sure. But there was a purpose to his stance, a determination in the solid body she'd come to intimately know.

Her chest constricted painfully. She knew this man. She'd shared his secrets, her dreams, but she hadn't shared all of herself. She'd been too afraid. She knew that now. And that was all he'd ever asked for. The one thing she'd been unable to give and didn't know if she ever could. He deserved better.

She lowered her head, no longer able to bear the look of disappointment in his eyes.

"What will you do?" she managed to ask, but wanted to know what she would do without him.

He shrugged, picked up some papers on the desk as if they'd suddenly become important. "Travel a little, relax a lot." He offered a bittersweet smile. "Maybe I'll go visit my brother Calvin in San Francisco for awhile."

"Will—I see you? Talk to you?" She wouldn't cry.

"That's really up to you, Leone. Maybe when you figure out what you want."

"What makes you think that I haven't?"

"I'd say that was pretty obvious, wouldn't you?" He took his jacket off the hook. "I have some errands to run before the first set."

He moved past her toward the door. With one word she could stop him, convince him that this was all wrong. But she didn't.

The door closed quietly behind him.

FOURTEEN

"He said he'd finish out the month," Leone mumbled into her second cup of coffee for the morning.

Antoinette sat on the opposite side of Leone's kitchen table. "Out of the blue?" The absurdity of the situation raised her voice a notch. "That doesn't sound like the Cole I know."

Leone nodded in agreement, still unable to digest it all herself.

"What's happening with you? How do you feel about it? What did you tell him?"

Leone hesitated, ashamed almost of what she was about to say, but most of all confused by the way she had handled the whole thing.

"I'm not sure how I feel," she admitted. "On the one hand, I'm hurt and disappointed. On the other, I keep thinking that maybe it's for the best, that somehow I made it happen." She gazed into Antoinette's eyes searching for understanding.

"I'm with you on the first part, but I'm having some trouble with the second half. That sounds like some of the garbage Steven used to put in your head. Everything that went wrong, wasn't right or could have been better was your fault. How do you figure this is your fault?"

Leone took a long breath. "I guess I knew all along that I wasn't putting all my energies, my total heart, into our relationship. I took it for granted that Cole would always be around."

"Listen, girl, let's be honest. Steven put you through the wringer with his petty jealousies and constant campaign to undermine your self-esteem. He did everything he could to control your life, Lee. And whether you want to admit it or not, you haven't fully recovered from the effects."

Leone took a sip of her coffee. She knew Antoinette was right. Steven Weathers looked like a dream, and to the casual observer he acted like one. Everyone who'd ever seen the two of them together always commented on what a wonderful looking couple they made. No one really knew, except Antoinette, what went on behind their closed doors. And in the early days of their courtship and marriage, Leone was too blinded by love and awe to notice what was really happening to her. It was the little things, at first.

She remembered one date in particular. They'd been seeing each other for about six months and had been invited to a major fund raiser for the development company Steven worked for. She'd spent weeks shopping for the perfect dress and shoes. She'd had her nails done and hair cut into what she believed was an attractive style. She'd even spent half her morning getting a facial and new makeup. She wanted everything and herself to be perfect when Steven arrived.

Promptly at seven o'clock her doorbell rang. She was living in a studio at the time, and although it was beautifully furnished and perfect for one person, she longed to finish her RN training so that she could make some real money and get a bigger place. But maybe she wouldn't have to. If things kept moving along the way they had been between her and Steven, she might just become Mrs. Steven Weathers with a house of her own.

She took one last look in the mirror on her way to the door. Taking a breath, she pulled the door open, eager to see the look of pleasure on Steven's face when he saw her.

"Hi," she beamed, smiling with all the eagerness that raced around inside her.

Steven shot his pristine white cuffs and checked his watch. "We're going to be late if we don't leave right now. I thought I'd asked you to meet me downstairs." He glanced around, his smooth, pale brown features congealing in distaste as if he'd suddenly smelled something rotten. "You know how I hate to come through that lobby, not to mention that pissy, smelly elevator." He brushed off the sleeves of his midnight blue jacket, ridding it of imaginary lint.

Leone was a flower, wilting, withering under the scalding heat of his scorn that rained down upon her. One by one her beautiful petals fell to the earth, until there was nothing left but a thin bare stem ready to be cast aside.

"Come on, let's go. You know I hate walking into any place late."

It didn't occur to him that they couldn't leave until he had arrived, which he'd just done, Leone fumed, on the verge of tears. I have to walk through the same lobby and ride the same elevator, she thought, grabbing her purse and evening jacket.

For the entire evening while Steven charmed one guest after the other, Leone was left by herself, not introduced to anyone. And as the evening dragged mercilessly onward, the more insignificant she felt, shrinking by degrees into the floral patterns of the wall covering.

She should have left him then, but she didn't. She married him instead. Because Steven, being the charmer that he was, would always find ways to make it up to her. He'd take her home and make love to her as if she were the last woman in the world, the most incredible creature he'd even been with. He'd send flowers out of the blue, or surprise her by being parked outside of the hospital when she got off work. And she'd forget the hurts, the slights, the bouts of insecurity. Until she couldn't take it anymore. Couldn't take the arguments, the accusations, the ridicule.

"Why did you marry me, Steven?" she'd shouted. "If I'm such a disappointment to you, why did you marry me?"

He turned calmly toward her and delivered his parting line as calmly as a weather forecast. "You needed someone like me to take care of you, Leone. I felt sorry for you." He'd walked down the hall and shut the bedroom door.

In all her life she'd never felt so empty. She couldn't even feel hurt or anger, just nothingness. The following morning she found a lawyer in the Yellow Pages and filed for a divorce.

Antoinette was right. She hadn't gotten over the pain, the destruction. And because of it, she'd been afraid to truly love again. Now it was too late for her and Cole and it would be unfair of her to ask him to wait for her. Wait for her to heal.

"Don't cry, babe," Antoinette whispered, stroking Leone's head.

Surprised, Leone wiped her cheeks and found them damp with tears. She shut her eyes and sniffed. "What am I going to do, Nettie?"

"You're going to deal with it, day by day. You're going to get to know yourself, Lee, who you are and what you really want from life and a relationship. And if it's Cole that you really want, you'll make that decision when the time comes."

"Suppose he doesn't wait?" Leone asked, her voice coated in a child-like plea to make everything all right.

Antoinette knew what Leone wanted her to say. But she'd never lied to her friend, and she wouldn't start now.

"That's a chance you're going to have to take, Leone. Win or lose."

"I suppose." She took a deep breath. "You haven't heard the best part yet."

"What's that?"

"Ray is taking over the band until they find someone permanent."

"Oh, shit."

"My sentiments exactly."

"So what's going to happen with the band, brotha?" Parker asked as he wheeled his dove grey Mercedes CLK onto the Brooklyn Bridge on their way to Ray's house.

"Cole talked like he was hoping somebody was going to step up to the plate when he dropped the bomb, but nobody did."

Parker frowned. "Man, pleeze, what's the problem? That's every musician's dream to have their own band. Come on."

"Not these brothers. I guess it's because they all have families and regular day jobs to think about. Taking over a band, managing one, ain't easy. You know that."

"Yeah, yeah. You're right, I guess." He impatiently drummed his fingers along the steering wheel as they crept through the rush-hour traffic. Suddenly he snapped his head in Ray's direction.

"What about you, man? You sure don't keep a day job, and unless you've been holding back on the 411, you don't have a wife and kiddies to worry about."

Ray had wondered how long it was going to take Parker to leap onto that tidbit of information. He'd hoped to share his news over a couple of drinks. But the way the traffic was inching along, it would be time for him to start work before they got to the other side.

"He asked me to do it," Ray finally confessed.

"He asked you?" Parker couldn't believe it. "You mean he asked you after everyone turned it down, right?"

"No."

"What?"

"Actually, he asked me before he broke the news to everyone else."

"Get outta here. You've only been with them a couple of months. What gives? You're not that good," he added, emphasizing each word. Ray was wicked on sax, but Parker measured his accolades with a teaspoon.

"Thanks. And since that's the way you feel about it, I'll keep the details to myself."

"Aw, come one. That's not something you keep to yourself. This is big. Something you've been waiting for most of your life."

That much was certainly true. It had been a long-term dream to have his own band, something he could settle with, write music for and possibly record with, instead of the intermittent recording gigs he sat in on when needed. It was cool, but not solid, steady. That's what he was looking for in his life now. He realized it more each day.

"You gonna tell me or what?" Parker questioned, easing around a turtle-moving station wagon and just making the light across the Flatbush Avenue Extension exit.

"All right, all right. Don't beg. I got to the club early one night last week, wanted to run through some numbers, you know. When I arrived, Cole was already there, which wasn't really unusual. But he seemed like he was caught up in his own world. He was just sitting at the piano, staring at the keys, didn't even hear me the first time I spoke to him."

"Hey, man," Ray greeted while propping his sax case against the side of the stage. He peered at Cole's profile, wondering if he had just been ignored or if the brother really didn't hear him.

"Fleming. You all right, man?"

Cole blinked, and slowly turned his head in Ray's direction. "Hey, what's happening?" His voice was flat, dull like a floor that had been waxed one time too many. He aimed for a smile, but it missed its mark.

Ray stepped closer, slid his hands in his pants pockets. The club was only partially lit, casting shadows in some spots, plunging others into darkness. The view of Cole seated at the piano was obscured by the play of light that moved across his face. Yet Ray could still identify the mask of a troubled man.

Ray crossed the expanse of the stage. "Everything cool?" he asked while he pretended to look for some music sheets from the stand tucked away in the corner.

"Yeah. Yeah. Takin' it light. How about you?" Cole swung back toward the piano keys.

"You know how it is, still trying to get used to staying in one spot," he chuckled.

"I hear ya."

Cole cut his eyes in Ray's direction. "I know you must have a lady by now. You're real popular around here," he prodded.

"No one steady."

"Hmm. But I'm sure if the right opportunity presented itself..."

"Sure. If all the elements were right." The conversation was beginning to make him edgy. Did Cole sense his attraction to Leone? He'd tried to be cool, stay out of her way. But he got the impression that Cole was digging for something, but he couldn't figure out what.

"Let's say you had a steady gig, decent pay, great crib and the perfect lady, would you ever consider, hmm," he shrugged, "settling down, maybe heading up your own band?"

Ray's eyebrows met each other in the middle. Where was this going? Was he feeling him out to discover if he was planning to quit? He turned the question around in his head. Hey, the brother asked, so he must want to know the truth.

Ray pulled up a stool, slid it between his thighs and sat. He braced his palms on his knees and stared Cole directly in the eye.

"Fleming, as long as I can remember, having my own band was what I dreamed about. I've been all over the country, in and out of more dives than I could ever count. I've played with great bands and ones that should pack up their instruments and get day jobs."

They both laughed.

"I want to secure that dream. Yeah, I do," he said, his voice taking on the hush that fills you when real passion is the catalyst.

Thoughtfully, Cole nodded in agreement. He understood that gut feeling, that euphoria that lifts you, drives you, until nothing else matters but the sound, the perfect

note. He wanted to feel that way again, and because he did-
n't, he knew it was time to let it go.

"I was hoping that's what you'd say." Cole studied Ray
a moment. Ray Taylor was on his way to greatness. He
could see it, hear it, feel it. It was only a matter of time. "I
want to make you an offer…"

"Just like that, huh?" Parker asked, finally making a left
onto Atlantic Avenue. They passed one antique shop after
another, the occasional restaurant, the YWCA on Third
Avenue and then a string of Islamic bookstores and eateries.
"So he offers you the deal of a lifetime, knowing that the
other dudes won't take it?"

"Yep. He made his announcement, asked if anyone was
willing to take over. When he got the negative response, he
put my name up as his temporary replacement."

"Why you though?"

"'Cause I'm good at what I do," Ray tossed back.

"I suppose," Parker said with grudging admiration.
"What did the rest of the band say?"

"They actually seemed relieved." He chuckled lightly.

"Man." Parker shook his head in disbelief.

Ray paused a beat. "We need a piano player."

The car jerked as Parker accidentally pressed too hard
on the gas. "What are you saying?"

"I'm making my first executive request. You gonna help
a brother out or what?"

Parker pursed his lips as if he was annoyed and totally put upon. "Thought you'd never ask."

Ray laughed.

"What about boss lady? What did she have to say?"

"Beats me. She hasn't been in for the past few days."

"Probably pissed and trying to regroup. Didn't you say the two of them had a thing going?"

"Yeah."

"Hey, maybe this is a bigger blessing in disguise than you thought it was."

"What's that supposed to mean?" He didn't want to think about what he just knew Parker was going to say.

Parker turned right on Flatlands Avenue, thought about detouring into the car wash, saw the line and changed his mind.

"It means, my brotha, the playing field is now open." He turned toward Ray and winked.

FIFTEEN

It was Sunday. The end of a long, tension-filled week. When Leone awoke she felt as if her body had been twisted into knots. Lying in bed, she stared up at the ceiling; the sounds of Raven's usual morning music was missing.

Friday evening she'd finally told Raven about Cole's leaving. She hadn't fully realized, or better yet, accepted how deeply Raven had become attached to Cole until she saw the pain on her face, heard it in her voice.

"Why?" Raven asked, her voice a whisper away from breaking. She wrapped her arms tightly around her thin frame as if she were trying to hold herself together. Her eyes filled and she blinked rapidly to stem the tears.

Leone lowered herself into a seat at the kitchen table, pressing her palms against the cool surface.

"He said he needed to make some changes in his life."

"I don't understand. He always seemed happy. He loves working at the club. He told me so." She dropped her arms defiantly to the side. "It's because of your relationship, isn't it?" she challenged. "He told me he wanted to marry you and make us a family."

"Things change, Raven. People change. That doesn't mean Cole stopped caring about us."

Raven stared at her mother for a long moment. "Where's he going?"

"He said he wants to go to San Francisco for a while to visit with his brother."

"Fine. Good riddance." She turned on her heel and stormed out of the room.

She probably could have handled the whole situation better, Leone thought. But the truth of the matter was, she didn't know what to say. For the most part, she was as confused as Raven. Although she was pretty certain her lack of being able to commit was part of the problem, she couldn't believe that was the only reason for Cole's abrupt announcement.

Leone turned onto her side. It had been nearly two weeks since he'd made his declaration. Although they were polite and pleasant to each other, the strain was unmistakable. And now that Ray was band leader and manager, they were thrown together more often than she would have liked. It certainly didn't make it easier on her with him turning up every minute. Sometimes she would be in the storeroom taking inventory and she'd feel his presence. She'd turn and he'd be standing there in the doorway, claiming that he needed to ask her a question. Or she'd be working in the office and he would pop up, earlier than the rest of the band for rehearsal, and sit with her until the guys arrived.

She hated it and anticipated it at the same time. When he wasn't around she would be disappointed, annoyed almost and let down. The whole thing was making her crazy. What did that say about her feelings for Cole? If she could feel herself heat from the inside out when Ray Taylor entered a room, was what she felt for Cole ever real? The more she thought about it, the less she knew.

She frowned. Cole had even gone so far as to tell her that she should be the one to teach Ray the business end of Soul to Soul, so that he would understand their system and help her out since he was leaving.

It was almost as if this were some divine plan of Cole's to put Ray solidly in her path. But why? She shook her head. That was just crazy thinking on her part.

Sighing, Leone peeped at the bedside clock. It was nearly noon and she had yet to rouse herself for the day. Tossing the light blanket aside, she pushed herself into a sitting position.

The new guy that was to take Cole's place on piano was supposed to sit in on a special rehearsal session later that afternoon, Leone recalled as she headed to the master bath for a shower. She was to be there as well to hear him play. She wasn't looking forward to it. It just made everything so final. In her mind no one could replace Cole.

She turned on the shower full blast. The more she thought about it, the more she realized that she was losing her enthusiasm for the club, for everything in general. She usually made it a point to visit the hair salon once a week, get her nails and toes manicured, and pick up at least one trinket for her and Raven in celebration of the end of the week. She hadn't done any of those things since Cole made his intentions known. Her bedroom, which she generally kept immaculate, showed signs of neglect. Clothes that should have gone to the cleaners had taken up residence across the chaise lounge. And she and Raven had eaten either pizza, Chinese food, or McDonald's for the past two weeks, since she didn't feel like preparing her usual full course dinners. Funny, Raven didn't seem to care or notice. It was if a general malaise had settled over both of them.

Leone pulled her soft green gown over her head and hung it on the back of the bathroom door. Little by little, day by day, she dreaded going to work. At first she thought it was because of the tension between her and Cole.

She stepped beneath the pulsing spray. But what she'd begun to understand was that much of her joy over the past year at the club had been because of Cole. His nurturing, attentiveness and love had been much of the driving force that kept her going. Falling in love with him had been an added bonus, yet one she had let slip away because of battles within herself.

Lathering her body with her favorite peach-scented soap, she realized with a deep sadness that settled like an anvil inside her stomach, that with Cole's leaving, her entire life was about to change.

Moments after Leone finished drying off, she heard the faint sound of the doorbell. Usually, the bell or the phone was Raven's cue to yell, "I got it!"

Leone listened. Nothing. Shaking her head, she quickly pulled a powder blue t-shirt over her head, zipped her jeans and slipped a pair of black leather mules on her feet. It was probably one of Raven's friends anyway.

Raven's withdrawal and anger were really worrying her. She'd had no idea that Raven would react so strongly, take it so personally. But she should have expected it. Raven's attachment to Cole over the past year was nothing short of phenomenal. His influence in her life had made her bloom, mature in a way. She was more focused on her schoolwork. Her choice of friends had dramatically improved and her sense of self as well as her blossoming womanhood were daily becoming apparent. She'd become more open, actually happy. Not the strident, bitter girl who'd been abandoned by her father at a time when she needed him most. It wasn't so much the fact that her parents were divorced. It was that Steven, in his inherent selfishness, had divorced himself from his daughter as well. If he called once a month in the years since he'd moved out, it was a lot. That alone had devastated Raven in a way that Steven would never understand. But somehow Cole did.

Leone headed downstairs. Maybe she should give Cole a call and ask him to talk with Raven. Perhaps coming from him, some assurance from him that he still cared, that it wasn't her fault, she'd accept it better.

The bell rang once more, just as she entered the foyer.

"Coming!"

As she approached she could just make out Cole's form through the beveled glass window of the door.

For an instant, her breath seized in her chest, escalating the beat of her heart. It was that old feeling, the sensation she'd experienced when they first met. Too late now, she cautioned herself. She took a breath, straightened her shoulders and opened the first door. Stepping into the vestibule, she put a smile of sorts on her face and opened the outer door.

"Hi," she greeted, suddenly feeling awkward and unsure. The light but manly scent of him, that familiar scent, filled the small space that separated them. His cool, brown complexion was smooth, his hair trimmed, his mustache neat, gently outlining the lips that had touched her in the most intimate of places. Her pulse raced as she tried to beat back the rush of emotions that suddenly sprung to the surface, rekindling the smoldering embers that she had let die down. *Too late,* she cautioned herself. *He's made his decision.*

She kept her hand on the door frame, searching his rugged face for some clue as to why he'd come, then wondering if he still read her mind.

"I know I should have called. I was just cruising around and thought if you wanted—I could drive you to the club to listen to rehearsal," Cole said in that voice that could have easily been Barry White's equal. She'd often teased him about that, he recalled, and in return he'd croon some of her favorite Barry White hits and they'd roll all over the bed laughing in each other's arms. He swallowed as the knot of recollection welled in his throat. That wasn't why he was here—not to dredge up old memories. She had to want and need him as much as he wanted her. He needed to hear her say the words. But he wouldn't settle for anything less, not at this stage in his life.

"I—was going to call you," she said.

"Were you?"

His tone was skeptical, Leone noted, but she couldn't blame him. "Yes. About Raven, actually."

Cole's features tightened as if a string had been pulled beneath the skin. "What happened? Is something wrong?" He looked beyond her shoulder into the house as if the answer rested just beyond his line of vision.

Leone angled her head toward the interior. "Come in."

"She's completely shut down, and shut me out," Leone concluded as she sat opposite Cole at the island counter in the kitchen. "She's yet to come out of her room for the day."

"Dammit!" he suddenly exploded, slamming his palm on the surface. "I hadn't thought about how this might affect Raven. I figured she'd probably shrug it off like most teenagers do about things."

"I guess you didn't realize how important you are to her." She didn't mean to sound bitter and accusatory, but she couldn't help it. Being hurt was one thing. She was an adult and would deal with it. Raven, on the other hand, was still impressionable, still forming her values and ideals about men and relationships. And the only examples Raven had seen were failed ones. Her mother's.

Leone saw the pained look on Cole's face. She should apologize, she thought. But she didn't. She was hurting in a way she couldn't explain and she wanted him to hurt, too.

Cole averted his gaze. "Do you think she'll talk to me?"

Leone's right eyebrow rose in question. "Maybe. I can ask."

"Would you?"

She nodded in agreement and stood. She headed for the living room which led to the stairs. Just before she mounted them she stopped and turned back toward Cole.

"She loves you, you know," Leone said simply, needing him to understand the power that he held over her child.

"And I love her, too."

Leone pressed her lips into a tight smile and went in search of Raven.

Several moments later Raven appeared in the archway, body tense and expression sullen. Leone waited several feet behind her.

Cole stood, greeting her with a tender smile. "Hi, hon. How are you?" He wanted to hug her, take the look of sadness out of her eyes. But he dared not.

"Fine." She folded her arms and rested her weight on her right side.

"I thought you might want to go for a drive."

"For what?"

"Raven!" her mother snapped. "Don't be rude."

Cole held up his hand. "It's okay, Lee."

"Sorry," Raven mumbled.

He looked at Raven. "So, how 'bout it?"

Raven pouted for a moment, then glared at her mother. "All right. I need to change clothes."

"Take your time. And bring a jacket. It's pretty cool outside."

Raven trotted upstairs, leaving Cole and Leone by themselves.

Cole rose and began to pace the kitchen floor, needing to create some distance between him and Leone. Their close proximity was getting to him. The scent of her freshly scrubbed body was like an aphrodisiac. He wanted to take her in his arms, feel her weight against him. Would she let him if he tried? His spirit couldn't risk the rejection. Instead, he talked about mundane things.

"I can't believe how chilly it's gotten so quickly. Winter will be here before you know it."

Leone focused on his back that was turned to her. "You'll miss all that in California," she said.

Her words penetrated him like the plunge of a butcher's knife.

"Yeah, I suppose. Just have to deal with the occasional earthquake," he said, attempting to make his voice light.

"Hmm. Would you like something to drink?"

"Naw. I'm good." He turned. "So how have things been with you? We really haven't had a chance to talk lately."

"Fine. Busy," she responded, noncommittal. "And you?"

He shrugged. "Just trying to get everything together for this move." He chuckled. "You don't realize how much junk you accumulate until you get ready to relocate."

A tightness pulled in her chest. "You're taking everything?" she asked, suddenly realizing that this was no temporary jaunt to the coast.

"Whatever I can. What I can't, I guess I'll get rid of."

"So...this...isn't temporary? You intend to stay there."

Cole slid his hands into the pockets of his khaki slacks. "That's the plan, Leone. Make a clean break and start over."

She looked away. In her mind she'd always believed that it was just for a visit, short-term. That he'd come back and somehow they would work out whatever it was that had gone wrong. Give each other some time and space to listen to their hearts. She hadn't been willing to accept the idea that it would be for long, for good. She swallowed as an incredible ache gripped her insides, twisting them into a painful knot. Her eyes began to burn.

"I see." She exhaled and forced a smile. "I'm sure you'll love it out there. I hear it's wonderful."

"Yeah. I have some job offers lined up." He waited a beat. "Actually, I heard from one of them on Friday. It's a nightclub in Vallejo."

Her heart banged in her chest.

"They want me to come down next week. Rehearse with the band."

Her eyes widened. "Next week?"

He nodded. "That's the real reason why I stopped by, Lee. I, uh, I'll be leaving on Saturday."

Saturday. Too soon. Too soon. I'm not ready. She clenched her hands. "I see. Well," she breathed, "I'm, uh, glad everything is working out, that you're getting what you want." She rose and walked toward the cabinets, needing something immediate to do.

"Did you say you wanted some tea? I think I'll make some," she rambled, her thoughts and emotions in disarray.

All you have to say is don't go, Cole, and I won't, he thought as he watched her go through the motions of putting on the tea. Say it, Lee. Say it, he silently begged her. But she didn't.

"Sure you don't want some? I found this great cranberry blend." She felt as if she were coming apart, seam by seam as if someone had inadvertently pulled the single thread that held her together. Leave, why don't you? she wanted to scream. Just get out and go. Go to California. Run, don't walk. But she couldn't say anything.

"I'm ready," Raven announced, cutting through the tension that held the room and its occupants captive.

Cole stole a glance at Leone, hoping to see some sign, some inkling that there was still a chance. But she'd turned her back to him.

He took in a breath. "Then let's get going, kiddo." He crossed the room and put his arm around Raven's shoulders. "You hungry?"

"Always," she giggled.

"How 'bout some Mickey D's for starters?"

"Super size," she warned, gazing up at him.

Cole glanced over his shoulder. "See you later. At rehearsal."

All Leone could do was nod her head.

SIXTEEN

Leone didn't wait for Cole to return. She couldn't take the chance that if she was alone with him, she'd beg him to change his mind; humiliate herself by pleading for his love; use her body to make him stay; whisper promises so that he wouldn't go.

So instead she got in her car and drove. She had no destination in mind and drove by rote, barely noticing the stroll of lovers, mothers with children in tow, hurrying home from church to fix Sunday dinner, the determined joggers, or the outlandish clothes and hairstyles of the teens who traveled in bands of three to ten.

In the middle of all things familiar, she felt lost, disconnected, as if someone had spilled coffee on the roadmap of her life, smearing all the landmarks. The street in front of her became cloudy, and she realized that she was crying, silently weeping for what was and what might never have the chance to be.

Reaching the mouth of downtown Brooklyn, Leone took the exit onto the Brooklyn Queens Expressway, better known as the BQE to traffic-weary New Yorkers. The spanning highway wrapped around the boroughs, linking the multi-ethnic hub of Queens to the plethora of cultural expansion in Brooklyn. However, in the back of her mind good sense prevailed and she quickly remembered how easy it was to get lost on the streets of Queens. It seemed that each little community had a secret society dedicated to confusing drivers and pedestrians with a multitude of similarly numbered streets, roads, places and lanes. She took the next exit, which put her onto the Belt Parkway East.

As she sped along the familiar roadway, she drove abreast of the shoreline. On the horizon she could see the water dotted with the colorful sails of small crafts, the boardwalks lined with would-be fisherman—even though the fish were not fit to eat, fishing was still a pleasant pastime. She passed the riding stables and caught a glimpse of equestrians in training. Much farther ahead she saw the peaks of the towering buildings that comprised Starrett City, the complex built on what was once the swamplands of Brooklyn. Winding her way around, she spotted in the distance the houses that ran along the waterfront. The scene brought to mind a sleepy village and she wondered what it really looked like close up. Seeing an exit coming up, she veered right and got off, now with a destination in mind.

Somehow she found her way into the Flatlands, each street number in consecutive order with winding cul-de-sacs and dead ends hidden by towering trees which hung like green canopies across the roads and the exquisite homes.

It was a part of the city she'd never ventured into before and she roamed aimlessly, taking in the beauty until she realized she'd pulled into a neat cluster of four homes that were braced by the water. She pulled to the end of the drive and was in the middle of making a U-turn to get out when she spotted someone coming out of the house to her right.

For an instant her heart stopped, then began a rapid beating. Ray.

This was a private community, which was one of the reasons Ray had finally decided to settle down there. He never had to concern himself with the blare of police sirens, loud music and bands of high-strung teens. Yet with all the privacy the area afforded, he was less than five minutes away from the rest of the world. The owners of the four houses that sat in the circular cocoon all knew each other and looked out for trespassers. So the sight of an unfamiliar vehicle, with its engine running, immediately caught his attention.

He stood on the edge of his property and tried to get a closer look without being too obvious. After all, whoever it was could be a visitor for one of his neighbors. He dropped his bag of garbage into the can but didn't take his eyes off the car which was beginning to look familiar. He squinted, hoping to get a better view of the occupant, because he was certain it couldn't be who he thought.

Oh, Lord, Leone thought. How in the world am I going to explain this? I know he must recognize me by now. He probably thinks I'm staking out his house or something. She turned the car around with the intention of speeding off as if she didn't see him, when he suddenly smiled and waved.

Briefly she shut her eyes. When she opened them he was coming toward her, with that swagger straight out of a shoot 'em up Western. As he drew closer, she could see the light of surprise sparkling in his eyes. He leaned down and she reluctantly lowered the window.

He grinned broadly, truly surprised at seeing her. "What are you doing around here? Visiting?" He braced his forearm on the doorframe, his face inches away from hers.

"Uh, no. Actually I was just driving around. I, uh, spotted the area from the highway. I'd never been around here before…"

"Well, come on out. I'll give you a tour."

She shook her head as she spoke. "No, really, I…"

"Come on." He angled his head to the side. "Personal tour? Can't beat that."

She mulled it over a minute. What harm could it do… really? After all, she was there already. "All right. Where can I park?"

"Just pull up behind my car in the driveway right there." He pointed toward his house and stepped back so she could pull her car around.

At least she looked halfway decent, she thought, cutting the engine. Well almost, except for the fact that her eyes were probably red and swollen from crying. She took a quick peek in the mirror and cringed. She could always blame it on allergies.

Taking her bag from the passenger seat, she opened the door and got out.

Ray took her in with one long glance. He wished he understood what it was about Leone that had him walking on eggshells. Around her he felt inept, inexperienced, as if he somehow had to try to prove his worth to her. A part of him believed that she saw him as a talented but unambitious skirt chaser with nothing more on his mind than a good time. He didn't know why what she thought of him was important, but it was. That Sunday afternoon that they'd spent in the club together had definitely broken the ice, but even after that she still remained reserved and aloof. Almost as if their whole conversation, the trip home and what almost happened, never transpired.

Maybe it was best, he thought, watching her long legs bring her closer to him. After all, regardless of the circumstances, she was still Cole Fleming's woman. And until somebody told him otherwise, he would make every attempt to act accordingly. However, he really had to question the fates for having dropped her virtually in his lap. What was that supposed to mean?

Leone's legs felt like strings of cooked spaghetti, and she wondered if she looked as wobbly as she felt. She plastered a smile on her face.

"You really don't have to do this, you know," she said immediately.

"Of course I don't. But I'd like to. Come on inside."

Ray stepped ahead of her and she took a deep breath and followed him in.

When she crossed the threshold, she would have sworn she'd stepped into the virtual world of Architectural Digest or House Beautiful. Wood and glass dominated the two-story structure, beginning with a sunken living room that boasted rafters and track lighting, and a wrought iron, spiral staircase. The open-air living room gave a clear view of the dining room, the kitchen, and the water beyond. And if she wasn't mistaken, there was a small boat docked right behind his house. Built-in smoke glass units contained cut crystal and china on one wall and CDs, cassettes, a massive stereo system, and bar on the other.

The deep carpet was such a pale beige it was almost white, which was in sharp contrast to the deep forest green leather furniture that dotted the space. Art was strategically placed along the winter white walls leading to the floor above and surrounding the living space.

"Wow," was all she could finally mutter. Her gaze continued to wander around the room.

Ray chuckled. "That seems to be the first response from everyone who comes here. You get used to it after a while." He headed for the bar and opened the glass door. "It's comfortable, fills my need for the ultimate in style…and it's private." He took out a bottle of Scotch. "Can I fix you a drink?"

"No. Nothing for me, thanks." She stepped down and moved toward the couch.

"Sure? Soda, water?"

"Hmm. Well, maybe a Coke if you have it."

"Comin' up."

"Great art," she commented, twisting her hands in her lap while noticing Basquiat, Catlett, Biggers and some Cynthia St. James originals. Impressive.

"Yeah, I try to collect things in my travels." He poured a glass of Coke, then turned on a John Coltrane CD. "Ice?"

"Yes. Thanks." She began to clutch her purse as if she could squeeze out the tension that ran through her like electric charges.

Ray handed her the glass of Coke and joined her on the couch. "You want to talk about it?" he asked softly. "I'm a pretty good listener."

"Talk about what?"

"Whatever drove you out of your house on a Sunday afternoon for starters." He took a sip of his drink.

"Maybe I like driving around."

"True. I know with me, when I get in the car with no specific destination in mind it's usually because I need to clear my head. Driving does that for me. What about you?"

Leone stared into her glass, watching the ice cubes swim around in the brown, bubbly liquid. "I suppose," she mumbled.

"Did it help?"

"What?"

"The drive."

Leone shrugged. "Not really," she admitted. She released a breath. "I guess it's too complicated."

"Sometimes talking helps. But if you'd rather not, I understand." He leaned back against the cushions of the couch.

"I thought you were bringing in the new piano player today."

"I am." He checked his watch. "We're supposed to meet at the club at six. I still have a few hours."

"Oh."

They were both quiet for a moment, the strains of Coltrane's sax wafting in the background with his rendition of "My One and Only Love."

"We never really had a chance to talk again...since that Sunday afternoon...in my car."

Leone swallowed.

Ray eased a bit closer. He knew what he was about to do was wrong, but he didn't want to think about it because if he did...

He took her chin between his fingers and turned her to face him. "I wanted to kiss you then, Lee." He searched her eyes, let his gaze trail down her face to her throat and saw the tiny pulse beat there. "I want to kiss you now. I want to know what it feels like."

She should stop him, just get up and leave. Her car was right outside. But she could no more stop his lips from meeting hers than she could stop the racing of her heart.

They were soft, moist, experienced as his mouth played with hers, gently urging her to open her lips, let him explore her depths. And by degrees she did.

Their tongues met in an explosive dance that shot straight to her head. White light blinded her and she ceased to breathe as she swallowed the deep moan that he exhaled. It settled inside her, gentle at first then building like a volcano ready to erupt, building, building.

His fingers, long and sinewy, trailed along the sides of her face, across her shoulders, then down her arms until he gathered her against him.

She twisted her body to get closer, closer as the heat between them intensified like flames fanned by a roaring wind. The exquisite power of it made her lose all sense of reason and all she knew for certain was that she wanted more. She wanted to feel his hands on her body, on her bare flesh. She wanted to touch him.

Tentatively her fingers played with the buttons of his denim shirt. Ray clasped her hand and held it against his heart. She took his other and placed it against hers.

"Lee," he whispered against her mouth. "Tell me it's okay," he uttered in a voice so deep it was hardly recognizable.

"Yes," came her ragged reply.

His fingers splayed, covering her right breast, and she gasped as a tremor shot through her.

Little by little he increased the pressure until his touch became an ever-escalating torture. He eased back and looked into her eyes as he lifted her T-shirt over her head before freeing her breasts of the confines of satin and lace. He tossed her shirt and bra onto the floor.

For several moments he simply stared at her, transfixed by her soft beauty. Like one in awe, he touched the twin swells and she shuddered, her eyes slamming shut when his mouth covered the nipples that had hardened into dark fruits.

His mouth was hot as it took her in, his tongue laving the sensitive peaks until she whimpered with hunger. Cautiously he eased her back until his body covered hers.

She immediately felt the hard knot of desire throb between her thighs that had grown wet with need and anticipation.

Slowly he moved against her, pressing his flesh into her, offering a mere sample of what it would feel like buried within her.

She was literally on fire. Every nerve ending pulsed as if electrified. And then his mouth, his tongue danced along her stomach, dipped into her navel even as he unfastened the button and zipper of her jeans, easing them down her thighs.

All that separated him from her was a thin band of baby blue fabric. Tenderly he touched her there and her body tensed.

"It's okay," he soothed, stroking her as he placed tiny kisses all along the dark triangle that shadowed the near sheer fabric.

Her inner thighs quivered. And then suddenly she was alone. Her eyes flew open and Ray stood above her, staring down at her with a dark, brooding longing that was almost frightening in its power.

He unbuttoned his shirt and threw it to the floor, pulled his wallet from his back pocket and removed a sealed condom before stepping out of his pants and boxers.

He was beautiful, she thought, dizzily watching him cover his throbbing erection with the latex sheath. His body was a study of rippling muscle covered in a smooth brown satin. His thighs bulged like those of a runner, his stomach flat and firm, and for a brief moment she thought of her own. Nothing like it once was. Nothing like what she was certain he was accustomed to. And she knew her breasts no longer had the firm fullness of her youth. And suddenly she felt old. Old compared to this man who was ten years her junior.

"You're absolutely exquisite, Leone," he whispered, pushing aside her doubts. "More beautiful than I could have imagined." He lowered himself above her. "I'll make you happy." He separated her thighs with his own, bracing his weight on his arms.

Instinctively, she raised her knees, tightening them against his waist.

"I promise," he said before his tongue delved into her mouth and he eased deep into her warmth in one smooth stroke.

Her hips arched high against him, taking him in farther…more…letting him reach the deepest recesses of her body, filling her until there was nowhere to go…but in and out…try it again, over and over.

Ray kissed her mouth, her neck, suckled her breasts, whispered how good she felt in her ear, moved in a slow but steady rhythm into her body, marking his place time and again until she thought she would go mad if release didn't come.

He held her, it seemed, at the precipice where she was able to look into the lush valley of fulfillment, but he wouldn't let her take the plunge…not yet. He wanted her to remember this time between them, burn it into her body and her mind, as he knew it would be indelibly seared into his.

The feel of her beneath him, around him, had his mind swimming, his emotions raw. He'd been with many women in his life. All kinds of women. But not like this. Not like Leone. And the strength of it scared him. Scared him because he'd allowed his emotions to overrule his mind. He'd broken an oath that he'd promised himself he'd never break—sleep with another man's woman. Yet, knowing that, he couldn't help himself. Didn't want to. Consequences be damned. He'd waited all his adult life to feel like this with a woman...complete.

She rocked her hips against him and he sank deeper as the strangled cry of his name spilled from her lips.

He buried his face in her neck to keep from sobbing as the waves of an unspeakable climax surged through him, hardening him even further until it was only seconds before release shot through him, and the rhythmic pulse of her own orgasm sucked out the last of his life-giving fluids.

He collapsed against her and they held each other in a satiated silence. Their bodies shuddering with the aftereffects of their lovemaking. He looked into her eyes and saw tears glistening on her lashes. Gently he kissed them away.

Leone felt his weight, the wetness between her thighs, the throb that continued to pulse there, the tingle that still held her nipples taut and sensitive to the touch. Still their bodies moved against one another in tiny after-thrusts, seemingly unable to douse the fire. And in the midst of the wonder of it all, her mind screamed: What have I done?

The heat of his breath purred against her throat while he steadily caressed her hip in a slow circular motion.

Involuntarily her insides gripped him and felt him swell until his arousal peaked, filling her.

He groaned in sublime agony as wanton desire seized him. She lifted her pelvis rocking against him.

Ray raised his weight onto his arms and gazed into her eyes while he moved in an erotic dance. "It's all right," he whispered, sensing her doubts, her struggle with guilt. Gently he kissed her, gathered her tightly into his arms, sealing their bodies, their souls together. "I promise you."

But how could it be? Leone wondered, even as the electric waves of sensation spread through her limbs. Yet, feeling Ray, being with him, sharing herself in this way, seemed all too right, to be wrong.

"I didn't plan for this to happen," Ray said as they sat next to each other on the couch. He twirled a strand of her hair around his finger.

"But I'm glad that it did," Leone said, tucking his shirt around her body, suddenly feeling naked. She glanced across at him. "And I wasn't stalking you," she said with a hint of nervous laughter.

"Now I'm disappointed," he quipped. He waited a beat. "So, what are we going to do now? What are you going to do?"

Leone flinched. She didn't want to think about that part. For as long as she could, she wanted to hold onto the fantasy with Ray. And that's all that it was, a fantasy. They were both adults. Something between them had clicked and they'd connected. That didn't mean they had to be life partners. They could both walk away, back to their lives and leave these past few hours behind. Couldn't they?

Leone cleared her throat, and tried to sound very 90s, like the women she was sure he was used to. "Really, it's no big deal. What happened, happened." She shrugged. "I mean, this isn't the first time for either of us," she continued with bravado. "And I'm sure it won't be the last—with other people," she qualified. "I say we move on. Take today as a great memory and move on." She pulled the shirt a bit tighter.

Ray stood, totally unconscious of his nude body, or the effect it had on her.

"Cool," was all he said. He crossed the room to the stairs. "I'm gonna take a shower, get some of this sweat off," he said in a way that suddenly made Leone feel dirty. "There's a guest bath just behind the kitchen if you want to do the same thing." He shrugged and smiled bitterly. "But, hey, maybe you don't."

He trotted up the stairs and didn't look back.

For several moments Leone simply sat there, unable to move. She'd never felt so cheap and ashamed in her life. Even at her lowest moments with Steven, she'd never felt so totally dehumanized.

She heard the sound of the shower beating against the walls, and her current situation became clear.

With determination, she gathered her clothing, took a shower, got dressed and into her car. When she pulled out of Ray's driveway, she had no intention of ever revisiting this day again.

Ray watched her pull away from between the slat of his bedroom blinds. Didn't she feel anything? he wondered. Couldn't she tell that with her it wasn't some casual fling? He expected that kind of response from some of the other women he'd been with, but not from her.

He turned away from the window and began to get dressed. He shouldn't be hurt, he thought, pulling on a black T-shirt. But he was. For the first time in his life he'd wanted to be more to a woman than a great lay. He wanted her to care, really care—about him.

Most of the time it didn't matter. He zipped his black jeans. But this time it had. He stepped into his black leather loafers.

But, he concluded, looking into the mirror and running a brush across his hair, if she can dismiss what happened between them as nothing more than a fling, then so could he.

The last place Leone wanted to go was to the club. She didn't think she could look Cole in the face knowing what had transpired between her and Ray.

And what of Ray? How could she face him as well? What must he think of her? It was obvious by his attitude afterward that he thought very little.

"Oh, God!" She slammed her palm against the steering wheel, inadvertently sounding the horn, much to the annoyance of the driver in the car ahead of her. When had she turned into the kind of woman who let her hormones make her decisions?

She took a shaky breath. Well, as the saying goes, she sniffed, you made your bed, now lie in it. "Or couch," she mumbled sarcastically as a tear of regret ran down her cheek.

Stopping for a red light, she reached for her cell phone and hit the programmed code for her house. After the third ring, Raven picked up, sounding rushed and breathless.

"Hi, hon, it's me. How was your afternoon with Cole?" Her heart thumped.

"Fine. I just got back and heard the phone."

"Oh…uh…is Cole with you?"

"No. He dropped me off. Said there was a rehearsal with the new piano player."

Leone flinched. "Right. I'm on my way over there now." Silence.

"Cole said I could come and visit him in San Francisco anytime I want and he'd pay for my ticket," Raven quickly added, assuring that money would never be a reason for her not to go.

"That's really nice of him."

"He said maybe I could convince you to come sometime, too."

Her throat tightened. The light turned green.

"Uh, I'll talk to you when I get home."

"Sure." Raven hesitated, then rushed the words out. "I don't know what happened with you and Cole, Ma, but whatever it is, you can still fix it. He really loves you."

Leone knew if she stayed on the line a minute longer, she'd burst into tears. Whatever repairs could have been made, it was too late now. Even though she and Cole weren't officially together, there was still that unspoken tenet that the possibility remained, and a tenuous thread still holding them together. If anything could have broken that thread, what happened today was it.

"I've really got to go, Raven. You know how nervous talking on this thing while I'm driving makes me. I'll see you later. Okay?" She pressed the "end" button and slipped the phone back into its slot.

Leone moved along with the traffic and headed toward the club and uncertainty.

SEVENTEEN

"You did what?" Parker asked while he put on his jacket.

Ray paced back and forth across the wooden floor. "I slept with her," he repeated.

Parker shook his head in disbelief. "Hey, man, when I said the field was open, I didn't think you'd take me up on it." He picked up his knapsack from the corner by the couch and slid the straps over his shoulders. "So now what?" He opened the door.

Ray followed him outside. "I guess it's like she told me, we just move on."

"That's cool with you, man?"

Ray shrugged. "Sure, why not?"

Parker looked over his shoulder. Ray might be a lot of things, Parker thought, but a good liar wasn't one of them. "You like her a lot. And I don't think you're taking it as light as you want me to believe."

"Hey, it was what it was. No biggie." He shut the door behind himself.

"If you say so, man. But I don't believe you." Parker walked toward his car and opened the door. "My question is, how are you going to be able to look Cole in the face with her in the same room?" He gave Ray an arched look and slid behind the wheel of his Mercedes.

Ray got into his own car and started the engine. How was he going to face Cole? How could he hide his true feelings for Leone, especially now? He pulled out behind Parker and into traffic.

An anvil of guilt slammed down in his chest. Cole didn't deserve this. Not like this, even if everything wasn't perfect between him and Leone. He had no right to muddy the waters. Leone was vulnerable and at a shaky point in her life. And as much as he wanted her, making love with her wasn't the answer to what brought her to his door. He knew that, and yet, he'd let emotion instead of reason take over. He felt as if he'd taken advantage of her. Her need for him was not borne of genuine caring, but rather insecurity and the desire to be cared about, have her issues soothed by touch. She'd needed to feel wanted and worthwhile. At least, maybe, he'd been able to do that much. But at what cost?

Getting involved with another man's woman, be it a tenuous relationship or not, was something he'd never done. And, now, without question, he knew why.

Leone pulled onto the block of Soul to Soul, drove by looking from one side of the street to the other. She didn't spot Ray's car. She felt a momentary reprieve. Maybe he wouldn't show up, she thought in a silent prayer. But just as quickly, she knew that was an impossibility. Ray would show up. It wouldn't be like him not to, no matter what the circumstances.

She found a parking space around the corner from the club. For several minutes she sat in the car trying to get her thoughts and emotions in order. She took a quick peek in the mirror and dabbed at her eyes.

Maybe she should just go home. Put this off until she could think clearly.

"No," she said aloud. "Twenty-four hours or twenty-four days isn't going to change a thing."

She sucked in a deep breath. What happened between her and Ray was a done deal. They were two adults, she counseled herself. She and Cole hadn't slept together in nearly two months. They both knew that things had shifted between them but neither had been willing to let go. Maybe they didn't want to. In her heart she knew she didn't, but Cole had made up his mind and she didn't believe it was her right to change it, especially when her own emotional focus and level of commitment was so uncertain.

Taking her purse from the passenger seat, she opened the door, shut it behind her and walked toward the club.

You can do this, she repeated over and again in a silent mantra.

She took the keys from her purse and opened the club door. "You can do this," she whispered to herself one last time, and stepped inside.

Cole was seated on a stool on the stage chatting with the guys in the band. He turned in her direction when he heard the door.

The instant he saw her, he felt that old familiar heat warm his insides. God, he loved her and always would.

Leaving her was the hardest thing he'd ever had to do. But he knew he must for his own emotional salvation.

Maybe with some time and space she would realize that they were meant to be together. But he knew he couldn't hang around. He couldn't stand knowing and seeing the looks that passed between her and Ray Taylor, or live with the thought that Ray might touch her the same way he had, only better.

Maybe if he moved out of the way, gave them some space, she'd see that Ray Taylor could never give her half of what he could.

Ray was still young and ambitious. Still full of himself and his own dreams. He didn't honestly believe that Ray was truly ready for a serious commitment to anyone other than himself, no matter what he'd told him before.

Yet, he could be all wrong about Ray. He might be the man for Leone. It was risky, what he was doing. But it was a risk he was willing to take because he loved her. And above all else, he wanted Leone to be happy, even if her happiness was with someone else. At least he would know he'd tried.

Leone put on her best smile and hoped that in the dimness of the club, no one would see the tremulous edges.

She walked confidently toward the group.

"Hey, fellas."

There was deep chorus of hellos.

She put her purse down on a nearby table. "Just getting started?"

Cole stood. "We're just waiting on Ray and the new guy." He hopped down and stood in front of her. As soon as he did, he felt the change in her, the shift in the heat that her body gave off, the eyes that wouldn't quite meet his, and his heart stood still. Slowly his eyes glided over her but not in that tender way he usually reserved for her.

Could he see through her pretense? she wondered as her heart hammered in her chest.

"How are you?" he asked. "When I brought Raven home you were gone."

Her gaze darted away, roaming the room. She cleared her throat of the lie that sat there. "I just went for a drive. Ran some errands."

Cole stared at her a moment. "Oh, Raven was worried."

She turned back to him. "I called her." She paused. "Raven said you two had a good time."

"We did. And a good talk." He wanted to touch her as he used to, somehow uncoil the rope of tension that had wrapped around her body. "I think she understands."

"Does she?" she asked caustically. She could feel her anger and frustration rise to the surface. At least those were emotions she could handle.

"Don't do this, Lee," he cautioned, lowering his voice.

Her eyes snapped up and locked on his face. For an instant her heart softened and all she wanted to do was let him take her in his arms and make things between them the way they were. But she couldn't and neither could he.

"Do what? Be real?"

"No. Make this harder than it already is."

"For who, Cole? You or me?" She spun away, leaving him standing there, and retreated into the back office.

She shut the door firmly behind her and leaned with her back against it. Steeling herself she walked across the room and sat down behind the desk. She covered her face with her hands and cried.

"This is it," Ray said as he and Parker approached the door to the club. "Just be cool," he warned, tapping on the glass.

"Don't know any other way to be, brotha. You be cool."

Ray glanced over his shoulder at Parker and sneered instead of smiled.

Earl, the band's drummer, opened the door. "Hey, man," he greeted, giving Ray a pound.

"Earl, this is my man, Parker."

The two men shook hands. "Good to meetcha. Come on in. We've been waiting on you guys."

Once inside, Ray made all the introductions and the band took their places. Behind them, near a corner of the stage, Al unzipped the protective case on his upright bass. The lanky chocolate man whistled the melody of "Autumn in New York" as he set up behind the others.

"I was thinking we'd do an all 'Bird' tribute tomorrow night," Cole suggested. "Some of the old bop standards."

Ray busied himself with adjusting the thick Rico reed on his shiny Selwen sax, not looking at anyone. The avoid-

ance of eye contact was not lost on Cole, who pulled a fistful of charts from his leather tote.

"What tunes did you have in mind, Mr. Ivorys?" Al
quipped, feeling the uneasy tension between the pair.

"Maybe 'Confirmation,' 'Ornithology,' 'Funky Blues,'
or 'Au Privare,'" Cole said, a curious expression of bewil-
derment on his face.

"That's cool," Mel, the trumpeter, chimed in. He was
always late and usually blessed out on Scotch, but his playing on brass easily matched the pyrotechnics of Dizzy, Fats,
Little Jazzy or Miles.

"What do you think, Ray?" Cole asked, staring the
young saxophonist in the face.

A silence followed, which only heightened Cole's certainty that something was wrong. Ray's eyes held an odd,
faraway look, as if he was recalling a memory of joy in his
head.

"Ray…Ray…Ray. Earth to Ray," Cole teased. "What's
up, man? You're off on another planet. What do you think
about the 'Bird' idea?"

Parker watched from the distance, ready to intercede if
necessary. His boy was not putting on a good show.

"Yeah, I'm down with it," Ray answered absently, now
staring in the direction of Leone who'd reentered the room.

The look, the distracted reply, the returned expression
on Leone's face, made Cole even more uneasy. Something
had happened between the two of them. He felt it.
Thoughts flooded into his mind, sinister thoughts, forbidden thoughts, painful thoughts.

EIGHTEEN

Cole's gaze shifted from Ray to Leone, who'd both moved like shadows to opposite ends of the rehearsal space, as if by distance they could snap the band of tension in half.

Parker stepped forward, a human shield between Cole and Ray. "You want me to sit this one out, Cole?"

Cole blinked, and slowly focused on Parker.

"Naw, lemme hear what you can do."

Cole stepped down off the stage, but instead of taking a seat at the table with Leone, he sat two tables away. He leaned back in the chair, resting it on its hind legs.

"Ray, it's your show, man." He cut a look at Leone. "Go for it."

Ray moved to center stage. He placed the horn to his pursed lips, checking the reed and his embouchure. The room quieted suddenly. This was not big band Ray or even small group Ray; this was Ray alone. Solo.

His eyes closed and his entire body seemed to shudder before he launched into the soft, lyrical Ellington ballad, "Satin Doll."

Mel nodded in unison to the cute little phrases, the agonizingly beautiful lines full of a variety of feeling and mood.

Parker leaned back on the piano and smiled, taking in every improvised note and shift.

The music stroked Leone's battered soul, gentle, tentative, like the brush of a feather along a sensitive spine. So sweet, yet a cry of exquisite torment, a need unrequited in each note, tumbling over her like pebbles skipping over water.

She was swept away, captured and helpless. Yet she didn't want to be released. It was as if Ray was speaking to her, pouring out his heart, emptying his soul. But he couldn't be. She wouldn't let him. But she felt him as surely as if his hands were on her bare flesh, scorching her, igniting every nerve.

Rocking slightly to the melody, Ray seemed to be deconstructing the song, adding in a host of new twists and turns. But as soon as the group grew accustomed to this gentle music that broke the rules, coming from somewhere deep in his soul, he cut loose, turning his sound into something hard, harsh and terrible. A roar that held a fierceness, a boldness that no one had ever heard in his playing before, not even Parker. Sounds that were a mix between Coltrane and Ayler.

Leone shut her eyes and trembled.

Mel stared into the bell of his trumpet, almost as if he was ashamed to witness this raw, naked part of Ray's inner terrain. No one said anything.

A long rush of caresses followed—something that spoke of confusion, frustration and pain. Ray bent over like a boxer who'd been sucker punched, reaching for more squawks and shrieks that made the hair stand on Leone's long, lovely neck. She sat there with tears in her eyes, glistening in the amber glow of the stage lights.

Cole rocked back in his chair, transfixed by what he was hearing. He never knew Ray had such deep feelings in his soul, never knew the young man could be so revealing, so honest. He also knew that this was not just magic, but a confession of love, of guilt, of betrayal.

Ray returned with his soft, molasses voice, the bass-throated tone that made the women sigh, before firing off a series of blues-colored notes in a long cluster, before howling like a man possessed, before finally ending in a raw sexual cry.

Cole observed Leone's expression shift from rapture to despair. She sat staring, mesmerized, as tears flowed down her cheeks. Suddenly, she heaved a sigh and hurried from the room.

Cole watched her leave, then turned back to face Ray on the stage. The young saxophonist abruptly stopped playing, holding the horn, Coltrane style, across his chest. For a moment, he locked glances with Cole, and once seeing the recognition of his sin in Cole's eyes, pivoted and walked off the bandstand. He didn't stop walking until he left the club.

No words were needed then. The truth had been told.

The room was suffused in a winter silence. The kind of quiet that settles in the morning hours after a long night of snow—serene—almost painful in its chilling beauty.

Cole slowly rose, shedding the cold cloak of his new reality.

"Guess it took Ray someplace else," he said quietly, not looking at anyone in particular. He tugged on his bottom lip with his teeth. "Heavy piece of work."

"I'll go get him," Parker announced.

"No. I'll go. Why don't you run through the next number. See what you can do with it, Parker."

All eyes followed Cole as he stepped outside.

When Cole came through the door, Ray was leaning against his car, arms folded, head bowed.

"Nice piece of work you did in there," Cole said, appearing in front of him.

Ray's head rose slowly, his gazed latched onto Cole's countenance, but wouldn't meet his eyes. He didn't respond.

"It takes a helluva man to do something like that— reveal yourself." A flicker of a smile appeared then vanished.

Ray looked away. "Yeah," was all he uttered.

Cole pulled out a pack of Newports from his shirt pocket. He lit a cigarette, and blew a cloud of smoke over Ray's head. "People say the eyes are the windows to the soul. I think music is the window," he said, his words trailing the white vapors. "When we open ourselves to it, it admits everything. Too much sometimes. Even the things we try to hide. Not everyone can understand the words being said through the notes…except maybe another musician."

Ray met his eyes for the first time and in them stood understanding. Perhaps not forgiveness, but acceptance.

Cole stamped out his cigarette, grinding it into crumbs on the gray concrete, turned and reentered the club, leaving Ray with his thoughts and his conscience.

NINETEEN

It had been nearly three weeks since that fateful afternoon at the club, and two since Cole had said his goodbyes. He'd refused to allow Leone to accompany him to the airport, saying that it was best. The last time she saw him, he was packing up his music sheets and having a final drink with the gang.

Leone sat on the edge of her bed, lost in the storm that her life had become. She felt adrift, as if her anchor had been removed and she'd been cast out to sea with no destination.

What had she done? she asked herself for the umpteenth time as she walked toward the window. She pushed the pale green, gossamer curtains aside and stood framed in the window.

A light rain fell—mist really—casting a pall across the city. Ghost-like canopies hung above the homes, creating an image of the surreal.

The tip of her finger drew circles in the hazy moisture on the window, aimless circles until the glass was clear. Yet her vision beyond remained the same, cloudy and uncertain.

She hadn't heard from Cole since he'd relocated to San Francisco and as much as she needed to hear his voice, perhaps his way was better.

What was it about her that kept her incapable of giving totally, of speaking her real feelings, allowing another's love to help her wounds to heal?

There was so much bottled inside, brimming to the surface, ready to overflow. But each time the words rose to her lips, she'd swallow them back. To allow them to surface, to be spoken, would ultimately reveal her weakness. And weakness, need, had nearly destroyed her once before. And she was terrified to risk that kind of hurt again.

She turned away from the nothingness beyond her line of sight and sat on the chaise lounge.

She understood now what it really was that had happened with her and Ray. It was a coupling, yes. It was the making of love, yes. But more than that, it was the one way she knew to release her inhibitions, shed her armor. And somehow, she believed Ray understood that. Accepted it, even though, she also knew, he wanted more. And if he understood that about her, accepted the flaw of who she was, was he the man for her? The one who wouldn't ask for more than she was willing to give?

It was Cole, in his insistent gentleness, who needed all of her, not just the bits and pieces that remained.

Would she ever be capable of that level of giving, ever again, to Cole or to anyone before it was too late?

In the distance she heard the faint ringing of the doorbell. Raven had gone out earlier, with the intention of spending the dreary Saturday afternoon in the company of her friends.

The relationship between the two of them since Cole's departure had been polite, but distant. In Raven's silence was her loud accusation that it was Leone's fault that Cole was no longer in her life.

Leone missed the warm friendship that she and Raven had begun to build over the past year. Now it was as it had been before, a tenuous truce that with the slightest provocation could be broken.

The bell rang again. Finally she sat up and peeked out of the window. Antoinette's car was parked out front.

Securing the belt of her robe around her waist, she hurried down the stairs to the door. She'd skillfully avoided Antoinette over the past couple of weeks, not yet able to speak the words of confession that she knew her friend would demand to know.

But Antoinette, being who she was, would never allow Leone to sink alone in her own ship of confusion and doubt.

Leone pulled in a breath, pasted on a smile and opened the door.

Antoinette stood there with her head dipped to the side, her hand planted on her full hip.

"I figured the only way we were going to talk was for me to just crash the party in person, since you haven't returned my calls."

"Oh, girl, please. You know how busy I am," Leone said lamely.

"Don't 'oh, girl' me. You gonna let me in or what?"

Leone stepped aside and Antoinette sashayed in, dripping water from her Kenneth Cole umbrella. She deposited it in the silver bucket by the door and stripped out of her raincoat, hanging it on the matching coat rack.

"Where's Raven?" she asked, heading for the living room.

"She went out."

Leone trailed Antoinette inside and took a seat on the couch, tucking her bare feet beneath her.

Antoinette plopped down on the love seat and stared Leone in the face. Suddenly all the fronting was gone. Her face and voice softened. "Tell me what's going on, Lee. That's why I'm here."

Leone's nostrils flared as she took in a reinforcement of air. How could she explain when it was all so twisted in her head?

"Doesn't matter how you put it, just get it out," Antoinette gently coaxed, seeing the lines of tension draw between Leone's troubled eyes.

"He's gone, Nettie." Her voice cracked and her eyes filled. "And I let him. It's my fault. I hurt him and I don't think I can ever make that up to him." She sniffed and heaved in short, staccato breaths.

"What really happened, hon? It's okay. This is me."

Leone pressed her lips together, then leaned her head back against the cushions of the couch, closing her eyes.

Behind her closed lids, segued all the images of the past few months; from her steady withdrawal from Cole, to Ray's entrance into her life, to the afternoon they came together, to his painfully beautiful musical confession, to the day Cole boarded his plane. The scenes all danced together in an almost macabre frenzy—a movie reel out of control.

One scene faded into the next until they all became one brilliant cacophony of light and sound.

Slowly, Leone told it all, like one in a dream state, leaving nothing out, not her deepest secrets or her worst fears. She confessed her role in it all, succumbed to and accepted the flaw in herself. She shared the pain of loss between her and Raven, Cole, Ray. She told it all until she exorcised all of the demons that had tormented her, leaving her empty, but sadly not cleansed.

When she opened her eyes, Antoinette was seated next to her.

"That's one helluva story, girl," she said, wiping the line of tears off Leone's cheek. "The question is, now that the deeds are done, what are you going to do about it? You can't spend the rest of your life in mourning. You can't let Raven slip away again because you can't get yourself together."

Leone lowered her head.

"The sad reality is, Cole is gone. That was his decision, whether you played a role in that decision or not. You could call him, tell him to come back. But back to what? What's going to be different about you that would make him stay?"

"Nothing at the moment."

"Exactly my point. Like I told you before, Lee, you never really gave yourself time to heal after Steven. Sure time passed, but you never addressed the real issue, you.

And until you do that, nothing will ever be any different with Ray, with Cole, with anyone."

"That's comforting," Leone said sarcastically.

"Have you and Ray talked since…"

Leone shook her head. "No. Not really. He's tried. He's asked me out. Wanted to know if he could call me. But I keep putting him off. If I even think for a minute that we might somehow be alone, I find a quick exit."

"That's real womanly, Lee. What are you so afraid of?"

Leone crossed her arms and huffed. "What should I do, then?" she asked, her voice rising in frustration.

"For starters, why don't you see what the man has to say. If he did what you said he did up on stage in front of all those people, he has to be a man of substance. Maybe he'll understand more than you give him credit for. Give him a chance."

Leone was thoughtful for a moment. Ray did deserve to be heard, she reasoned. After all, what happened with them wasn't just about her, and although he seemed to go along with her program, she knew it wasn't how he truly felt. Maybe it was time she really listened.

She blew out a breath. "I'll try."

"That's a start. And at some point, you need to talk with Cole, Lee. Really talk to him, even if it means going out to San Francisco to do it."

She slowly shook her head. "I—I don't know about that, Nettie."

"I'm not saying tomorrow, but at some point. You can't go through life with all the threads trailing behind you.

You've got to tie off those loose ends, so they can stop tripping you up."

Leone grinned. "You and your metaphors."

"Hey, whatever works. But one thing at a time."

Leone nodded, then exhaled. "You know, Ray started this jam session thing."

"What's that?"

"We rent out the space on Saturday afternoons before the club opens to let a couple of bands work out. Those that don't have rehearsal space."

"Not bad. Get any takers?"

"Takers! The phone hasn't stopped ringing since the word went out."

"Seems like Mr. Man has a business head on his shoulders, too."

Leone smiled tightly. "Yeah, he does. Last weekend was the first session."

"Did you go?"

"No. But I heard...Ray told me...it went according to plan."

"Oh." Antoinette arched a brow. "You two talk about anything else you haven't told me about?"

"No. I've kept it strictly business."

"Hmm. Nuff said on that subject. But ...what about Raven?"

"She's just so angry, Nettie. Angry at me."

"She can't stay that way forever." Antoinette got up and went into the kitchen. "Want something to drink?" she shouted from the other room.

"There's some iced tea in the pitcher. That's fine with me."

Antoinette returned shortly with two glasses and handed one to Leone, who relaxed and took a sip. "At some point you're going to have to find a way to get through to her. You can't sit around and let your relationship with her deteriorate. Whether you realize it or not, your daughter is more like you than you're willing to admit."

Leone frowned. "Raven, like me? No way."

"Raven balls up her feelings inside, never really says what's in her heart. She just acts out. She gets that from you. You are one of the most closed people I know."

"I talk to you."

"Yeah, after I beat you over the head. And Raven talked to Cole. He was her outlet. We all have somebody."

"I never really looked at it like that. I suppose that's why it's always been so hard for us to get along. We're both too busy hiding our feelings, and never really talk to each other except to lash out and be angry."

"Exactly. She learned all that from you. And you have to be the one to break the pattern."

Leone lowered her head. She was at the root of so much that was wrong. She'd let the circumstances of her life completely reshape her. And ultimately, it had affected her daughter. Casualties of war, she thought morosely.

She turned to Antoinette. "Thank you."

"For what?"

"For knocking me in the head. At some point, I'm going to have to take that first step if I ever want things to get better. But most of all I have to do this for Raven. She's the most precious person in the world to me, Nettie. I don't want to see her grow up to be a bitter woman, incapable of feeling the joys of loving someone and being loved in return."

"The next step is deciding where to begin."

Leone nodded, pondering her options. The phone rang. "Excuse me," she said, getting up to answer the phone in the kitchen.

She returned shortly. "That was Raven. She wanted to spend the night at Terri's house." She shrugged. "I told her we needed to talk."

"And?"

"And…she said, 'Can't we do that when I get home tomorrow? I'm really having a good time here. Terri's mother is showing us how she frames and mats portraits.'"

"So of course you said yes."

"Call me a coward and get it over with. She sounded like she'd rather be with Terri's mother anyway." Leone crossed the room to the other side and leaned against the mantle.

Antoinette twisted her lips. "Maybe because Terri's mother talks to her, Lee."

Leone glared at her. "And so will I." But even as she defiantly said the words, she wasn't sure how she would ever begin.

TWENTY

For the better part of the night, Leone replayed in her mind the conversation she'd had with Antoinette. The more she thought about how much she could lose by remaining the way that she was—locked inside herself—the more determined she was to take the steps toward change. Raven was her catalyst. Finally, during the early morning hours, too weary to think any further, she drifted off into an exhausted sleep.

By the time she was able to pull her eyes open, the bedside clock showed it to be noon. Slowly she pushed herself up, listening for sounds in the house, and heard none.

Raven had yet to return. But being a teenager, she and Terri had probably stayed up the entire night and were still asleep.

Hmm. When was the last time Raven had invited her friends to spend the night? When had she last spent a full day with her daughter just doing mother/daughter things? She couldn't remember. It had always been easier to just set down rules and have expectations.

Suddenly, she felt terribly sad. She'd become so ladened with her own life, her own sorrows, that she'd completely forgotten that Raven needed her too. Just because she was growing up and didn't need changing or to be fed every two hours didn't mean that she didn't need her anymore. How long had she been in this vacuum that had become her life? Too long.

She swung her legs over the side of the bed and padded barefoot into the bathroom. All that stops as of today, she determined, turning on the shower. Somehow she would find the words to make things right. One by one. Step by step.

Less than a half hour later, she was out the door. She wanted to be in the best frame of mind when she talked with Raven. And being in the club on a quiet Sunday afternoon always helped to clear her head.

She decided to walk. The crisp, early November afternoon was part of the remedy she needed. She inhaled deeply of the sharp air, observed the turning of the leaves that were now a myriad of orange and gold, set against a stark white sky. Changes, she thought. The evolution of time, turning what was into something new, a shedding of the past.

Leone turned up the collar of her trenchcoat against the sudden gust of wind and slid her hands into her pockets. Yes, changes, she thought again.

When she arrived at the club, she was surprised to see the light on inside. She sucked in a breath of annoyance. They'd obviously been left on from the night before, leaving her with an astronomical light bill. Ray was going to hear about this. What if she hadn't come by? They would have stayed on until Monday afternoon when the kitchen staff arrived.

Leone stuck her key in the door and tossed it open. Furious, she stormed inside and found it, as she suspected, empty. Out the window went her thoughts of coming here for some quiet solitude and regrouping. She was too pissed off to think about anything other than snatching the neck of the person responsible. She stomped across the room and stopped short when Ray came from the back, wiping his hands on a towel.

The corner of his mouth curved into that smile of his, a cross between seductive and boyish, depending on the recipient's frame of mind.

"Hi." He came toward her.

Her chin jutted upward. "What are you doing here?" Her heart began to race as he drew closer.

He held up both hands in surrender. "Hey, I'm sorry. I just wanted to go over the schedule for the jam sessions in the upcoming weeks and lay out the numbers for tomorrow's rehearsal." He tossed the towel onto the bar. "I'll be out of your way in a minute, just let me get my things."

She tugged in a breath. "Fine." She spun away and took a seat at a shadowed table in the corner. She could kick herself. There was no reason for her to treat him that way. What had he done besides come there to work and say hello to her when she came in? She tried to swallow down her stupidity but it clung like lint in her throat.

"I'll see you later."

Her head snapped around. She hadn't heard him come up behind her.

"I locked up in the back." He gently worked his jaw from left to right as if he was trying to shake the words loose.

"Thank you," she whispered.

"Not a problem." He slung his bag on his shoulder and moved toward the door.

"Ray." Leone stood. "Wait."

He turned but didn't speak. He looked at her and waited.

"Can...we talk...for a minute?"

"I have something to do."

She swallowed. This was her out. She should just let him go. Forget it.

"It won't take long. I promise." She twisted her hands in front of her.

She watched his expression tense, his eyes narrow in suspicion. He worked his jaw again, contemplating.

He looked briefly at the floor, then moved back in her direction. He stood directly in front of her, forcing her to look up at him.

Ray adjusted his knapsack on his shoulders. "I'm listening."

"Can we sit down?"

Ray pulled out a chair and sat without responding. He dropped his knapsack on the floor between his knees.

Leone searched the room with her eyes, trying to buy some time while she formed the words in her head.

Finally, she focused on her entwined fingers, so symbolic, she realized, of her own life.

"This is really hard for me, Ray." She stole a brief glance at him, catching the unreadable expression on his face. "Umm, that day...at your house, I, uh, I didn't mean what I said."

Ray remained stoically silent. He had no intention of making this easy for her. Not after the emotional hell she'd put him through.

"Aren't you going to ask me about what?" she asked, totally rattled by his uncharacteristically chilly demeanor.

Ray folded his arms, looked at her from beneath his lashes and slowly shook his head.

She blew out a breath. "Fine." She raised her chin in that way Ray found so endearing. "I didn't mean that what happened didn't matter to me," she said in short clips. "I'm not one of those young," she emphasized the word, "non-conventional women you're used to dealing with." Her voice and her eyes softened. "I—I've never done anything…like that before. And, I guess I figured the easiest way not to feel like an inexperienced teenager was to…act like it didn't matter."

Leone swallowed over the tightness in her throat. Finally, she looked him square in the eyes. "It did matter. A great deal."

Ray glanced up at the ceiling for a moment, needing to compose his thoughts and his emotions.

"That's all I ever needed you to say to me, Leone—that it mattered. That I wasn't some quick lay to fill in some empty space."

He pulled his chair closer to the table, the sound of its wooden legs scraping across the floor reverberated throughout the silent space.

"Listen, let me just say this. I care about you a lot, Leone. More than I expected and more than you realized.

When I made love with you, it was like some dream of mine had come true. For as long as I can remember, I've wanted to feel the way I did with you when I was with a woman. That what we had was making a difference." He blew out a derisive breath. "When you said what you did, it really blew me away. I guess it was my own past coming back to haunt me."

Leone gave him a tight smile.

"I'm not going to sit here and lie to you, Leone. I want you. I want to be with you, really get to know you, and let you know me." He reached across the table and cupped her chin, gently caressing her jaw line with his thumb. His eyes skimmed over her face. "But I also know that deep inside, your heart is somewhere else, not really with me. I care about you a lot, but I'm not in love with you. Cole is. And you're in love with him."

She looked away and bit down on her lip.

"It's okay, Lee. It is. And I don't want to compete with that. I can't. Cole is a decent man, one of the best I've met in my life. You have no idea how much he sacrificed because of how he feels about you."

Her eyes widened. "What do you mean?"

"That's something you and Cole need to talk about. Whatever went wrong between the two of you that made room for us can still be fixed. It's not too late. I really believe that."

Her eyes filled. "I've made such a mess of things, haven't I?"

He gave her that smile again. "Yeah, you have. But there is a bright side to all this."

"What?" she sniffed.

"I'm still young. I can recover. But you two…well….time is of the essence—"

Leone swatted him on the arm. "What are you trying to say?" She swatted him again.

He held up his hands, begging for mercy. "Nothing, nothing," he laughed between swats. "I swear."

Leone eyed him and pursed her lips. "That's better," she said, fighting down the urge to laugh.

For a few moments they looked at each other with a tenderness reserved for those who have shared intimately of one another, and they knew they'd both be all right.

"We should have done this a long time ago," Ray said soberly.

"I know. And I'm sorry for treating you so badly. You didn't deserve that."

He took her hands between his. "What do you say we just forget the past—well, not everything." He grinned wickedly. "And start from today as friends. Nothing more, nothing less."

A soft smile lit her face. "I like the sound of that."

Ray leaned closer, looking deep into her eyes. "I'll never forget what we shared, Lee. And don't you ever think for a moment that it wasn't important to me," he said, still holding her hands.

"I won't forget either," she whispered.

Gently he touched his lips to hers, once, twice.

The sensation of another presence in the room caused them to suddenly spring apart.

Leone gasped when she saw Raven standing in the doorway staring at them.

"I thought I'd find you here," she said coldly. "I figured I'd stop by so we could talk." Raven's breathing was coming in short bursts. Her throat worked up and down.

Leone slowly rose from her seat as she sensed the explosion that was about to erupt.

"You remember Ray, don't you?"

Ray stood. "Good to—"

"Haven't you taken enough already?" she suddenly lashed out. "First it's Cole's job and now my mother! What did he ever do to you?"

"Raven!" her mother warned, walking toward her daughter.

Raven pointed at Leone. "You just leave me alone. How could you do this? With him? He's young enough to be my big brother. How? That's sick." Leone flinched under the barrage of accusations. "You knew how much Cole loved you and how much he loved me. And you ran him away, just like daddy. I hate you. You always leave me with nothing!"

She whirled away and ran out the door.

For several seconds Leone stood in the shadows of the club, paralyzed with humiliation and by the intensity of Raven's outburst.

"Oh, God," she suddenly expelled, covering her mouth with her hand. "I've got to go get her." She turned back toward the table to get her purse, her vision clouded with tears.

"Slow down, Lee." Ray put his arm around her shoulders and felt her entire body trembling. "I'll go with you."

She turned wide eyes on him. "No. Please." She pressed her hands to his chest. Briskly she kissed his cheek. "Thank you," she said in a hushed voice, turned and hurried out.

TWENTY-ONE

Leone ran out onto the sidewalk and looked frantically from one end of the street to the other. Raven was nowhere to be seen. She turned and headed home.

As Leone walked swiftly along the sidewalk, she wished now that she' driven to the club. She sent up silent prayers that she could find a way to make things up to Raven. Her own insecurities and old scars had not just affected her, they'd affected Raven and Cole. And because of that, she stood the risk of losing the two people most dear to her—for good.

Maybe this whole mess was a blessing in disguise. It had forced her to take a hard look at herself, objectively, and although she didn't like what she saw, she believed she could make the changes necessary for a new beginning.

When she finally reached her street, Leone's heart was hammering as she approached the house.

"Please be there," she whispered as she quickly jogged up the steps. But the instant she put her key in the door and went inside, she knew she was alone.

Dropping her bag on the table in the hall, she went straight to Raven's room in hope that perhaps she'd left a note or something.

She scanned the room in all the obvious places and found what she expected—nothing.

Retracing her steps, she headed for her bedroom, went directly to her nightstand and pulled out her phone book.

She'd made it a point early on to have the phone number of all Raven's friends. She began dialing, starting with Terri.

Twenty minutes later, she hung up the phone for the last time. No one had seen her. Or at least that's what they all said. The only one she hadn't reached was Ron. When the answering machine came on, she opted not to leave a message.

She'd talked briefly with Terri's mother who assured her that if Raven turned up she'd make sure she called.

Leone walked to the window and peered outside. The sun was already settling down behind the buildings. It would be dark soon.

She folded her arms, warding off the sudden chill that had crept up her back. What if Raven had run away? What if she never came back, just to punish her?

Leone pushed her fist to her mouth. Where would Raven go? She didn't have any real money to speak of. Since she'd refused to allow Raven to work after school until she'd gotten the first semester under her belt, she was sustained only by her allowance. Which always had to be replenished before its due date.

She crossed the room, heard a car pull up out front and ran back to the window.

Her hopes quickly dissipated. It was only her neighbor.

There had to be something she could do, she worried, her panic level rising with each passing minute. Right now she didn't even have the luxury of calling Antoinette, who she was sure by now, was on a train to Washington, D.C.

for another computer installation job. As Antoinette's career had grown by leaps and bounds over the last year, she'd turned more and more to Cole.

Had this been any other time of crisis with Raven, she would have called him. He would have calmed her down and worked things out with Raven. She'd grown to depend on him, accepted the fact that he was an integral part of their lives. As much as she reveled in her independence, her sense of freedom, she secretly enjoyed the security of knowing that Cole would take care of things. Take care of her.

The phone rang.

Leone ran across the room before it could ring a second time.

"Hello?" She held her breath.

"Everything okay?"

She plopped down on the bed. "Ray. Hi. No, it's not. She didn't come home."

"Did you—"

"I called everyone," she said, heading off his question. "No one's seen her."

"She have a boyfriend?"

"Sort of. Ron. I called but only got an answering machine."

"She's probably just out walking, Lee. Working things out in her head. She'll be back. She didn't take any of her things, did she?"

An electric charge of fear shot through her. She dropped the phone on the bed and ran down the hall to Raven's room. She pulled open her closet and tried to determine if anything was missing. It all seemed to be in place, the best she could tell.

She checked beneath the canopy bed. Raven's suitcase was still there.

Mildly satisfied, she went back to her room. Seeing the phone on the bed she guiltily remembered that she'd left Ray hanging on.

"Ray, you still there?"

"What happened? I was about to hang up and come over there."

"I'm sorry. When you mentioned missing clothes, I realized I hadn't thought to check her closet and had a panic attack."

"And?"

"It looks like everything is there."

"That's a good sign."

"Is it?"

"Sure. The three times I ran away I took clothes. When I wasn't serious, I just took my basketball."

She held back a chuckle, trying to imagine a young Ray Taylor. "Please don't explain. But I'm sure there's a moral in there somewhere."

"What I'm saying is, wherever Raven decided to go, she doesn't plan to stay." He paused. "She'll be back, Lee. Just relax and be there for her when she comes home. She has some real issues on her mind."

"You really think she'll be back?" she asked, needing to hear the reassuring words again.

"I know so. I'd stack my sax on it!"

"Then it must be true."

"Call if you need me. It's not a problem."

She gulped down her reservations. "Thank you. I will."

"You need to call your mom, Rae," Ron said as they walked hand in hand down South Oxford Street.

"I don't have anything to say to her."

"Maybe it wasn't nothin'. You just blowin' it up."

She snatched her hand away. "You don't get it, do you?"

"Get what, Rae? You been blaming your mom for everything that's wrong in your life since I met you."

Raven stopped short and propped her hand on her hip. "She is the cause! My dad left because of her. Cole left because of her. She never really talks to me about anything, just tells me what to do. She never listens."

"Maybe you need to think about somebody besides yourself for a change, Rae. You ain't no kid no more. Your mom is probably feelin' it too."

"Since when are you on her side?"

"It ain't about side, Rae. It's about right." He dug his hands into the pockets of his oversized jeans, pushing them farther down on his narrow hips. "I like you. Like you a lot. You know I'd do anything for you."

Raven loosened her defiant stance and focused on the pavement.

Ron's voice gentled. "Go home, Raven. Talk it out."

She twisted her lips to the side. "How'd you get so smart?"

"Been through it with my old man. Last year of high school. We used to battle about everything."

"Really? You and your father seem so close."

He nodded. "Take my word for it. Being out on the street ain't worth it. Your mom is awright. Give her a shot."

Raven stared at him for a long moment. The prospect of sleeping in Fort Green Park was not an enticing prospect. She knew she couldn't stay with Terri. Her mother would make her call home as soon as she walked in the door.

Raven stretched out her hand. "Walk me home?"

"Not a problem, babe."

Ron took her hand and they walked back toward the house. At the foot of her steps, Ron asked, "You want me to come up with you?"

Raven thought about it for a minute. "No. I should go up by myself."

He nodded. "Cool. I'll call you later then."

"Maybe it's best if you call tomorrow," she said with a crooked smile.

Ron kissed her lightly on the lips. "Just be cool, Rae. And honest."

Raven blew air through her teeth. "I'll try." She turned away and went up the steps.

The instant Leone heard a key in the door, the tight, suffocating feeling she'd lived with for the past few hours finally loosened its hold. She ran to the top of the stairs just as Raven came through the door.

Leone's hand flew to her chest in concert with a gush of air that rushed from her lungs upon seeing that her daughter was safe and in one piece.

Slowly she came down the stairs, meeting Raven at the door.

Raven looked away, not sure what she would see in her mother's eyes. She closed the door behind her. "Hi," she mumbled under her breath.

"Are you okay, Raven?"

Raven tugged on the inside of her mouth with her teeth. "No."

"Neither am I," Leone admitted, and realized that it felt good to say the words.

Raven's smooth brown features bunched into a frown at her mother's admission. In her entire life she couldn't remember her mother ever admitting that anything was wrong, that she ever felt anything other than "fine."

"Come on inside. We need to talk, really talk. Starting with your father." She put her arm around Raven's stiff shoulders and guided her into the kitchen.

In the hours that she'd sat in her room waiting for Raven's return, she'd thought about how to approach the subject of her ex-husband. She could easily sugarcoat it, keep him the invisible hero that Raven believed him to be, or she could simply avoid the entire painful topic as she'd always done.

But she was slowly coming to understand that Raven needed to know the truth. Perhaps not every gory detail, but the truth, so that she could free herself from the fantasy of Steven and see things as they really were. Avoiding the things that hurt, avoiding the issues that raised uncomfortable feelings had been the elements that brought them to this place. Neither of them would ever be whole, be better if it continued. And it was up to her to make the first move.

So, she did. Little by little she spoke of her blind love and faith in Steven, of her own fragile sense of self and how she'd allowed a bad marriage to feed her insecurities.

"I don't believe that your father is a bad person, Raven," Leone said, hoping to put a balm on the wound that she'd opened. "I just think that, unfortunately, the two of us brought out the worst in each other. We fed off each other's weaknesses. And that's not what real love is about."

Leone took Raven's hand. "But my battle didn't stop there. I turned all that hurt and sense of failure as a woman on myself. I withdrew. From you, from my friends, from life." She pushed out a thoughtful breath. "I guess I thought if I didn't ever let anyone get close to me, know my feelings, my thoughts, I couldn't ever be hurt like that again."

"Me, too?" Raven asked incredulously.

"Not intentionally. But questions about your father, questions about how to live, how to be a young woman, make choices; all those things became threats to me."

"Why?"

"Because it reminded me how incompetent I felt about dealing with them."

"So you shut me out, too."

"Yes," she uttered. But her answer was more than a confession, it was a plea for forgiveness. And somehow, Raven in her seventeen-year-old wisdom, understood it.

"And I shut out Cole."

"What are you going to do about that?"

Leone's brows flickered in contemplation. "I'm not really sure yet. I know I need some time to work through some of my issues, try to be more open, willing to share in a partnership before I can think of me and Cole in any concrete way."

"But what if he stays out there and finds someone else?"

"That's a chance I'll have to take. I won't be in another relationship with anyone if I can't be all there. It's not fair to me or to them."

Raven turned a plastic cup around and around on the table. She met her mother's steady gaze. "Ron was right."

"Ron? Right? About what?"

"He was the one who convinced me to come home, to really listen."

"He did?" She couldn't have been more surprised than if she'd won the lottery. She obviously had very much underestimated Ron. Out of the mouths of babes, she thought.

"It's kind of nice, too," Raven paused, "talking like this with you."

Leone felt her heart swell with love when she realized how much she'd missed by shutting out this wonderful young woman from her life. She vowed to never let it happen again.

"I kind of like it, too."

Raven propped her elbows on the table and rested her chin in her palms. "So does this mean we can talk about anything, now?"

Leone's right brow arched suspiciously. "Hmm. I suppose," she said with caution.

Raven waited a beat. "Is there something going on between you and that guy, Ray?"

Leone thought about it for a split second. "No. He's just a friend and a great bandleader. That's it."

Raven angled her head to the side, checking for any chinks in the story. "Okay. Just asking. 'Cause if it was…well, I guess it would be all right. I guess."

"I'm glad I have your blessing, but I don't think it's anything for you to concern yourself with."

They were both silent for a while, caught up in this new relationship they were forging. Finally, Raven spoke.

"I'm sorry about going off like that at the club. That wasn't cool."

"You're right. It wasn't. But you're forgiven. As long as it doesn't happen again." She pinched the tip of Raven's nose, then pushed up from her seat. "I'm starved."

"Me, too. Terri's mom taught us how to make curried chicken," she said excitedly. "Want me to show you?"

Leone's eyes widened in a combination of surprise and alarm. Raven had never set foot in the kitchen for anything more complicated than sitting down to eat, or warming something up in the microwave.

"Sure," she finally stuttered.

Leone watched her daughter move expertly around in the kitchen, taking out all the preparations like a pro. She shook her head and smiled.

Changes. One step at a time.

TWENTY-TWO

For the first time in almost two months since Cole moved to the West Coast, Antoinette had a full day off. She and Leone had been keeping in touch by way of the telephone. So with some down time, they decided that with Christmas only weeks away, they'd spend Saturday morning doing what they considered early shopping.

"I can't remember the last time I actually shopped with more than a week until Christmas," Antoinette commented, examining a silk scarf in Saks Fifth Avenue. She placed her two overloaded shopping bags at her feet.

"You and me both. It's usually a mad dash two days before for me. If I'm lucky. What do you think of this for Raven?" She held up a two-piece pants suit in navy blue.

"Hmm. Raven is so picky about her clothes. I don't know, Lee," she frowned.

Leone hung the suit back on the rack. "You're right. I never know what the latest fad is from one month to the next. Maybe I'd be better off getting her some CDs."

"Now you're really treading on thin ice."

Leone laughed. "True. I can't understand a thing half those so-called singers are singing about."

Antoinette picked up her bags and they continued strolling through the store. "Tell you the truth, I think it's supposed to be that way.

"Yeah. Hey, maybe some boots."

"That's safe." Antoinette peered into a jewelry case lined with gold bracelets. "How are things between you and Raven?"

Leone smiled. "Great, actually. I think the incident at the club was a real turning point—for both of us." She side-stepped a woman with a double stroller. "We talk now. Really talk. And she's not so eager to run out of the house anymore. When I'm home, we actually hang out together."

"That's an improvement." She paused a beat. "What about Cole? Heard from him lately?"

"Not recently."

"Have you tried to contact him?"

"I've thought about it. He sent a card for Thanksgiving and gave me his address and phone number."

"So why haven't you called? You know you miss that man."

They walked toward the exit and out onto the busy Manhattan streets. A light snow had begun to fall, and the mass of humanity moved through it in picture-perfect fashion.

Leone shrugged at Antoinette's question, and tightened the cashmere scarf around her neck. "I don't know. Scared, I guess."

"Of what?" Antoinette jostled her packages and slipped on her gloves.

"That he might not be interested anymore."

"Sorry excuse. You'll never know unless you try."

Leone didn't respond.

"How have things been with you and Ray? Any more sparks flying?"

"Things have been fine with us. And no—no sparks. What happened is in the past. End of story."

"Oh. I was just wondering if maybe that was the real reason you haven't called Cole"

Leone jerked her neck back. "What's that supposed to mean?"

"Let's go into Rockefeller Center and see the tree," Antoinette said, momentarily dodging the question.

But Leone wouldn't let it rest. "Come on, what are you really saying?"

"I'm just wondering if you've really put out the flames with Ray. That maybe you do care about him and think it might interfere—again—if you got back together with Cole."

They walked together in silence as Leone processed Antoinette's comments.

There might have been a time when she would have completely agreed with Antoinette. But not now. She would admit that she did like Ray. They'd developed a solid friendship over the past few months, an honest one. She had no illusions that there was a future for the two of them. Underneath his claim to want stability, Ray Taylor still had some wild oats to sow. He told her as much when they'd shared lunch together several days earlier, which is what she told Antoinette as they entered Rockefeller Center...

She and Ray had gone to her favorite African restaurant on Fulton Street. Leone was determined to get him to try the vegetable pita sandwich, although he swore he was a devout meat eater and marvelous cook, and that vegetables weren't what he considered full course meals.

"This better be good," he grumbled, helping her out of her down coat before taking a seat.

"Just relax and don't be a crybaby." She snapped open her menu for emphasis.

"That's not one of those age jokes, is it?" he quipped, picking up his own menu.

"No, it's an experience joke. You've got to broaden your horizons, try new things," she said loftily.

"Yeah, okay. Just as long as it wasn't an age joke," he replied, wagging a finger at her.

Leone chuckled and shook her head.

Abruptly, he put down the menu and leaned forward, bracing his sweater-covered arm on the table.

"You know what, Lee?"

"Hmm?" she responded absently, still scanning the menu.

"That Sunday...at my house."

Her stomach took a quick dip as her gaze rose above the top of the menu. They hadn't discussed that afternoon since it happened and the resurrection of it suddenly heated her with embarrassment.

"What about it?" *Please don't tell me you have something I could have caught.*

A waitress appeared at the table like an apparition. "What will you both be having?" she asked in a heavy Senegalese accent.

"Uh…"

"She's the expert," Ray said, pointing an accusing finger at Leone. "I'm at her mercy." He flashed Leone a wicked smile and a wink.

"Two steamed vegetable pitas and two salads with carrot dressing." She caught the pained look on Ray's face and added insult to injury by ordering carrot juice.

"Right away," the young woman said, jotting down their orders. She removed the menus and whisked away as quietly as she'd appeared.

"As I was saying…" Ray continued, undeterred.

Now, if she were the old Leone, she would have quickly stated that it was over and done with and she didn't want to discuss it. But if Ray could eat a vegetarian meal, she could live through discussing "that" day.

"Yes."

"I've done a lot of thinking since then, about you, but especially about me."

Leone reached for her glass of water and hoped her hands wouldn't shake. She took a long swallow.

"But you know the one thing we never talked out is why it happened." He reached for his glass as well but didn't drink, only held it in his hand. "You don't have to tell me your reason, but I want you to know mine."

Leone held her breath and waited.

"For a while, even before I met you, I'd begun to feel like my life was running away from me, that I needed to nail it down." He took a breath. "I began to think I was wasting myself, that I needed stability, and having one woman would do the trick. I blamed everything on that…"

The waitress arrived with their salads. Ray curled up his nose, but Leone dug in, needing something immediate to do to keep from hearing some awful truth.

"Anyway," he continued, pushing his salad around with his fork, "when I met you, I locked in on you. I guess because you were so different from any other woman I'd known. Somewhere in the back of my head I believed being with you would miraculously change me, make things different for me."

She swallowed a forkful of salad, afraid to ask the question that hung on her lips: Did I change your life?

As if reading her mind, he answered. "You did change me. But not the way I'd imagined. What being with you made me realize was that the change has to come from me. I can't hang my hopes on someone else. That's the wrong kind of expectation."

Ray finally took a tiny morsel of salad and moved it around in his mouth. Suddenly his eyes widened in surprise. He dug his fork in again and took a sizeable chunk. "This is actually good," he said, chewing and swallowing.

Leone gave him an arched I-told-you-so expression, but refrained from rubbing it in.

"Anyway," he wiped his mouth with the cloth napkin, "what I'm trying to say is, with you I was able to discover who I was, who I still am. Deep down I love my life the way it is, and when the time is right, the circumstances are right, I'll know it."

"So you're saying I was just an experiment."

"No. Not at all. What I'm saying is, when I'm ready I know what I want."

"What's that?"

"A woman like you, Leone. Don't think any less of yourself because of what happened with us. You're an incredible woman. Any man would be lucky to have you." He reached across the table and put his hand atop hers. "Don't blow it, Lee. Figure out what you want and go after it. You can't get back time lost, but you can still move forward."

Even though he didn't come right out and say it, she knew he was talking about her and Cole.

"That being said," Ray suddenly announced, "I have to break down and admit that this salad is great. If these veggies things taste half as good, I'm hooked."

"Then you're in for a treat. How are the jam sessions going?" she asked, thankful to change the subject.

"Great. Great. As a matter of fact I wanted to run this idea by you."

"Sure…"

"So, you're going to have these blow-out jam sessions during Christmas week," Antoinette enthused. "What a fabulous idea."

"Yep. Ray worked it all out. He has all the groups lined up and we have a reservation list that will take us well past the new millenium!"

"I know you put me down, right?"

"I'll have to check my records," Leone teased.

"Don't play me, girl. Besides, it will give me a chance to meet this Ray character and see what kind of skills he has."

Leone had a brief erotic vision, shook her head and laughed.

The week leading up to the Christmas extravaganza was over-the-top hectic. The entire staff was running around like insane people, barking orders and bumping into each other. The chaos began when word "slipped out" to the press that Soul to Soul would be holding the music event of the year with a week-long array of jazz bands and guest performers, a feat that had never before happened in a local Brooklyn club.

Two television stations had called wanting to tape the shows, and the local cable station, BCAT, would be taping the entire series for continuous broadcast.

The concept had blown up to monumental proportions, and although making all the arrangements and being sure everything was in place was driving her crazy, she loved every minute of it. Raven, Terri and Ron were even pitching in since school was closed for winter recess. Their real reason for being so accommodating was the hope that they'd be seen on television. But Leone didn't mind. She could use all the help she could get, plus it gave her and Raven a chance to bond on yet another level.

Leone had just sat down in her office after spending the morning supervising the painting of the formal dining room, when the phone rang. She exhaled an exhausted breath and picked up the phone.

"Soul to Soul, Leone Weathers speaking…"

By the time she got off the phone ten minutes later, she'd agreed to have the Christmas show broadcast live on WBLS.

She still held the phone in her hand, her thoughts frozen, when there was a knock on the door.

"Come in," she said absently.

Ray opened the door and stepped in, looking GQ perfect in his black ensemble.

"Hi. Listen, I'm going to start the next set of rehearsals in about an hour. Do you think the kitchen would mind doing lunch for them again today?"

"I don't see why not. You want me to ask?"

"If you wouldn't mind."

"Not a problem. Oh, I just got a call from WBLS radio. They want to broadcast the Christmas show live! Can you believe it?"

Ray grinned like a kid. "Of course. This is the event, woman. You're going to be on the map, Lee!" He slapped his hands together.

"Thanks to you."

"Hey, I'm a small piece of the puzzle. Cole was the key to the whole thing. If he hadn't hired me, this would have all been a moot point."

Cole. Her throat tightened. How would she get through Christmas without him? As much as she'd tried to put him out of her mind, she couldn't. There was so much of her life during the time they were together that he had been a part of; from the design of her office to the layout of the club, to the way he smoothed things over with Raven, to the way she drove her car, to how she expected to be treated.

She missed him, dammit. She missed being able to look up and see him walk through the door with that smile of his. She missed his strong fingers instinctively finding all the tension knots in her shoulders. And she missed sitting out in the audience and not seeing him behind the piano, playing something just for her.

"Are you okay?"

Leone blinked, pressing her lips together. "Yes," she said, her voice sounding strained.

Ray looked at her for a long moment and could tell by the wistful look in her eyes what was going through her head.

"Live, huh?"

"That's what they said," she replied, attempting to sound cheery.

"Then I guess we'll have to make it extra special."

Leone looked at him curiously. He winked and walked out.

TWENTY-THREE

Christmas was coming on a Saturday this year. One more day to go and the whirlwind that the past week had been would mercifully be over. Thank the heavens, Leone thought, painfully stepping out of her black heels.

Every night had been a sell-out. Even though they did honor reservations, if guests were more than twenty minutes late, they lost their table. There had been a line down the block and around the corner every single night.

Leone literally collapsed across her bed. She couldn't begin to imagine what tomorrow was going to be like. The local cable station and the radio station people would be there from mid-day on, checking equipment, finding the best locations, and making general nuisances of themselves.

As she drifted off to sleep, still clothed in her Versace cocktail dress, she wondered if fame and fortune were all they were cracked up to be.

After eating a huge Christmas breakfast and ripping open Christmas presents, Leone and Raven dressed in their new cable knit sweaters, jeans and matching boots and headed for the club, their evening wear slung over their shoulders in garment bags.

When they arrived, there was already a line forming in the hope of getting a reservation for the final performance, which promised to be something to remember long after the night was over. Ray wouldn't even tell her who the lineup was.

"That's all part of the hype of effective promotion," he'd told her when she practically begged for details. "Give them just enough to whet their appetites." With that tidbit of information, he'd strolled off with a victorious look in his dark eyes.

Sometimes she could strangle him, she thought as she and Raven wended their way around the line and eased inside.

The instant she set foot in the club, it was non-stop action, from soothing the ruffled feathers of her staff, the news and radio crews, to checking on menus and putting in orders for rush supplies of paper goods.

When she sat down to catch her breath, she looked at the clock and it was already five-thirty. She dropped her head on her arms and squeezed her eyes shut. At that precise moment she felt eternally grateful that Cole had had the foresight to install a mini shower in the office bathroom. It had come in handy on many a night.

A slow smile spread across her mouth when she recalled the steamy lovemaking sessions she and Cole had shared in the office after the staff was gone for the night. Then they'd squeezed into the narrow shower stall and start all over again.

She sighed. For the New Year, she was going to take a trip to San Francisco. The hell with this. She'd sent him a card for Christmas, but she hadn't heard from him. Well, she pushed herself up from her seat, if she had anything to do with it, that was all going to change. Soon. Come Monday morning, she was going to the travel agency and purchase her ticket. She didn't care if she was going to have to eat crow, she was going to make all this up to Cole, tell him how much she loved and missed him and that her life was hell without him in it.

She took her garment bag from the hook on the back of the door, locked the door and headed for the bathroom. A hot shower was just the remedy she needed at the moment. She had a long night ahead of her.

From the instant the doors opened for the first set, the house was packed. Leone had had to hire extra kitchen staff as well as three more waitresses and two bartenders in order to handle the crowds during the past week and it still didn't seem like enough.

She was standing in the back of the room scanning the glitter of the throng when the house lights dimmed and Ray took center stage.

"Good evening ladies and gentlemen. As you may or may not know, I'm Ray Taylor and this," he waved his hand expansively behind him, "is the Cole Fleming quintet."

The club erupted into applause. And Leone's heart thumped in her chest with the mention of Cole's name.

"Thank you." He held up his hand for quiet. "It was because of Cole and the owner of Soul to Soul, Leone Weathers," he peered out into the crowd and upon spotting

Leone pointed her out, "that this glorious week of non-stop jazz has been possible. And in tribute to the both of them I'd like to welcome none other than the incomparable Herbie Hancock!"

Leone's mouth dropped open and the audience went ballistic.

Herbie glided onto the stage, dressed in traditional black with his trademark round, wire-rimmed glasses and took his place behind the piano. He smoothly swung into "Driftin'," which he'd originally recorded with Dexter Gordon on tenor sax. And Ray played his stand-in role with ease.

Heads bobbed and fingers popped. Leone was so excited she thought she'd burst with delight. This was absolutely incredible. Antoinette was out there somewhere with her latest boyfriend, but she couldn't spot her.

The cameras were capturing every minute and the radio station was pumping out every note to the listeners across the city.

Everything was perfect, more than she could have ever imagined. Well, almost perfect. Suddenly she had a wave of melancholia. She looked around the room. Everywhere that her eyes landed she spotted couples, couples. Couples hugging, couples holding hands, couples with their heads close in conversation.

This was the kind of night, the kind of moment you shared with someone important in your life, someone you loved. And for all the glory of the evening, in the total success of the series, she didn't have that one thing that would make it—

"I always wished I could play like Herbie."

Her stomach lurched and her heart seemed to stumble in her chest. The voice was right in her ear, in that familiar spot that would send shock waves running along her body. She was almost afraid to turn around because of what she might not find.

She could feel her legs tremble as she pivoted around, and she looked up into those warm, caring eyes. He wore all gray, the silk sweater stretching across his wide chest. She reached up and caressed his cheek before she spoke, needing the reassurance that he was real and not the lights and sounds playing tricks on her.

"Cole," she whispered.

"Hey, babe." He smiled down at her and even in this crowded room, she was the only one he could see.

"How...when? No one told me."

"Ray found me through the musicians' union."

"Ray?" she asked incredulously.

"Yeah, told me I still had some unfinished business...with you. Is that true, Lee? Is there anything we need to say?" He stroked her shoulder, needing to touch her.

"I love you. I made some mistakes and I want to make it up to you. If you'll let me. I need you, Cole, more than I was willing to admit—because I was scared." She gazed up into his eyes, as Herbie segued into his piano solo version of "My One And Only Love."

Cole ran his finger down her chin. "Do you know how long I've waited for you to say that?"

"Too long. But I promise you, you won't have to wait ever again. I'm going to remind you every day, in every way I can, how much I love you."

Cole slid one arm gently around her waist and pulled her flush against his body. "I'm going to hold you to that," he uttered before lowering his head to touch his lips to hers.

Instantly she felt her spirits soar and she was suffused with an unexplainable joy. She eased closer, reveling in the feel of him. She didn't care who was watching. Because all she could think about at that moment was that she'd been given a second chance.

She'd doubted herself as a woman, a mother, a partner. She'd allowed herself to believe that in order to be whole you needed to be validated by someone else. But it wasn't true. That came from inside. She knew that now. And she thanked her stars above that Cole was wise enough to give her that space she needed to be all she could be—to herself and to him.

Ray stood on the far side of the club, leaning casually against one of the pillars, watching the embracing couple who had all but shut out the world. He smiled with contentment. That's what love was all about, he thought—loving enough to let go.

Raven eased up beside him and gazed happily at her mother and Cole. She looked up at Ray. "Thanks a lot for what you did for my mom and Cole."

Ray slipped his arm around her shoulders. "That's what friends are for. That's what friends are for."

ABOUT THE AUTHOR

Donna Hill lives in Brooklyn, NY with her family and works by day as a Public Relations Associate for the Queens Borough Public Library system. She was recently contracted to write her first feature screenplay. She conducts writing workshops and seminars for community colleges and other venues and produces author-centered events under her promotional management company, Arnod Productions. She has been featured in *Essence Magazine*, *Newsday*, the *Daily News*, *Publisher's Weekly*, *Black Enterprise*, the Washington *Post*, the *Amsterdam News* and *USA Today* among others. She has appeared on B.E.T., "The McCreary Report," "Good Day New York," Lifetime Television, and numerous cable and radio programs across the country.

2006 Publication Schedule

January

A Lover's Legacy
Veronica Parker
1-58571-167-5
$9.95

Love Lasts Forever
Dominiqua Douglas
1-58571-187-X
$9.95

Under the Cherry
   Moon
Christal Jordan-Mims
1-58571-169-1
$12.95

February

Second Chances at
   Love
Cheris Hodges
1-58571-188-8
$9.95

Enchanted Desire
Wanda Thomas
1-58571-176-4
$9.95

Caught Up
Deatri King Bey
1-58571-178-0
$12.95

March

I'm Gonna Make You
   Love Me
Gwyneth Bolton
1-58571-181-0
$9.95

Through The Fire
Seressia Glass
1-58571-173-X
$9.95

Notes When
   Summer Ends
Beverly Lauderdale
1-58571-180-2
$12.95

April

Sin and Surrender
J.M. Jeffries
1-58571-189-6
$9.95

Unearthing Passions
Elaine Sims
1-58571-184-5
$9.95

Between Tears
Pamela Ridley
1-58571-179-0
$12.95

May

Misty Blue
Dyanne Davis
1-58571-186-1
$9.95

Ironic
Pamela Leigh Starr
1-58571-168-3
$9.95

Cricket's Serenade
Carolita Blythe
1-58571-183-7
$12.95

June

Cupid
Barbara Keaton
1-58571-174-8
$9.95

Havana Sunrise
Kymberly Hunt
1-58571-182-9
$9.95

Bound For Mt. Zion
Chris Parker
1-58571-191-8
$12.95

2006 Publication Schedule (continued)

July

Love Me Carefully
A.C. Arthur
1-58571-177-2
$9.95

No Ordinary Love
Angela Weaver
1-58571-198-5
$9.95

Rehoboth Road
Anita Ballard-Jones
1-58571-196-9
$12.95

August

Scent of Rain
Annetta P. Lee
158571-199-3
$9.95

Love in High Gear
Charlotte Roy
158571-185-3
$9.95

Rise of the Phoenix
Kenneth Whetstone
1-58571-197-7
$12.95

September

The Business of Love
Cheris Hodges
1-58571-193-4
$9.95

Rock Star
Rosyln Hardy
  Holcomb
1-58571-200-0
$9.95

A Dead Man Speaks
Lisa Jones Johnson
1-58571-203-5
$12.95

October

Who's That Lady
Andrea Jackson
1-58571-190-X
$9.95

A Dangerous Woman
J.M. Jeffries
1-58571-195-0
$9.95

Sinful Intentions
Crystal Rhodes
1-58571-201-9
$12.95

November

Only You
Crystal Hubbard
1-58571-208-6
$9.95

Ebony Eyes
Kei Swanson
1-58571-194-2
$9.95

By and By
Collette Haywood
1-58571-209-4
$12.95

December

Let's Get It On
Dyanne Davis
1-58571-210-8
$9.95

Nights Over Egypt
Barbara Keaton
1-58571-192-6
$9.95

A Pefect Place to Pray
Ikesha Goodwin
1-58571-202-7
$12.95

Other Genesis Press, Inc. Titles

A Dangerous Deception	J.M. Jeffries	$8.95
A Dangerous Love	J.M. Jeffries	$8.95
A Dangerous Obsession	J.M. Jeffries	$8.95
A Drummer's Beat to Mend	Kei Swanson	$9.95
A Happy Life	Charlotte Harris	$9.95
A Heart's Awakening	Veronica Parker	$9.95
A Lark on the Wing	Phyliss Hamilton	$9.95
A Love of Her Own	Cheris F. Hodges	$9.95
A Love to Cherish	Beverly Clark	$8.95
A Risk of Rain	Dar Tomlinson	$8.95
A Twist of Fate	Beverly Clark	$8.95
A Will to Love	Angie Daniels	$9.95
Acquisitions	Kimberley White	$8.95
Across	Carol Payne	$12.95
After the Vows	Leslie Esdaile	$10.95
(Summer Anthology)	T.T. Henderson	
	Jacqueline Thomas	
Again My Love	Kayla Perrin	$10.95
Against the Wind	Gwynne Forster	$8.95
All I Ask	Barbara Keaton	$8.95
Ambrosia	T.T. Henderson	$8.95
An Unfinished Love Affair	Barbara Keaton	$8.95
And Then Came You	Dorothy Elizabeth Love	$8.95
Angel's Paradise	Janice Angelique	$9.95
At Last	Lisa G. Riley	$8.95
Best of Friends	Natalie Dunbar	$8.95
Beyond the Rapture	Beverly Clark	$9.95
Blaze	Barbara Keaton	$9.95
Blood Lust	J. M. Jeffries	$9.95
Bodyguard	Andrea Jackson	$9.95
Boss of Me	Diana Nyad	$8.95

Other Genesis Press, Inc. Titles (continued)

Bound by Love	Beverly Clark	$8.95
Breeze	Robin Hampton Allen	$10.95
Broken	Dar Tomlinson	$24.95
By Design	Barbara Keaton	$8.95
Cajun Heat	Charlene Berry	$8.95
Careless Whispers	Rochelle Alers	$8.95
Cats & Other Tales	Marilyn Wagner	$8.95
Caught in a Trap	Andre Michelle	$8.95
Caught Up In the Rapture	Lisa G. Riley	$9.95
Cautious Heart	Cheris F Hodges	$8.95
Chances	Pamela Leigh Starr	$8.95
Cherish the Flame	Beverly Clark	$8.95
Class Reunion	Irma Jenkins/ John Brown	$12.95
Code Name: Diva	J.M. Jeffries	$9.95
Conquering Dr. Wexler's Heart	Kimberley White	$9.95
Crossing Paths, Tempting Memories	Dorothy Elizabeth Love	$9.95
Cypress Whisperings	Phyllis Hamilton	$8.95
Dark Embrace	Crystal Wilson Harris	$8.95
Dark Storm Rising	Chinelu Moore	$10.95
Daughter of the Wind	Joan Xian	$8.95
Deadly Sacrifice	Jack Kean	$22.95
Designer Passion	Dar Tomlinson	$8.95
Dreamtective	Liz Swados	$5.95
Ebony Butterfly II	Delilah Dawson	$14.95
Echoes of Yesterday	Beverly Clark	$9.95
Eden's Garden	Elizabeth Rose	$8.95
Everlastin' Love	Gay G. Gunn	$8.95
Everlasting Moments	Dorothy Elizabeth Love	$8.95
Everything and More	Sinclair Lebeau	$8.95

Other Genesis Press, Inc. Titles (continued)

Other Genesis Press, Inc. Titles (continued)

Other Genesis Press, Inc. Titles (continued)

Midnight Peril	Vicki Andrews	$10.95
Misconceptions	Pamela Leigh Starr	$9.95
Montgomery's Children	Richard Perry	$14.95
My Buffalo Soldier	Barbara B. K. Reeves	$8.95
Naked Soul	Gwynne Forster	$8.95
Next to Last Chance	Louisa Dixon	$24.95
No Apologies	Seressia Glass	$8.95
No Commitment Required	Seressia Glass	$8.95
No Regrets	Mildred E. Riley	$8.95
Nowhere to Run	Gay G. Gunn	$10.95
O Bed! O Breakfast!	Rob Kuehnle	$14.95
Object of His Desire	A. C. Arthur	$8.95
Office Policy	A. C. Arthur	$9.95
Once in a Blue Moon	Dorianne Cole	$9.95
One Day at a Time	Bella McFarland	$8.95
Outside Chance	Louisa Dixon	$24.95
Passion	T.T. Henderson	$10.95
Passion's Blood	Cherif Fortin	$22.95
Passion's Journey	Wanda Thomas	$8.95
Past Promises	Jahmel West	$8.95
Path of Fire	T.T. Henderson	$8.95
Path of Thorns	Annetta P. Lee	$9.95
Peace Be Still	Colette Haywood	$12.95
Picture Perfect	Reon Carter	$8.95
Playing for Keeps	Stephanie Salinas	$8.95
Pride & Joi	Gay G. Gunn	$15.95
Pride & Joi	Gay G. Gunn	$8.95
Promises to Keep	Alicia Wiggins	$8.95
Quiet Storm	Donna Hill	$10.95
Reckless Surrender	Rochelle Alers	$6.95

Other Genesis Press, Inc. Titles (continued)

Red Polka Dot in a World of Plaid	Varian Johnson	$12.95
Reluctant Captive	Joyce Jackson	$8.95
Rendezvous with Fate	Jeanne Sumerix	$8.95
Revelations	Cheris F. Hodges	$8.95
Rivers of the Soul	Leslie Esdaile	$8.95
Rocky Mountain Romance	Kathleen Suzanne	$8.95
Rooms of the Heart	Donna Hill	$8.95
Rough on Rats and Tough on Cats	Chris Parker	$12.95
Secret Library Vol. 1	Nina Sheridan	$18.95
Secret Library Vol. 2	Cassandra Colt	$8.95
Shades of Brown	Denise Becker	$8.95
Shades of Desire	Monica White	$8.95
Shadows in the Moonlight	Jeanne Sumerix	$8.95
Sin	Crystal Rhodes	$8.95
So Amazing	Sinclair LeBeau	$8.95
Somebody's Someone	Sinclair LeBeau	$8.95
Someone to Love	Alicia Wiggins	$8.95
Song in the Park	Martin Brant	$15.95
Soul Eyes	Wayne L. Wilson	$12.95
Soul to Soul	Donna Hill	$8.95
Southern Comfort	J.M. Jeffries	$8.95
Still the Storm	Sharon Robinson	$8.95
Still Waters Run Deep	Leslie Esdaile	$8.95
Stories to Excite You	Anna Forrest/Divine	$14.95
Subtle Secrets	Wanda Y. Thomas	$8.95
Suddenly You	Crystal Hubbard	$9.95
Sweet Repercussions	Kimberley White	$9.95
Sweet Tomorrows	Kimberly White	$8.95
Taken by You	Dorothy Elizabeth Love	$9.95

Other Genesis Press, Inc. Titles (continued)

Other Genesis Press, Inc. Titles (continued)

Order Form

Mail to: Genesis Press, Inc.
P.O. Box 101
Columbus, MS 39703

Name _____
Address _____
City/State _____ Zip _____
Telephone _____

Ship to (if different from above)
Name _____
Address _____
City/State _____ Zip _____
Telephone _____

Credit Card Information
Credit Card # _____ ☐ Visa   ☐ Mastercard
Expiration Date (mm/yy) _____ ☐ AmEx   ☐ Discover

Qty.	Author	Title	Price	Total

| | Use this order form, or call
1-888-INDIGO-1 | Total for books _____
Shipping and handling:
$5 first two books,
$1 each additional book _____
Total S & H _____
Total amount enclosed _____
Mississippi residents add 7% sales tax |